IN BABYLON

MARCEL MÖRING

IN BABYLON

Translated from the Dutch by Stacey Knecht

Perennial

An Imprint of HarperCollins*Publishers*

First published in English in 1999 by Flamingo, an imprint of HarperCollins
Publishers, 77-85 Fulham Palace Road, Hammersmith,
London W6 8JB.

First published in Holland in 1997 by J.M. Meulenhoff bv.

The Publishers gratefully acknowledge the financial support of the
Foundation for the Production and Translation of Dutch Literature.

The first U.S. edition of this book was published in hardcover in 2000 by
William Morrow, an imprint of HarperCollins Publishers.

First Perennial edition published 2001.

The Library of Congress has catalogued the hardcover edition as follows:

Möring, Marcel.
    [In Babylon. English]
    In Babylon / Marcel Möring—1st ed.
      p. cm.
    ISBN 0-688-17645-3
    I. Title.
PT5881.23.O75I5132000
839.3'1364—dc21   99-053531

ISBN 0-06-095963-0 (pbk.)

01 02 03 04 05 BP 10 9 8 7 6 5 4 3 2 1

To Hanneke and my parents

Contents

PART ONE

Travellers   3
Sauerkraut   13
There is a God   32
The Kotzker   40
Who's There?   48
A Land of Milk and Butter   80
Zeno   142

PART TWO

On Our Way (to the Middle)   153
The Second Law of Thermodynamics   171
Lacrima Christi   212
The Tower   242
Quid Pro Quo   247
This is Germany   272

PART THREE/FOUR

Punishment   291
A Fairy Tale   298
Long Ago and Far Away   314
Fathers and Sons   326
The Depths of the Depths   342

PART FIVE

Stranger   391

'Trees have roots. Jews have legs.'

ISAAC DEUTSCHER

'Our civilisation is characterised by the word "progress". Progress is its form rather than making progress one of its features. Typically it constructs. It is occupied with building an ever more complicated structure. And even clarity is sought only as a means to this end, not as an end in itself. For me on the contrary clarity, perspicuity are valuable in themselves.

'I am not interested in constructing a building, so much as in having a perspicuous view of the foundations of possible buildings.'

LUDWIG WITTGENSTEIN, *Culture and Value*

Part One

Travellers

THE LAST TIME I ever saw Uncle Herman, he was lying on a king-size bed in the finest room at the Hotel Memphis, in the company of six people: the hotel manager, a doctor, two police officers with crackling walkie-talkies, a girl who couldn't have been more than eighteen, and me. The manager conferred with the policemen about how the matter might be settled as discreetly as possible, the doctor stood at the foot of the bed regarding my uncle with a look of mild disgust, and I did nothing. It was just past midnight and Herman lay stretched out, his white body sinewy and taut, on that crumpled white catafalque. He was naked and dead.

He had sent up for a woman. She had arrived, and less than an hour later his life was over. When I got there the young hooker, a small blond thing with crimped hair and childishly painted lips, sat hunched in one of the two white leather chairs next to the ubiquitous hotel writing table. She stared at the carpet, mumbling softly. Uncle Herman lay on his back on the big bed, his pubic hair still glistening with . . . all right, with the juices of love, a condom rolled halfway down his wrinkled sex like a misplaced clown's nose. His pale, old man's body, the tanned face with the shock of grey hair and the large, slightly hooked nose evoked the image of a warrior fallen in battle and laid in state, here, on this dishevelled altar.

I stood in that room and thought of what Zeno, with a touch of bitterness in his voice, had once said, long ago, that you could plot family histories on a graph, as a line that rippled up and down, up and down, up and down; people made their fortune, their offspring benefited from that fortune, the third generation squandered it all, and the family returned to the bottom of the curve and began working its way back up. An endless cycle of profit and loss, wealth and poverty, rise and fall. Except for the history of our family, Zeno had said, that was a whole other thing. Our family history could best be compared to a railway timetable: one person left, and while he was on his way, another returned, and while he was busy arriving, others were setting out on a new journey. 'Normal families stay in the same place for centuries,' said Zeno. 'If they do ever leave it's a major historical event. In our family it would be a historical event if, even after just half a generation, we associated suitcases with a holiday instead of a new life.'

'Right,' said the doctor, who probably wasn't much younger than the victim himself. 'Let's get to work.' He placed his bag on the writing table, opened it, stuck his hand in the gaping leather mouth, and pulled out a spectacle case. The glasses gave him an air of efficiency, like a tailor about to pin up a hem. He went to the bed, moved the body over so he could sit down, and began poking and prodding. Then, peering into the dead man's clouded eyes, he asked what had happened. I turned to the girl, who was still hunched over in her chair. She seemed to sense my gaze, and lifted her head. She looked extremely unhappy. 'The doctor would like to know whether you noticed anything unusual.' She shook her head. 'Well?' said the doctor. 'Nothing,' I said. 'She didn't notice a thing.' The doctor frowned. 'Are you saying he just popped off?' I looked back down at the floor. She shrugged. Sighing, the doctor got to his feet and took off his spectacles. His eyes travelled around the room. Then he went up to the girl. He stood before her and, jabbing the air with his glasses, said, 'What were you doing to him?' The girl clapped her hand to her mouth and ran out the door. We heard her in the bathroom, quietly retching.

It was around one in the morning by the time the four of us emerged outside, in the moonlit doorway of the hotel. A hearse glided soundlessly by. The wind rustled the tall oaks around the patio, there was faint music in the distance. The doctor and the hotel manager reminisced about a man who had once been found tied to the bedposts, the girl and I watched the police car as it turned onto the road in a cloud of flying gravel. The doctor and the manager said goodbye and we were left behind. We stood outside the door listening to the music. It sounded like Ives.

'I think he would have enjoyed dying that way,' I said. 'In a hotel, with a young woman at his side.'

She started retching again.

I stared into the half-darkness of the city and thought, for the first time in years, about the future, which had once lain before me and now, now that I was old and worn, lay behind me.

'He was a traveller,' I said.

The girl turned to me and opened her mouth. The heavy lipstick was smeared along one cheek, which made her whole face look lopsided. She breathed out quick, small puffs of steam and shivered in her baseball jacket.

'We were all travellers,' I said.

She turned away and looked at the empty street and the light that hung yellow and still beneath the tall trees. I saw her glance at me from the corner of her eyes, hurried, fearful, like someone who has found herself with an unpredictable psychopath and doesn't know which would be better: to stay or leave, respond or ignore.

There was a pale blue haze around the moon. A gentle breeze rustled the treetops. As if Uncle Herman's soul had dissolved in the night, I thought, and now, the final matters settled, the remains of his life carried off, had disappeared in a last contented sigh. On its way, forever.

And at that very moment, there, outside the hotel where Uncle Herman . . . had lost his life, at that moment I saw myself for the first time in maybe twenty years, and the image that loomed up out of the labyrinth of my life was that of a face in the crowd, a man nobody knows, yet is there nonetheless, an eyewitness, a stowaway in time.

―――――――

The fire in the hearth burned peacefully, like a flower with red, orange, and yellow petals, swaying in the wind. The mahogany claw of a chair leg jutted out of the flames, as if we had been sacrificing some wooden animal.

'Are you asleep?'

I looked sideways, at Nina, who sat cross-legged in the big arm-chair next to me. She was sitting on a sleeping bag, her long red hair hanging down, and leaning on the palms of her hands.

'No, I'm not asleep. But I might just as well be. I've rarely felt as old as I feel today.'

She nodded. 'What were you thinking?'

'Nothing special.'

'Come on, N. If we're really going to be snowed in here for the next few days I don't want you playing the mystery man. Do your *Decamerone*. Give me the *Canterbury Tales*. You're a fairy tale writer. Amuse me.'

'You want to hear fairy tales?'

'Maybe later. All I want to hear now is what you were thinking.'

'I was thinking about Uncle Herman. I suddenly remembered the last time I saw him.'

'When was that?'

'When he was dead.'

'Oh, that.'

'My God, how times have changed. You say: Oh, that. For me . . . it was a shock, I can tell you.'

'After the sixties? I thought all you men ever did in the sixties was fuck and get high.'

'Them, niece. Not me. I would've liked to. But I'm a Hollander. Nathan Hollander. A respectable man. I eat my poultry with a knife and fork, I hold my wine glass by the stem. I've never fucked around or used drugs.'

'Nuncle, would you mind not calling me "niece"? It sounds like grey woollen skirts and sensible shoes.'

We grinned.

'But haven't you ever . . .'

'Oh, sure. Hash. Long time ago. Not my style. I like being in control.'

She sighed. 'The two-glasses-of-wine-five-cigarettes-a-day man.'

'That's me.'

'And the sex wasn't so hot either?'

'Nina! I'm your uncle. I just turned sixty. That's not the sort of thing you're supposed to ask old people.'

'Old people . . . You're not old. What's sixty anyway, nowadays? You're still in great shape.'

'Thank you. I only said I was old to hear you say I wasn't.'

'And that's why I said it.'

'No, I haven't had a very thrilling sex life. Certainly a lot less thrilling than Uncle Herman's.'

Nina stared into the fire. It was burning low. I stood up and threw on a few more chair legs and a piece of the piano lid. When I was sitting back down again she said, 'With all that traipsing around the world I reckoned you must have had a sweetheart in every port.'

I shook my head. 'I'll tell you what I've learned in the past sixty years. If you really want to get someone into bed, fast, don't ever start talking to them. I talked. My mistake was that I thought you had to get to know each other first, at least well enough to carry on a conversation. By the time I had my hand on the bedroom doorknob, the women around me were only interested in more talking. I became a friend, not a lover.'

She nodded, as if she could imagine that. 'So you were the only one in that crazy family who didn't get enough.'

'Oh, I wouldn't exactly say . . .'

'Herman did it with call girls.'

'Once. We know he did it once with a call girl and that was after Sophie died. I believe he was faithful to Sophie all his life.'

'As if that were normal! Faithful to your brother's wife.'

I shrugged. 'Zeno . . .' I said. 'We know he did it at least once. Had . . . er . . . sex, I mean. You're proof of that.'

'Zeno,' she said. Bitterness tugged at her lips. 'And Zoe thrived on it.'

I sighed.

'Manny.'

'My father was undoubtedly . . . active,' I said, 'but only after he and Sophie were divorced. Zelda, on the other hand, almost certainly died a virgin.'

'A bunch of loonies,' Nina concluded.

'And you? Now that you've defined the rest of the family in sexual terms, what's your story?'

'Imagine asking a young girl such a thing, an old man like you . . .'

We laughed.

I looked at Nina. Shadows leapt about in her face. In the firelight, her pale skin had a warm, rosy glow. Her curly red hair even looked like fire, a churning mountain stream of arabesques and garlands. Nina? No, she would never have trouble getting what she wanted. I gazed at my niece with the satisfaction of a father who sees that his daughter has blossomed into an attractive young woman: intelligent, sharp, well-dressed and well-bred. Even now, in the old clothes we had found in Herman's wardrobe, corduroy trousers that were much too large for her and cinched at the waist with a leather belt, a jumper with the sleeves rolled up four times, thick woollen socks, even now she looked like the sort of tubercular, red-haired beauty the Pre-Raphaelites were so mad about. Her lightly rounded lips were freshly painted. There was a shimmer of rouge across her cheekbones. The green of her eyes was pure enamel.

'We have got to eat,' I said. 'I'll go and cook us something.'

'Cook?'

'That's what I said. There's plenty of food. Enough supplies to last us through the next world war.'

She looked at me blankly.

'I'll show you,' I said. 'But only if you promise not to be frightened.'

I picked up a candelabra and we walked out of the library. In the stone-cold hall the warmth was driven instantly out of our clothes. Nina shivered. I felt her hand in my back, and even though I was still shaky from all that sitting, I hurried to the door of the cellar. At the top of the stairs, shadows bolted into the darkness of the second floor hallway. Sofas, chairs, tables, a wardrobe, a pustule of furniture swelled and shrank as the light glided across it. Nina rushed up beside me, grasping my arm so firmly that I nearly bit my tongue.

Then I opened the cellar door and went ahead of her down the small flight of steps. When my feet touched the concrete floor I stopped and waited for her to follow. I raised the candelabra and let the light do the rest. Nina was halfway down the stairs, but the last step seemed to take forever. It was as if she were suddenly moving in slow motion. She clapped one hand to her mouth and, holding closed the collar of Uncle Herman's jacket with the other hand, looked about in stunned silence.

'Sauerkraut,' I said. 'Do you have any objection to sauerkraut?' She shook her head. I handed her the candelabra and walked past the shelves of provisions, where I chose a tin of beef sausages, a bag of dried apples, condensed milk, a jar of stock, potatoes, a packet of sauerkraut, spices, mustard, a rectangular piece of dried meat, and a bottle of Pinot Gris.

'What . . .' She was still looking around. 'What's all this?' The candlelight glided over the towering walls of cans and jars. 'My God. There's enough here for . . . for . . .'

'For the next world war,' I said.

'Was he some kind of fanatical hoarder?'

I shook my head. 'No. There was always an adequate supply of food in the cellar, but nothing out of the ordinary. I have no idea where all this has come from or when these shelves were stocked.'

Nina went over to one of the racks and picked up a tin. She turned it around in the light of her candle, squinting. Then she picked up another tin, a glass jar, a box, a crackling bag of pasta. 'I'd say a year, maybe a year and a half. Not much more. Tins and jars usually have a shelf life of two to three years.' She handed me a tin of peas and showed me the date on the bottom. Their edibility was guaranteed for at least two more years. 'You can tell best by looking at the coffee. Here. This packet'll be good for three more months. That means it couldn't have been bought more than a year ago.'

'Smart girl,' I said.

She put back the tin and looked at me impassively.

'Come on, I think we should go back upstairs,' I said. 'It's much too cold down here. There's a fire going in the kitchen.' I opened the door and let her go first. With the swaying globe of candlelight before her she walked to the kitchen. There, in the pleasing glow of the Aga, which I had lit earlier that afternoon, I set out the ingredients. I handed Nina a knife and let her peel the potatoes, while I arranged the apples in a baking dish and poured myself a glass of wine. I slid the dish into a lukewarm spot in the oven.

'What's going on, Nathan?' she asked after a while.

I filled a large pot with an inch or two of water and placed it on the stove.

'What do you mean? This house? The barricade? The supplies? I don't know. I have no idea. And what's more: I can't imagine how any of it got here.' I cut the dried meat in thin strips with one of the large knives from the block. The meat was as hard as a wooden beam and tasted like Bressaola, as the Italians called their dried fillet of ox.

'Mrs Sanders?'

Mrs Sanders managed the house during Uncle Herman's absence and played housekeeper whenever he was there.

'Why would she bother? Uncle Herman left the house five years ago. I haven't been back here in all that time. Besides, when we did use to come here, Uncle Herman had everything delivered fresh.'

Nina handed me the potatoes and leaned against the counter. 'But how . . .'

I cut the potatoes in four, tossed them into the pan and topped them with the sauerkraut.

We stared silently at the dark sky behind the kitchen window. Now and then a cloud of snow was hurled against the glass, as if someone were playing Mother Holle and shaking out a feather pillow.

The water boiled, I added thyme, salt and rosemary and moved the pan to a part of the stove where the sauerkraut could simmer gently.

'I don't like it,' said Nina. 'I don't like it one bit.'

I poured a generous dash of Pinot Gris and the contents of the jar of stock over the sauerkraut and covered the whole thing with the dried apples.

'So I'd noticed.'

Slowly the odours began to fill the kitchen. Wine-tinged fumes curled up along the lid and droplets of steam began forming on the windowpanes. I pricked the potatoes with a fork: time to add the shredded meat. I slid it off the marble chopping board I had found in a cabinet and stirred it into the sauerkraut. At the bottom of the big cupboard, where it had always stood, was the little saucepan. I emptied in the tin of sausages and put it on the back burner. I opened the can of condensed milk, added a few heaped spoonfuls of mustard (whoever had stocked these shelves certainly knew their condiments: it was Colman's), and mixed it all together. A dash of the wine, a spoonful of cooking liquid from the pan. I stirred and tasted.

The windows were steamed up. Those farthest from the stove were already beginning to freeze over. I took two plates out of the cupboard, put them in the sink, and poured hot water over them from the kettle standing on the back of the stove.

'This is the story of my life,' said Nina. 'I'm snowed-up in a haunted house with a fairy tale writer who's writing the biography of his mad uncle, and he's making sauerkraut and potatoes. My mother was right. I wasn't destined for happiness.'

'It could have been worse,' I said. 'I might have been an accountant. Then what would you have done for the next few days? Read my ledger?'

'What do you mean: then what would I have done?'

I tipped the water out of the plates, got a dishtowel out of the cupboard, and began drying them. The towel smelled like it badly needed airing.

'Now that we're stuck here you'll have plenty of time to read Uncle Herman's biography.'

She heaved a sigh.

I took some wood out of the basket next to the stove and threw it in the Aga.

'Do we have enough firewood to last us a while?'

I nodded. 'After we've eaten we'll have to chop some more, but that barricade is so huge, it'll go a long way.'

She looked at me glumly.

Sauerkraut

WE HAD ARRIVED in the winter to end all winters. That morning Nina had been standing at the appointed place, behind the gate in the arrivals hall, left arm flung around her body in a half embrace, the other raised and waving, her long, deep red curls a torch above the dark blue coat.

'N,' she had said, as her cold lips brushed my cheeks.

'N,' I had answered.

In the car, leaning forward slightly to adjust the heat, she asked if I'd had a good trip, and didn't I think it was cold, fifteen below ... Had I heard there was more snow on the way? And she had turned the car onto the motorway, as the chromium grin of a delivery van loomed up in the corner of my eye. Without thinking, I jerked back in my seat. Nina straightened the wheel and sniffed as the van barely missed us and slithered, honking, into the left lane.

'Trolls,' she muttered.

The further inland we drove, the whiter the world became. There were cars parked along the roadside, a pair of snowploughs chugged along ahead of us. Halfway there, we stopped for coffee in a snow-bound petrol station, full of lorry drivers smoking strong tobacco and phoning their bosses to ask what they should do. After that the snow began falling with such a vengeance, you could hardly tell the difference anymore between road and land. The snow banked up and blew in thick eddies across the whitened countryside. Nina and I leaned forward and peered into the whorls.

After more than three hours we neared our destination. The car danced a helpless cakewalk on the rising and falling country roads. Nina sat motionless, one hand clamped around the wheel, the other on the gearstick, eyes narrowed and fixed on the horizon. We were going less than twenty miles an hour. Her hair blazed so fiercely, I could almost hear it crackling. Her pale skin was whiter than ever.

'Another fifteen minutes or so.'

Nina nodded. She turned the wheel to the right. The car drifted into a side road.

'Do you mind if I smoke?'

'Not at all. That is, as long as it isn't one of those filthy cigars.'

'That was Uncle Herman, dear girl. And they weren't filthy cigars. He only ever smoked Partagas and Romeo y Juliettas.'

'It's like setting fire to a pile of dry leaves.'

I grinned.

'I can't believe you still do that,' she said, as I lit up my Belgian cigarette and blew the smoke at my window.

'I'm too old to stop. It's too late for me anyway.'

She shot me a sidelong glance.

'Sixty,' I said. 'When this century retires, so will I.'

Nina frowned.

'When we bid farewell to the twentieth century, I'll be sixty-five.'

I gazed out at the picture book of white fields and paths, and smoked. Every so often we dipped down, into a shallow valley, and the *akkers*, the fertile slopes for which this region was famous, spread out before us, only white now, gentle curves beneath the endlessly falling snow.

'Hey, was that a joke?'

I looked sideways. 'About the century, you mean?'

She shook her head. 'What you said over the phone, that Uncle Herman's biography has turned into more of a family chronicle.'

I rested my head against the cold doorjamb and closed my eyes. Even then, I could see the whiteness slipping past us. I pulled at my cigarette and blew more smoke at the window. I knew that Nina was truly interested, not just in the family history, but also in the things I made. She was the only one of the Hollanders who had read everything I'd ever written. For several years now she had even been my European agent. As a result of her efforts my fairy tales were leading new lives. A number of them had appeared as cd-roms, a group of Scandinavian television stations had banded together to turn them into a thirty-two-part series, and in the Czech Republic a director had bought the rights to *Kei*. He had phoned me one night, in Uncle Herman's Manhattan apartment, and I had listened in amazement. He wanted to film *Kei* as a realistic story. 'Let us forget that fairy tales belong to the realm of fantasy,' he said. 'Let us accept them as an expansion of our own limited reality.' In the nearly forty years that I had travelled the world as a fairy tale writer, he was the first to speak about my work as something that could be taken seriously.

I looked at Nina. 'A family chronicle. *Almost* a family chronicle.'

'But why put so much work into it? Fifty pages would have been more than enough.'

'I think Herman's little plan worked.'

She squinted again and peered through the windscreen. This far away from town they didn't sand the roads, or at least, not any more. The road that, a few miles back, had wound through the whiteness like a black river, was now nothing more than an indentation in a landscape that had been stripped of all distinguishing features.

'What little plan?'

I told her. That one of the terms of Herman's will, a biography of him in exchange for the house, had been his final attempt to lure me away from the domain of the fairy tale. That he had always thought my work was a waste of talent and, all my life, had tried to change me. 'And now, after fifty years, he's actually done it. I can't get away with some fake biography. But I can't see myself writing a real one either. *The Life and Works of Herman Hollander* . . . No. Somehow or other I have to tell everything. From Great-Great-Grand-Uncle Chaim up until this very moment. Like that story about the English explorer who finds himself in an Indian tribe in the Amazon. Never seen a white man. He and his travelling companions receive a royal welcome and that night around the fire the tribal sorcerer tells them the history of his people, from the moment the gods created the first Indian out of a crocodile, up until the moment that three white-skinned, red-headed Englishmen walked into the village.'

'The Creation of the World, and everything that goes with it. By Nathan Hollander.'

'Something like that.'

Nina sighed.

We had reached the end of a long, sluggish dip in the road and were now moving slowly upward, up the Mountain that wasn't a mountain. Conifers, heavy with snow, jostled along the narrow path. Now and then the car skidded and Nina had to shift down to get it back on course. The woods grew denser, the road narrower, until all that remained was a path that bore like a tunnel through the thick hedge of tall white firs. It twisted left to right and the car glided right to left. I looked sideways and, in a flash, saw ghosts among the trees. They were hurrying along with us to the top. Uncle Chaim, Magnus, Herman, Manny, Zeno. They dashed through the thick white forest like a pack of wolves. The road curled once more, the car wriggled, groaning, into a curve. It was as if we were driving so slowly because we were laden down with history, as if my family was indeed running along the edge of the wood, while the weight of their stories hung from the rear bumper.

'Shit.'

With a thud, the car veered into a snowdrift. The engine screeched and died. The snow scurried around us and the windscreen wipers stuck out through the layer of down that was forming on the glass. Nina opened the door and looked outside. Then she turned to me in amusement. 'We're stuck.'

I rolled down my window a little and tried to inspect our surroundings through the veils sweeping by. 'It's not even supposed to snow this hard around here.'

'Yes, but when it does you get an instant seventeenth-century winter landscape.'

'What are we going to do?'

'The only thing we can do,' said Nina. 'Walk.'

'Don't you think you'll be able to get us out?'

'I can try, but it doesn't look hopeful.'

'I'll push.'

I got out. Nina started the car, put it into reverse, and slowly released the clutch. I leaned against the bonnet. The wheels churned through the snow, the car glided slowly backwards. When she had manoeuvred it to the middle of the path, about thirty feet back, I went around to her door and leaned over. Nina rolled down her window and began laughing. 'You look incredible.'

'We'd better walk the rest of the way,' I said. 'It'll take hours to get past that bank and I think it'll only get worse higher up the Mountain.'

'What do we do with your luggage?'

'I can manage, it's just one bag.'

She got out of the car. I took my suitcase out of the boot, and then got out the tow rope. I tied one end around Nina's waist, the other around my own. She arched her left eyebrow, but said nothing.

It snowed. It snowed it snowed it snowed. When we looked back after sixty feet or so, we could hardly see the car anymore. In a few hours' time it would be a barely visible bulge in a high white bank.

From where we were stranded the path went up and to the left. It was only recognizable as a path because it was fringed with trees. I had no idea exactly where we were or how much farther we had to walk. We waded through the knee-deep snow, hampered by our long coats and slippery shoes and the shrieking snowstorm. Now and then I felt Nina tug on the rope and I turned round and waited until she signalled for us to move on.

After half an hour's walking the path disappeared. In a whirling white vortex of snow, half visible, fast asleep behind the shuttered library and hunting room windows, stood the house.

'Well, here we are . . .' said Nina, her shoulders hunched in the snow-covered coat.

The storm seemed to have subsided, slow fat flakes were falling, creamy tufts of white that floated down with such ease, they seemed to be saying: No need for us to hurry, there are so many of us, we have all the time in the world. I looked at the house and felt something stirring inside.

Even though the snow lay thick upon my shoulders and was

falling so steadily that it nearly robbed me of the view, my thoughts slipped readily into the lake of memories that encircled this place, and instead of white, white, and more white, I saw the long wooden table that had been set out in the garden when we spent our last summer here all together: the tablecloths hanging down in the tall grass, wine bottles here and there, half-empty, half-full, the flowers Zoe had strewn among the dishes and bread baskets, the gentle confusion of empty chairs around the table. At the back of the garden Zelda and Sophie, our mother, were playing badminton, Zeno lay asleep on the garden seat, smiling like a buddha, and Zoe and Alexander – I think it was still Alexander in those days – walked hand in hand in the soft twilight at the edge of the lawn, where the woods began. Bumblebees buzzed above the wine glasses, way, way up in the sky swallows were chasing thrips, and the smell of resin and dry wood wafted down from the treetops.

'I'll tell you what you're thinking,' said Uncle Herman. He blew out a grey-blue cloud of cigar smoke, a Romeo y Julietta, so fragrant it made my head swim. 'You're thinking, if only things could always be this way.'

We were sitting side by side on the red-tiled verandah, a table with ice bucket and bottle between us.

'If only things could always be this way, that's what you're thinking. You're such a sentimental bastard. A little sun, some wine, the family in the garden, and you think: *Une dimanche à la campagne.* I know you.' He puffed at his cigar. 'Where's Mrs Sanders?'

I turned around and looked inside. 'No idea.'

'Are you planning to stay and work here?'

A pretzel-shaped smoke ring floated off and didn't dissolve until it was very far away from us.

'Yes,' I said. 'If it's all right with you.'

'You didn't get the key for nothing. And if you can keep your mouth shut I'll even tell you a secret . . .'

Zoe and Alexander came walking towards us. They looked like two characters in a French film. My sister was wearing a long white linen dress, Alexander a cream-coloured suit and a battered straw hat. They were still walking hand in hand. Zoe worked for *Elegance.*

If she was wearing this now you could be sure that the Summer-in-the French-Countryside look would be all the rage the following year.

'Just don't tell me you're engaged,' said Uncle Herman, 'because if you do I'm going down to the cellar and staying there until everyone's gone.'

'We're engaged,' said Zoe.

'*Une dimanche à la campagne,*' I said. 'Need I say more?'

Alexander turned his questioning gaze to Zoe.

'Where the hell is Mrs Sanders?'

Zoe pointed. Uncle Herman turned round and jumped when he saw that she was standing right behind him. 'Good God, woman, don't sneak up on me like that.' Mrs Sanders lowered her left eyebrow. 'The engagement cake,' he said. 'It's time for the engagement cake!' Zoe began laughing. Alexander opened his mouth, looked at Uncle Herman and from him to me and then back to Zoe, and closed it again.

When Mrs Sanders had cleared the table and set out the huge cake, the coffee, and the plates and cups, I went to get Zeno. He was still lying on the garden seat, nestled in a cloud of cushions. The sun filtered through the leaves of the apple tree. His body was dappled with tiny golden flecks. 'Raised by leopards, he was, all the years of his youth,' I said, after I had stood there for a while watching him. Zeno opened one eye. He observed me coolly. 'For a kabbalist, you're far too poetic, N,' he said. He shut his eye again and for a moment it was as if he were drifting away. I could see him lying in a paper boat, gliding away over an unruffled lake that was red with evening sun. 'The cake's ready,' I said. Zeno groaned softly. 'Is it that time again?' He opened both eyes, so slowly I almost envied him.

At the table the coffee had already been poured. Zelda turned halfway round in her chair and beckoned to Zeno. He sat down next to her and whispered something in her ear that made her laugh. He was the only one who could. Uncle Herman once said that Zelda's great tragedy was that she had been born a nun in a Jewish family.

19

'Hollanders!' cried Uncle Herman, jumping up from his chair and waving the cake knife, as if he were about to make the traditional sacrifice. 'Here we are, all together again, as we are nearly every summer, and here is the engagement cake . . .'

'. . . as it is nearly every summer,' I said.

Zoe smiled indulgently.

'As it is nearly every summer,' Uncle Herman affirmed. 'But why, you should be asking, Zeno, why is this day different from all other days?'

'Why should I be asking?'

'Because you're the youngest, you moron.' Zeno nodded at Zoe as if to thank her.

'This day is different from all other days, because I have a few important announcements to make. A: I'm giving up the house.'

None of us were prepared for this. My mother shrank back, her right hand on her chest, mouth slightly open. Zelda gazed intently at Uncle Herman. Zeno narrowed his eyes. I looked to the left and stared up at the sky. The dying light of the setting sun caressed Uncle Herman's white hair, 'the Einstein halo,' as my father used to call it.

'I'm too old to look after the place,' he said. 'And for that reason: point B, I'm leaving Nathan in charge, not only of the Fatherland . . .' Cheers rose. Zeno said something I didn't understand. 'But also . . .' He held up one hand to silence his audience, '. . . in charge of the house. That is, if he's willing to accept the responsibility. Each of you will have the right to spend time here now and again.'

There was another burst of applause. Uncle Herman didn't move a muscle. He waved the knife, and when it was quiet he opened his mouth again. 'And now we cut the cake, the traditional engagement cake, in the hope that this will be the last. And finally: regards to all of you from your father. To the happy couple!'

He stuck the knife in the cake and sliced it in two, so resolutely that he really did seem to be finishing off a sacrificial beast.

Later, when the sun had gone down, we sat in the library, Uncle Herman, Sophie and I. The rest, Zoe and Alexander, Zeno, and

Mrs Sanders, were in the kitchen, where my sisters and brother drank wine and the housekeeper plied Zeno with bread and cheese. Even though it had been a hot day, Uncle Herman had asked me to make a fire and move the large chesterfield over by the hearth. 'Fire is good for books,' he said, 'as long as it doesn't get too close.' The glow of the flames enclosed us in a swaying red globe of light and shadow.

'It's been a fine day,' said Sophie.

'After a day like today, a person could die happy,' said Uncle Herman.

'Actually, I was thinking of trying to get some work done,' I said. 'One last glass of wine, cup of coffee . . .'

'That's exactly why I'm leaving you the house,' said Uncle Herman. 'You're such a Calvinistic bastard.'

'Leaving him in *charge* of the house,' said Sophie.

'Leaving him in charge. But when I die, the house is his. He's the only one of you who has any use for it. Besides, where else would he put all these books?'

My eyes travelled from the fire to my uncle. I was aware that my mouth had dropped open.

'You get the house, N.'

I wanted to say something, but got no further than a vague sort of stammering.

'Herman, how can he keep up a house like this? The boy can hardly even support himself.'

Uncle Herman raised his glass and peered at the red spark floating in the wine. 'It has always been my conviction that you should give a man bread when he's hungry, but let him provide his own butter. Stimulates the initiative.'

My mother looked at me with a worried expression.

'Sophie,' said Uncle Herman, 'if it's the others you're concerned about . . . I'm sure they'll see reason, and if they don't, they obviously don't have the sense of family loyalty they should. And besides . . .' He straightened up in his chair and took a gulp of wine. 'Nathan will have to do something for me in return.'

I looked at him without saying a word. In the reflection of the flames the white wreath of hair had taken on a faint red glow. The gently hooked nose stuck out like a beak and the wilful mouth was crinkled into a benevolent smile. He wasn't very tall, my Uncle Herman, five foot eight at most, but sometimes, like now, he gave the impression of being twice his size. Perhaps it was the coarse tweed jacket with the suede elbow patches, or his rather slow-emphatic way of moving, or his penetrating gaze. Or perhaps it was the way he spoke. The way Uncle Herman talked always sounded as if he were pronouncing judgement on the validity of the logical-positivistic viewpoint in this day and age or something similar, even if he was only asking you to put the cork down next to the bottle after you'd opened it. On the few occasions that I had accompanied him on one of his lecture tours, I'd been impressed by his talents as a demagogue. For the first time I had understood why the great minds of our time spoke with and listened to him as if he were their equal.

'This house,' said Herman, 'is no ordinary beautiful house in the woods. And this library . . .' He made a sweeping gesture with his arm to indicate the walls of books that surrounded us. '. . . is no ordinary library. This is a line in the sand. A boundary. The black hole through which we can navigate that other dimension.'

'Herman . . .' I said.

'And nothing less than that.'

'Okay.'

'No, not: okay. Do I speak in tongues? This. This. This. Here! This is your ship to the other world. You don't know it yet, but you'll find out.' He emptied his glass and rose unsteadily from his chair. 'That is, if you're made of the same stuff as . . .' His voice dissolved in a peal of laughter that rang out from the kitchen. 'Listen,' he said, raising his right hand, 'they're enjoying themselves. Fine. That's fine.' He tapped on the pockets of his jacket, glanced down at the table next to his chair, and then rested his eyes on Sophie. She stood up hurriedly. 'Come,' he said. 'Let's all laugh. This way, ladies and gentlemen, to the gas chambers. Everything's fine.' He offered Sophie his arm, and as they stepped into the darkness that lay outside the circle of firelight, he tapped me on the shoulder.

'Yes. Laugh. But just remember where it all came from and where it's going. Don't ever forget . . .' He paused to enhance the dramatic effect of what he was about to say. '. . . we're still a family of clock-makers!'

They strode off into the dusk. My mother cast a confused glance at me over her shoulder, but when I grinned back, she frowned.

And so, speaking in tongues, more than a little tipsy, leaning on my mother's arm as if he weren't my uncle at all, her brother-in-law, but an ageing Casanova, finally at peace in the company of the woman with whom he would spend his last years, my Uncle Herman left the library, never to return, and I was left behind, staring at the slow flickering of the fire, painfully aware of the walls of books that seemed to be whispering softly, 'You're all ours now. It's you and us and the house. We'll never let you go.'

When I left the next morning Mrs Sanders was standing in the front doorway, at the top of the whitewashed stairs. She had one hand on her hip and the other raised halfway above her head, but she wasn't waving. I waved to her, hoisted my suitcase onto my shoulder and walked down the path, towards the trees, on my way to the bus that stopped at the bottom of the hill. When I reached the edge of the forest I looked round one last time. Mrs Sanders had gone back into the house. The shutters on the first floor windows were closed and the library curtains drawn to keep out the morning sun. In the late August light, the house looked like the head of a giant whose body was the hill I now descended. I could see him, the Titan, crouched, his arms around his knees, sound asleep for centuries. Moss, grass, shrubs, and finally trees had sprung up all over his body. But there would come a day when he would feel the blood flowing through his limbs once more and his body would stir beneath the earth. The trees would shake and the thick layer of humus and woodland soil would burst open. He'd flex his muscles and rise up and look out over the lazy, elfin landscape of the East, over the rippling farmland, the slopes overgrown with broadleaved trees, the mossy banks and the drowsy little villages at the place where two roads meet.

'Here we are . . .' Nina had said, when the house came into view.

The snowstorm screeched around us. Nina's hair flew about wildly, only her pale forehead, and now and then part of her face, were visible in the stream of red flames.

'This is it,' I said.

I crunched my way to the entrance, a green door at the top of a flight of stairs that was no more than a ripple in the snow, took the big key out of my pocket, and jiggled it in the lock.

In the hall, where the air was grey with snowlight, the stale smell of emptiness leapt up and hurried towards us. I leaned over and began untying the rope around Nina's waist. I sank down on one knee and tugged at the rope with stiff, cold fingers. I blew on my hands and fiddled with the knot, which had been pulled tighter by our struggle through the snow. Nina didn't move. She stood bolt upright. When I looked up after a while to apologize for my fumbling, I saw her gazing down at me patiently. Several more minutes went by before I had freed her, and it felt as if I had set myself free. The warmth of her body escaped from her coat and glided around me. I was amazed, so much warmth from such a slender woman. As if she were ablaze, as if it were no coincidence that the red hair kept reminding me of fire, but the visible manifestation of a heat raging within her. I straightened up, the rope still in my hands, a hangman who suddenly lacks the conviction to fulfil his task. Nina laughed like an anaemic angel.

We stood on the black-and-white marble-tiled floor and looked around in silence. The twilight hung about us like vapour, the cakes of snow that had fallen from our coats lay on the floor without melting. It was nearly as cold in here as it was outside. I took a few steps forward. 'Welcome to Bluebeard's Castle, Ninotchka.' She followed the theatrical gesture with which I tried to encompass the space, our presence, everything that determined this moment. When my hand was poised somewhere above my head, her face froze.

Upstairs, where the staircase ended, the staircase that plunged down from the first floor like a waterfall of turned wood and scroll-work, rose a solidified tidal wave of wood and upholstery. The landing was crammed full of cabinets and chairs and lamps. I saw a large sofa, a linen cupboard, the red plush sofa from the bedroom that overlooked the garden, the secretaire, a sideboard, chairs-chairschairs. I took another step forward, in order to see better. My right foot landed in a patch of snow and I slid across the slippery marble. As I fell over backwards, my arms flailing, I saw something black shooting through the air. Nina's arms slipped under mine and slowly we sank to the floor. Only then, half in Nina's embrace, my eyes still on the ceiling, did I see, looking down on us, unmoved, impassively gleaming in all its black sovereignty, the piano, the lid slightly open, and behind that lid, barely visible in the murky light of the stairwell, but I knew they were there, the grinning row of black and white keys, the rotting teeth of the music beast.

'What . . .' said Nina, 'what . . . is . . . that?'

We scrambled to our feet and stared up at the protuberance of furniture, the piano that hung there like an ebony cloud, a Dali vision come to life.

I shook my head.

In the grainy light I could see the faint lines of two thick ropes that had been tied around either side of the piano and disappeared behind it by way of a hook on the ceiling. I walked up a few stairs, until I was standing under the instrument, and peered through a gap between two pieces of furniture. The ropes ran down along the wall of the stairwell and had been secured to one of the pieces of furniture that formed the front of the barricade. One tug at the sideboard, the secretaire, or the linen cupboard, and the piano would come crashing down and flatten anyone standing below it.

A trap, I thought, this is a trap. Everything was so precisely wedged together that it was impossible to push anything aside to get through. If we wanted to get past this barricade, we would have to deal with the piano first. It was the only way to prevent it from crashing down unexpectedly. Someone must have dragged the whole interior, piece by piece, to the stairwell, and then, slowly and deliberately, re-arranged it all. It must have been someone who knew Uncle Herman but didn't have his best interests at heart. I ran my index finger along the sideboard.

'Maybe we'd better sit down,' I said. Nina was still staring at the barricade. I took her arm, pulled her along to the hunting room, and offered her the bed as a chair.

The shutters at the front of the house were closed and the hunting room was so dark that the huge four-poster bed, where Uncle Herman used to sleep, stood in the shadows like a solid block.

'N?' Her voice came from far away. 'What is that up there at the top of the stairs?'

'I don't know. I haven't been back here in five years.'

'Why?'

'Why all that junk?'

'Why haven't you been back in all that time?'

I looked around me, at the furniture that seemed so lifeless and grey. 'It's not the same any more,' I said. 'And I didn't feel I should come back until I'd earned it. Now the biography is almost done. Now I'm allowed.'

She was silent.

I looked into the darkened room. 'Whatever's up there, it hasn't been there very long.' I lit a cigarette and blew out a puff of smoke. 'There's not much dust on that furniture. Someone's been in here and . . . It couldn't have been Mrs Sanders. She's not strong enough to drag all those . . .'

'Then who? A burglar?'

'I don't know. The lock was intact. He would've had to come in through the back . . . But why? Why would a burglar build a barricade?'

I held the cone of ash from my cigarette above my cupped left palm and looked around.

'The fireplace,' said Nina.

'What?'

'You could throw it in the fireplace.'

I went to the hearth and flicked the ash into the blackened hole. 'Listen. You stay here, I'll check around the back. And I'll try to find some wood while I'm at it. If we don't make a fire in here, we'll freeze to death.'

She stared down at the floor. 'I've got to go back,' she said.

'You can't.'

'Let's call someone.'

'There's no phone.'

She raised her head and looked at me, her face expressionless. 'I've got to get out of here.'

'You'll never find the car, and if you do it'll probably be buried in the snow by now.'

I walked out of the room. When I looked back through the doorway, she was still sitting, motionless, on the big four-poster bed. She was peering down at her feet, as if she could see something that simply wouldn't let her go.

The house smelled like an auditorium. I inspected the kitchen and then from the kitchen window, the white lawn with the wooden shed where the gardener kept his tools. The thermometer on the windowsill read seventeen below zero. It must have been about five below in here. None of the doors at the back of the house had been forced, none of the windows were broken. I went to the library and stared into the murky light at the flood of books. The shutters were closed, the windows appeared to be intact. When I was back in the kitchen, I opened the door to the cellar. Behind the door, one foot on the stairs, I fiddled in vain with the light switch. I took the box of matches out of my pocket, lit one, and groped my way into the receding darkness. Slowly the floor came into view, and then the walls, and glass and tin, walls of tin cans, glass jars, bottles, shelves piled high with provisions, a fat red Edam, a smoked cheese, dried meat, sugar, salt, onions, dried apples, a string of garlic, crackers, candied fruits, toilet paper, a large cardboard box with bottles of detergent, bars of soap, indeterminate tubes of toothpaste, two bottles of calor gas with burners and detachable parts, and an assortment of candles. I stared, in the light of the dying match, at the display. Outside of a supermarket, I had never seen this much food at one time.

I dropped the match, it went dark. I sat down on the stairs, elbows on my knees, hands folded, and let the chilly darkness stream around me, the cool, sweet smell I remembered.

Uncle Herman never kept much in stock, because he never stayed at the house for more than three months at a time, and if he was there, he had Mrs Sanders order in as much fresh food as possible. Now the shelves were filled.

'Herman,' I said, 'Nuncle, what the hell is going on here?'

I struck another match, stood up, and walked on. The vaulted cellar extended over the length and breadth of the entire house, divided into rooms that were separated by white stucco walls with semicircular passageways. The first room, a kind of central hall beneath the real hall, was once filled with virtually empty shelves. Now they were crammed. I unpacked the candles and stuck a few in my jacket. I lit another and in the flickering light I inspected the vault to the left of the main hall. One half was taken up by a mountain of potatoes, held together by three partitions. In addition to that: tin cans and glass jars of baked beans, carrots, kidney beans, corn, red cabbage, beets, sauerkraut, ravioli, macédoine, pickled mushrooms, salmon, tuna, sardines, corned beef, canned brie and camembert, dried apples, condensed milk, powdered eggs, chicken soup, stock, green peas, candied fruits, herring in dill sauce. And in addition to that: packets of rice, pasta, potato starch, flour, jars of coriander, dill, thyme, rosemary, marjoram, pepper, oregano, ginger powder, chilli peppers, capers, horseradish, pesto. The vault to the right of the entrance, the wine cellar, was as I remembered it. Racks from floor to ceiling, not a single free patch of wall. Thick, white-grey shreds of cobweb, and fine dust, powdery as ash. There was no cellar book here, but no one would have trouble finding his way around. Everything was carefully arranged, white on the left, red on the right, subdivided by country of origin (France, Spain, Italy), province (Bordeaux, Burgundy, and so on), region (Saint-Émilion, Médoc, Pomerol, Chablis, Margaux) and year.

A barricade at the top of the stairs and enough supplies in the cellar to survive an atomic war. I couldn't believe that Mrs Sanders had dragged all this into the house by herself. And why should she? Uncle Herman was never coming back and I hadn't been here in ages. But what disturbed me most was that it looked as if that huge stockpile was there in preparation for something that was yet to happen. I turned round and went back from room to room. Jars and cans, neatly in rows, packets of sugar one behind the other, as if it had all been stocked by a diligent shop assistant. I couldn't tell whether any portion of this enormous quantity of food had ever been touched. What I did see, when I got back to the stairs, was the old transistor radio I had brought along with me on one of my visits. It was lying behind the bottom step, half-covered with a spider's web. I switched it on and heard the soft rustling of empty ether. I tucked it under my arm, blew out the candle, and went upstairs.

In the kitchen, I turned the aerial this way and that and twiddled the large dial until I picked up the sound of voices. It was the local station. I put the radio on the counter and listened to the babbling. After a minute or two there were a few bars of music and a bronzy male voice. 'This is Radio East, on air twenty-four hours a day. We're here for you. Give us a ring and tell us how you're enjoying the storm!' Then I heard a man and a woman, who took turns answering calls from people who were stranded or had something exciting to share with the listeners. A couple of people snowed in at a petrol station phoned to say they had been living on coffee machine coffee, soft drinks, and chocolate bars since the night before and longed desperately for bread and cheese. A police spokesman reported that entire villages were cut off from the outside world, columns of trucks were stranded and disbanded in the middle of nowhere. Everyone was advised against using their cars. Then came the weatherman from the airport. The snow would continue all day and possibly into the night, he said, and the temperature, for the time being, would remain at around fifteen degrees below zero. That night he expected local temperatures to drop to twenty-five below. I stood at the counter and looked out at the endless snow. We had to get wood.

In the horizonless white world that was forming outside, the blizzard snarled and shrieked. I stood knee-deep in the snow. The trees were white, the sky hidden behind a curtain of flakes so thick it was impossible to look up. The wind had blown drifts nearly three feet high against the wall of the verandah. Where the logs should have been, where they had always been, under the lean-to behind the kitchen, I found only the sawhorse and an empty brown wicker basket.

I went to the little gardener's shed, to the right of the house. There was no wood, but I did find tools, an axe wrapped in burlap, a couple of rakes, a hoe and a shovel, a grindstone, and empty wooden crates that had once held flower bulbs. There were still a few onion-like skins at the bottom. I picked up the crates and the axe and went back out into the snow, towards the kitchen. I stopped briefly to take shelter on the verandah. There, blinded by the blizzard, I wondered what to do. Chop down a tree? How long did you have to wait before green wood was dry enough to burn? White whirlpools spun through the air, snow that had fallen was whipped back up and formed new drifts in other corners. I clasped the axe firmly under my arm and went inside.

In the kitchen I laid the axe down on the counter and looked at the cold gleam on the blade. I picked it up and slowly turned it around. Then I lit the candle again, tucked the axe under my arm, and went to find Nina.

'I'm home . . .'

I opened the hunting room door a hand's-breadth and peered in through the crack. There was no answer. I pushed the door open a bit further. 'Daddy's ho-ome . . .'

The hunting room was empty. The yellowy candlelight glided across the walls and bed. Where Nina had been sitting the covers were rumpled, but she herself was nowhere to be seen. I walked inside and laid my hand on the bed. Cold. She must have been gone for a while now. She had probably left after I'd gone down into the cellar.

Why had she left without saying anything? What could possibly make her want to sneak back through the icy wind to her car, through a forest she barely knew? I blew out the candle, put the axe on the bed, and went into the hall. In the doorway, with the wind blowing me straight in the face, I peered out at the snow-covered stairs. Not a footstep in sight. I pulled my coat tighter around me, closed the door, and walked down the path, to the forest.

For half an hour I plodded through the white storm. Although it was much less windy among the trees, Nina's footsteps had vanished. It wasn't until I had reached the spot where we had left the car that I saw the first sign of her presence. Under the white film of snow that covered the path glimmered the tracks of a car that had backed out, turned, and disappeared, skidding, towards the bottom of the hill.

On the way back my feet went numb. It was as if my shoes were full of cement. Each time I took a step I felt the dull thud of something coming down too hard. I had left Nina alone while I went to look for wood and make a fire, and God knows we needed it, but now, on my third trek through the snow, as my feet and calves got soaked for the third time, I was beginning to reach the point where one is no longer cold, but scared. If my toes, fingers or ears froze, I would lose them. There was no chance of me reaching civilization on foot. I had to warm up, fast.

The last stretch I began to run, half stumbling, nearly falling, towards the house. For a moment, on the great white lawn, I rose up out of myself. I saw a tiny figure, swathed in black, fighting its way through the whiteness. The house stood motionless in the whirlpool of snow and the little man in the depths ran and ran and ran.

There is a God

IN THE LIBRARY, by the fire, we ate with our plates on our laps. The Pinot Gris was at perfect cellar temperature and fragrant as a meadow in summer. The sauerkraut was steaming hot, but we were so hungry we gobbled it down.

'Sauerkraut with mustard sauce and apples,' Nina said after a while. 'This is the first time you've ever cooked for me.'

'You could be right.'

She sipped her wine, squinting slightly. 'It's delicious. I didn't know you had it in you.'

I bowed my head in gratitude. 'When I was a boy I used to cook for the whole family. I didn't think Sophie was any good at it.'

'And was that true?'

'Was she good at it, you mean? Oh, she was alright. She'd just lost interest over the years. If you have to cook every day of the week, it's no fun anymore.'

'But you cooked every day, too. You just said so.'

'It was different for me. I cooked so I could think up fairy tales.'

Nina had put her plate down on one of Uncle Herman's mobile bookcases and was holding the glass of wine in her hand. 'I think it's time you told me why we're here,' she said.

'Why we're here? You're here because you gave me a ride and can't get back. Though you certainly did your damnedest to escape. I'm here because . . .'

'Not the old Uncle Herman story again. What's going on here?'

'I don't know, Nina, I have no idea.'

'Then let me ask you something else. What were you just doing with that cup of water? What were you saying?'

Before we sat down to eat I had filled a cup with water and poured it out over my hands, three splashes over my right hand, three over my left. 'The blessing over washing the hands and eating,' I said. 'A Jewish ritual.'

'Never heard of it. I didn't know you were religious.'

'Religious . . . I'm not religious. I'm a sceptic.'

She looked annoyed. 'So what're you saying? You pray but you don't believe in God?'

'The berakhah, the blessing, isn't praying. It's talking to God.'

'Whatever. If you ask me it's like sitting on your bike and saying vroom-vroom.'

'So?'

'So it's nonsense. It's illogical.'

I shrugged my shoulders. 'Sex is nonsense and illogical, too. For the preservation of the species it's enough just to . . .'

'Nathan, shut up. What's the point of doing all that if you don't believe in it?'

'Because I don't believe in believing. That's what I call nonsense. But the rituals, the washing of hands, the berakhot over bread and wine, we've been saying them for centuries. They don't serve any particular purpose. We only say them because we want to say them. It's an exercise.'

'Exercise?'

'In self-perspective. In humility. In transcendence. When you say the berakhah over bread, you're reminded of what a miracle our daily bread really is. You didn't make it yourself. You didn't till the land. You didn't sow the seeds and reap the grain. You didn't grind the wheat and bake bread with the flour. But it's there.'

'You worked for it. You bought it.'

'But it's still a miracle. People in other countries work for it, too, but they can't get it.'

'You're a believer.'

I shook my head. 'I'm a non-believer, through and through. I distrust every form of religion. But that doesn't mean I don't see what's extraordinary about the world.'

'The world is there.'

'And the world is extraordinary. Such a sophisticated . . . machine. So many people. So much technology. So many structures and forms.' I hesitated. 'For something that complex, it runs amazingly well.'

I leaned over and piled up the empty plates. 'I'll be right back.'

Nina nodded. She lay curled up in the chair, one side lit by the orange glow from the hearth, the other bathed in shadow.

In the kitchen, with only a faint glimmer of light from the chinks in the oven door, it was a while before I could see anything. As I waded through the darkness, something shot past the window. I froze. I stared at the black square above the sink, searching. For the first time today it fully dawned on me where I was: in an enormous hunting lodge in the forest, on top of a densely wooded hill in the middle of the countryside, a hill straight out of some dark fairy tale. A bird, I thought, it was a bird flying past the window. I put the plates down on the draining board and went into the hunting room to light a fire in the big stone hearth. If Nina hadn't returned I would have wrapped myself in a sleeping bag and spent the night in the chair in front of the fireplace in the library.

'We're running out of wood,' said Nina, when I came back in. 'There are a few more of those black chunks, but not an awful lot. What is that anyway, that black stuff?'

'The piano.'

'The . . .' She was remembering the piano. I could tell by the look on her face. The image loomed up deep within her of the black colossus that had been hanging above the stairs, like a guard before the barricade of chairs and cupboards and tables. 'My God, how did you get it down?'

'Let it fall,' I said. 'Sliced through the ropes and let it fall.'

'Wow . . .' A glittering flickered in her eyes. 'What a shame I wasn't there.'

'Yes. You don't know what you missed.'

It had been quite spectacular. Under any other circumstances, if

I hadn't been so cold and it had been of my own free will, I'd probably even have enjoyed it.

After I had abandoned my hunt for Nina, I'd staggered up the stairs like a wounded deer and immediately begun throwing things down. Fire. The word blazed before my eyes. I grabbed chairs, seizing them by the legs and hurling them to the ground. One of them smashed to pieces on the stone floor of the hall, another bounded up and down a few times like a young stag on mahogany hooves, and then broke. It was followed by a hatstand, a stool and the drawers from a sideboard.

The sideboard was the first piece of furniture blocking the way upstairs, a sturdy oblong, four drawers high, old oak, wrought brass handles. I knew nothing about antiques, but it looked Dutch, early nineteenth century. On top of the sideboard was a small red sofa, covered in plush right down to its squat wooden legs. On the seat were marks left by the chairs I had already hurled into the depths. Various odds and ends were scattered over seats and tabletops: a pendulum clock, a pile of framed photographs (Uncle Herman and Enrico Fermi, our family on board the ship to America, Sophie, Molly, my first wife). To the left of the sideboard my way was barred by a secretaire, and above that, a wooden colonial-style desk chair with padded green leather seat. The space on the right was completely filled by a mahogany china cabinet, taller than I was, the colour and gleam of fresh dung. I lifted up the desk chair and flung it over the banister. For a brief moment it occurred to me that I was standing here before a collection of antiques which had not only been assembled with great care, but which was also quite valuable, and that I had judged this construction of chairs, cupboards and knick-knacks on its wood content alone.

It had taken me a while to decide what to do next. The barricade was as much of a puzzle as it was an obstruction. If I removed the sofa, I'd have access to the linen cupboard, I could bash in the doors and side panel and dismantle the rest. Then I could cut through the ropes and the piano would go crashing down without hurting anyone. I reached forward, grabbed one of the sofa legs and tugged carefully. The sideboard under the sofa groaned. When I looked up at the piano, slow patches of light were gliding across the gleaming black lacquer and the sideboard began to move. The piano needed the sideboard to stay up, the sideboard needed the sofa to hold it down.

I walked downstairs to gather up the bits and pieces of wood, carried them into the kitchen, lit a fire in the Aga, and went outside.

It was snowing harder than ever. I had to grope my way to the gardener's shed. There, tired and wet and cold, I rummaged through the tools. I chose a rake, a hoe and a shovel, cranked up the grindstone and placed the blade of the hoe against the grinding face. Minutes later it was sharp as a knife. I threw a hammer, a chisel, a pair of pincers, and a couple of screwdrivers into a burlap sack, tucked the tools I had set aside under my arm, and walked back.

Lucky for me, the shed was only about a hundred feet away from the kitchen door and I wasn't so tired that I'd lost my sense of direction, but even at this short distance, anyone else would have been in serious trouble. The icy wind whipped up thick whorls of snow and drove the flakes in high banks against the back of the house. If it continued snowing like this, in a few hours' time I'd no longer be able to get the doors open on this side. I'd have to climb out the window to dig a passageway through a bank. From what I could tell, the snow was about two feet deep, much deeper in places where the wind had blown drifts. That shovel would certainly come in handy.

Back inside, at the top of the stairs, I climbed up onto the sideboard and the sofa. I straightened up and, balancing precariously, raised the hoe. Night hadn't fallen yet, but dusk hung heavy in the hall and I could barely see the ropes. It was a long time before I finally got the blade in the right place. If I cut through the left rope, the one farthest away from me, the right side of the piano would come down. The piano would land next to me on the stairs or, by the force of its own weight, tighten the rope around the left side and hang there, at least for a while. Then I could cut through the remaining rope and let the piano fall on the stairs. I pushed the hoe upward and began to make cutting movements. The blade was so sharp, it sliced through the rope in almost a single stroke. There was a loud bang, the creaking of wood, the groaning of the rope as it was pulled tighter. But the piano didn't just hang there. It swung forcefully to the right, seemed to come to a standstill, and then, with a powerful heave, came swooping back. It was a terrifying sight, the great gleaming black instrument swinging back and forth up there from the ceiling. The rope groaned loudly and you could faintly hear the singing of the piano strings. Then the barricade began to move. The sideboard shifted. Wood moaned, slid past more wood and made the disagreeable sound of things being slowly pulled apart. I aimed my hoe at the other rope, which was quivering with the strain, and pressed down. The rope was hard as steel. I took a deep breath and leaned my weight against the handle. Suddenly, before I knew what was happening, a black beast came raging down from the heavens. I fell sideways, grabbed hold of the sofa, which began tipping, and let go of the hoe. The roar of breaking wood, a crash as if a complete symphony orchestra had been hurled into a cellar. The whole house was filled with sound, piano notes echoed from wall to wall, pieces of wood that had flown up came back down again.

It was a full minute before the rustle of silence had taken possession of the hall once more. Down below, the stone floor looked like the scene of a shipwreck on a South Sea island beach. The piano had exploded in a cloud of brushwood. Only the harp and lid had survived the fall. The rest lay strewn over the marble tiles in chunks the size of a hand or a forearm. I grabbed the rake, walked downstairs, and began clearing up the mess. On the way down I saw the marks of the piano's descent. It had hit the banister, gouged out a piece of wood, then bounced off the stairs and shattered to bits. The staircase looked as if someone had rolled down from the first floor in a tank.

Downstairs I picked up the piano lid. I leaned it against the staircase, grabbed the axe, and split the wood into strips thin enough that I could kick them to pieces. When I was finished I divided up the wood between the library and the kitchen. In the library hearth I built a fire with crumpled newspaper, the remains of a splintered crate, and the thin strips provided by the bottoms of the drawers. The wind shrieked through the chimney and tugged at the front door, which was pounding wildly in its latch. I arranged a few of the larger chunks of piano on top of the little heap of paper and splinters, and lit a match. The draught in the chimney sucked up the burgeoning fire out of the newspaper, through the brittle wood, to the larger pieces.

The hearths in the library and hunting room, green catafalques of Italian marble, were deep enough to sit in. You could build a huge fire in those hearths, and I would have done so, if I hadn't already known that Uncle Herman had made the same mistake when he spent a winter here in the fifties. The heat had burst the frozen flue and they'd had to send for a man from one of the neighbouring villages to repair the damage.

By the time I got back to the kitchen, it was fairly comfortable. The fire in the huge stove had driven out the worst of the cold. I picked up the basket I had found in the gardener's shed, went down to the cellar and filled it with several bottles of wine, a box of crackers, a wedge of cheese and butter, a tin of powdered milk, jars of spices, a coffee pot and filter, salt and sugar, and a handful of candles. In the library, in front of the fire, I sat and ate. I could still hear the front door rattling in its latch. High above me, where the wind played the chimney like a flute, rose a low, plaintive moan. I imagined snow whirling around the house, curling along the windows and walls and settling in banks that grew higher by the hour. I put the remains of the piano lid on the fire and watched as the flames tasted the black wood. The lacquer began to wrinkle, here and there a tiny bluish flame danced on a splinter. Then the fire shot into one of the chunks, and then another, and another. It gave off a delicious warmth. I closed the heavy curtains, put the plate of crackers and cheese that I had prepared on my lap, and poured a glass of wine, an ice-cold Nebbiolo d'Alba. The glow of the flames lit the room. Candles stood on either side of the mantel-piece, others here and there on top of a cupboard. Slowly, I began to warm up. My joints thawed, the wooden feeling in my knees disappeared.

Nina had left at around five. It was now nearly seven. I had spent about three hours in the house. I was dead tired. The cold, lugging all that wood, the chopping and splitting, had worn me out. As I sat there by the fire, my eyes grew blurred and I was overcome by a metallic feeling of exhaustion. The flames illuminated the green marble scrolls on the mantelpiece. The hearth began to look like a gateway. Beyond that gateway I saw the soot-covered wall of the chimney, the paler spots where the fire couldn't reach and the blackened patch in which the brickwork was no more than a tarnished bulge. The fire murmured and sighed. I heard the banging of the front door in the hall as the wind yanked it back and forth. I closed my eyes and thought about the fairy tale I had been working on for the past few months. It was as if something toppled over inside my head.

The Kotzker

HE WHO WORKS his way past five mangy chickens, Yankel Davidovitz's bony cow, and the massive stench of the rubbish dump behind the house of Schloime Kreisky, the hide trader, will be rewarded with a view of the sagging door of the Kotzker shul. It hangs in its cracked leather hinges like an unwashed dishrag, begging for a lick of paint, yammering for a little consideration, and maybe a nail or two. Around the door the walls of the shul struggle to hold each other up. The mortar between the bricks is brittle and crushed, the beam anchors rusty, the high windows black with soot. But even before his fingers have touched the door handle, a glob of snot dangling from the wood, even as he stands upon the threshold, trying to decide whether this wretched pile of bricks could possibly still be in use, his ears are graced by the gentle singsong and soft murmuring of the morning service, his nostrils teased by the smell of books, candied ginger, smoking oil lamps and the wax with which the rebbe's wife polishes the tables, the chairs, in short, the entire shul.

Which brings us to the rebbe, the Reb, or simply, Menachem Mendel, the spiritual and social leader of the motley crew that constitutes Kotzker Jewry. Thirty years ago he came here from Pzysha and has been the rabbi of Kotzk ever since, thirty long years, the past ten of which he has spent in utter solitude, in the unrelenting, self-imposed confinement of his study. The last his followers ever heard from him, and that was seven years ago, was a furious, incomprehensible shout. Schloime Kreisky was the cause of this outburst, stinking Schloime, doomed to walk the earth amid the reek of rotting hides, hog's piss and mouldering bark, Schloime, who had taken himself to the place of silence to ask the Reb what it meant when a slice of bread fell to the ground butter-side down, and was told in no uncertain terms that he was a 'stinking swine's tit'. Inquisitive as they are, those Kotzker Jews, the last-recorded words of Menachem Mendel were discussed at length, pondered, weighed, held up to the light, sucked on and chewed over until, at the end of a long night, Yankel Davidovitz slammed his palm down on the long wooden table in the middle of the study-house and roared, 'But Schloime *is* a stinking swine's tit!' Whereupon the deeply wounded Schloime leapt to his feet and screamed at Yankel that while he might smell a bit unusual, at least he, Schloime Kreisky, hide trader of Kotzk, didn't have daughters who disgraced the village by flirting shamelessly with every straw-haired fat-bellied Polak and that he could swear with his hand on his heart that he, Schloime Kreisky, would never milk an innocent cow dry like 'some people around here', to which Yankel shrugged his shoulders and said that his troubles were his own concern and that his cow, even if, God forbid, she should die, was still too good to serve as merchandise for a certain 'hide trader'. From that day on, the silence between Schloime Kreisky and Yankel Davidovitz had been as profound as that surrounding Reb Menachem Mendel, and would have remained so, had not the Lord of the Universe in his immeasurable wisdom decreed that Schloime's youngest son Mendel should fall in love with one of Davidovitz's wanton daughters.

Mendel fell for Rivka like a rotting oak before the woodsman. He was young, barely eighteen and, like most lads his age, preoccupied with finding some rhyme or reason in this madly spinning world. His eyes drifted searchingly through the tops of the drooping oaks around Kotzk and sometimes, in autumn and spring, but now it was autumn, Mendel could feel his heart pounding wildly and he had to stifle the urge to sing and shout. Not that singing or shouting (in Kotzk there wasn't much difference between the two) would be considered strange, on the contrary, but Mendel was afraid of what might fly from his lips. There was a tumult raging in his breast that he thought it might be better to suppress.

One autumn morning, Mendel arrived at the watering place along

the road to Worki with his daily load of bark. He had been journey-
ing since daybreak, and now that the sun was up and the sky had
changed from purple to red to orange, he felt it was time for bread,
water, and rest. He flung his load under an oak tree, scooped up
water in the bowl of his hands, drank, sat down against the bundle
of bark, and fell asleep. He began dreaming, something about the
pile of hides behind the workshop. They rose up and came running
after him, and he fell and they started dancing around him, but then
he awoke and saw that he was surrounded by seven young women,
all looking down at him and smiling. At first he closed his eyes,
because he thought he had been captured by dybbuks and that his
life on earth was at an end, but then he realized that their faces, a
few of them at least, looked familiar.

'Wait till your father hears about this!' cried one of the girls.

Mendel opened his eyes. Before him stood Rivka Davidovitz. He
had seen her once or twice in the women's section at the shul, a
hazy figure behind the wooden grating.

'And when your father hears you've been talking to me . . .' said
Mendel, but he couldn't think of what might happen because he
had the feeling that Rivka Davidovitz's sparkling eyes were pulling
him to his feet.

'Then what?'

Mendel swallowed. He opened his mouth and made an unintelligible sound.

The girls laughed and then ran off, Rivka last of all. He watched
her go, she looked back, he smiled unhappily, she waved. He sank
back against the bundle of bark and raised his eyes to heaven.

Mendel and Rivka had met and, as young people who in some
strange way are meant for each other often do, they sought each
other's company again and again in conspicuously inconspicuous
ways. They met at the watering place, outside the shul, at Aaron
Minsky's wedding, and when spring had come and summer and
then a year had gone by, the whole village, except for the fathers,
knew that these two were courting.

This went on until Yom Kippur, the time when one forgives the
sins and misdeeds of others and repents for one's own, when the

poor Jews of Kotzk felt even more insignificant than they already were. On this High Holy Day the men of Kotzk sat in the shul in their shrouds, thinking glumly about all that had happened to them and all that they had done to others. Yankel Davidovitz was among them, brooding over the feud between himself and Schloime Kreisky. When he had brooded long enough and the silence between him and the man sitting opposite him had taken on outlandish proportions in his guilt-ridden mind, he got to his feet. He offered Schloime his hand and said, 'I'm the miserable swine's tit, Schloime, forgive me.' But Schloime, who had borne the smell of hog's piss, tree-bark, and rotting hides ever since he was a boy – his father had been a hide trader, too – could not forget the affront. He jumped up, jabbed a forefinger into Yankel's chest and yelled that he had nothing to forgive a man who, as far as he was concerned, didn't even exist. Yankel, whose mind was shadowed by a breathtakingly dark cloud of sin, clapped his hands together and bowed his head. As he stood there before Schloime, who was trembling with rage, a voice rose from the group of men that had gathered around them. It was Aaron Minsky. 'Stop this childish nonsense!' he shouted. 'The two of you can't even make peace, when your own children have been courting for more than a year!' It was as if Schloime had swallowed a shovelful of live coal. He dropped down onto a rickety bench, gasping for air, his head shaking, and asked if it were true, that his son Mendel, pure as the driven snow, was courting one of those Davidovitz witches, and which one . . .

The commotion in the shul carried on until late that evening, until after midnight, when an exhausted Schloime and a shattered Yankel stood outside the door of the rebbe's study, shuffling their feet like two boys who know they're about to be punished for stealing apples. For a long time it was quiet, until finally Yankel took half, not even half a step forward and softly whispered the rebbe's name. It remained silent inside the room that had swallowed up Menachem Mendel ten years before. 'Reb?' Yankel asked again. Nothing happened. Schloime, who had bags under his eyes from weariness and care, shoved Yankel aside, pounded on the door, and cried, his voice breaking, 'Open this door, you moth-eaten brushface, miserable sod, tapeworm...' Yankel stared at him in amazement. From behind the closed door came the sound of slow footsteps. Yankel made ready to flee, but Schloime's hand bit into his kapok coat. The door opened slowly and the amused face of Reb Menachem Mendel appeared.

'What did you say, Schloime?'

'Monkey's arse, slimy old shoelace, piece of...'

Reb Menachem Mendel looked at Yankel and, tilting his head towards Schloime, asked, 'What's the matter with him?'

Yankel told him what had happened ever since Menachem Mendel had called Schloime 'a certain name' and what he, Yankel, had said and that they hadn't spoken to each other since, but that their children were now courting and that since it had been Yom Kippur, he, Yankel, had wanted to make amends, but that Schloime had not, and that Aaron Minsky had said they should purge the water at its source and they thought...

'... that this was the source,' said Menachem Mendel.

Yankel nodded.

When Yankel Davidovitz and Schloime Kreisky came out of the shul later that morning, a group of weary men stood there waiting for them, in silence. Aaron Minsky who, since his marriage, had grown in many ways and had emerged as the village spokesman, stepped forward, raised his eyebrows, and said, '*Nu*, Yankel and Schloime?' But Yankel shook his head and walked straight past him, while Schloime stared at him with vacant eyes and an astonished expression and then, shaking his head, trudged off down the road.

In Kotzk the days slipped by and grew shorter and shorter, until December came and preparations were made for Chanukah, the festival that relieves the long winter gloom and points hopefully to the inevitable budding of trees and flowers, the festival that brightens the Jewish year like a light in the distance when a man has lost his way and is searching desperately for a place to shelter from the cold of a winter's night. At Yankel Davidovitz's house, spirits were high. The kugel was browning in the oven and the gleaming menorah stood on the table. The master of the house, surrounded by his seven daughters and wife, lit the first candle. Yankel stood before the menorah and stared into the swelling flame until it had stopped smoking, and then turned to Rivka. 'The time has come,' he said, 'to speak of you and Mendel Kreisky.' Rivka pricked up her ears. If what she thought were true, she would finally hear what all of Kotzk had been eager to know for the last two months.

'When Schloime Kreisky and I were at the rebbe's . . .' began Yankel. His eyes strayed to the dancing candlelight. He shook his head and sat down in the chair at the head of the table. The eight women followed him respectfully.

'We found ourselves in a room where books were piled high, on tables, on chairs, on the floor. The bookcases along the wall reached all the way to the ceiling. Books, papers, everywhere you looked. The rebbe cleared two chairs and invited us to sit down and then came and stood before us. Behind him was an oil lamp. The light seemed to wrap itself around him, like a tallith. "So, you've come to find the source?" Schloime nodded, a bit guiltily. His unceasing river of abuse had run dry the moment he saw the room. "Well then," said the rebbe, "here is the source."'

Yankel turned to Rivka.

'There's no stopping the love between two people, Rivka. Even if Schloime and I hadn't been to see the rebbe, you and Mendel Kreisky would have been allowed to marry. Even a pauper with one cow and a stinking hide trader know that much.'

Rivka opened her eyes wide.

'What the rebbe said had nothing to do with either of you, or with that senseless silence between Schloime and me, or with any of the other trifles one finds along the way. "What gives you the right," said the rebbe, "to drag a man out of ten years of silence?" We bowed our heads. Schloime cleared his throat. "You're still our rebbe," he said. Menachem Mendel shook his head. "I haven't been your rebbe for ten years. A rebbe is a teacher, not a hermit. I have nothing to do with you. I am the billygoat." He's lost his mind, I thought. He said, "Do you know the story of the holy billygoat?" We nodded.

Yankel looked around at the eight faces gazing back at him, glowing with excitement. 'You know the story, too. The old man

who heads for home one winter's night and the snow is falling and
the wind is blowing so hard, he can barely see the road. He walks
for an hour and then stops to catch his breath. He gropes around
in the bag over his shoulder and realizes he has lost his tobaccobox.
He tears his hair, he beats his breast. Ayyyyy, he wails, my tobaccobox! Here I am, lost in the storm, and now my tobaccobox box is
gone, too! He shakes his head and sinks down in the snow. There
he sits, his head in his hands, like a weary horse that knows its end
is near. Suddenly, in the distance, he hears a heavy drone, as if the
very earth is shaking. The trees tremble, snow tumbles from the
highest branches, the night is filled with sound. The old man looks
up, and there, standing before him, is the holy billygoat. Enormous.
The biggest billygoat he's ever seen. His curved black horns reach
to the stars. The man claps his hands to his eyes and starts praying.
But the holy billygoat bows his head and says: Cut off as much of
my horns as you need for a new tobaccobox. Trembling with awe,
the old man takes his knife and cuts out a piece of the gigantic
horns. He thanks the creature and runs the rest of the way home.
Nobody believes him, of course, but from that moment on, each
time he opens the tobaccobox, people flock around him and cry:
Doesn't that tobacco smell delicious! Where did you get it?'

Yankel stared into space. 'Schloime and I knew the rest of the
story: after a while everyone starts going to the billygoat to get a
piece of horn for a tobaccobox, until finally the goat is walking the
earth without any horns at all. But Menachem Mendel said: "I am
that billygoat. You carve up my horns to make boxes in which the
tobacco will smell as delicious as that of the first man who saw me.
But has anyone ever asked themselves where that smell comes from?
No one. You search, you hunt, you explore. You think: To find
the billygoat, one must suffer. Or: One must be humble. Or you
interpret the billygoat's every word, every movement, and think:
The world is a whole, everything is connected to everything else,
or you think that seeing the billygoat is some rare privilege. Nonsense, all of it. I ask you: where does that smell come from, what
is it made of?" Schloime and I shrugged our shoulders. "I'll tell
you," said the rebbe. "That smell doesn't come from the billygoat, it

doesn't come from its horns, it has nothing to do with the encounter between the goat and the old man. That smell is in us, we smell what we are." Schloime shook his head. "I don't understand," he said, "why can't we smell that smell, or –" and then he looked at me, "why doesn't anyone ever smell anything but stinking hides?" The rebbe lifted a pile of books off the chair behind a large table and put them on the ground. He sat down and gazed into the light of the oil lamp. "That is because, Schloime, we only *think* we can smell. We walk past the house of a hide trader and what do we smell? Hog's piss, tree-bark, rotting hides. That is also what we smell when we talk to Schloime Kreisky because he, and his father and his father's father, have spent their lives surrounded by hog's piss and tree-bark and rotting hides. But do we smell Schloime? Do we smell the life he leads? Do we smell his soul? No, we smell only what is around him, what he holds in his hands, what lies about in his yard. The smell of Schloime himself, which is heavenly and sweet like cinnamon, is masked by whatever else wafts our way. And we allow this, just as we allow the world to churn in our eyes, but never really see, just as we open our ears to every random scream, but never really hear." The rebbe stared straight ahead and closed his eyes. "The secret," he said, "is not to smell, not to hear, and not to see, and then, when all roads to the mind are closed, to open the heart and make the world anew, to see it anew, hear it anew, smell it anew." '

Yankel looked at Rivka. She swallowed hard.

'Rivka,' he said, 'never call a person what he seems. Try to hear his true voice, smell his true smell, and see his true face.'

The girl nodded.

'And another thing,' said Yankel, turning to his wife, 'the kugel's burning.'

Who's There?

WHEN I AWOKE, the fire had died down to a smouldering heap. I got up from my chair and began piling wood on top of the remains. There was still enough life left in the red embers at the bottom of the hearth. The chimney drew the glow through the new layer of wood, and five minutes later the room was lit red once more by a roaring fire. I did my best to keep it low, but the draw was so strong that the flames shot into the chimney on the least provocation. In the hall, the door was still rattling. I picked up a few large chips of wood and walked out of the library to go and secure it. On the threshold, I stopped. The library had been heavy with the twilight of closed shutters and drawn curtains, so I hadn't realized how dark it was outside. Here, in the hall, the sky behind the windows above the door was blackish-grey. An ominous, dull rumble echoed. From this close it was as if the wind itself had fists and was pounding on the door, demanding to be let in. Without knowing why, I looked up, at the barricade. I didn't expect to see anything, no translucent ghost, no wild apparition in tattered robes with streaming black hair, yet my gaze was drawn to the first floor. Then I heard a voice. It came from far away, muffled. It was a voice that no longer had the strength to cry out, yet cried out all the same. I shook off my hesitation, ran to the door, and turned the key.

A vortex of snow and cold flew in, wrenching the door handle out of my hand. I was pushed backwards. The freezing air tore at my clothes, flakes whirled around my head and I heard nothing but the howling, raging, whistling and wailing of the wind. Just when I had got my foot behind the door and was about to push it closed again, a dark figure blew inside.

Nina lay on the marble floor like a fallen bird. She wasn't moving. Her lips had a bluish sheen and her face was nearly as white as the snow that caked her jacket and legs. She had no shoes on and her stockings hung in shreds around her ankles. I took her in my arms and carried her into the library, where I lowered her into the arm-chair in front of the hearth. Then I ran to the hunting room. There, in the big linen cupboard, I found the sleeping bag Uncle Herman sometimes wrapped around his legs when he felt like sitting outside on a chilly night. The thing smelled strongly of mothballs. Back in the library I peeled Nina out of her coat and slid her into the downy envelope. She didn't move; she didn't even shiver. I threw more wood on the fire, took a candle and went into the kitchen, where I pushed open the outside door, filled the percolator with snow, and put it on the back of the stove. As the water bubbled up, gurgling and sputtering, I stared out the window. Now and then there was a lull in the endless storm and I saw the garden glowing blue in the moonlight. But then the wind would scoop up some snow and hurl it towards the kitchen and the dark hole above the lawn would turn white. I leaned over the sink and peered into the darkness. The drifts under the window and against the garden house were at least three feet high by now.

The water in the percolator began to turn brown. I got out mugs, spoons, and sugar and went into the hunting room. In the cupboard, Uncle Herman's old clothes lay in neat piles waiting for someone who was never going to come back. I chose a pair of corduroy trousers, a jacket, thick woollen socks, and a jumper. Then, the clothes under my arm and mugs of hot coffee in my hands, I returned to the library. In the cabinet where Uncle Herman kept his liquor, I found a bottle of Irish whiskey. I poured a generous swig into the coffee. Nina was sitting in the chair by the fire, the sleeping bag up to her chin. Her eyes were open and her teeth were chattering loudly. I held the mug to her lips and helped her sip.

I had barely had time to think since she blew in. Now the first questions started coming. How, why? How long had she been pounding at the door? Why had she left? And then returned? What would have happened if I hadn't heard her? I put the mug down on the table next to my half-eaten meal and looked her over.

'Cold. I. Thought. I. Was. Going. To die,' she said.

I kneeled down in front of her, unzipped the sleeping bag and pulled her feet towards me. 'These stockings will have to come off.'

Her head sagged jerkily downward in slow, stiff arcs. Her eyes were open wide, the pupils deep holes in the sparkling green of the iris.

I slipped my hands under her skirt and tugged so hard on the pantyhose that she nearly slid off the chair. She kicked feebly and wriggled her way back up.

'Can you put these on yourself?' I asked. I held up Uncle Herman's clothes.

'Yes,' she said. 'Yes.' She got to her feet, shakily, stepped into the trousers and pulled them up.

'Better take off that skirt.'

She nodded.

'That coat, too.'

When she had changed and was sitting in the chair with a fresh mug of coffee and whisky, I took hold of her feet. I slid her right foot under my jumper, next to my bare skin, and began rubbing the left one. It was like massaging a block of ice. The foot under my jumper was so cold, I could feel it burning against my skin. Nina dropped her head back and closed her eyes.

After a while I helped her out of the chair and sat down in her place. I pulled her onto my lap, laid the sleeping bag over us both, and clasped her tightly. She sat on my knee like a mannequin, cold and stiff. It wasn't until she had warmed up and the whisky began to take effect that she relaxed.

Half an hour passed before the colour returned to her cheeks. Her forehead was beaded with sweat, her teeth had stopped chattering. The scent of her body rose from the sleeping bag. Her wet hair began to dry, the dark damp streaks grew lighter. I wriggled myself out from under her, tucked her back into the sleeping bag, and busied myself with the fire. It was a fire to be proud of, large pieces of wood that burned evenly and cast a fierce heat. In the library, black shadows danced against the orangey-red glow from the hearth.

'What's in this?' she asked, after I had brought fresh coffee and sat down in the chair next to her.

'Coffee in mine, coffee and whisky in yours.'

She smiled drowsily. Her cheeks were glowing now, her eyes were slightly moist, and they glittered. 'I can't,' she said. 'I'll get drunk.'

I picked up the plate next to my chair and fixed her some crackers and cheese. She wolfed them down with the gusto of someone who hasn't eaten for a very long time.

'I thought you were going to rape me,' she said with her mouth full.

I dug my cigarettes out of my jacket pocket and stuck one between my lips. 'I always let my victims warm up first. I'm no necrophiliac.'

'A cigarette. I *must* have a cigarette.'

Her voice was unsteady, the alcohol had set her adrift from the anchor of control. She leaned towards me and stared into my face. I lit her a cigarette, avoiding the piercing black pupils that were trying to bore their way into my eyes. She flopped back in the cracked leather and blew out smoke.

'Why did you come back?'

At first she didn't seem to understand my question. Then she raised her right hand and drew on her cigarette. She wrapped herself in a cloud of smoke and shook her head. A shiver ran through her. 'I was nearly at the bottom of the Mountain. I drove into a snowbank.'

'You walked back up? All the way to the top?'

She looked at her watch. 'Eight o'clock?'

'Sounds about right.'

'I drove away and then . . . what d'you call it . . . walked right back. It can't . . . be that late.'

'It took you almost two and a half hours to get back here.'

She picked up the sleeping bag, which had slid onto the floor, and pulled it around her. 'Less. First I tried to turn the car round. I revved the engine for at least half an hour, but I couldn't get it out of the snow.' She stared straight ahead. Her long hair glowed in the light of the flames. 'First it moved, but then it got stuck. I sat in the car for a while, with the engine running. To keep warm. And then I got out and headed back. Kept on falling. The whole time. The wind was blowing so hard I had to hold on to the trees. I was scared that if I lost my way I'd freeze to death.' She took her cigarette and breathed in the smoke as if it were pure oxygen. I could picture the trek over the snow-covered paths, the light slowly turning to dusk, the wall of trees on either side of the path and the icy whirl of the blizzard. If I had had to bet on the outcome of that journey, I would never have put my money on her.

'And then I got here and practically beat down the door, but you didn't open it!'

'I was asleep.'

She shook her head. 'Could I have another cigarette?'

I felt around in my jacket until I found them. 'We'll have to ration them. There are twenty left. That means we can smoke five a day.'

'I don't normally smoke, you know.'

'Normally . . .' I handed her a cigarette and lit it for her. We drank and stared into the fire.

'Five. What do you mean, five? You think we're going to be here for five days?'

I nodded. 'Maybe. Three, at least. I heard it on the radio this afternoon. This isn't just another snowstorm, this is a national disaster. Entire villages are cut off from the civilized world, people are stranded in their cars, in weekend cottages and service stations. The snowploughs won't get up the Mountain until last. If they ever get here at all. No one knows we're here. This house has been vacant for five years, more than five years. Why should they even be looking, and why here, of all places?'

'So . . .'

'So we have to improvise. And ration. And plot. And . . .'

She sighed.

'As long as we're here and it stays this cold, we'll have to keep gathering wood and keep the fires burning.' I stood up and threw another piece of Louis XV in the hearth. 'This is going to be the opposite of a holiday.'

'Why,' said Nina, 'do I get the feeling that you don't mind?'

I shrugged my shoulders, picked up the bottle, and filled our glasses. The fire licked at a gleaming, dark brown chair leg, almost as if it were teasing me about this compulsory iconoclasm, the burning of Uncle Herman's collection of 'family heirlooms'. A soft hiss escaped from the fire and the wood began to burn.

'Let's make a deal,' I said, my eyes glued to the dancing flames. 'You tell me why you took off this afternoon and I'll read you my version of Uncle Herman's life.'

She was quiet.

'Or we could always just not talk to each other for the next few days.'

'You think I'm here for the fun of it?'

'No, I don't think you're here for the fun of it. You'd much rather be somewhere else.'

I tried to tear my eyes away from the hearth, but couldn't. At the centre of the flames, a hollow formed. The room around me turned red. A tunnel of black bored through the tinted glow. I peered down the tube and saw, way off in the distance, something glimmering, a fragment, no more than a speck. The walls of the tunnel began moving past me. The red faded, the walls moved faster and faster until they were streaking past and as I stared into the half-light at the end of the tunnel something began to take shape. I squinted and leaned slightly forward. I felt my body moving sideways, as if part of me wanted to fall and part of me didn't.

When I finally looked up, Nina was staring into space. She sat as still as an alabaster statue. Total serenity, even her eyes had stopped gleaming. She blew out cigarette smoke with the clumsiness of a non-smoker.

'Regret,' Zeno had once said, 'is the most destructive human emotion. You only feel regret when it's too late. If something can be restored, there's no question of regret. Remorse, perhaps, or guilt. But regret, what I mean by regret, is mourning for the irreversibility of things.'

I picked up my mug. As I drank, staring into the black mirror of the coffee, the image of the tunnel returned. I put down the mug and took a deep breath. The smell of coffee mingled with my fear of what lay at the end of that tunnel. I reached for the cigarettes and pulled one out of the pack. My hand shook as I brought the tiny match flame up to light it. Nina was watching me. When the match went out, I threw it in the hearth and lit another. I looked at Nina. No, not at her, at what she was.

'Listen,' I said. 'If we want to stay alive, it's time to gather wood. I'll go and pull down part of that barricade.'

'Bar –' She remembered the pile of furniture at the top of the stairs. 'I want to get out of here,' she said.

I was already at the door. 'You'll have to wait until the storm clears, Nina, and the way it looks now that could take several days.'

She groaned softly. 'There's no phone, the car's stuck. What *do* we have?'

'Nothing. No water, no electricity. We never had gas to begin with. We're Robinson Crusoe in the wintertime.'

She got up from her chair and started pulling on the socks that were still on the floor. 'I lost my shoes.'

'I'll catch a goat tomorrow and make you a new pair.'

'Very funny.'

I grinned. 'Uncle Herman used to have a pair of those indestructible hiking boots. They're around here somewhere. If you wear two pairs of socks, they should fit you. He didn't have very big feet.'

'There's no light in the hall, is there? Are there any flashlights?'

'None that I know of.'

'Why exactly isn't there any electricity?'

'I had it disconnected, years ago.'

Nina shook her head. 'If you're not here and you don't use anything, it doesn't cost anything, either.'

I was silent. Suddenly I thought of the calor gas burner that I had seen in the cellar. It wouldn't give much light, but certainly more than a candle. Nina could hold it up while I wrenched loose part of the barricade and threw it downstairs.

'Was there a lamp fixture?' she asked, when I had explained my plan. She got up from her chair and came walking towards me.

'A what?'

'You use that sort of burner when you go camping. If you attach a lamp fixture, you've got a lantern.'

'I don't know. Didn't see any.'

Nina picked up a candelabra and followed me. There were four of us in the hall. To our left, against the staircase and the high white walls, huge, misshapen shadows walked along with us. I heard Nina shudder. 'It really does look like a haunted house,' she said. 'All we need now are a couple of burning torches and some creepy organ music.'

'Or a corpse in a closet.'

'Hey! Would you stop that?'

'You don't have to be scared of the dead,' I said. 'The living are much worse.'

'God. You really know how to put a person at ease, don't you?'

In the box of gas canisters Nina found a wide glass tube and a burner with a kind of wick. 'This is it,' she said. 'You attach it to the bottle and then . . .'

'. . . there is light.'

She observed me for a while, then smiled.

At the foot of the stairs I attached the lamp to the gas canister. Nina held the candles and gave instructions. I put the canister down on the stairs, turned on the gas, and held up a match. The burner started raging and cast a blinding white light all around us. 'Isn't this cosy,' I said. 'I suddenly remember why I never liked camping.' Nina blew out the candles, put the candelabra on the floor, and picked up the lantern we had made. I grabbed the tools, the axe and the sharpened hoe, and we walked upstairs. My shadow glided across the ceiling, the brightly lit staircase, the hole in the barricade. When Nina came and stood next to me, the black figure shot away to the side of the hall.

'What're you going to do?' she asked.

'I think we should go left.'

'What's left?'

'Two bedrooms, two bathrooms. My bedroom and my bath-room.' I stared at the heap of chairs and tables. 'And this.'

'Not much wood,' she said.

'No. I'm counting on the bedrooms. If we can reach even one of them and chop up a bed . . .'

'Isn't there any other way to get wood? There are such beautiful things here. Can't we save any of it?'

I shook my head. 'We've got to hurry. It's much too cold here. We have to think of ourselves first. If we start lugging all those beautiful things downstairs, we'll never keep the fire going. The only other choice is to burn up the library.'

Nina looked at me. 'Uncle Herman's library.'

'And mine,' I said. 'And Zeno's.'

Her face clouded.

I stepped forward and pulled a chair out of the pile that was blocking the way to the bedrooms. Nina came up behind me with the lantern. Shadows wheeled around us, patches of black leapt up between the chairs, cupboards, and other pieces of furniture, and disappeared once more. When she was standing beside me, I raised the chair, a fragile affair on slender legs, and threw it down. It crashed against the marble stairs, the sound of breaking wood ripped the darkness below us.

'What's that?' whispered Nina.

In the distance was a faint rustling noise. 'An echo,' I said, 'the echo of . . .'

The rustling came closer.

'*Who's there?*'

We both ducked. The lantern went clattering down the stairs. In the sudden darkness we heard the voice for the second time, a voice from the depths of something dark and far away.

'*Who?*'

A rustling like the sea.

'*Nathan?*'

My heart exploded in my head. I reeled and stepped into the emptiness above the stairs. As I began falling, my right hand felt for something to hold on to. My fingers groped about in the void, where once the sideboard had stood, but found nothing. Then I felt Nina's hand. She grabbed hold of my sleeve and pulled me up.

'Who's there?'

I could smell Nina's hair. Cinnamon, I thought.

'Nathan, for God's sake ... What ...'

'Who?'

'What?' I cried.

'Nathan?'

A rustling like the sound of the wind in your ears as you fall and ...

I could feel Nina shivering beside me. 'Zeno?'

'Who's there?'

I relaxed. I put my finger to my lips. 'Listen,' I said.

'Who?'

'A tape,' I said.

Rustling. 'Nathan?'

'A ... God. A ... tape. Zeno.' Nina was breathing heavily, in and out. She let go of my jacket and leaned back, I heard the dull groan of wood.

'Who's there?'

I stood up and walked down the stairs. It was a while before I found the burner: I had to feel my way along the cold marble, listening to the escaping gas. I turned off the valve and inspected the lantern – the glass was cracked, the tank dented. I let out a thin stream of gas and lit a match. The white light shot up again. High above me I heard the distorted voice still intoning its fractured sentences. Who's there. Who. Nathan.

When I got back to Nina, I saw the glistening snail's trail of a tear along her nose. I reached out my hand, towards her arm, but she turned away. Her back was tall and straight. I put down the lantern and began furiously throwing down tables and chairs.

For half an hour, three quarters of an hour I was at it and all that time I heard the questions that Zeno kept asking me from the other world. If the voice hadn't been drowned out every so often by the sound of shattering wood, I would have fled or, in a blind rage, seized my axe and leaped into the tangle of chair legs and armrests, chopping like a madman until I had found the tape recorder.

When we were back in the library – I had added more wood to the kitchen stove and the fire in the hunting room – we stood for a while in front of the hearth.

'How long will that tape keep on playing?'

'No idea,' I said. 'We'll just have to wait until the batteries run out.'

'N? What's going on here?'

I stared into the flames and tried to remember whether she used to call me that in the past, when she was a child. N. All the members of my family did, had done, though I never knew why. No one had ever addressed Zoe or Zelda or Zeno as Z.

'You tell me,' I said.

She didn't answer. Only the greenish-blue gleam of her eyes, the perfectly tranquil face and the red wreath around it.

'I don't know,' I said. 'I don't recognize this house at all anymore.' I saw her gaze grow vague. 'It's as if I've woken up after being asleep for a hundred years and I look around me and there are things I recognize, but everything is different, just different enough to make me doubt what I thought I knew.'

There was a silence. Now and then a piece of wood snapped in the hearth, or part of the burning pile caved in with a sigh.

'How did that tape get there?'

'I really don't know. What's the matter? Do you think I planned all this? Nathan Hollander's mystery weekend?'

'A film,' she said. She lowered her voice slightly: 'He's searching for the secret of his past, but the past doesn't want to be found. Coming soon, to a cinema near you: Nathan Hollander, the movie.'

'Starring . . .'

'Dustin Hoffman, as Nathan Hollander.'

'I'm twice his size.'

'Okay, Jack Nicholson then.'

'I don't have those acrobatic eyebrows. Besides, then we'd need a love interest.'

She looked at me for a while. 'I don't know any red-haired actresses.'

'Hordes,' I said. 'Nicole Kidman. Lucille Ball. There's also this slightly whorish, but very charming redhead I once saw in the film version of *Hotel New Hampshire*. And there's a beautiful Italian woman. The same hair as you, that fan of red curls. What was her name? Domenica . . . She played in that Tarkovsky film and at one point she begins to unbutton her dress and you see this magnificent alabaster breast. My God.' I stared at the fire.

'I think we'd better forget about that love interest. I haven't got magnificent alabaster tits and your eyebrows can't dance. Let's do something.'

'What did you have in mind?'

'Don't you have anything in mind?'

I shrugged.

We fell silent. 'The fairy tale writer doesn't know,' said Nina. She sat down and stared into the fireplace. I smiled wrily. She drew her legs under her and settled back into the chair. Then, her face raised to me, like a sleepy cat, her eyes narrowed, she said: 'I expected you to at least tell me a fairy tale about it.'

'I thought you wanted to know why we were here.'

'I don't want to think about the snow. I don't want to think about that tape. Or about the barricade. Or about all that food.' She opened her eyes until they were so wide that it was impossible for me to miss the import of her words. 'And I don't want to talk about Zeno, either. Didn't you say this was a great opportunity for you to read me Uncle Herman's biography?'

'Out loud? I thought I'd just hand you the manuscript. It's a long story.'

She smiled.

'And a tall one.'

She nodded.

'It's all about arrival and departure and Zeno . . .'

Nina's gaze strayed to the fire.

'. . . and the atomic bomb and . . .'

'The what?'

'The atomic bomb,' I said, 'I know everything there is to know about that.'

'The atomic bomb ... You say it the way most people would say: I know everything there is to know about cars. Or football. Books, even.'

I could feel the wine, and the glow of the hearth.

'Are you going to keep avoiding this? I told you before: do your *Decamerone*, give me the *Canterbury Tales*, unexpurgated. You've promised me stories galore, but so far all I've had are coming attractions. Please begin. What is the beginning, anyway?'

'The beginning,' I said. I went to the reading table, behind the chairs, and opened my bag. The packet of paper I had printed out the week before felt cool, almost as though it didn't belong to me.

'Should I get some more wine?'

I nodded. The beginning. I sat down, the manuscript on my lap, and stared into the flames.

Here I am, I thought, a fairy tale writer. A memory that stretches back to the seventeenth century, though I myself was born midway into the nineteen-thirties. Son of an inventor, who was the son of a physicist, who was the son of a clockmaker, whose forefathers had all been clockmakers, ever since the invention of the timepiece. Nephew of Herman Hollander, *the* Herman Hollander, nephew and sole heir. Brother of Zeno Hollander, *the* Zeno Hollander. Son of a failed painter – my mother – brother of two sisters, one of whom fluttered through life like falling cherry blossom and the other who was born with the soul of a nun and the body of a Jewish bombshell. I was the only normal one in my family and I'm the only one, except for Nina, who is still alive. When I die, no more Hollanders. What a relief that'll be. Travelling for centuries and finally arriving. Nothing gained, but at least, oh Lord of the Universe, peace.

The end of the century, I thought, is this – the door handle in one hand, my other hand on the light switch. I look round and see the room. Soon I'll turn out the light, shut the door behind me, walk into the hall, open the heavy front door, cross the threshold, and leave the house.

The beginning. What I've seen in the part of the century that I've lived through, and what I've heard about the part when my parents and my uncle were alive. Those who don't know me will think that I've been everywhere a person has to be if he wants to say anything valuable about these last hundred years. But that isn't true. No one has less knowledge of people, my kind of people, the country in which I lived and the world in which I grew up, than I do. This life is a mystery to me. I close my eyes and let the newsreel of my, *our* history, go by – images of departing steamers (why do I remember the ship, that distant past, in black and white?), flashing neon signs in the desert, the glow-in-the-dark hands of Mickey Mouse on an alarm clock, a house like the head of a giant and Gene Kelly in *Broadway Melody*, I close my eyes and see nothing that kindles even the tiniest spark of light in me. This century, this life, the history of my family, it has all passed me by and left me, like a mouse in the middle of Times Square, in total bewilderment.

The beginning. Uncle Chaim once said, 'Beginning? No beginning. We're clockmakers. One big family of clockmakers. People of time. Time has no beginning.'

If there's one thing I do know about, it's beginning. Although Uncle Herman didn't share that opinion.

'What's this?' he once asked me. He had taken down a book of mine and opened it. 'This is a beginning? "Kei was in love with the miller's daughter and the miller's daughter loved him, but one day Kei's love disappeared. He gazed, as always, at his young wife, but her hair was like straw, her eyes, dull grey pebbles, and her skin, unwashed linen. Kei knew this wasn't so, but that was how he saw her. He decided to go in search of his love." What sort of nonsense is this? In and out of love in a single line. Where's the development?'

I had answered what I always answered (because the question was the same as the previous year and the year before that): 'Why do I have to explain why love disappears between a man and a woman? Half of world literature is already about that. I'm concerned with the other phenomena.'

'What phenomena?'

'The obscure ones.'

'What obscure ones?'

'I don't know, they're too obscure.'

At that point Herman would always start tugging at his hair.

(Once he pulled mine too, when I was about seventeen, but he was so sorry afterwards that he took me into town and treated me to as many books as I wanted.)

Uncle Herman didn't like obscurity. He had worked all his life towards the clarification of things that were uncommonly vague and in the wake of that pursuit he regarded every form of art, even one as trivial as mine, as an ideal way of gaining insight. That insight wasn't supposed to boil down to the fact that things were obscure.

But they are. Between 'Once upon a time . . .' and 'They lived happily ever after . . .' the fairy tale unfolds, and even though it may seem that the reader, or listener, is transported by the events between the first sentence and the last, it is these two sentences alone that do the trick. 'Once upon a time . . .' and 'They lived happily ever after' reflect the way in which we see the world: as an event with an obscure beginning and, for the time being, an obscure end. Between them is our story, and our limitation, and although every fairy tale tries to weave together various events in order to reach that magical moment when all will be revealed, we are always aware that what we have read, or seen, is that which was already visible or readable, the representation of something obscure.

I felt the weight of the manuscript on my lap. Uncle Herman's story, the story of the entire family, the history of departure.

There's a group portrait in my mind. Left, Uncle Herman: his white hair standing out on all sides, his eyes coal-black, glittering like mica. Herman is eighty-five years old. He's naked, white as freshly cooked spaghetti, pubic hair glistening. (A detail I can't seem to forget.) Then Emmanuel Hollander, my father: a cross between Walter Matthau and Billy Wilder. He's wearing a straw Bing Crosby hat, a pair of trousers that are slightly too short, so you can see his white sports socks, and below that, ridiculous gym shoes. He hasn't got his shirt tucked in. Manny, as he likes to be called, is seventy-one. A pencil-stub glimmers behind his right ear. It's easy to spot, because there's no hair poking out from under his hat. Manny was the only man in our family who went bald instead of grey. Next to him stands Uncle Chaim, our great-great-grand-uncle, although that title isn't entirely accurate. He was born in 1603 and died of woe in

1648. Chaim has something in his hand, the right hand, but it's hard to tell what. A small man dressed in a peculiar collection of clothes: battered boots, a pair of trousers badly in need of mending, a coat like an old dog. Magnus, Chaim's nephew, is standing beside him. Straight-limbed, lean and alert, about twenty-five years old. He has a wooden chest strapped to his back. In that chest are his clock-maker's tools and a small pendulum clock. Then there's me, Nathan Hollander, who everyone, except Uncle Herman, calls N. Once I was a little boy with bristly black hair, all knees and elbows, small for my age, skinny, as only little boys can be. Here, in this portrait, I'm a sinewy man. Six feet tall. Sharp features, deep-set eyes, a face that, as time went by, grew weathered and creased. The long limbs, head bent slightly forward, always someone to lean towards and listen to. The hair, bristly and grey, an unruly tussock of rimed grass. Next to me, far right, Zeno. He's Magnus's age here: as old as he was the last time I spoke to him. His hair has the soft coppery sheen that I remember like nothing else in this life. The eyes, I can see them as if he were sitting here opposite me: large brown eyes with moss-green flecks that, when they catch the sunlight, shimmer like water plants beneath the surface of a murky pond. His skin has the soft gleam of wax, his lips are slightly tensed.

My group portrait.

I call it 'Travellers'. Because that was what we were. Each and every one of us. We came from the East, we travelled to the West. Uncle Chaim and his nephew Magnus, my most distant forefathers, lived in the region that now forms the border between Poland and Lithuania. There, in the dense primeval forest, where the bison still roamed and wolves and bears waylaid those who travelled from one village to the next, they made clocks. Whenever my grandfather, my Uncle Herman, or Emmanuel, my father, wished to explain or justify our presence in this place or that, they would say: 'Clock-makers, every one of us. Travellers. Came from the East, on our way to the West.' As if to say that the East was a sort of mythical birthplace, the womb of our . . . line, and the West, our Occident, the destiny towards which we, sometimes willingly, sometimes reluc-tantly, were headed. Travellers. Uncle Chaim journeyed through the kingdom of the night, from then to now, and later, in the company of his nephew. Magnus left the East, roamed for twenty-one years all over Europe, in search of Holland. Uncle Herman led us, my father and my mother and my sisters and I, out of the old Europe, into the New World, and never stopped travelling. Manny brought us from the east coast of America to the west, from the edge of history to its heart. I myself never had a home and Zeno, my young brother, removed himself from the face of the earth.

They're all dead. And all of them, I have known and loved. Uncle Chaim and his hazy nephew Magnus, too, even though, by the time I was born, they had been history for nearly three centuries. They're the only ones who are still with me.

I used to be awakened by voices in the night, cries that were so clear and sounded so close that they echoed in my head long after I had sat up in bed. 'Nathan!' My name, clear as day. 'NATHAN!' But no matter how often I was jolted awake, looked around, turned on the light, or didn't, I never saw a thing. For a long time I thought it was God calling to me across the black waters of darkness and sleep. I'm the sort of person who bears such possibilities in mind.

It wasn't until I was about ten years old that I discovered why I was hearing those nocturnal cries. We were living in the camp on the Hill, in New Mexico. In our cramped wooden house, I shared a room with Zeno, who had just turned one.

I was awakened by a creaking sound. When I looked up I saw an old man sitting at the foot of my bed. There was a full moon and its bluish light bounced off the hard desert ground, through the curtainless windows, into my room. One side of the old man's body was sharply defined and I could see that he was wearing a shabby black suit. His back was slightly bent. Something glistened in his eye, a small, gleaming tube that was aimed at his lap.

'Bah,' he said. A shard of moonlight shot across his stubbled jaw as he turned his head to me. He grinned broadly and raised his eyebrows. The tube fell out of his eye, he caught it without looking. 'Too dark. Can't see your hand before your eyes. Nice clock you've got there.' He shifted his gaze to my night table. I looked sideways, at the green fluorescent arms of Mickey Mouse.

I didn't have to ask who he was. He didn't have to tell me. Great-Great-Grand-Uncle Chaim, no doubt about it.

'How are you, my boy?'

'Fine,' I said. 'Thank you.'

'Magnus here yet?'

'No,' I said. 'I haven't seen him.'

'Young people . . .' He winked. Because he smiled at the same time, his face turned into a bluish white wad of paper, a ball of creases and shadows.

There was a shuffling noise in the receding darkness and out of the wall came the ghost of a wanderer. He emerged from what seemed, for a moment, to be a forest path, and all at once he was standing in the middle of the room.

'Speak of the devil . . .' Uncle Chaim said.

Magnus looked around and scratched his head.

Uncle Chaim pursed his lips, shook his head, and gave me a meaningful glance. 'Young people,' he said again.

'I'm young, too, you know,' I said.

He stared at me, and then smiled. 'You,' he said, 'are the eldest.' He turned to Magnus and raised his head. 'Have the two of you already met?'

Magnus, who was busy winding up the propeller of the biplane hanging under the lamp from a piece of fishline, jumped. 'Nathan, isn't it?'

I nodded.

'Magnus Levi,' he said, 'Currently going by the name of Hollander.'

Uncle Chaim chuckled.

I was now sitting straight up in bed, my hair, a wild shock, my face pale with sleep.

'What are you looking at?' Uncle Chaim asked.

I turned around and saw that I was still sitting in the same place, but that at the same time, I was standing in the room looking at myself. 'Is that me?' I asked. I looked back at the bed and saw the little boy sitting there and rubbing the sleep out of his eyes. Zeno lay in his own bed against the opposite wall, sound asleep.

'Happens from time to time,' said Uncle Chaim. 'They'll think up a name for it some day. No doubt that joker from Vienna could explain it.'

'Calling Freud a joker is not only unfair, it disclaims the great strides he made in . . .'

'Oh, Magnus, shut up.'

'Sorry.'

Here I was, in my room, surrounded by the things that made up my universe, the airplane with the rubber-band wind-up motor that my father had built, the Mickey Mouse alarm clock with radioactive hands, two fossilized sea urchins, a cupboard full of books, and a map of the world on which I kept track of the Allies' progress with tiny flags, here I was and I was twice myself and in the company of ancestors who had been dead for three centuries.

'We can go about this in two ways,' said Uncle Chaim. He was fiddling with the copper tube that had fallen from his eye. It rolled between his thumb and forefinger, from top to bottom and back to the top and when it was on top it spun round on its axis and rolled back down again. Warm yellow patches of light shot across its surface, liquid stars that seemed to float between his fingers. 'We decide on what this is and you tell us what you think of it, or we forget the explanation and pretend this is all perfectly normal.'

'Uncle,' said Magnus, 'I don't want to interfere . . .'

'Have you ever noticed, Nathan, that people who are about to interfere always begin by saying that they don't want to interfere?'

'. . . but perhaps it would be a good idea if we first told the boy how we got here to begin with.'

Uncle Chaim tilted his head to one side and looked at me expectantly.

I shrugged.

'Do you think you've gone mad?'

'No,' I said.

'Do you think that other people will think this is normal?'

I shook my head.

'Then that's that,' said Uncle Chaim. 'Have you seen this?'

I stepped forward and saw, for the first time, what he had been working on when I awoke. In the palm of his left hand lay an open pocket watch. I came closer and looked at the jumble of cogs. A wisp of wire, fine as a hair, was sticking up through the spokes of a tiny slender wheel.

'Overwound. Always the same. Scared to lose their grip on time, so they wind up their watches like they're wringing out the laundry.'

Magnus bent over Uncle Chaim's hand. 'An anachronism,' he said. 'This is a waistcoat-pocket watch, late nineteenth century.'

Uncle Chaim turned to me and said, 'Magnus is very particular about these things.'

'Anachism . . .'

'Anachronism,' said Magnus. 'That's when something turns up in the wrong time . . .'

'Like us,' said Uncle Chaim.

'For example,' said Magnus irritably, 'if you read a story about the eighteenth century, and there's a car in it.'

'Anachronism,' I said.

'Exactly,' said Magnus. 'And in a way, we are too, just as Uncle Chaim said.'

'It all depends on how you look at it,' said Uncle Chaim.

'Why are you here?'

Uncle Chaim snapped shut the hand holding the watch. He stretched his face into a broad grimace. 'Well,' he said.

'To help,' Magnus said.

'Bah,' said Uncle Chaim.

'To tell you how it all began and . . .'

'Hm,' said Uncle Chaim.

'We were there when Herman was a boy, too,' said Magnus.

'Herman,' said Uncle Chaim. 'Don't talk to me about Herman.'

'But Herman didn't want us.'

'Herman,' said Uncle Chaim, 'only believes that things exist if you can pinch them.'

Magnus laughed. 'Your Uncle Herman,' he said, 'believes what he thinks, but he doesn't think what he believes.'

Uncle Chaim shook his head.

'Isn't that true?' said Magnus.

'What?'

'That Herman only believes what he thinks but doesn't think what he believes . . .'

Uncle Chaim opened his hand and looked at the watch. 'I'm not so philosophical,' he said. He turned to me, the 'me' that was standing before him, not the little boy on the bed who sat, his hands on the sheets, staring straight ahead. 'We're here because we're here.'

'Ah. Old Testament!'

Uncle Chaim spread his fingers. The watch leaked out in copper-coloured droplets. 'What do you mean, Old Testament?'

'That's what God calls Himself: I'm here because I'm here.'

'Magnus. Nephew. God calls Himself something very different – I am that I am. Which can also mean: I'm here because I'm here. Or: I am who I am.'

'Yes, Magnus.' He shook his hand. The last few drops of the melted watch splattered about.

'Talk about anachronisms,' Magnus said to me, nodding towards Uncle Chaim's hand.

'We'd better hurry, Nephew. It's nearly daylight. Nathan?'

I looked at him with, I would say now, the candour of a child with an overactive imagination. Uncle Chaim smiled and laid his hand on my hair.

Magnus came closer. 'What did you want to say, Nuncle?'

Uncle Chaim kept looking at me. I saw his eyes grow small, then large and gentle. He shook his head. 'What a life,' I heard him mumble, 'what a world.' Magnus stood beside him, nodding gravely. Uncle Chaim sighed and stared down at the floor. Just as I was about to follow his gaze to see what he saw there, he straightened up and his face turned into the crumpled wad that it had been before, all grins and wrinkles.

'You know what we do with firstborn sons, don't you?'

I frowned.

'Firstborn sons belong to God, says the Torah. That you know. You've read it.'

I nodded.

'But parents can keep their children by redeeming them. The

father pays five shekels, five silver rijksdaalers. His debt is settled, he no longer has to part with his firstborn son.'

'In our family,' said Magnus, looking appropriately solemn, 'that has never happened. In our family, it's become traditional *not* to settle the debt to God.'

'Probably,' Uncle Chaim took his hand off my head and stared somewhere into the half-light of the room, 'one of our forefathers was just too stingy, or he forgot, or, even more likely, he was too stubborn. A stubborn family, that's what we are, Nathan. The sort of Jews that say: Yes, but . . .'

'Whatever the case, we don't do it,' said Magnus, 'and that means that we, firstborn sons of the house of Hollander . . .'

'Levi, we're Levites as well, priests . . .'

'. . . that the firstborn sons of the house of Hollander belong neither to themselves nor to their family.'

'They belong . . .' Uncle Chaim hesitated. He shrugged his shoulders and looked at Magnus, then wriggled his eyebrows and leaned towards me. 'They belong . . . to God.'

Magnus's eyes rested on me expectantly. I looked around, at the little boy in bed. He looked like someone who wasn't there.

'Okay,' I said.

Uncle Chaim placed both hands on my shoulders, then kneeled down heavily so his face was on a level with mine. 'Nathan,' he said, 'Nathan. Don't say "okay". It's not "okay". It's not nobility. Not a privilege. Highly dubious privilege, at best. You can go back. You can ask your father to redeem you. He won't know what it means, but if you ask him he'll do it for you. It's possible, you're allowed. Think about it.' His face was a white-grey-yellow haze. I smelled his breath, a whiff of thyme.

'It's okay,' I said, after a while.

Uncle Chaim shook his head.

Magnus shuffled closer. They were both standing so close now that it was as if I was lying under the blankets and sawheard-smelled nothing but the hollow I had made in the bed. Magnus was hay, fresh hay. 'We'll be back, if that's what you decide,' said Magnus.

'We'll be back,' said Uncle Chaim.

They stood there all around me and I shut my eyes in the scent of thyme and hay and the heat of their bodies, the feathery touch of their hands on my shoulders and head and . . .

'Nuncle,' I said to Uncle Chaim.

'Yes, child,' he said.

'Can you see the past?'

'Yes.'

A cloud slid in front of the moon. It grew dark in the room and then light again, lighter than before. It was nearly morning.

'And the future?'

There was a very long silence.

'Yes,' said Magnus, 'we can see the future. But we don't know if what we see is right.'

'Okay,' I said. 'Okay.' The heat from their bodies was so intense that I felt myself gliding away in the paper boat of sleepiness.

'God,' said Uncle Chaim, 'why this child?'

'Shhh,' said Magnus. 'It's okay. He's right.'

Just before I reached the land of slumber and my body went limp, I heard Uncle Chaim sigh, 'Oh, Magnus . . .'

Not that I had an image of God. Not that I even believed in such a thing as God. I was a child who read the Old Testament with the thirst of a desert traveller and the hunger of a fasting penitent. At night, when the Hill was swathed in velvet darkness, no wind, no voices, now and then the scuffling of a lizard on the roof, the crackling of stones in the desert, at night I lay in bed and looked at the green hands of Mickey Mouse, who kept the time in my alarm clock. And through my bedroom, in the space between Zeno's bed and mine, the Old Testament caravans trekked from Mamre to Canaan. On the Indian rug that covered the wooden floor, Jacob fought with the angel and lay in his well, staring up at the starry night. I believed in stories. I was a believer of stories. The question of whether or not God existed didn't interest me. God was the least of my worries.

A family of travellers, yet I never told anyone where I went each night with Uncle Chaim and Magnus. Life was confusing enough as it was. Manny worked day and night on something we knew nothing about and when he came home he fell asleep at the table. Sophie sat during the day with the other wives at Mr Feynman's calculators, and my sisters, Zoe and Zelda, had reached the age when they were turning from girls into women and were practically unapproachable. And so I kept silent. I kept silent and I listened and as I listened I lost the distinction between then and now, here and there, reality and fantasy. That wasn't so bad. Later, much later, I would make it my profession to be of another time, and as a child, in an environment where no one paid any attention to me, it wasn't so bad to be considered a dreamer.

And so I became a fairy tale writer, all because of Great-Great-Grand-Uncle Chaim and Cousin Magnus. Hand-in-hand, we travelled through the forest of stories. 'The only way to understand the world,' Magnus once said, 'is by telling a story. Science,' said Magnus, 'only teaches you the way things work. Stories help you understand.'

The only person in the family who ever opposed my choice of career was Uncle Herman. I can vividly remember the moment when he first heard what I wanted to do with my life. That was in Holland.

I was about fifteen and Herman, who had come to visit, asked my mother, his sister-in-law, whether she had found a school for me yet.

'He's been at school since he was six,' Sophie had answered.

'University,' said Uncle Herman. 'Have you given any thought to what the boy should study?'

Sophie had looked at him in amazement. 'Herman,' she said, 'young people decide for themselves what they should study. Who they marry, too.'

At that last remark, Uncle Herman had gone slightly red in the face. He turned to me and asked what I had in mind. I said that I had nothing in mind.

'You're not the only one,' he said. 'But the question is: what do you want to be when you grow up?'

'A fairy tale writer.'

We were sitting in the sun lounge. It was the middle of summer. The doors were open and from the garden came the sound of late birds who were letting other late birds know where they were.

'Fairy tale writer,' said Uncle Herman.

'Fairy tale writer,' I said.

'Lord of the Universe,' said Uncle Herman.

'I'm good at writing fairy tales,' I said.

'Just how do you intend to do this?'

'What?'

'Become a fairy tale writer! What are we talking about here?' The subject made him rather hot under the collar. He slammed his hand down on the armrest of the wicker chair in which he was sitting, his lips pressed firmly together.

I looked at my mother.

'N,' said Sophie, glancing worriedly at Uncle Herman, 'I think what you're supposed to do now is tell him what you'd like to study.'

'Oh,' I said.

Uncle Herman closed his eyes and leaned his head against the back of the chair. He took a deep, slow breath. After a long while he straightened up again and after another long while he opened his eyes and looked at me wearily. 'All right,' he said hoarsely. 'What do you plan to study, Nathan? Are you going to university?'

'To become a fairy tale writer? I don't think that exists,' I said.

'No, of course it doesn't exist!' he shouted.

'Herman,' said Sophie. Her mouth had settled into a disapproving frown. 'If you can't behave yourself, go back to your big house so you can play lord of the manor.'

Uncle Herman bowed his head and nodded. There was a brief silence, and when he looked at me again it was as if he were seeing me for the first time. I turned around on Sophie's painting stool and tried to look interested in a charcoal sketch on the easel. 'Nathan,' he said finally, 'you've got to do what you've got to do, but if you do something, then do it well. What I mean is that you shouldn't just piddle around and see if it works. Think up your own course of study, your own training, so that you can choose from different skills and won't be restricted by some accidental talent.'

'Hold on,' said Sophie, 'talent is no small thing, I mean . . .'

'Talent, Soph, is the curse of anyone who really wants to do something. Talent is the greatest handicap you can have. Why do you think you're giving painting lessons to frustrated housewives instead of exhibiting at the Stedelijk? All you've got is talent.'

Sophie looked at him with an expression that gave new meaning to the word freeze-dry.

I didn't understand what Uncle Herman was talking about. I wanted to be a fairy tale writer, because I had discovered that I could do it. What more did he want? That I should first be unable to do it so that I would want it all over again?

As I thought this, I slowly began to realize the significance of Uncle Herman's words.

That was probably the most important day of my life. Not only did I learn that you had to mistrust talent if you truly wanted to discover anything, I also realized that I had stumbled upon an outlook on life which may or may not have been Uncle Herman's, but which certainly seemed worth a try.

And so I wrote my fairy tales and the longer I wrote, the deeper Uncle Herman's strange paradox sank in and the harder it got. By the time I was eighteen I couldn't do a thing. If I had to make a shopping list – the household chores had been divided up and I was the cook – I spent an hour at the kitchen table mulling over the correct sequence of butter, cheese, and eggs. It was the year when we ate almost nothing but omelettes and pasta with red sauce. I had long since stopped writing fairy tales by then. I cooked, stared at the pans on my stove, the sauce bubbling, the eggs setting, the garlic browning and the blue steam rising from the slow-warming olive oil, while inside me, the words formed mile-long caravans that trekked through the desert of my authorship.

The fact that it turned out all right in the end, I owed to Uncle Chaim. One night I was sitting in my room, reading, when he stepped out of the bookcase and posted himself next to my chair.

'Kabbala . . .' he said after a while, breathless.

'The *Zohar*,' I said.

'Forbidden,' said Uncle Chaim. 'Not until a man is forty.'

I rubbed my sandy eyes and bowed my head. 'Nuncle,' I said. 'Didn't you once tell me I was the eldest?'

He tore himself away from the book in my lap and looked at me. 'A good memory,' he said, 'can be a blessing. And a curse.'

I closed my book and let my head sink down onto the back of my chair. 'I know, Nuncle, I know. But it's there and there's nothing I can do about it.'

'The head,' he said. 'Must be covered. With Kabbala, always covered. Always.'

I nodded.

Uncle Chaim waited while I stood up and got my yarmulke from the shelf of Jewish books.

'Good,' he said. 'But now: why?'

'Why Kabbala?' I shrugged. 'Maybe I'm just looking for the path to enlightenment.' I realized that I sounded somewhat bitter. Uncle Chaim had heard it, too.

'Write, child. Don't read. Write.'

There was a stumbling noise behind us. When we looked round, we saw Magnus standing by my bed.

'You're still awake,' he said.

I spread my arms.

He walked towards us. When he was standing next to Uncle Chaim, he cast a quick glance at the book in my lap. He pursed his lips and looked at his uncle.

'Write,' said Chaim again. 'A writer writes, he doesn't read.'

'Cooks eat, too,' I said.

Uncle Chaim shook his head. 'To keep from starving. To taste. To know. But not to while away an evening.'

'He can't write anymore,' said Magnus. 'He's searching for True Writing.'

'Isn't any,' said Uncle Chaim. 'Just stories.'

Magnus drew himself up. 'Flaubert said . . .'

'Shah! That's after your time, Magnus. And before his. Nathan only has to worry about himself. He has to do, not think. Listen.

74

Two men are on their way from one town to another. Just happen to meet. One rich. One poor. Time for the evening prayer and one of them recites the *Shemona Esrei*, from memory. Long. Very long. The other man puts his hand over his eyes. Recites the alphabet. The first man laughs at his companion: "You call that praying, you ignorant fool?" The other man says: "I can't pray, so I give God the letters and he makes a prayer out of them." That night the first man falls gravely ill. As if his life is pouring out of him. Cries out to God: "What have I done to deserve this?" He hears a voice that says: "This is because you mocked my servant." The sick man says: "But he couldn't even pray!" The voice: "You're mistaken. He could pray, for he did it with all his heart. You know the phrases and words, but you're all mouth and no heart."'

He's right, I thought. The motivation is important, too.

And so, by way of a detour through the Kabbala, which I read because there was nothing more I could do, I dug out my old stories and got back to work. Two years later my first collection of fairy tales was published.

The beginning.

There are so many beginnings.

Beginnings?

Beginnings.

Six. All six, somewhere else. All six, at a different moment. And for a clear understanding of our history I shall have to tell them all at the same time.

Uncle Chaim's beginning began in the spring of 1648, that of his nephew, Magnus, in the autumn of that same year. My father began in 1929, midsummer night. Uncle Herman's beginning, I'd place in 1945, in the springtime. Zeno began when he ended, in 1968, and I myself have only just begun, this morning. Out of the plane, blinding snow everywhere, the pier a white catafalque, and the travellers shuffling, groping their way inch by inch through the wind-driven curtains. This is Holland, but the wind is Siberian and the snow, from distant polar regions. Cold, my children, cold as a terrible dream about explorers lost in the wilderness. Roald Amundsen travelling on foot to the South Pole. Nobile, stranded with his dirigible. Scott and his starving, frozen men, waiting to die. We lean into the wind, our coats held closed at the throat, and struggle through the snowstorm. Come. Come, we're off. To the beginning.

———————

'I don't know what sort of bottle this is,' said Nina, 'but it looks intriguing.'

It was as if my chair had suddenly shot forward, like someone sitting in the car of a roller coaster, the long-drawn moment of motionlessness at the top of the rails and then, bang! down he goes. A tremor coursed through my body, so violent that Nina ran to my side. The manuscript lay around my feet like a landscape of ice floes.

'N?' She laid her hands on my shoulders and bent forward, her face close to mine. 'What is it? Everything all right?'

'Huh.' I couldn't speak. The breath sank in my chest and I leaned my head on the back of the chair. 'Yes,' I said. 'I was lost in thought. I . . .'

'For a moment I thought you were sleeping.' She put the bottle on the table between our two chairs and crouched down in front of me. 'You were sitting here, completely limp,' sliding the papers together, 'but I could see you had your eyes open, so . . .'

'I was far away.' Uncle Chaim, Magnus, Herman, Zeno – they echoed in my mind, they were like wisps of smoke, slowly dissolving. 'Very. Very far away.' I shut my eyes and breathed deeply. 'I'm back now,' I said, when I had opened them again.

'N?' She left the manuscript for a moment and put her hands on my thighs. She looked at me closely. 'Have you ever had this before?'

'I'm a fairy tale writer,' I said. 'It's my business to be far away.'

Nina jumped to her feet. 'Why the hell can't you Hollanders ever give a straight answer?'

'Yes. You're right.' I reached for the pile of paper and began putting the pages in order. When I turned round Nina was sitting cross-legged, her arms folded, in her chair. 'I'm sorry. Yes, I've had it before. Many times. But it's got worse. Has its advantages, though.' I picked up the bottle she had brought in and looked at the label.

'What kind of advantages?'

'Sometimes I get lost in a story.'

'What kind of story?'

'A fairy tale.'

She looked at me with the expression of a lab technician who can't quite believe that this just came out of the test tube. 'Are you telling me that you . . . that you drift off and then dream a fairy tale?'

'Daydream.'

'Daydream.'

I nodded.

'I've always wondered where you got them from. Good thing you're not married.'

'What?'

'Married, you know? To a woman?'

'You mean that I wouldn't make a very companionable husband.'

'Companionable . . .' she said. 'No, I mean you're just unconscious half the time.'

'Where did you find this?' I held up the bottle.

'In the cellar. I spent a long time poking around. It was somewhere down at the bottom.'

The bottle was grey with dust, but I recognized it immediately. It was the red Aloxe Corton I had once given Uncle Herman for his birthday.

'The corkscrew is still in the kitchen.'

'I'll go and get it.'

She was already at the door, when I called to her. 'Aren't you afraid, all by yourself?'

'Of course I am, but there's not much point in thinking about it. And I've just spent about half an hour alone in that cellar. I've already stood the test.'

I had thought that she had been gone for five minutes. Half an hour. I had lost half an hour of my consciousness. As if someone had thrown a switch and I had disappeared from 'now' and sunk away into my family's past. The line between the world of the living and the dead, I thought, is growing thinner all the time.

When Nina returned with the corkscrew I cut the seal off the bottle and said, 'This wine is nearly twenty years old. It might be past its best by now. The white . . .' I began twisting the metal spiral into the neck. '. . . the white is renowned. One of the greatest . . .' The cork was wedged in tightly. '. . . white wines. Charles the Fifth used to drink it, I've been told.' It came out in one piece. Because the bottle had been lying in the rack for so long there was some deposit on the cork, but I saw no crystals. I picked up a glass and poured, the light of a candle behind the bottleneck. The wine was deep red in colour, not a trace of cloudiness. As I turned the glass around and looked at the liquid, I felt Nina's gaze. I leaned over and sniffed. Then I took a careful sip. Somewhere in the distance a forest loomed up, with plenty of wood for chopping. I immediately thought of a story, 'Blueberries', by Tolstoy. Deep in the slow whirling of flavours and aromas I could clearly taste them: blueberries.

'There is a God,' I said.

'N,' she said, 'you're whining.'

Uncle Herman had good taste, completely unlike his brother, though I could certainly appreciate Manny's preference for corned beef sandwiches with mustard and dill chips and a large glass of Budweiser. The difference was, I thought, as I drank my wine, that one sense of taste had a deeper richness, and the other, a more superficial one. When you got right down to it, I thought, that was probably the difference between America and Europe. We were accustomed to the struggle to reach the depths and, once there, to seek the things we were searching for. The Americans had brought that depth to the top and created a surface that was far richer and more complex than ours. For a moment I wondered what that meant for me, a product of both these cultures.

'The tape is still running.'

'I'm not surprised.'

'Should I throw more wood on the fire?'

'Please. But be careful.'

She got a few bits and pieces and added them to the blazing pile in the hearth.

'Now,' she said, when she was sitting down again. 'The story.'

'What would you like to hear? Everything, from the very beginning, or would you rather I choose something?'

'Something about yourself, then. Don't you think that would be appropriate?'

'I don't really play a part in the story of my family. I was there, that's all. That's my second talent: I'm always there.'

'Then tell me where you've been.'

'The atom bomb, for instance.'

She looked at me, and when our eyes met I saw that a trace of fearful doubt had crept into her gaze.

'I know it sounds ridiculous, but I was there at the first test explosion.'

'In Japan?'

'No, that wasn't the first. In the desert, near Alamogordo, New Mexico.'

'Okay,' she said. 'Supposing . . . no, I believe you, but . . . would you please begin at the beginning?'

'The problem is, you never quite know where the beginning is, in this family . . .'

'Somewhere,' she said, louder now. 'Begin somewhere, anywhere, and work your way forward. Chronologically. All this jumping back and forth is driving me mad.'

I drank my wine and tried to forget Tolstoy's blueberries. Nina sat curled up in her chair, head bowed, the heavy red hair like a hood around her face and over her shoulders. I filled our glasses, we drained them. We smoked another cigarette. Outside, the wind grabbed hold of the shutters and ran its hands along the house looking for chinks, holes, some way to get in. It wailed and moaned like a restless spirit. Around us the darkness bowed over the glow of the flames and it was as if we were sitting in a cave: the storyteller and the last member of his tribe, waiting until the fire, and finally they, too, turned to ashes.

A Land of Milk and Butter

IT ALL BEGAN with Great-Great-Grand-Uncle Chaim Levi and his nephew Magnus. Uncle Chaim was a clockmaker, Magnus came walking all the way from Poland, his tool chest on his back, to build a new life for himself in the Lowlands. My great-grandfather, who was also a clockmaker, and my grandfather, the physicist, prided themselves on the fact that the men in our family, since the prehistory of clockwork, had all been people of time. Whenever my grandfather was holding forth and wanted to lend weight to his argument, he would bring up Magnus. Magnus Levi had learned the trade from Uncle Chaim, who had invented the pendulum clock, an innovation that made so little impression in seventeenth-century Lithuania that Uncle Chaim had flung it under his workbench, forgot about it, and was promptly forgotten himself. According to Uncle Herman, that pendulum clock was the first example of a familial talent to be in the wrong place at the wrong time.

Clockmakers, that's what we were, even in the days when time was a rare commodity. Ragged tinkers who travelled from town to village and village to town, the clocks in a chest on their back, the little tools rolled up in canvas. Always on the road and always the tinkling of the bells of the wall clocks, the faint thrumming of the rods in the mantel clocks, the chickechickechick of the pocket watches. They carried time on their backs. Time travelled with them. Time was what they lived on. And for some, time was why they died. A distant ancestor once repaired a steeple clock, somewhere in the East, in a provincial capital on the edge of a Steppe. The clockwork had run riot and every few minutes you heard the sonorous chiming of the quarter hour or the rich blur of strokes that told the hour. The smith, at risk to his own life, had tried to disconnect the striking mechanism, but had got no further than muffling the sound with an old gunnysack. By the time the clock-maker arrived, he had nearly been beaten to a pulp. In the village, no one (except the deaf sexton) had slept for two days. Men, women, children, even animals had bags under their eyes and snarled and snapped at each other. Happy marriages threatened to dissolve, many women had fled to their relatives in other villages, the cows had stopped giving milk. There wasn't a bird to be seen for miles around.

The clockmaker was received by a hoarse-voiced village elder. They shook hands, drank a glass of tea, and listened as the old man shouted out the details of what had happened. Then he plugged up his ears with wax and climbed the tower. The smith went with him. But when they reached the top, the clock would not be silenced. The two men climbed back down again, went to the village elder, and told him what was wrong. 'We'll just have to wait,' the clockmaker said, 'until the works have wound down.' The village elder shook his head and said that wasn't possible. Tomorrow was the annual fair and if the clock hadn't stopped by then, the merchants would all go running. The village would lose such a large portion of their income that they wouldn't be able to afford the sowing seed for the following year. The clockmaker looked at the smith, spread his arms, and climbed back up. There, between clock and clapper, he met his death.

Uncle Chaim was a taciturn man. He sat in his little wooden house, repaired timepieces, and shrugged his shoulders. 'History,' he told the young Magnus, 'is like a clock. You think it's getting later, but the hands are always moving in the same circle. What's on top today, is on the bottom tomorrow.' Magnus, who often came to see him in the little house at the edge of the woods and helped him out, or leafed through the old books that lay under the bed, Magnus would think back on what had happened, when a band of Cossacks had struck off the head of Chaim's wife because she happened to be standing outside the door with a basket of washing when the horsemen thundered past. And he also thought of the village on the other side of the forest that, one day, was no longer there – burned to the ground.

Whenever Magnus was with his uncle, in the shaky wooden house, hidden among the trees at the edge of the forest, Chaim sat him down on the cracked bench beside the door and told him about the past, wading back and forth across the grey wooden floor, taking up clocks, picking up a screw here and there and putting it in one of the many drawers and boxes on the table under the window. Magnus sat down on the bench, which was so old it gleamed like dung, and listened. They drank tea out of glasses white with lime.

The old man told him of the days when there weren't any Cossacks and everything was green and fields of sunflowers bloomed just outside the village, green stalks as thick as your arm with heads as big as wheels and in those heads the black spiral that nearly sucked you in, right into the heart of the sun . . . Magnus listened and thought: It's all nostalgia, regret for lost time.

Great-Great-Grand-Uncle Chaim's favourite story took place in the days when he was just a boy and lived in a town in the North, on the river harbour. His parents owned a modest house on the quay. At the end of the cart track that ran along the house, where the deep furrows branched off to the right and disappeared in the first hesitant overgrowth of the great forest, stood a small wooden structure that looked like a cowshed and was inhabited by a woodsman and his three daughters. Chaim spent nearly all his days in the woods behind that odd-looking house, where he and the eldest of the three girls would think up long, perilous adventures.

'It wasn't a very big forest,' he said. 'Maybe two days around, but when you're ten years old you can wander about a forest like that for a week and think you're in another country. We usually pretended we had to make a dangerous journey, on horseback, straight through the Carpathians, through the forests of Lithuania. Early in the morning I would come for Freide and we'd go to the kitchen and fill a knapsack with provisions: some bread and cheese, a bottle of water. Then we'd mount our horses, the ones we didn't have – we were just pretending – and ride out. First a long way over the firebreak, but soon we were among the trees, where it was dark and quiet. Usually we wouldn't be home until suppertime, when it started getting dark. I can't remember us talking much. We rode and rode, and were especially careful when our horses had to go downhill. Such fun we had. But the best part about the forest was clearing the land.

'At the end of the summer,' said Chaim, 'we'd all go into the forest. The woodsman, Freide and her sisters and I would spend the whole day gathering brushwood. We sawed down sick trees, cut back gnarled branches, cleared the paths ... In the afternoon we ate in the open field, right next to the lane, and in the evening, when we were done, we brought our brushwood there and made a big fire. You mustn't forget, it was getting colder by then. Late September. During the day the sun still shone brightly, but the evenings were cool. We wrapped ourselves in blankets and the woodsman and I built a campfire. First a pile of dry leaves, covered with twigs, then a sort of wigwam made of branches, and on top of that heavy, gnarled boughs, as thick as an arm and often still green. After a while we had a big cone of wood. We left a small opening at the bottom where we could stick in a dry, burning branch. The campfire began to burn from inside out, from little to big, from dry to wet. It usually wasn't long before we had a huge fire, and we roasted potatoes in the ashes. Above us, and in the forest, it had gone completely dark and we sat in that clearing, lit by the flames. Shadows danced among the trees. The sparks from the fire flew up to the treetops and burst into pieces. We would sometimes feel a little scared. As we pricked our potatoes on sticks and held them in the ashes, the woodsman told us ghost stories. I wish you could have seen it.'

That's what he always said, Uncle Chaim: 'I wish you could have seen it.'

Magnus saw other things. One day when he arrived at Uncle Chaim's house he found a bare patch with smouldering stumps of charred wood where the house had been. The clockmaker was nowhere in sight. Magnus walked among the half-burnt pieces of wood, through the ankle-deep layer of damp ash, but found nothing to remind him of the little house. The bench was gone, the table, the shaky wooden bed with the old books . . . He picked up a stick and poked around in the blackened mess. Just as he was about to leave, he saw something lying in the scorched coppice, under an oak. It was Chaim's instrument kit, the chest he used to carry on his back when he travelled about the country repairing clocks in remote villages and towns. It had been cast aside, landed in the bushes, and been forgotten. Magnus slung the chest onto his back and set out on his journey.

'Cossacks,' said Uncle Chaim, when I asked him once what had happened. 'Beware of Cossacks, my boy.'

'There are no more Cossacks,' I said. 'Not here.'

'There are always Cossacks.'

Here was America, where we were already living, the land where Uncle Chaim thought that people lit their lamps with a dollar bill and nobody ate potatoes.

'Cossacks and potatoes,' said Uncle Chaim. And he sang, to confirm his loathing for potatoes:

> *Zuntik – bulbes,*
> *Montik – bulbes,*
> *Dinstik un mitvokh – bulbes,*
> *Donershtik un fraytik – bulbes,*
> *Shabes in a novene:*
> *– a bulbe-kugele!*
> *Zuntik – vayter bulbes.*

Sunday, potatoes. Monday, potatoes. Tuesday and Wednesday, potatoes. Thursday and Friday, potatoes. But on Shabbat, a special treat: potato pudding! Sunday, more potatoes.

'The food alone should have been reason enough for me to leave that country,' Uncle Chaim once said. I had reminded him that this would have made him an eligible candidate for the Hollander Top Ten List of Terrible Reasons to Make Drastic Decisions.

'Pah!' he said. 'Don't compare me to your father, who left Europe because he didn't want to wear a tie. Or Magnus, who left because he was looking for a wife without a moustache.'

That was what Magnus had said, that all the women in their region had moustaches. 'Moustaches and hairy legs.' He had shivered at the thought. Uncle Chaim had looked at him sideways, his left eyebrow lowered. 'Hairy legs? When did you see a leg?' Magnus, inhabitant of the spiritual realm for nearly three centuries now, had blushed like a young girl. '*Nu*, Magnus, Nephew. Where in all those parts did you ever see a leg?' Magnus had mumbled something about moustaches and that he had certainly seen *them* before and that you could only assume . . . His uncle's eyebrow remained firmly lowered and it was a long time before he looked away. Finally he turned to me and shrugged.

But neither hairy legs, nor upper lips, were the reason for Magnus's departure. It was the last Cossack raid, when Uncle Chaim's house was burned to the ground. There, among the stumps of wood and lumps of charred straw, like rotting teeth in a blackened mouth, he had tightened his belt, knotted his puttees, and left.

The year was 1648.

————

Magnus Levi, as he was still called at the time, reached, after more than twenty-one years of travelling, the easternmost part of the Lowlands. And there he stayed. Not because he was tired, which he was, or sick of travelling, which he also was, but because he arrived in a town on Market Day. He wandered among the stalls looking at blushing apples, pears as big as a man's fist, cabbages like cannon balls and bulky rolls of worsted. He could smell contentment in the air and he felt something settling inside him, going slowly round and round, the way dogs do when they have found a place where they want to lie down. Magnus tried to resist this unfamiliar feeling, but it was strong, almost overwhelming. He jumped when a cloth merchant called out to him.

'What're you selling, friend?'

He could vaguely make out what the man asked, because the dialect in which he spoke sounded much like the Plattdeutsch he had picked up along the way.

'*Uhren.*'

'Clocks?'

Magnus nodded.

The man beckoned him to come closer and then gestured to him that he wished to see what was in the wooden chest. Magnus placed the chest on the merchant's stall and opened it. Hanging among his neatly arranged tools was the little pendulum clock he had made. The man pursed his lips and nodded admiringly.

'*Schön,*' he said. He looked back at Magnus, his head slightly tilted, and asked, '*Deutsche?*'

'*Deutsche?*' Magnus shook his head. '*Weiter östlich. Polen.*'

'*Pol . . .*'

Once again Magnus shook his head. '*Da gewohnt. Nicht Polak.*'

The merchant shrugged his shoulders and pointed to the pendulum clock. '*Wieviel?*'

Magnus named his price and the man on the other side of the stall began busily converting. Again he pursed his lips.

Meanwhile a small group of curious onlookers had gathered around them. People asked the merchant where the traveller had come from and the merchant, who suddenly felt like a true cosmopolitan, told them the story. Just as Magnus was taking the pendulum clock out of the chest so that they could see it better, the cloud of spectators parted. A lady and her companion walked through the space they had made. Magnus, who hadn't noticed a thing, was busy letting the clock chime. The melodious cooing of the rods and the first four lines of the song Friede always used to sing rose up in the clear spring air. He had worked for months to get the eleven copper rods just the right length that they would produce the proper tones, and before that he had slaved many, many months to build a mechanism that would allow the tiny hammers to hit the rods at just the right tempo, and in sequence. He stared dreamily at the little clock. He didn't notice that anything had changed until he saw the merchant give a deep nod. At first he grinned, taking the nod as a sign of appreciation and admiration, but when it remained silent and everyone appeared to have shifted their gaze, he looked sideways. Standing next to him was a young woman in a dress of midnight-blue. A black crocheted shawl was draped across her shoulders. She was in the company of a servant girl in a white lace cap.

'What song is that?'

She had dark eyes, the colour of polished, gleaming walnut, and curly black hair, tied back in a ponytail.

He stammered out something that even he didn't understand.

'*Deutsche?*' she asked.

The merchant explained to her where the clockmaker had come from and then Magnus told her that he had been on the road for twenty years now and had travelled through Poland and Bohemia and Moravia repairing clocks and in one big city had even built a timepiece for the mayor.

When he had finished speaking, the young woman asked how much he wanted for the pendulum clock. Magnus looked at the timepiece. The sloping sides were like the curve of a woman's hip, the wood was the colour of . . . He named a price that was barely half what he had named earlier.

'What?' cried the merchant. 'You told me . . .'

Magnus, who realized he had let himself get carried away and was about to be laughed at, picked up the pendulum clock and tucked it back into his wooden travelling case. He smiled unhappily, shrugged his shoulders, and said, in even clumsier German (if that were possible), something that was meant to explain his peculiar behaviour. The young woman leaned towards her maidservant and whispered something in her ear. Then she gave Magnus a nod and asked the merchant to measure off two yards of white linen.

The group of onlookers dispersed and Magnus slung the chest onto his back. He walked between two stalls and made his way to the large church in the middle of the market square. There, in the shelter of the buttresses, where it stank of rotting vegetables and old fish, he had a serious word with himself. How could he have been so stupid? To let himself be carried away by a pair of beautiful eyes? Imagine selling Reisele for a price that wouldn't even cover the cost of . . . You're in a strange land, Magnus Levi. You've got to keep silent and listen, instead of bragging and swooning. When he had

gone past the church the sun came out again, and in the clear spring
light he walked out of the market square, into an alleyway between
two large white houses with stained glass windows. Behind the glass
he saw a row of plants in white and blue pots. They bore red flowers,
as big as apples. He had seen many things on his journey to the
West: he had been in prosperous regions, but nowhere had he seen
such abundance as in this place, nowhere had it been as clean,
nowhere did the brass door knobs gleam as brightly as they did here.
Behind the white houses was a cobblestoned street lined with clipped
trees and tidy flower beds. As he walked among those little trees he
heard the click-clacking of a woman's heels. When he looked around
he saw a servant girl, who had gathered up her skirts and was running
towards him.

When she had caught up with him, she stood there for a while,
panting. He waited for her to catch her breath, trying to look
friendly. This wasn't easy, because he was frightened. He had recognized her as the servant girl he had seen with the young woman
who had been standing next to him at the market, and he was afraid
she had come to tell him that he had behaved in an unseemly manner
and that she would have him run out of town. That had happened
to him before, somewhere in a Prussian village. He had never quite
been able to discover what he had done wrong, but whatever it
was, he had nearly been thrown in prison for doing it.

'My mistress asks if you would be so kind as to repair the clocks
in her father's house,' panted the girl.

He looked at her without quite understanding what she meant.
She was young, maybe eighteen or nineteen, and she didn't seem
to find him at all threatening or strange. But that still didn't set his
mind at rest. *'Ich geh weiter,'* he said. *'Andere Stadt. Muß gehen . . .'*

The servant girl sighed and shook her head. 'They'll pay you
well,' she said. 'She wants you to come, sir. She's seen your clock.'

Pride is like the sun that peeks out from between two clouds.
Magnus felt the agreeable warmth of recognition.

'Die Dame ist nicht böse?' he asked.

The servant girl shook her head. 'You may come this evening,
seven o'clock,' she said. She told him the address and made him

repeat it three times. Anyone, she said, could show him the way. Her master's house was known to all.

For the rest of that day Magnus wandered about the town. He looked at shops, peered through the open doors of coffee houses, and stood for a long time gazing at mothers as they walked with their young children across a grassy field. Ducks waddled along the banks of a pond, deer stood poised on a hilltop, a jay skimmed carelessly over his head. Everything was small and clear and still. Magnus had arrived in a fairyland.

That night, in the little town in the east, Magnus was to meet the woman of his life. Her name was Rebekka Gans and she was the daughter of a prosperous cattle dealer. The shy clockmaker had moved about the house behind the Grote Markt like a cat walking on new-fallen snow. He didn't dare sit on the brocade chairs, and he stood there clutching his travelling case for so long that the young lady finally asked if he wouldn't rather put it down. Where? Magnus had thought, looking around the high-ceilinged room with the gleaming wooden floor. She had walked up to him, taken the chest, not flinching when she felt the weight of wheels and tools, and leaned it against the green-veined marble of the hearth. Then she had looked at him with her grave, impassive face and rung for the maid.

He had examined every clock in the house that night and as he did so, had drunk tea out of cups so thin that the light from the oil lamp shone right through them and had eaten almond curls so fine and meltingly sweet that they flitted about in his empty stomach like butterflies. When he left, after an hour or two, his head felt as light as those biscuits.

'Eyes like a moon calf,' said Uncle Chaim. 'In love. In love? Bewitched!'

That was how it felt, in any case. And Magnus knew just when it had happened. Not at the market, where he was 'Smitten by the sight of her,' as he himself once said. Not when he was in the house, nibbling on those fluttering cookies and watching the flicker of candlelight under the teapot. Not when he had placed the small black-lacquered clock before him on the table. 'Salomon Coster,

The Hague,' it said on a silver plate behind the glass door. The young lady had stood beside him and watched as he studied the movement. It was a pendulum and, as far as he could tell, one of the first applications of that technique. He had asked three questions, enough to determine that the clock was about ten years old, that it was based on the theory of a certain Huygens, who had invented the pendulum clock. At that moment Magnus had realized that Uncle Chaim had invented the very same thing fifteen years earlier. He had looked up, young Magnus, stared into the lamplit twilight, and let his eyes wander. The waste of it all. The clock that Uncle Chaim, shaking his head, had flung under his workbench after Wolschke, the German forester, had informed him that the count had called it a 'diabolical piece of rubbish' and didn't want it in his house. The capriciousness of an age that allowed two, maybe even more, to come up with the same invention, yet clasped only one of them to her bosom. If Uncle Chaim had been credited with the invention instead of Mr Huygens, the history of Chaim and Magnus, perhaps even of the entire continent, would have turned out differently. And then he had met her eyes, at the end of the journey his eyes had made around the room. The oil lamp lit them from the side and he saw tiny stars in the blackness, the veil of her lashes, the soft yet clear-cut line of her jaw, and he wanted to turn away but couldn't. Her bound hair curled rebelliously at her temples, a few strands had come loose above her left eye and before he knew what he was doing his hand was on its way to . . . That's when it happened. A shadow of a smile had stolen across her face (not just her lips, he remembered later that night, as he wandered through the town, brooding and pondering, it hadn't just glided over her lips, that smile, but over her whole face, the . . . the memory of a smile, a barely perceptible 'yes,' an 'if circumstances were different . . .') and he had felt his hand clench, had, so slowly that it seemed to last for hours, called it back ('Here! Here, you mongrel of a hand! Down!') and the hand came back towards his own face and – by that time his neck was damp with sweat – suddenly the hand was coming towards him at full speed. The next thing he knew, he was lying on the floor. He had boxed his own ear. The lady tried to control herself, but even he felt relieved when, not two seconds later, she burst into peals of laughter.

Outside, under the spring moon, drifting from one alleyway to the next, he had wallowed in his shame like a pig in the mud.

'The history of love. Write about that, a big fat book. Kings. Princes. Abraham and Sarah, ah . . . Solomon and the Queen of Sheba. David and Bathsheba. And one special chapter for the man who boxed his own ear,' Uncle Chaim said. 'And all because he was scared of hairy legs. Bah!'

By morning, Magnus had walked around the town three times and knew it as well as the village where he himself had grown up. The streets, the houses, the market square, the shooting grounds, they were all like the movement of a trusty clock. He bought bread at the baker's and ate it on the bank of a ditch strewn with buttercups. The dew left the fields, birds flew up to the clear blue sky like tinkling bells. The smell of cow dung rose up from the ground and tickled his nostrils. A milkmaid came by with two wooden buckets on her yoke and saw him chewing his butterless bread. She put down her buckets, drew a dipper out of the milk, and gave him a drink. He thanked her in a mixture of languages he had learned along the way and she laughed like a man as she walked on. He gazed after her, the broad hips in the long striped skirt, the plump back, the full, rounded arms. A land of milk and butter. The milk he had drunk was nearly yellow with cream. He was no farmer, but even a layman could see how succulent and tender the grass was here.

Halfway through the morning he tugged on the copper bell at the merchant's house and was let in by the servant girl. She gave him milk in a mug and set a plate beside it with a buttered brown slab. The milk was sweet and hot, the slab of brown was called *koek* and tasted of anise. After he'd eaten he was shown into the parlour – but no one was there. The table had been cleared and laid with a coarse linen cloth. He went and fetched, under the maid's supervision, the clocks he had seen earlier, and set about his work. Although the clocks were a different shape from those he knew, he was familiar with the works, and by noon he had cleaned and oiled two of the four. Then the maid came for him and in the kitchen, where a portly cook was stirring a pot, he was given bread and cheese. It wasn't until he had closed up the last clock that the lady of the house walked in. The maid followed her carrying a tray with a teapot, a blue and white plate of butter biscuits, and a little tower of porcelain. Magnus cleared off the table, cleaned his instruments, and packed up his chest. All that time the young woman watched him gravely. Then she removed the cloth from the table, set it, and had him sit down again.

'Nu,' she said. 'Lomir redn.'

So. Let's talk.

The maid left the room. Magnus, his mouth a carriage house, stared at the woman in amazement.

They spoke. They spoke like the tea that flowed, fragrant, from the spout of the teapot, like the biscuits that crumbled between their teeth and left a buttery film on their fingertips. They spoke until the windowpanes turned grey, blue, and finally indigo. They spoke, and it was, as Magnus would later say, as if he were emptying and filling at the same time.

Then the merchant came in.

'A beard,' said Magnus, many centuries later, 'a beard like a cluster of bees. A head of hair – he was my future father-in-law but there's no other way to describe it, I'm sorry – a head of hair like a witch's broom. My heart didn't just stop: it was no longer there.'

'Becky,' the giant had said. ('A giant, Nathan,' said Magnus. 'I didn't even know that Jews could be so big. A voice like the great clock in Worky.') 'Becky, I didn't know we had guests.'

'Tatele,' she said. 'This is the clockmaker.'

And Magnus had jumped up, knocking over his chair, clicked his heels (as he had learned in Germany), bowed from the hips, and cried, 'At your service, Your Grace, Magnus Levi!' And he thought, Tatele? Little Papa?

Becky and her father had laughed like the rain: he, a gusty cloudburst of deep, sonorous tones, she, a spring shower on a velvety meadow.

A clockmaker, even though he travelled about and carried all his

wordly possessions in a chest upon his back, was good enough for
Rebekka Gans. Her father, Meijer, a dealer in livestock, had also
started from scratch. He knew that the Jews in neighbouring countries, and even in some parts of the Lowlands, lived by the grace of
the good-naturedness of their local administrators. He had been in
the North, where no more than three Jewish families were allowed
to live in town, where Jews were only allowed to be butchers,
tanners, or peddlers, and were forbidden to build synagogues. The
tolerance in this region, and especially in the prosperous West, had
made him a wealthy man, but he had never forgotten his own
humble beginnings.

That was why, even though Magnus was poor and had no home,
Meijer Gans looked at the character of the man who wanted his
daughter and not at his position or means. He peered into Magnus's
soul, seeking ambition and a spirit of enterprise. He was pleased
with what he found.

The couple were given Salomon Coster's clock and a dowry in
silver when, two months later, they left for West Holland. In Rotterdam, a cousin of Meijer Gans's who dealt in grain helped them find
a house. The widower himself – Rebekka's mother had died of
childbed fever shortly after her birth – remained behind in the East.
He would miss his daughter the way a man misses an arm, yet he
wished her happiness and good fortune, things that, in his opinion,
were best found in the West. Magnus embarked on a new life and,
as if to show how much he wanted to be and belong here, he
changed his name to Hollander. He knew of no better way to stress
his wholehearted devotion to this rich land of luscious grass, creamy
milk, and golden yellow cheese.

A son was born, one, whom they named Chaim. He became a
clockmaker and met a girl called Zipporah Leib. The son married
the Leib girl. They had a son, who was named after Grandfather
Meijer and, scarcely three years after his birth, died of galloping
consumption. Chaim thought he had provoked the Lord of the
Universe by not giving his firstborn son the name he should have
had, and so, seven years later, when another son was born, he was
called Heijman, the Dutch version of Chaim, which means 'life.'

The boy was strong and healthy and, like his father, became a clockmaker. He married, as had every other man in the family, late. He took Chava Groen as his wife, and when they were nearly forty she had a son whom they called Heijman. He married Lenah Arends, and from their alliance, too, came one son: Heijman Three. He took Rebecca van Amerongen as his wife, who bore him Heijman Four. The nineteenth century was two years old by then. Heijman Four and his wife, Esther de Jong, had a child at the age of forty-three. It was a son: Heijman Five. This descendant of the house of Hollander, a clockmaker, married young. He was twenty-three when he met Anna Blum and twenty-four, Anna twenty-five, when they knew the joy of offspring: Heijman Six.

The tide of time (Magnus's words) had driven the Hollanders to the West, to Rotterdam, that boisterously expanding merchant city on the North Sea coast, and there it seemed as if they had finally landed in a peaceful haven. Seven generations of Heijmans (if we count the first, who was called Chaim) grew up there. Magnus and Rebekka lived to see their children's children, but could sense that the younger generation were ashamed of the family's humble origins; embarrassed by Magnus's old work-coat, the wooden chest Rebekka had hung on the wall and the modest trade in matzos, dried fruit and nuts that she and her friend Schoontje ran from a little shop in the Jewish quarter.

'That's the way it goes,' said Magnus, in keeping with the analysis that my grandfather, the last Heijman Hollander, liked to make of The Journey to the West. 'You start with a stone, a piece of rope and a threadbare coat, and you build a house so your children will have a roof over their heads, a safe place to live, but once they've grown, they say: Come, Father, throw away that stone and that rope and that old coat. Everyone wants a house, no one likes to be reminded of all the grief that came before it.'

The last Heijman in the series took Sarah van Vlies to be his bride. He didn't succeed his father in the clockmaking business, but studied physics instead and eventually became a professor in Leiden. His parents had left him a jewellery shop and renowned repair studio, and enough money to enable him to take his doctoral degree.

Heijman became a respected, though not exceptional, physicist. His greatest claim was the development of a standard formula for bridge construction. At a time when physics was becoming increasingly experimental, he was more of an engineer than a researcher, more of a clockmaker than a thinker.

And so, eight generations of the family started by Magnus and Rebekka had been born in Rotterdam. They had lived, prospered, prayed, sung, and died there. They had seen the fishing village grow to become the second merchant city of Holland and ultimately – after the Nieuwe Waterweg had been dug and another Jew – Pincoffs – had founded the Rotterdamse Handelsvereniging and had the harbours built on Feijenoord – the largest harbour in the world. They had prospered, the Hollanders, just as the city had prospered, and, like the city, had set their sights on the West, on all that was modern and new. Together, they had opened themselves to the world, yet felt deeply and firmly rooted in that land of Holland. When, in 1939, the eighth and ninth generations stood on board the ship that was to take them from Rotterdam to New York, their departure was more than the leaving of a place. It was the resumption of the journey, the loss of the place that had allowed them to take root in the world. It was the loss of a place that was just like them, a city that, unlike Amsterdam, had never boasted about her tolerance for the Jews, yet was often more tolerant. Rotterdam had become their heart and they had felt cherished in her arms. Moving on was second nature to the Hollander family, yet for eight generations, from Magnus's son Chaim to the last Heijman, they had been Rotterdamers, born and bred. They had all but forgot where they began.

1648 was the year Magnus slung his pack on his back, turned round, and left the region where he had been born, raised, and expected to die. Twenty-one years later he arrived in the Lowlands.

'Twenty-one years to walk from Poland to Holland?' I once asked him, amazed at the duration of the journey.

'He lost his way,' said Uncle Chaim. 'Didn't know he was going to Holland. Knew he was headed West. Took a wrong turn.'

'I . . . Things were different then,' said Magnus.

'I understand that. But twenty-one years?'

'Magnus,' said Uncle Chaim. 'Dear dear dear . . . nephew. Worthless boy scout.'

So for twenty-one years Magnus was on his way and what he did in all that time no one really knew. He himself said that he worked a bit here, stayed for a while there, turned South when he thought he was going West. A journey . . . If you were to try and draw the route, you would end up with a tangle of wool.

Two and a half centuries later, in Rotterdam, my father and mother met.

'The Lord of the Universe, whether you believe in Him or not,' was Uncle Herman's version, 'decided in 1927, or, God knows, perhaps even from the genesis of creation, to bring together the light and the darkness, and that He would do this in the form of a marriage. That is why – pay attention! – He arranged for your parents to fall into each other's arms during the fireworks on Midsummer Night. Good fortune, some people would call it, bad luck say those who know better. Others (by that, Uncle Herman was referring to himself) call it a disaster. He came from a family of clockmakers and physicists, she was old money. He was a promising engineer, she, a young lady who had life figured out long before life understood her. He lived in the shadow of his father, your grandfather, who placed physics above all else, and she thought that physics was merely re-inventing the wheel. She was a free spirit.'

Uncle Herman had the tendency to devote quite a bit of attention to the setting in his stories, the backdrop against which a particular event took place. Perhaps this is something peculiar to sociologists. Whatever the case: ever since he first told me his version of the downfall, I was impressed by the way in which he linked the fate of our family to the history of this century, particularly because he proved to be right.

It was Midsummer Night, 1929 (not 1927, Uncle Herman wasn't very good at dates) and above the park, rockets were flaring and fading in chrysanthemums of red, yellow, green and blue sparks.

The upturned faces of the spectators and passers-by shone in the light of the fireworks, and the tall oaks and chestnut trees looked lovelier than ever. Outside the little white inn at the edge of the park, men stood with a glass of beer in one hand, the thumb of their other hand hooked in a waistcoat pocket, legs slightly apart. Women hung on their arms or whispered to one other. Each time a rocket exploded, their dresses flashed white in the darkness.

'Hollander! Hollander!' someone shouted. His voice was half lost in the booming of the fireworks, but my father had heard it and looked around, searchingly. He met the equally searching gaze of a young woman standing nearby. They looked at each other, turned away, and continued hunting.

'Hollander!'

Once again my father and the young woman looked at each other. Then she frowned, cast one last glance behind her, and marched up to my father.

'My name is Hollander,' said my mother. In her voice, my father told us later on, was a touch of indignation. As if she had meant to say: Why are *you* responding to *my* name?

'Mine, too,' said my father.

'Ridiculous,' said my mother. (She had already become a Socialist by then and had learned to dispense with bourgeois formalities. These had been replaced by a directness that made most people blush.)

'Emmanuel Hollander,' said my father, hurt. 'Pleased to meet you.'

My mother shook her head and crossed her arms.

At that moment a man came walking towards them. He had large brown eyes in a full, oval face. With his short, thick curls and round metal glasses he looked much younger than he actually was. 'Hollander,' he said. Only now did my mother hear that her surname was being pronounced with a German accent. *'Wie geht's?'* My father bowed lightly to the man and introduced him to my mother. 'Frau Hollander,' he said. Then he turned to her and introduced the stranger, 'Mr Paul Ehrenfest.'

'I didn't know you were married, Hollander,' said Ehrenfest.

My mother stamped her right foot on the ground. (Always her right foot. Zeno once asked why she never used her left foot, which baffled her for days afterwards; it was the sort of question you ask someone with a long beard, whether he sleeps with it above or below the blankets). My mother stamped her foot and let the light of the fireworks glitter in her eyes. 'I have nothing to do with this man,' she said. Ehrenfest looked at her in confusion.

'She just came up and started talking to me,' explained my father, who didn't have much of a knack for social intercourse.

My mother stamped her foot again. 'How dare you!' she cried. She raised her right hand and soundly boxed my father's ear.

Ehrenfest, who was a colleague of my father's and had lectured at the University of Leiden for the past seventeen years, watched her as she disappeared into the flickering darkness.

Heijman and Sarah Hollander, my grandparents, had always befriended the foreign professors who taught at the university. The young Enrico Fermi, during his three-month stay in Leiden, had been one of the family. He had aroused Sarah's interest in Italian food, not by cooking for her, but by talking about the delectable dishes his Mama used to make. Heijman, who wasn't at all pleased about his wife's sudden interest in such exotic cuisine, said that Fermi wasn't staying long and there was no reason to pamper him: the national Dutch meal (potatoes, overcooked vegetables, and leathery meat) was good enough. But that wasn't what mattered to Sarah. Uncle Herman, who was the same age as Fermi and spent a lot of time with him, said that his mother was fascinated by the passion with which a grown man like Enrico spoke of his Mama's cooking. That, said Uncle Herman, was how Sarah wanted to be remembered, too. (And she was. According to Herman, no one had ever roasted a chicken like his mother, golden yellow, with a crispy crust and succulent, piping hot meat underneath. Her cakes, he said, were so delicious that once, in the kitchen, he had run his finger along the swirls on a mocha cream cake and not stopped until he had polished off the whole wagon wheel. It had cost him a night of indigestion and three weeks' house arrest.)

Ehrenfest was older than the Hollander brothers. That night, in the park with the fireworks, he was forty-nine years old, at the peak of his career and, according to Albert Einstein, 'the best teacher I know of in our field.' He stood there before Emmanuel and didn't quite know what he had said wrong. The son of his host had introduced someone to him as 'Frau Hollander' and the young lady in question had walked off in a huff. Dutch etiquette could be extremely complicated.

'Excuse me, Mr Ehrenfest,' said my father. 'I have to put something right. I've made a stupid mistake.' He held up his hand and went racing after my mother's cotton dress, leaving Ehrenfest behind under a shower of yellow drops of fire, victim of a misunderstanding that would never be resolved. Not long afterwards, grief-stricken by the developments in Germany, he took his own life.

'They met again,' said Uncle Herman, 'your father and your future mother, at the ice cream vendor's cart, in that field on the east side of the park. I was standing there, too. I saw Manny grab a woman by the arm and I was greatly surprised. He'd never been much of a ladies' man. She turned round and said something – nothing very nice, that much was clear even from a distance, and he started talking with his hands, turned halfway round and pointed into the darkness, towards the restaurant, and talked and talked and talked. At first I thought: I didn't even know Manny had a girlfriend, and then: I certainly didn't know he'd had a girlfriend for so long that they're already fighting.'

Uncle Herman moved as inconspicuously as possible towards his brother, but hadn't gone ten steps when his name rang out in the darkness.

'Herman Hollander! Where were you?'

My father looked up. My mother looked up. Herman bowed his head and tried to become invisible.

'It was a woman,' he said. 'Let's just say: a woman I was trying to avoid.'

'She was the wife of one of my father's colleagues,' said my father, 'and she and Herman had had a fling. Probably started out for him as an exciting little game, but when the fun was over for him, it had only just begun for her. She chased him all over the place! I think your grandfather was even more upset by the whole thing than either Herman or the woman's husband.' After that my father would always fall silent for a moment, and then conclude with: 'Beautiful woman. A really good-looking woman.'

They ended up, Herman and his ladyfriend, one avoiding, the other pursuing, right next to my father and mother. Herman took a deep breath and said, 'May I introduce . . .' He looked at my mother. She sighed and said, 'Sophie Hollander.' Herman's lady looked surprised. 'I didn't know you had a sister, Herman.'

'No . . .' said my father.

'Oh, I beg your pardon,' said the lady. 'Your wife . . .'

'I think I'm going mad,' said my mother. She looked around and then sank down onto a post.

The light and the darkness, said Uncle Herman, but he meant: his light, his darkness. That night in the park, my father fell for my mother (she, discerning as always, hadn't yet fallen for him), but Uncle Herman was the one who felt the earth move under his feet. That was the difference in the Hollander Brothers' feelings for Sophie. One fell in love, the way many people fall in love, the other lost his heart. The first few months everything was fine. The three of them spent a lot of time together, so much that it soon became impossible to imagine them as anything but a threesome. They strolled down the Binnenweg, under the trees, past Hoboken. They sat in the grass of Zocher's Park and held heated political discussions (that is, Herman and Sophie did; Emmanuel, in the meantime, would be building something out of twigs and Herman's pipe cleaners) or walked along the Boompjes and looked at the slow, wide river, the Wilhelminakade on the other side, where the great American-bound ships moored and unmoored and which was often swarming with emigrants.

My father and my uncle were not the only young men who wanted her. Sophie was a real catch. She was pretty and proud and came from a family of wealthy stockbrokers and merchants. Sophie was involved in politics, had been active in the Socialist movement ever since she was a girl, something her family had never thanked her for. ('What are you trying to do?' her father had asked after hearing from a colleague that his daughter had been seen with the Reds. 'Make us poor with our own money?' She had answered him calmly and confidently, and was so convincingly eloquent that, a month later, her father went to a meeting himself and, less than six months after that, joined the party). Although her leftist tendencies were a blemish on the otherwise excellent reputation of her family, Sophie Hollander was considered by many families to be a fine match. She did paint, of course, but that was an innocent enough pastime for a young lady. Most of the mothers were certain that these strange fancies, that Socialist claptrap and that painting of hers, would end once she was married to their son and had children of her own. Sophie disagreed. She took the things she did seriously. She was a socialist, because she couldn't see how the God of Abraham, Jacob, and Isaac was making the world any better. She painted . . . because she was a painter. If she were to marry – and at the time she ran into the Hollander Brothers she was extremely doubtful that this would ever happen – it would have to be a man who regarded her as his equal and thought it only normal that a woman should have her own opinion, her own work, and most of all, her own life.

So the young Messrs Hollander both courted this headstrong woman and it was Herman who decided whom Sophie would choose.

'There have been a few moments in my life,' Herman said later, 'when I should have kept my mouth shut. This was one of them. If I hadn't been such an arrogant know-it-all, who had to blurt out everything that popped into his mind, I'd have won her.'

'If,' I said. 'Everything in this family is "if". Manny says: If I'd only been able to cash in on the drill that wasn't a drill, I'd be filthy rich. Zelda says: If I'd only been able to take care of Zeno, what happened never would have happened. Zeno says . . . Hang on a minute: won her? Your mistake was in thinking she could ever be won.'

He had muttered something unintelligible, Uncle Herman, his eyes fixed on the horizon.

'The point is,' he said after a while, 'I've travelled the whole world over, met more people than most, but I've never met anyone like your mother.'

'Thank you.'

He looked at me from under a bushy frown. 'Do you find that inappropriate, Nathan?'

I shook my head. I knew how fierce the battle had been between my father and my uncle, and how Uncle Herman had lost.

One evening we were sitting in Café Loos. Sophie and Herman were discussing the situation in Germany, where the Weimar Republic was crashing down. Herman, who had just raised his hand for two more glasses of beer and tea 'for the lady,' said: 'Man is the offal of Creation.'

'The what?' said Sophie.

'The excrement of Creation,' said Herman, who was being slowly borne along on the stream of his metaphors. 'Stupid, selfish, and bad to the core. A creature that imagines itself to be moral, but only ever uses morality to account for so-called "good" deeds, or to justify "necessary evil." If you ask me, we're better off without it.'

'Without what?' asked Sophie, bewildered.

'The human race,' said Herman. And in one and the same breath he gave the waiter his order.

'How,' said Sophie, 'can you be a socialist if you don't believe in the goodness of man?'

'Dear girl,' said Herman, 'socialism, contrary to what you and your fanatical friends might think, is not a surrogate religion. It's a scientific approach to the problem of social inequality.'

'Dear girl?' Sophie snorted.

'Underground transportation,' said Emmanuel. 'Now there's something you can believe in.'

Sophie and Herman both looked at him. Then they turned back to each other and Sophie said, 'Dear girl? What do you think I am, Herman Hollander? Some romantic little twit who runs around with socialists to burn off excess energy?'

'Most people would just call it charity.'

'Why you arrogant . . .' Sophie couldn't quite think of the word that characterized Herman at that particular moment.

'It was a serious mistake in judgement. I thought that Sophie had been looking for a social life and ended up doing charity work because it suited her character.'

'But Sophie wasn't like that.'

He had shaken his head. 'No. Socialism was her form of . . . the way in which she hoped to make the world a better place.'

'So it *was* a surrogate religion.'

A finger stabbing in my direction. 'But that's where I was wrong! I didn't see the sincerity of it. I was an atheist. There wasn't a single form of religion that I took seriously. And Sophie was a true believer. She simply chose the twentieth-century version.'

In later years he would write an article about this, 'The Tradition of Progressive Thinking', in which he described an unbroken line that ran from the Torah, by way of the prophets and the various messianic movements, to socialism. It was, he said, a development that had its origins in the primitive amazement at 'a world that wasn't good' and had led to increasingly practical and pragmatic methods of making the world better. Socialism was, my grandfather would have said, the zenith of that development.

Emmanuel stayed out of the discussion altogether. He sat by the window of that strange, round cafe, gazing out at the traffic, and imagined a world in which all transportation was underground and people whizzed about in stainless steel capsules propelled by compressed air. At times his abstractedness had had a negative effect on our history, but that night his musings about new, smaller, better machines had been the start of our family.

'Emmanuel,' said my mother, when I myself was about twenty, 'may have been a worthless husband, but he was just the man I needed.'

'Because he was a worthless husband,' I said.

She had shaken her head. 'No, because he knew what it meant to start out with nothing and to make something out of it. And because he knew, without ever even having thought about it, that making something is equally important to both men and women. He knew the passion of creation. A person who truly devotes himself to his task, N, will have total respect for another person who does the same. Herman isn't a creator. He's . . .'

'A dissector. An analyst. You think it's the difference between synthesis and analysis?'

'Yes.'

And so, describing my father in the past tense, because she had long since stopped seeing him as a creator, my mother accounted for her ultimate choice, for a man who focused all his attention on nuts and bolts, and smaller things still.

Emmanuel Hollander worked at, and believed in progress, but progress was not a religious notion for him, as it was for his future wife. He was an engineer and knew that every machine began as a rickety prototype, held together with paper clips and string, but gradually improved, little by little. His mistake was in concluding that the world was no different: a huge, exceedingly complicated machine perhaps, but that didn't mean you couldn't make it better. It just took a bit longer.

Progress, to Emmanuel's way of thinking, was the art of making things smaller, and he could still clearly remember when The Realization had hit him.

Walking down the Binnenweg in Rotterdam, somewhere near Hoboken, which was bathed in the dazzlingly bright light of the high summer sun, he had heard his father talking with Professor Lorentz. 'Smaller, Hollander,' said the Nobel Prize laureate. 'Smaller is the future.' They were strolling under the trees at the edge of the field, the two gentlemen in their black suits and the little boy – my father in his knee-breeches. He watched the ladies parading past the tall houses with the turrets. The grass smelled sweet. Herman was running around with a couple of other boys and, in the distance, a lap dog was sniffing at a German shepherd three times its size.

That night, when the professor had gone home and his father was about to retire to his study, Emmanuel asked who Smaller was.

'Smaller?'

'Mr Smaller. The one who's the future.'

Heijman Hollander laughed and tousled his son's hair. 'Not Mr

Smaller, Manuel. The professor means that the future lies in making things smaller. He means that we can now invent all sorts of things, but that they're all too big and require too much energy. The first internal-combustion engines were so big and heavy that they had to spend an enormous amount of energy on themselves, just to drag themselves along. It wasn't until they were smaller that we could we use them for boats and cars. That's what Professor Lorentz means. He thinks that everything can be smaller. Smaller and smaller and smaller. Smaller is a sign that things are getting better.'

'Smaller,' my father was to say later, years later, 'that's what it's all about. This is the age of miniaturization. Some people say communication. But communication only became profitable when we found a way to build such small appliances that the ordinary consumer was able to use them. Miniaturization is a sign of progress.'

That was why my father became an inventor instead of a scholar, because he was fascinated with making things smaller, not with the way they worked.

'Why,' Uncle Herman once said to me, 'do you think I went to so much trouble to get Manny to come with me to America? Yes, we were brothers. Good answer.' (I hadn't even given him an answer.) 'But we weren't all *that* close. Perhaps I thought he would be a comfort to me, in that far-off land of America. Fine. But that would hardly explain why I went to him night after night to try and persuade Sophie to leave. Well? Do you have any idea?'

I didn't need to have any idea. When Uncle Herman asked a question in this way, eliminating the undesired answers by first listing them all and then asking what I thought, it was clear that the only one who could possibly have any idea was him.

'I wanted your father to come,' said Uncle Herman, 'because I saw, knew, that he would do something. How did I know that, you're thinking.'

I wasn't thinking that at all (I was sure Uncle Herman would think it for me) but I nodded vigorously, because I was certainly curious.

'Your father,' said Uncle Herman, 'could have been one of the greatest physicists of his generation, if he wasn't so fond of tinkering.

He has an inimitable mind. But!' Up went the bony old finger. 'I don't mean that he's consciously original, or uncommonly brilliant. No. Your father never thinks. That's why he could have done important things.'

Can a person be a great physicist because he doesn't think? Uncle Herman believed so: 'Schliemann discovered Troy, or whatever it was, because he had a dream which told him exactly where to find it. Einstein assumed that a good proof was elegant. Fermi was called "the quantum-engineer" because he – mistakenly, I might add – was seen as a brilliant amateur mechanic, but a poor thinker. Leo Szilard, remember him, that skinny little fellow? Szilard's first achievement was taking out a patent for something to do with refrigerators.'

If that were true, and it seemed to be, my father could indeed have done great things. Because he hardly ever thought about his work, and if he did, it inevitably led to contraptions and inventions that he regretted long afterwards.

'In other words,' said Uncle Herman, 'you might think of genius as being proof of an extremely orderly mind, but such a mind is merely the reflection of something that lies deeper, and that "something", Nathan, is sheer chaos: premonitions, dreams, the human tendency to impose order, or to see it, when it probably isn't there. Your father, I've always thought, could have made optimal use of the chaos in his mind, if only he hadn't thought at all about what he did and worried more about the consequences.'

But my father, at crucial moments, had done exactly the opposite: he regarded his work as a game, and those rare occasions when he did take it seriously had led to catastrophes of historic proportions.

That man, an inventor who didn't think and relied on half-digested theories and wrongly heard remarks, and that woman, who had a gift for Messianism and opted for the Socialists, those two unequal quantities, Emmanuel and Sophie, had come together, and they married.

After the long line of Hollanders who had produced no more than a single child, and always a son called Herman, Emmanuel and Sophie exploded in a household that was out of proportion in more than one respect. Less than a year after the marriage, Zoe was born, two years later, Zelda, two years after that, me, and finally, after nine years, as a sort of reminder of something that had nearly been forgotten, Zeno.

Manny, who was still called Emmanuel at the time, earned his living as a mechanical engineering draughtsman for a crane factory. Although he had fixed up a small workshop in a shed behind the house, he hardly invented anything anymore. Sophie ran back and forth between the nappy bucket, the kitchen counter, the stove and the children's beds. Party meetings were a thing of the past. At night when the children were finally asleep, she could barely keep her eyes open. Her painting supplies, which she had carefully cleaned before storing away, lay in a cupboard gathering dust, between Zoe's and Zelda's dolls and my cars and boats.

No one was particularly happy, no one was noticeably unhappy. Inside the house the hearth blazed, the coloured glass tea light cast a warm red glow, there was challah and chicken soup on Friday, Manny made apple fritters on New Year's Day, and when the weather turned and summer settled over the land, the young family spent every Sunday on the Noordzee Beach. Herman nearly always went along. Manny often said that Sophie had got two men for the price of one.

But outside, darkness was falling. New Year's Eve 1938 was a quiet affair. There were the traditional apple fritters, which were carried on a huge platter to Herman and Manny's parents' house, and there were even fireworks, but the memory of *Kristallnacht*, which had raged in Germany not long before, was still fresh in their minds. Just after midnight Herman, Emmanuel, and their father stood outside watching the arrows of fire that fell from the sky. All three smoked a cigar and let the old year pass them by. And although none of them had reason to be dissatisfied, the cigars had lost their taste and the fireworks looked too much like the reflection of burning German synagogues in pools of broken glass.

———————

The decision to leave came several months later, on a Sunday evening at Heijman and Sarah's house. A wintery dusk hung in the parlour. There was only one light on, the standard lamp next to Uncle Herman, who sat with a half-closed newspaper on his lap and had long since stopped reading. In the back room, the stars from the tea light danced and the pale yellow cloud from the hanging lamp floated above the big round table. Sophie and her mother-in-law sat there, sliding sheets of white paper back and forth across the tabletop. Under the table, Zoe and Zelda were making their dolls fight out an argument that they themselves had begun. There was a horrible noise coming out of the radio. It sounded as if there were a kobold inside, a small, hideous creature hopping up and down on skinny little legs, steaming with rage. Every few minutes the voice coming from the Comedia would reach a shrill crescendo and the gnome would bite off the words that rolled out of his mouth. As if he were spewing out a long string of sausages and every so often, ranting and raving, would snap one off.

Outside a late winter rain began pouring down. The water streamed down the windowpanes and it grew even darker. Heijman Hollander got up from his chair and switched on the lamp on the sideboard. He paused at the window to look out at the rain. The street was already flooded. It was raining so hard that the water in the gutter looked as if it was boiling. Heijman sighed and sat back down.

Behind the tea-coloured linen of the Comedia the kobold had reached fever pitch. They were no longer words coming out of his mouth, not sausages either, but rough, grey-black cinders. Now and then his voice broke, hacked into the blackest ore, jagged chunks went flying. Then, as a surf of applause began rolling through the half-lit room, the gnome burst into his grand finale, a coloratura of grating and grinding and gnashing and . . .

'A ridiculous little man, that Hitler,' said Hollander senior. He leaned forward and pressed the ivory-coloured off-button on the radio. He sank back, sat with his legs slightly apart and frowned deeply at the fading green eye. The table lamp illuminated his balding crown and the wreath of white hair that stood out all around it. He stuck his thumbs into the pockets of his waistcoat and shook his head.

'If only that were true,' said Uncle Herman.

'What?'

'I said: If only he were just a ridiculous little man and nothing more.'

Grandfather muttered something. He leaned sideways and took a curved pipe out of the rack standing on a small table next to him. 'What do you mean: If only he were nothing more?' His hand glided over the tabletop, found the tobacco pouch, and stuck the bowl of the pipe into the leather muzzle.

Uncle Herman got up from his chair and folded his newspaper several times over. Grandfather lifted his head and looked at him, his left eyebrow slightly raised. Herman stared at him for a moment and then remembered the newspaper. He opened it out again and said, as he folded back the pages, 'This ridiculous creature is the spume riding on the tidal wave, he's the flotsam that washes ashore before the rest . . .'

The old man lit his pipe and disappeared in a ring of smoke. 'Don't romanticise,' he said, when he had reappeared. 'Analysis! Images only confuse the issue.'

'. . . hate incarnate, a demon evoked by the seance that the people have been conducting for years and years . . .'

'Images, stories . . .' said the cloud around my grandfather's head. 'Just like that pseudo-science you say you study.'

'Every new science is a pseudo-science,' said Herman.

He laid the newspaper on the seat of his chair, put his hands in his pockets, and looked down at the floor. 'I'm leaving.'

'It's raining.'

'Father!' cried Uncle Herman. 'Listen to me! Leaving. Leaving! The country. Anyone who has any sense is leaving the country.'

Grandmother appeared between the sliding doors. With the light behind her she was a figure consisting of three dark ovals, a large one on the bottom, then a smaller one, the smallest on top. 'Herman, I will not have shouting in my house.'

'Mama, come in for a minute.'

'I'm busy.'

'Mama . . . The edification of the diamond cutter can wait. I've got something important to tell you.'

'I must say, Herman,' said Grandfather, 'it hasn't improved your manners any, studying with those scatterbrains.'

'I was the only one in our whole damn family who saw that Europe was a sinking ship,' Herman was to say later, years later. 'As early as March 1939, when Germany invaded Czechoslovakia, I asked them to go with me. Begged them to go, threatened them . . .'

I had answered – we were sitting in the lobby of his hotel, he was over again from the States – I had answered that I knew that. After all, I had been there.

'Nathan,' said Herman, bending forward to pour the tea, 'I realize that your imagination knows no bounds and that this is how you earn your living, but what I'm talking about took place when you were a baby.'

'Four. Four and a half. I was four and a half years old. No milk.'

'Very foolish.'

'Foolish? I know exactly what happened. Would you like a complete run-down?'

'I meant the tea. Milk neutralizes the tannin.'

'It's like having a spoonful of warm butter in your mouth.'

Herman had poured the tea, pushed the plate of biscuits perfunctorily towards me and, when I didn't take one, made his selection. The plate would remain in front of him until it was empty.

'Fine,' he said, brushing biscuit crumbs off his jumper. 'Fine, you know exactly what happened then and then, at such and such a time. Congratulations. You have the perfect memory. You're blessed. But I'm not talking about registration. Insight, that's what matters.'

'I can remember Grandfather saying the very same thing.'

'Jesus.' Uncle Herman shook his head, grimacing. 'It's sick. A curse, that's what it is.' He grabbed another handful of butter biscuits and, distractedly, began to consume them. 'Analysis,' he said, 'analysis, no images.'

'No romanticising.'

'No romanticising . . . That too. Lord of the Universe! No romanticising, that's what he said.'

We drank our tea, the First Flush Darjeeling that Uncle Herman had brought with him and given to the hotel manager for safekeeping. It was a delicate, aromatic blend that, with each sip, evoked the image of rows of bowed tea-pickers in long, colourful garments, moving across the endless slopes of the Himalayas.

He was right, Uncle Herman. March 1939, and he had told his parents that he was leaving, even if they stayed behind. His father had laughed in his face and called Herman a half-cocked worrywort. 'Germany and the big four have divided up Czechoslovakia,' he said, 'because it's disputed territory. That invasion has nothing to do with us.' Herman's reply, that Hitler was depriving the Jews of their rights and locking up Socialists and Communists, fell on deaf ears. He had stood there in the middle of the room, Herman, a man, hardly more than a boy, and pleaded for the life of his parents. The horrors he depicted loomed up like phantoms in the darkening parlour. The Teutonic Hordes, as he called them, appeared in the clouds of smoke that rose from his father's pipe, disappeared, and were followed by new ghosts which, in turn, also disappeared, and were replaced by even more abominations. He conjured up a maelstrom of apocalyptic images. There, in the low light of the Dutch sitting room, the light of Rembrandt and Hals and Heda and Vermeer, there, in that light, observed by his silent parents, Zoe, Zelda, my mother and me, he had evoked his demons, and as he talked and talked and talked, he lapsed into the impassioned rhetoric of an Old Testament prophet. It would have come as no surprise if he had raised his right hand and said, in an imploring bass: 'Verily, I say unto you, in the name of the God of Israel, whose name is One: the day will come when you shall no longer be able to walk through your streets, you shall be hunted at every turn, like wild beasts, and if you seek comfort from your neighbour he shall betray you, he shall not know you. Those days shall come. The sun shall rise, the sun shall set, and in the light of day the people shall be crushed like ants!'

Perhaps he ought to have said that. They would have told him

– they were doing that anyway – that he was getting carried away by his own romantic image of reality, but at least then he would have had the satisfaction of prophecy.

But he controlled himself, he was reasonable, he pleaded and begged and lamented.

'Never again,' he said in the lobby of the Memphis Hotel, 'never again. When it was all over, in '45, I made up my mind never to control myself like that again. I'll preach, I'll prophesy, I'll sing, by God, if I think it'll do any good. But no more reasonableness when the world around me is being so unreasonable.'

The seance had ended with the front door slamming and Uncle Herman's footsteps receding down the street. We, my grandparents, my mother, Zoe, Zelda, who was crying, and I, remained behind in silence. It was a long time before my grandmother opened her mouth.

'Chaim,' she said. We all looked up. She never called him that. 'Chaim,' she said, 'would you ring for coffee?' My grandfather stared at her for a moment and then reached behind him, for the bellpull. He gave it a tug. In the distance we heard the little bell that alerted the maid. The silence in the parlour was solid marble. As we waited for her footsteps, I saw an amorphous army of sinister figures marching out of the shadowy corner of the room. Eyes flared in the darkness, the slow tread of the menace came thundering closer.

Although the past lived on in my family (my grandfather, a physicist who worked with the greatest minds of his day, without being a great mind himself, felt, above all, that he was the descendant of a long line of clockmakers, the zenith of an evolution that had taken place within our small circle of kinsmen. 'Clockmakers,' he always said, 'travelling hagglers who carried everything they owned upon their backs. That's what we were. Now we've reached our apex. We no longer wander, we dwell. We no longer do, we think.') – although that past of departing, arriving, and travelling on was still very much alive, the announcement of Uncle Herman's departure came as a shock. In my grandfather's eyes our forefathers had built a Tower of Babel, a work that reached to the heavens, and here was the last builder, the one who could finish the job, saying he was going down, leaving the tower. Here we were, in a land that was a zenith unto itself, the zenith of European civilization, the land for which we had named ourselves, where Huygens had invented the pendulum clock, here we were, risen, together with that land, from the murky waters of suspicion and mistrust, reaching for knowledge and understanding, and Herman was pulling on his coat to leave.

And he wasn't going alone. He walked out of his parents' house and marched resolutely to ours, where my father was sitting in the shed tinkering with a kind of mechanical hammer, a vicious-looking blue steel point that was forced down by a weight. When Herman walked in, the point had just shot through a sheet of iron and was stuck fast in the workbench. My father was trying to pull the thing out with a pair of pliers.

'Manuel,' said Herman, 'I'm leaving.'

'Leaving?' said my father. 'You just got here.'

'Lord,' said Herman. 'Why me? The country, Manuel, I'm leaving the country.'

My father put a piece of metal pipe under the pliers to make a lever. 'Holiday,' he said. 'Have fun.' He clamped the head of the pliers around the steel pin and pushed down hard on the other end.

Herman closed his eyes and tipped his head back. 'Brother,' he said, 'listen. Listen and use your brains.' And he told him what was going on 'outside.' By 'outside' Herman didn't only mean Germany. 'Outside' was the whole European world. 'Things are going wrong,' he said, 'and this time, it's serious. This is a sinking ship.' He talked of Carl van Ossietsky, how the winner of the Nobel Peace Prize had died in a camp. He told my father what German Jewish refugees had told him, that their shops had been plundered and their synagogues burned to the ground. 'But Herman,' said my father, licking the knuckles of his left hand, 'that's hundreds of miles away from here.' Herman had taken a good, long look at his brother. Then he said: 'Man is bad. That's terrible. Man is stupid. That's a shame. Those two traits make a dangerous combination, especially if it's rewarded. And that's what has just happened. The Germans have been given Czechoslovakia. The Germans aren't satisfied with

Czechoslovakia. Soon they'll want Poland and after that they'll want everything on the other side of their country. If you don't leave now, you'll be putting yourself at the mercy of the barbarians.'

But my father, the engineer, was barely listening. In his world of machines, things always got better the longer you fiddled with them. The German machine wasn't running very well at the moment. That would take care of itself. He didn't pay attention until his brother began depicting the possibilities to him of Life in the New World.

'We,' said Herman, 'are free men. You, as an engineer, just as much as I. Here, everything is fixed. If you happen to wear the wrong tie one day you can forget about ever becoming a professor or a manager. But in America everyone can be what he wants. Even if you never wear a tie in your life. There it makes no difference who you are or what you are, but what you do. What exactly *are* you doing?'

My father pushed down the pliers again and said, groaning, 'A way to make smooth holes. Without a drill.'

'Why?'

He let go of the pliers and rubbed his forehead. 'Drills make burrs. For some machines you need perfectly smooth holes.'

'What's the matter, you never heard of a file?'

'Herman,' said my father, picking up the pliers again, 'you take care of the state of world affairs, I'll make sure things work. With a file, a hole always ends up bigger than you meant it to be. I'm looking for a way to get just the right hole on the first try.'

Herman shrugged his shoulders and stared at the makings of my father's latest invention. 'Fine. But if I'm going to be responsible for the state of world affairs, I'd advise you to listen. The biggest and roughest hole you've ever seen is going to form right here, in Europe. If you and Sophie and the children don't leave, that hole will swallow you up.'

With Herman's help my father pulled the point of his mechanical hammer out of the workbench, and then they both went inside. They drank a bottle of wine and Herman told him once again about the New Homeland.

'So, in America you don't have to wear a tie and you can still be whatever you want?' Herman had nodded, without quite understanding. A country where what mattered was what you did, not who or what you were.

'So, no ties?' Emmanuel asked again.

'No ties,' Herman assured him.

'May the angels strike me down,' said Uncle Herman, his face in the fragrant steam that rose from his First Flush Darjeeling, 'your father left because he hated ties. It's taken me half my life to figure that out, but it's true. If I hadn't started blathering about ties that day, you wouldn't be sitting here now.'

I knew that Herman wasn't exaggerating. Once I had spent a summer holiday with my father and, tired and grumpy after the long journey, I'd asked him why the hell he had stayed in America. He didn't have to think twice before answering. He turned round, pointed in the direction of what he assumed to be the Atlantic Ocean and, beyond that, Europe, and said: 'Over there, everything is fixed. If you wear the wrong tie, just *once*, you can forget about ever becoming a professor or a manager. Here,' he said, with a wave of his arm, as if he were sweeping together his apartment, Manhattan, the entire continent, in one gesture, 'here you can be whatever you want. Even if you never wear a tie.'

My father may have been convinced, but my mother still had her doubts. A visit from three German refugees, arranged by Herman, made the necessary impression. Arjeh Pinkus, Josef Bamberger and Wolf Krohn had sat quietly at the big table in the living room, drinking Sophie's coffee, nibbling her assorted biscuits, and smiling uncertainly. Until Emmanuel put the bottle of gin on the table, poured out four brimming glassfuls, and asked them how they'd been. Sophie, who, since her early youth, had never been easily shocked, had spent half the evening with her hand over her mouth. That night Emmanuel received her permission to go to his parents and inform them that he and his family were leaving with Herman.

Heijman helped his sons with the travel expenses. Not because he agreed with Herman's ranting about 'Teutonic Hordes', but because he was a firm believer in the boundless opportunities awaiting his sons in America. He still considered Herman a deserter, about to drag his brother's family along in his romantic vision of evil, but after 'so many years of schlepping around,' what was one more westward-bound generation? All things considered, he said to my father when he came to tell him we were leaving, it hadn't done us any harm so far, that seemingly endless journey west.

There's a photograph showing the six of us posing in the traditional configuration of the emigrant family: Emmanuel and Sophie in the middle, Zoe and Zelda beside them, Uncle Herman, cross-legged, on the ground. I shine like a young prince in the Big Chair, Uncle Herman's lap. There are suitcases and trunks all around us. We must have just boarded. We look well-dressed and well-fed, privileged people in every respect. My father is wearing a dark grey, slightly crumpled suit, the thumb of his right hand hooked in his waistcoat pocket. My mother, in her dark red dress, is standing silently beside him, her face set in the serious frown still so fashionable in the thirties when people had their pictures taken. Zelda and Zoe are watching something out of camera range, and Uncle Herman, in a dark tweed jacket, his left arm around my stomach, is laughing at the photographer. I am peering nearsightedly, though no one knew that at the time, at the vague smudge in front of us. A fraction of a second later, after the magnesium flash had blinded us and the bluish cloud of smoke was clearing, I was to burst into tears.

The descendants of a family of clockmakers? You can't tell by looking at us. Anyone happening to go through the ship photographer's archives wouldn't even have noticed us: the umpteenth family on its way to the new Promised Land, not rich, not poor, not carefree, not desperate. The desperate went Third Class, in the belly of the ship, where it stank of hot iron and oil and the ceaseless pounding of the engines shook the walls. They were Jewish refugees from Russia, Poland, Czechoslovakia, Germany and Austria, who waited four, five, six, and sometimes more to a cabin, until that goyish hunk of steel had finally anchored and they could start once again on what they and their forefathers had done so often already: building a new life. Above them, way, way above them, those with hope and expectations and money travelled First Class. Industrialists, politicians, film stars, and singers paraded across the sun deck and spent their evenings in the dimly-lit lounge, wondering whether to round off the last few hours of the day with a Nuits Saint George or a whisky. We were in the middle, Second Class, too poor for the rich, too rich for the poor. Jews, yes, but the sort that no longer felt they had any connection with their forefathers – Abraham, Isaac, Jacob, those archetypal emigrants. None of us stopped to think that, if the truth be told, we had far more in common with those desert patriarchs than those leading the life of Riley on the deck above. None of us would ever have thought that we, like our mythical forebears, were characters in a never-ending story of arrival and departure.

Uncle Herman was the only one who still had a vague feeling of solidarity with the wailing, puking third class, but that was more the result of the socialism he had acquired during his sociological studies than any religious or ethnic affinity.

This was also the reason why, one night after dinner, we found ourselves sitting in the dreary Third Class dining hall. Herman and my father were drinking beer, my mother, tea from a lime-coated glass, my sisters and I, grenadine. Around us, men, women and children were sitting at the half-cleared tables.

'That fellow over there,' said Herman, pointing to a big dark man sitting on the other side of the hall, 'was important in the *Bund*. Fought against the Poles, against the rabbis, against the bosses, against everything that restrained him. He is the future. He is a free man.'

My parents and sisters looked over at the giant. He sat hunched forward, as big men do, slow and placid. They saw him as the incarnation of the New Man, the Man Who Fought Back.

'Free . . .' my father mumbled.

'Free,' said Herman. 'Free from religion, from the commandments of God and the rabbis, from the rest, the people around us. And there's more freedom on the way. You'll see, the world will change completely after the war.'

'What war?' said my mother.

'The one that's about to begin,' said Uncle Herman.

'There have been other wars,' mumbled my father, who had closed his eyes and was kneading the bridge of his nose, the way he always did when he was thinking something up.

'But none like this one. In ten or twenty years people will say that it was a war of absurd extremes, and that's probably true, but most of all it will be the division between the Old World and the New, between the heavy and the light, the shallowness and the depth.'

'What are you *talking* about?' said my mother.

'I'm talking about the end of the world as we know it, a world in which society is governed by tradition and morality, in which the classes are divided by knowledge and power and possibilities, and therefore, money.'

'Do you really think that socialism is going to take hold after this war?'

'Socialism,' said Herman, 'will be the only justice. After this war, no man who has fought for another will ever again accept that others are superior to him simply because they're superior to him. And the world can no longer afford the lazy life of the aristocrats. There will be a major redistribution of knowledge and power and money.'

My mother looked at my sisters who, in turn, looked at a couple of other children.

'Sounds like everything'll be fine once we get this war out of the way,' said my father absently.

'It will be an inferno,' Uncle Herman continued, 'the likes of which we've never known. What's about to happen over there . . .' He pointed towards the continent, invisible for nearly a week now, of Europe. '. . . will evoke demons that will live forever.'

My mother shuddered.

'All these ideas of yours, Herman, does this mean you don't believe a word of what we were taught?' asked Emmanuel. He drew a line through a circle and joined it to a parallelogram.

Herman smiled. 'God and Creation and us as the storm troopers of that Old Testament liege?'

'There's nothing wrong with religion,' said Sophie. 'And it's not

fair to present it as some childish fairy tale. You could say the very
same thing about socialism.'

'Yes,' said Herman, 'yes. But at least then it's a fairy tale we've
made up for ourselves.'

'That's probably what they thought back in the desert, too,'
mumbled my father.

Herman stared at him for a long time, then frowned.

We sat there, my mother talking to Herman, my father scribbling
all over the menu and occasionally letting a few words fall from
his lips that no one paid much attention to, Zoe and Zelda
quietly drinking their grenadine in the hope that they would go
unnoticed and not be sent to bed, and me, slumped against my
mother.

In the distance, Schlomo Minsky's gaze travelled over the hall.
When he saw me, his face broke into a smile. I waved, and he held
up one of his huge hands and waved back. Beside him, small, almost
transparent, red-haired Reisele was staring fixedly at me. My mother
looked down and gave me a nudge.

'Who are you waving at?' she asked.

'At Schlomo Minsky,' I said.

'At . . .'

'Schlomo Minsky,' I repeated.

'How do you know . . .' said Uncle Herman.

My mother gave me another nudge, and another, until I had no
choice but to look up at her. 'Nathan?' There was a question in
her eyes.

'I was down below,' I whispered.

'Below? Alo . . .' She looked over at my father, who was drawing
something unrecognizable on the menu.

'Emmanuel,' said my mother, so calmly that he looked up with
the frightened expression of someone being called to account for a
horrible deed he knows nothing about.

'What? What?'

'Nathan was down below, all by himself.'

'Hm?' He glanced at me quickly and smiled, relieved. 'Don't do
that again, son.' He returned to his menu. My mother's gaze

remained so firmly fixed that he looked up again almost immediately. 'What . . .'

'You promised to keep an eye on him. How can I mind three children at the same time?'

'Schlomo Minsky,' said Uncle Herman, pensively. 'How do you know his name, Nathan?'

I looked from my father to my mother. My father and my mother looked at me.

We had paid a visit, my father and I, to the ship's engineer, who always set great store by my father's coming. Not only did we bring cigars, the traditional Dutch way of breaking the ice, but both men also shared the same animal passion for machinery. Mr Ladenius was a small, immaculately dressed fellow from Groningen. His boiler suit may have been stained with grease and oil, but it always looked as if it had been washed and starched when he put it on in the morning. The red rag that always hung out of his pocket would shift, at the slightest provocation, from his right hand to his left and then to an up-and-down or back-and-forth-moving brass rod with a smidgen of grease on it that no one saw but he.

Ladenius was rather irritable that morning. Shortly before we arrived, he had detected a sound that he couldn't identify. He took the cigar my father offered him and put it in his breast pocket (usually they would give each other a light, sit down on the steel stairs that led to the droning machinery, and disappear in a nauseating cloud of smoke).

'Yes,' said my father, when the engineer had explained what was bothering him. 'I hear it, too.' He tipped his head to one side and listened for a while. 'The gasket.'

'You're not supposed to hear that at all.'

'No. Unless . . .'

Soon they were lost in a half-mumbled colloquy. I wandered up and down the staircases, from top to bottom and bottom to top, and when the two men disappeared into the hold, where the piston rods were sliding in and out of the pounding engine, I slipped out the door and began my quest through the labyrinth of the ship.

In the steel corridors, the chilly light of feeble bulbs glimmered along walls and ceilings. I stopped outside a steel door, open a hand's-breadth, and tried to make out the quarrelling voices from the room within. I had been standing there for a while listening when I heard footsteps heading in my direction. Without thinking, I ran off. Several doors down, I no longer knew where I was. Shadows leaped up in the long iron tunnel behind me, while in front of me the tunnel tapered off in a haze of strange sounds, muffled echoes and pale light. Somewhere, at the end of a long passageway that led to the crew's quarters, I ran straight into the legs of a young officer. Shrill screams rang out in the corridor. It was a while before I realized that I was the one who was screaming. The man in white, who smelled strongly of pipe tobacco and linen, grabbed me by the scruff of the neck and plucked me off the floor like a baby rabbit.

'Easy, lad. What's going on here?'

'. . . th-the too-hoo-tonni . . .'

'Calm down,' he said. 'Polack?'

I shook my head.

'Czech? Ruski? *Deutsche*?'

I was out of breath, my chest heaved. '. . . th-the too-hoo . . .'

The man picked me up and carried me on his hip to a door. Behind it was a large room with linoleum-covered tables. Right at the back was a kind of sideboard. Large chrome kettles stood on one end, and at the other, a man in chef's attire was stacking plates. The officer set me down on one of the tables and called out to him. 'Freddy! How about a nice glass of cold milk for this young fellow?' There was a clatter, the tinkle of glassware, and then the cook came walking towards us.

'What's that, sir?'

'A stowaway.'

They laughed.

'Jew?'

'Whatever he is, I can't understand him.'

I drank the cold milk and stared at the cook's stained apron. Now and then a dry sob welled up from my chest, but the fear that I had felt moments before was gone.

'Czech? Ruski? *Deutsche?*'

'Hollander,' I said. 'My name is Nathan Hollander, Captain.'

'Nathan Hollander. And by the way, I'm just a plain, ordinary seaman. Now then, what are you doing down here all by yourself, Nathan Hollander?'

I looked at my shoes, which were dangling a long way above the floor. 'I thought they were coming to get me,' I said. Another shiver ran through my chest.

'Who was coming to get you?'

'The Teutonic Hordes.'

'The . . .' The officer began laughing so hard that I shot back with fear. The empty glass slid across the table and the cook grabbed it just as it was about to go tumbling over the edge. 'The Teutonic Hordes.' They were both laughing now, though the cook was looking rather uncertainly at the other man. 'Where did you learn words like that?'

I explained that my Uncle Herman was always talking about them, that he had said Thank God we were at sea and headed in the right direction because otherwise we'd be crushed by the . . .

'Teutonic Hordes,' said the officer.

I nodded.

'So you're trying to escape?'

'Yes, sir.'

'And on which deck is your family travelling?'

I had no idea. I could find my way there from the dining hall and the promenade deck, but what it was called, what number it was, and where it was if you were coming from some other part of the ship, I didn't know.

The officer lifted me up off the table, beckoned, and led me back to the corridor where he had found me earlier. We hadn't gone more than sixty feet, when I put my hand in his. Way ahead of us I saw other figures in the dim light and behind us a faint echo made ready to follow in our wake.

After endless walking, downstairs, upstairs, and through so many corridors that I began to feel tired, we arrived in the working-class district that was Third Class. Laundry hung on lines that had been strung between the ceiling lamps. Men, women, and children sat in their cabin doorways, talking and quarrelling. There was a pungent smell of bodies, damp clothes, and onions. Voices shot up, doors slammed shut and swung open as we walked past, and running through that whirlpool of images and sounds was the swirling stream of words from the Diaspora. There, in that underworld, I was left behind. The officer patted me on the head, told me not to go wandering about the ship anymore, and disappeared behind a line of washing. Not long afterwards, Schlomo Minsky came home. The first thing he noticed was a group of excited children. When he came closer he saw that they were standing around a small boy from one of the upper decks and asking him questions in three or four different languages and, when he didn't answer, began jeering at him.

'*Schtil*,' said Minsky. He didn't need to raise his voice, there was instant silence. He laid a hamlike hand on the door, pushed his key into the lock, and let me in. The children who had waylaid me remained standing in the doorway and watched, their eyes wide. '*Gejh*,' said Minsky. The little group of onlookers dispersed.

He set me on top of a chest and seated himself on the only chair, an unpainted wooden thing that looked as if it were hurled down the stairs twice a day, thrown around the room, and then put back in place.

'Schlomo Minsky,' he said, laying his hand on his chest. 'Schlomo Minsky.' He pronounced his first name as 'Schloime.'

'Nathan Hollander,' I said, my hand on my chest.

'Nathan,' he said. There was a silence. Then he brought his huge hand to his mouth and made a drinking motion. I nodded.

He made tea on a small primus stove. His large body moved slowly, almost cautiously, around the cabin. He picked up a dented tin mug as tenderly as if it were a teacup of the finest china. After a while he brought me the mug. He put it down on the chest and said, '*Trink, majn Kind.*' I picked up the mug by the handle and blew on the steaming black liquid. It took a long time for the tea to cool off, so I just kept blowing and looking around, smiling at Schlomo Minsky, who followed my movements and, each time our eyes met, nodded and made faces.

'Reisele! Rivka!' In the doorway stood a woman and a girl my age. They both had red hair. 'This is Nathan, he has lost his way.'

The woman nudged the girl inside and looked me over, as Minsky kissed her on the hair. He nearly had to bend double to do so. They exchanged a few words in a language I couldn't understand, but when the woman began to laugh I realized that he was telling her what had happened. The girl stood behind her parents and watched me. Her large brown eyes shone softly and before I knew it I was lost in her gaze. It wasn't until Mrs Minsky clapped her hands that I returned to my senses. The girl, Reisele, sat down on the edge of the berth, still looking at me. I could do nothing but look back.

When I had finished my tea, Minsky brought me upstairs. Somewhere in the long corridor between the dining hall and our cabin he left me to continue on my own. He patted me on the back and said something I couldn't understand.

'So you've been to see Minsky . . .' said Uncle Herman. He looked at me thoughtfully.

'You were supposed to watch Nathan,' said my mother accusingly.

My father looked up in alarm.

'Do I have to do everything by myself? While all you do is sit around and daydream?'

'He just walked off,' said my father.

'All children walk off. Parents are there to make sure they don't get very far.'

'Stop it,' said Uncle Herman. 'The boy has a spirit of adventure.'

My mother hissed like a cat.

'And who's that pretty girl who keeps staring at you?' asked Uncle Herman.

'Reisele,' I whispered.

I could hear Uncle Herman smiling. 'Don't you think maybe you should go over to her?'

'Herman!'

Uncle Herman turned to my mother and gave his voice the implacable head-of-the-family tone that he had been adopting for some time now. 'Sophie. Give the boy a chance to see something more of life than our own sheltered little world. The Minskys seem like extremely respectable people.' He laid his hand in the hollow of my back and, giving me a gentle nudge, said, 'Go, Nathan. Try and learn something.' My mother sniffed. I took a step forward, hesitated, and then headed for the Minskys.

The rest of the evening I played with Reisele. Minsky and his wife sat around a table with several other Poles, while the two of us stood around an empty chair and played our own ocean voyage with two bottle caps and a burnt match. We couldn't understand each other, except for the occasional word, but we knew exactly what we meant. Now and then Minsky or his wife leaned over us to see what it was we were doing so quietly, then returned to the table and resumed their lively discussion.

When it was way past my bedtime, Uncle Herman came to get me. He stood there for a moment looking at Reisele and me, and when Minsky turned round, he nodded, held out his hand, and introduced himself. They spoke a language I didn't understand. Every now and then they laughed. After a while Uncle Herman laid his hand on my head and said it was time to go.

We had just returned to our table, when a man stormed into the dining hall. He stood in the middle of the aisle and shouted, 'Germany has invaded Poland!'

'When?' cried Herman. 'When did they invade?'

'Last night,' said the man. 'They've already reached Warsaw. The Poles can do nothing to stop them.'

My mother drew Zoe and Zelda close, my father pushed the menu he had been scribbling on a bit further away and looked at it with satisfaction. Somewhere in the room, but I couldn't tell where, a woman was murmuring '*Bubba, bubba*' – endlessly, tonelessly. My mother stood up. She took a deep breath. 'Sit down, Sophie,' said Uncle Herman. 'We can't do anything on this ship.' She shrugged her shoulders and jerked her head to one side, as if she were trying to jolt herself awake. 'War,' she said. 'Not yet,' said Herman, 'but it won't be long.' He looked at my father, who was adding something to the pattern of lines on the menu. 'What the hell are you doing? What is that? A message to the Almighty?'

My father shook his head in a distracted, pensive way. 'No,' he said, 'it sounds crazy, but I've thought up something I can't believe is even possible.'

'All right, what is it?' asked Herman.

My father looked up from the piece of paper. 'A way to make holes without a drill.'

Uncle Herman didn't move. He stared at his brother and waited. Nothing happened. 'Manny,' he said, 'we're out here in the middle of the ocean, on a ship, on our way to America, fleeing from Hitler. The Germans have invaded Poland and you've invented something to drill holes?'

'Without a drill,' said my father. 'The advantage is that you . . .'

'I don't want to hear it! I don't want to hear it! The world is caving in around your ears and you're messing about with a drill?'

'No, not a drill . . .'

'Manny!'

And so we sailed on, over the ocean that had seemed so peaceful and calm when we first set sail but had suddenly become the hideout from which The Enemy leered at unsuspecting travellers to the New World. There were frequent boat drills now and the crew didn't rest until everyone was in the lifeboats well before the required time. The atmosphere on board changed. Those who still had property in the Old Country, or shares in the New, stood in line outside the radio operator's cabin. Others, who had left family behind, pored over every news bulletin, however brief, and worried themselves sick listening to the rumours. And to make matters worse, the weather turned. Three days after the invasion of Poland the gentle swell, to which everyone was accustomed by now, changed to restless, choppy waves. They headed up into the wind, but once the storm finally reached us, even that no longer helped. The deck rose and fell. Emmanuel got so seasick that he was confined to his bed, Zoe and Zelda and I lay, green, in our berths in the adjoining cabin. Uncle Herman crawled along the floor of his cabin, groaning that he was going to die and wanted to make his will. Only Sophie remained on her feet. She had the time of her life. During the day she lolled in the sumptuous armchairs in the First Class lounge, at

night she drank champagne and Aloxe Corton in the empty restaurant. She ate at the captain's table with a few of the officers, an
American steel magnate, and a member of the Senate. In those wild,
tempestuous days – the stewards were sometimes stranded on their
way to the table when caught unawares by a particularly high wave
– she was the ship's mascot. Her eyes sparkled. Every night when
she walked into the dining hall, her hair smelled of salt and iodine.
She opened her oysters as if she had never done anything else. For
the first time in her life she learned the difference between eating
and tasting. The steel magnate, an old man who drank in her vitality
as if she were a walking elixir, let her taste a Petrus from before the
phylloxera disaster – a deep red wine, nearly black.

'Madame,' he had said, when the head steward had placed the
basket on the dazzling white damask, 'you are about to be among
the few people of this century to have partaken of this drink. This
is remembrance in a bottle. Remembrance of a time when the world
still held promise.'

And he had told her about the disaster that had laid waste the
French vineyards in 1863 and how it had taken nearly twenty years
for the French to accept the only possible solution: grafting indigen-
ous vines onto American rootstock. He told her that wine from
before the disaster was still considered the best that the industry had
ever produced. The Petrus, which was eighty years old when she
drank it, transported her, that night, to a world of fragrance and
hushed voices. At midnight she danced with the senator across the
empty floor, as a puking orchestra played a waltz. Afterwards she
stood in her rain-drenched coat in the doorway of the upper deck.
She clung to the brass rails of the gangway and bathed her face in
the salty spray. She could feel every fibre in her body – there was
life inside her, pure, irrepressible life. It was a feeling that filled
her with guilt and hope, both at the same time. As she stood there,
her face to the wind and the ink-black Atlantic night all around her,
she decided that she was going to paint again. No more housewife-
nanny-lover-cook. She would have a life, a life with the same
obligations, but the same privileges, too, as Emmanuel.

The storm moved on, towards Europe, the ship sailed on, to

America, and one by one the other passengers emerged from their berths. Once again, the kitchens began steaming, baking and roasting. The deck chairs were occupied by pale men and women who lay shivering under their blankets and blinking in the sun that broke through the clouds. Herman claimed that he had felt wonderful all along, he had just been a bit tired, and what a fine opportunity to catch up on his reading! Emmanuel scribbled over so many menus that the steward came and complained. Zoe and Zelda ran around the sun deck, played shuffleboard, and hid in the endless corridors in the bowels of the ship. I made my way below, where the air smelled of vomit and urine, to visit the Minskys. I played for hours with Reisele in the cramped cabin. Sometimes, when we were tired of playing, we would sit on her father's lap, she on his right thigh, I on his left, and listen to the stories he told. What Uncle Herman had hoped would happen – that Schlomo Minsky would show me a glimpse of the world of inequality and oppression and how a truly free man might cast off that yoke – did not. That didn't matter. The poverty, the hustling and haggling I saw in the overcrowded Third Class corridors, was enough to convince me for the rest of my days that life was not inherently just, and that it was up to us to bring justice into the world. So in a certain sense, I did receive the education that Uncle Herman had in mind for me. But at the same time I also drank from a well he would have preferred to keep hidden. Schlomo Minsky, however free and socialist, however much he resembled the square-jawed heroes of the revolution in those socio-realist paintings and posters from Russia, Schlomo Minsky, the 'New Man,' told us tales from the Talmud and Midrash and a whole new world opened up for me. Kabbalistic *wunderrebbes* flew through the air towards a God for whom they bore an almost physical love. Bearded tsaddikim stole out of the house at night disguised as farmhands and chopped wood for Polish maidens. There were golems, dybbuks, giants and horned men, the Angel of Death, the Archangel of the Countenance, a host of mystical beings from the Realm of Darkness. Somewhere, deep down, I must have known that Uncle Herman didn't appreciate this. Each time he asked me how it had been at the Minskys, I told him I had played with

Reisele. Sometimes I said that Schlomo Minsky had told us about wicked noblemen and pogroms. But the world of Kabbalistic amulets, miracle workers and sages, I kept to myself. A stowaway began growing inside me and he looked like a hunched Talmud and Torah Jew who had been raised on herring and blintzes, borscht and kreplach, black tea and Rashi.

And then, one bright, sunny day, the coast of the Promised Land appeared on the horizon and after a while we saw the raised arm of the Statue of Liberty against the white and blue marbled sky. Amidst a swarm of small barges and boats, our ship steamed up the Hudson.

We had, for the umpteenth time in our family's history, gone west to escape our fate and, for the umpteenth time, it looked as though we had made it.

When Emmanuel announced that he was going to America, his father saw his chance to intervene in the course of events. 'If you insist on going along with that pigheaded brother of yours, fine,' he had said. 'I'll pay for you both, but on one condition: that you continue with your studies.' Emmanuel had groaned when presented with this choice. He loved his work, and what's more he wasn't cut out for theory. But he was a good son, at a time when sons obeyed their fathers, and so, shortly after arriving, he went off to enrol at the nearest university. He started off at the front desk, was referred to someone else, and as he wandered around a university that was bigger than any he had ever seen, he got lost. Corridor after corridor passed him by, auditorium after auditorium appeared when he opened yet another door, but what he sought, he didn't find.

Or perhaps he did.

Somewhere in the depths of the building he met a man who looked strangely familiar. He began walking more slowly and noticed that the other man did the same. They gave each other an uncertain nod and were just about to walk on, when the stranger ran a hand

over his balding head, squinted, and cried, 'Emmanuele Hollander!'
He spoke with a slight Italian accent. My father, who, until that
moment, had had no idea why he thought he knew the other man,
suddenly realized who was standing here before him. It was Enrico
Fermi.

'Emmanuel. *Funiculi, funicula*! What brings you here?'

My father explained that his wife and brother were refugees and
that he was on his way to enrol as a physics student.

'And your father, where is your father?'

'He wouldn't come. He thinks it'll all blow over.'

Fermi shook his head. It would blow over, he said, the way a
hurricane blew over: leaving countless victims in its wake. 'You
must try to persuade him, once again. He's a Jew, and as a physicist
he's far too useful to the enemy to sit out the storm in the cellar.'

Fermi took Emmanuel by the arm and led him to his office. He
sent for tea and asked him about his plans.

Years later, many years later, my father would tell us how he had
felt that day, across the desk from the great Enrico Fermi, who sat
there and talked with him as if they were old friends. 'Like Moses
on Mount Sinai,' said my father. 'You know that part, Herman
always quotes it when he wants to show that the Jews are on such
good terms with God: And the Lord spake unto Moses face to face,
as a man speaketh unto his friend. That's how I felt.'

They drank their tea and talked, those two, about my father's
father, about Ehrenfest, about Dutch coffee, about Herman, who
was already moving in sociological circles, and about my father's
ambitions and plans.

'To be honest,' said Fermi, 'I don't really think your talent lies
in theoretical physics. I'd be happy to help you, but why should we
waste our energy if you already know that you would rather be an
engineer than a physicist? What were you working on before you
came?'

Emmanuel mumbled something about a drill that wasn't a drill,
which Fermi didn't find particularly interesting, but which did convince him that my father could make far better use of his talents as
a technician, an instrument maker. 'Our problem,' he had said, 'is

that we've entered a field which is still completely unknown and we're studying phenomena we can only visualize in our minds. All our equipment has to be specially built, because we're steering a course that has never been steered before. I believe you could make a valuable contribution.'

Emmanuel thought so too. A week later he started work as instrument maker-engineer for Enrico Fermi.

What was this drill that wasn't a drill, the instrument in which Fermi had not been interested, but which would ultimately be so closely associated with his work? Manny told me once, when I was visiting him in New York. It was a broiling hot summer and we had sought relief in an air-conditioned movie theatre, where we saw *An American in Paris*, with Gene Kelly. We were both big Kelly fans. After the film we were on our way to a delicatessen for a bite to eat, when I asked him what it was exactly, the drill that . . .

'When we boarded the ship to America,' he said, 'they were still busy loading up, so I went out on deck to watch, and that's when I saw the big winches turning. One of the axles was all worn down and wobbling like crazy, and I wondered how you could prevent that. I mean, I knew it was a question of forces being exerted on a static object and all you had to do was reduce or neutralize those forces, but it suddenly occurred to me that you could also use those forces. Imagine, I thought, if you could make a hole, not by eating away at the material, which is what a drill does, but by creating friction. You mustn't exert too much pressure, of course, or you'd destroy the material you're trying to drill. Friction, that was the main thing. And that's how I came up with the fire thorn.'

That was what he called the drill that wasn't a drill: the fire thorn. It was a triangular point that was placed on a sheet of metal and began turning at high speed. Under the point the heat became so intense that the metal started melting. The point then pushed the tiny puddle of melted metal onto the still solid layer of metal below it, gradually forming a hole that was extraordinarily even. 'If you've got the right material,' said my father, 'you can work with a point the size of a pin and make minuscule holes.'

I can't remember where we were walking, it wasn't all that often that I visited Manny, but I do remember the peculiar sensation of a night sky that refused to grow dark, the streaks of neon and splotches of headlight against the backdrop of the city.

'Sophie danced with him, you know,' said Manny suddenly. 'With Kelly.'

I turned my head sideways and looked at him, and when he didn't seem to notice, I asked him to repeat what he had just said.

'Sophie. She danced . . .'

'My God,' I said. 'Have you been seeing things? Am I hearing things? Where are we, anyway?'

'No idea.'

'At a party?'

'Huh?'

'Sophie. Did she dance with Gene Kelly at a party?'

'For a minute I thought you were asking if we were at a party.'

'I'm not that far gone.'

'She danced in *Ziegfeld Follies*.'

'Sophie danced in *Ziegfeld Follies* . . .'

'She's not in the credits. She was one of the scenery painters. That movie had a cast like you wouldn't believe. Fred Astaire, Cyd Charisse, Red Skelton, Lucille Ball, Esther Williams . . .'

'You said she danced with him . . .'

'One of the chorus girls was sick and she took her place at a rehearsal. But we knew him. He came to the house once or twice.'

'You're kidding!'

'Didn't he have something going with a friend of Sophie's? God, what was her name: Flo, Jo, Betsy . . . I can't remember. A very modest man. Crazy about Dutch coffee.'

'Gene Kelly is a very modest man and crazy about Dutch coffee.'

'He said: Soph, you make the best java I've ever tasted.'

'I'm definitely hearing things . . .'

'Your sisters thought he was God. I was pretty impressed myself.'

'Did he used to dance when he came over?'

'What, you think every time that man gets a cup of coffee he starts dancing?'

'For God's sake.'

'Funny you don't remember him. You must've been at least . . . oh, ten years old. You should ask Herman about it sometime. He thought the world was never the same after "Singin' in the Rain". He told him that, too. But that was later, I think.'

'And?'

'What?'

'What did Kelly say?'

'Nothing. He just kind of laughed. Herman knew that whole rain scene by heart. He knew exactly how many takes they did before it was done. Five, I think, something like that. Anyhow, great stuff. Herman thought it was basically an apocalyptic scene. He said that that long dance down that rainy street was actually a kind of rain dance, only the other way around, that somebody wasn't asking for rain, but already had it, was soaked to the bone in fact, and in spite of all that, was dancing and singing about being in love. That was just about the strongest indication of the end of a culture that Herman could imagine.'

'Isn't that a love song, "Singin' in the Rain"?'

'Yes, but according to Herman it was really the end of an era. "Singin' in the Rain," he used to say, was the moment when traditional notions of love and happiness were abandoned. Sun, smiling faces, beautiful countryside . . . In the movie it's pouring with rain, there isn't a tree in sight, some guy is dancing through puddles up to his ankles, a policeman arrives on the scene, but lets him do what he likes. Society bids farewell to her traditional mores. Er . . . The ultimate romanticization of urban society as inverted reality. Something like that.'

'Sounds like Uncle Herman, all right. A bit far-fetched.'

'Herman was pretty far-fetched himself in those days.'

'In those days?'

'Maybe he still is.'

'So, where did we have to turn left?'

'I, er . . . Here. Or maybe it was there, at that intersection?'

Finally we came to a deli, Sol's or Sal's, somewhere on 78th Street, I think. Manny had obviously been here before, because he greeted the waiters with the casualness of a regular and called out his orders to the boy in the white apron standing behind the counter. We sat down by the window and stared out at the city lights.

'That drill,' said my father, 'could've made me rich.'

'You *are* rich,' I said. 'You're the Mattress King.'

'I mean really rich,' he said. 'Rich beyond your wildest dreams.'

'But . . . ?'

'But out there,' he nodded his head towards the southwest, 'anything you thought up was government property. Somewhere there must be cupboards full of unused drawings and plans and sketches just waiting for an archivist with technical insight. All of them invented out there,' he nodded again.

'How old did you say I was, when he came to visit?'

'Who?'

'Kelly. Ten? Eleven?'

Manny blew upward, into the air, as if he were blowing a lock of hair out of his face. 'When was that, *Ziegfeld Follies* . . .'45, '46 . . . About ten. No, eleven. End of '46. You even sang for him.'

One of the waiters brought us our sandwiches and bottles of beer. My father tapped the forefinger of his right hand against his temple, in thanks. He opened the jar of mustard and began painting his corned beef yellow. 'Whoom wid a whew,' he said, when he had bitten into his sandwich and, staring out at the passers-by, began to chew.

'What?'

' "Room With a View." That's what you sang for him. At Uncle Herman's request. I think he even taught it to you. "Room With a View." Noel Coward tune, isn't it?'

I had sung "Room With a View" for Gene Kelly. Ten years old and I had, at the insistence of my entirely unmusical uncle, who had asked what I was really going to do with my life when I had told him I wanted to be a fairy tale writer, at his insistence I had sung that number for the God of the Song and Dance Act.

'Listen,' I said to my father, my bottle of Budweiser half raised. 'There seems to be some sort of misunderstanding. I thought I just heard you say that I'd sung a song for Gene Kelly and that Herman had taught me that song.'

Manny looked at me in amazement. 'That's what I said. Didn't I?'

'You mean it's true?'

He picked up his bottle and drank. 'Yep,' he said.

I grew posthumously nervous. 'What did he say? Kelly? What did he think of it?'

Manny shrugged. He picked up his sandwich and was about to take a bite when I laid my hand on his arm and gave him a piercing look. 'Nice, I think,' he said. 'Great tune. Something like that.'

'About me,' I said. 'What did he say about me?' I hadn't sung for years, but at that moment an answer to the question of what Kelly had thought of me seemed more important than anything else in the world.

Manny put down his sandwich and gazed into the restaurant. Laughter rose from the group of men sitting at the counter. Manny turned his face towards them and grinned. 'Your voice hadn't even broken yet,' he said. 'It was hard to tell, I guess. No, wait. I do remember something. The boy's got a voice. That's what he said. The boy's got a voice.' He looked down at his plate, but showed no signs of continuing with his meal. When he turned his eyes to me, I nodded absently. He reached for his sandwich again.

A mother who had danced in *Ziegfeld Follies*, a father who invented the drill that wasn't a drill, an uncle who was a world-famous sociologist and analysed a Gene Kelly movie in apocalyptic terms and . . . Suddenly I remembered the story of how Manny had run into Enrico Fermi at Columbia University and that Fermi had recognized him because he and my father used to sing *Funiculi, Funicula* together. Banality, I thought, is the backbone of history.

'Have you ever seen him since?' I asked.

'Kelly? No, when we went back to Holland he sent us a card and after that . . . not a word. Maybe we should've sent him a packet of Dutch coffee now and then.'

I grabbed my sandwich and started eating. Outside the traffic moved through the streets, men in shirtsleeves and women in light blouses glided along the sidewalk. In the distance, at the intersection, the traffic lights showed a slow succession of red and green flecks. My name is Nathan, I thought. I'm a Hollander in New York. My mind began to wander. Banality is the backbone of history. Or perhaps not banality. The insignificant, that which we forget, the inconsequential. What's visible, and what we regard as History, are the stories of kings and generals and archdukes and terrorists. But what supports those stories, the foundation, is the awkward side of life, someone who invents something to do with mattresses, a child stealing a guilder from his mother's wallet, the new boy at school, the failed marriage . . . There's a visible world, which we see in the papers and hear on the radio, which dominates film and TV, and a hidden world, the world that sees the visible world and thinks: that's where *real* life is.

'You're not eating,' said my father.

'I'm eating.'

'That's not eating, that's noshing.'

I bit into my sandwich and chewed. A vicious circle of seeing and being seen, of the awareness, or ignorance, of one's own import. That which is visible, I thought, believes itself to be of great consequence, while that which sees, yet is *in*visible, doesn't believe that it's of any consequence whatsoever. Except that what you *can't* see – just as with an iceberg – is weightier than you'd think. It's like what we Europeans say about America, that it's a land of banalities, of overstatement and superficiality and lack of culture, whereas our own gravitas – which we're so proud of – is nothing but the dead weight of past history. Since the Americans persist in believing that we're the core of their civilization, they confirm the notion of their own lightness, while Europe is true lightness, it's empty and motionless and . . . Europe, I thought as I drank my Budweiser, is a kind of historical Disneyland: if you don't believe in the fairy tale, there are only buildings and stories.

'Wow,' I said.

My father looked up.

'Nothing,' I said, 'I just ran my own continent right into the ground.'

My father made his eyebrows dance and then went on eating,

the jar of bright yellow mustard at his elbow. 'That drill,' he mumbled, 'was the best idea I've ever had in my whole life.'

———————

Every idea that had steered the course of our history, with the exception of Emmanuel's mattress invention, had led us farther from home and deeper into trouble. The last idea, the one that took us so far west that we were nearly back east, was that of a man from Budapest, a man whose life was as much of a journey west as ours.

He had fled Hungary when Bela Kun's Communists came into power, headed for Berlin, where he and Albert Einstein applied for various patents in the field of refrigeration technology, and left for England when the brown scum began flooding the streets of Germany. There, while waiting for a traffic light, he thought about what he had read in that morning's paper. It seemed that Lord Rutherford, during a meeting, had discussed the possibilities of nuclear energy in highly sceptical terms, calling the very idea 'moonshine.' As he, Leo Szilard, watched the traffic light change colour and stepped off the kerb, he thought that Rutherford might be wrong if, say, one were to find an element that, when split by neutrons, absorbed one neutron and released two. Such an element, provided one had enough of it, would be able to sustain a nuclear chain reaction. Under certain circumstances one could not only generate energy, but even make bombs.

Leo Szilard had this flash of inspiration in 1933. He didn't think of it again until he heard that Germany had placed an embargo on uranium from Czechoslovakia. That was in 1939. Evidently, he deduced, Germany had set up a secret atomic project. He went to Albert Einstein – they were both in America by then – and proposed to him that they try and beat the Germans at their own game.

Szilard's idea reached our family in the spring of 1943, when Manny, as Emmanuel had begun calling himself, came home one Friday and announced that we were moving the following week. Sophie, who was having an attack of Yiddishkeit (we were living in Brooklyn, among more Jews and certainly more Orthodox Jews than we had ever seen) had made gefilte fish and chicken soup with matzo balls, and was busy filling bowls from the big white tureen. Zoe, Zelda and I were looking suspiciously at the yellowish brown liquid with oatmeal-coloured lumps, and heard nothing. Sophie, waiting for her efforts to be acknowledged, didn't either. Only Uncle Herman responded.

'We?' he said.

'Chicken soup with *knaidelach*,' said Emmanuel approvingly, as Sophie set a bowl down in front of him. 'No, not you.'

Sophie sat down. Zelda and I looked at Zoe, who was slowly bringing the spoon to her lips.

'Not me . . .'

Manny tasted the soup and smiled contentedly. Zelda and I paid no attention to him. He ate anything, as long as it was on a plate. Zoe looked straight ahead, then let the soup glide carefully into her mouth, and shrugged.

'You can't come,' said Emmanuel.

'Can't . . .'

'What are you two talking about?' asked Sophie.

'Nothing. We're moving next week,' said Emmanuel.

Sophie began eating. Zoe, Zelda and I stared at her from across the table. Three spoonfuls later, it hit her. 'What!'

'Leaving. I've got to go somewhere else.'

' "I've got to go somewhere else"? "Next week"? Are you . . .'

Emmanuel tightened his lips and looked at her sharply. 'I can't talk about it. I'm not even allowed to say where we're going. It's government business.'

Sophie's mouth opened and closed. Manny and Herman began discussing something in low voices and very cryptic language. Sophie stared at the wall. Zelda, Zoe and I seized the opportunity to make our soup disappear.

A place 'somewhere in America,' said Emmanuel, that was where we were going. On the way there, our name would be De Vries.

'De Vries?' asked Sophie.

'De Vries.'

'Would you mind telling me what all this is about? We're moving to some godforsaken place, we have to change our name? What in the world have you been up to?'

'It's government business,' said Emmanuel wearily. 'A secret project.'

'But could you at least tell me which direction it is? And what about the post? How are we supposed to get our post?'

'We're going to New Mexico. All our post will be sent to P.O. Box 1663 in Santa Fe.'

Sophie looked at him as if she were seeing him for the first time in her life.

Herman sat at the table and stared broodingly ahead. 'Further west,' he said. 'Again.'

Manny shrugged.

A few days later Sophie went to the library to see where New Mexico was and what kind of place it might be. She came home later that afternoon with a frown on her face. 'It's very strange,' she said that night at the table. 'I'd taken down one of those WPA-books from the shelf, and on the borrowing slip were all names I knew, people I've heard you mention.'

'We're not the only ones who are going,' said Emmanuel.

Herman listened quietly.

'People I used to hear you mention,' said Sophie, 'who found new jobs. At least, that's what you told me.' Emmanuel said nothing. 'And then I ordered those train tickets, the way you asked me to, under the name of De Vries, and they gave me a very peculiar look. One man said, "What the hell's so special about Santa Fe? Why's everybody going there these days?"'

Emmanuel bent over his plate and stared at the omelette lying next to the bread. 'Nathan made supper,' said Sophie. 'I didn't have time.' He raised his head and smiled. He picked up his knife and fork and began eating as fast as he could.

At the end of that week we left with a huge pile of suitcases and two bulging backpacks. Herman, who had taken us to the station in a taxi, stood on the platform as we hung out the window calling out the sort of things people call out when they're about to leave.

'Yes, I'll write,' he said to Sophie. 'Goodbye, De Vries children. Take good care of yourselves, and each other.'

We waved and waved and then the train started moving and we pulled out of the station, on our way to the most westerly place we would ever go. All across the country Zoe and Zelda and I sang a song with only one line: 'We're going to Somewhere, we're going to Somewhere . . .'

The train took us to Lamy, a small town with a tiny whitewashed station on a double track. As the locomotive slowed and we got an extra good look at the scenery, Manny said, 'It's a cowboy movie, it's a goddamn cowboy movie.' The station was a simple little build-ing with a red-tiled roof and a wooden loading platform. When the train stopped and we got out, we could smell the dry, dusty scent of the desert. Behind us lay the sloping landscape, covered with scrub grass and sage. Further on was a mountain that looked like a giant molehill.

We started lugging suitcases, but before long a young soldier came over to help us. He loaded our bags into the pickup truck that was parked at the end of the platform. One of his fellow soldiers was busy helping other people.

'Sorry for the inconvenience,' he said, when he was finished and the other family had come over to join us. 'But we haven't got too many trucks at the moment. Folks are coming in every day and the roads are lousy, so a lot of the trucks break down. Why don't you sit up front, the kids can go in the back.'

In an office in Santa Fe, a woman gave us passes, food stamps, and instructions. Then we went up, to the Hill, as the woman in the office called it. After the train journey, which had taken more than a day, it took us another hour to reach the foot of the Hill. It was a table mountain, a mesa, which stood in the landscape like an altar. The climb was one long twist over a badly paved road where, around almost every bend, a truck stood waiting to give us right of way. The hot, stuffy air grew cooler and clearer. Finally, at the top, we saw the town: sheds, barracks, wooden huts, a water tower, people everywhere, the din of generators. After our passes had been checked, the truck drove the other travellers to their destination and then dropped us off at a low, rectangular building. It contained four apartments, was much too small for a family our size, and we were to live there until the day we left.

We lived in a camp, without Uncle Herman, and were never allowed outside the fence. During the day the sun hung in the sky like a piece of broken mirror and at night the rocks crackled with the cold. And then Zeno was born and it was as if I were standing in the wind and everything around me was moving and flying about but I didn't get hit, as if no one could see me anymore. For days on end I walked among the barracks. But no one spoke to me. The men in their khaki uniforms and white lab coats ran to and fro, women hung out the washing and played with their children, but no one saw me. When I came home Sophie would be leaning over the cradle, or staring so absently into space that I could walk back and forth across her field of vision and she wouldn't even blink. I was no longer put to bed, I was no longer read to. Every morning the alarm clocks jingled and everyone got up, but no one came in to tell me what clothes to wear that day, so I washed my face, put on two different socks, two-day-old underwear and a baggy shirt, ate a sandwich with an inch of peanut butter, and went outside, leaving behind a void that was filled with people who were no longer mine. When Uncle Chaim came to visit and told me I didn't belong to myself, but to God, I understood why everything was the way it was.

We were in Los Alamos, the place where a few thousand people were changing the course of history, most of them people who, like us, had fled the Old World. Here, on a flat-topped mountain in the desert of New Mexico, the bomb was being built that would end the war and burden the world, for the rest of the century, with guilt and fear. It was the farthest we had ever come.

Zeno

TIME SLIPPED BY like the shadow of a cloud over a corn field, there was light and darkness and light once more, the glasses were emptied and filled. Nina read and I dozed in the glow of the fire, got up, walked past the dark walls of books, took one down and put it back. Only after an hour, by which time Nina's hand was moving automatically to the right to reach for her glass, even if it was empty, did I look for something I intended to read. I picked up one of the candelabras and scanned the titles. At least half of Uncle Herman's library had been assembled by Zeno, the other half Herman and I had added. The result was a curious mixture of Kabbalah, philosophy, physics, and theology, a twentieth-century alchemist's library. It took a while for me to find the right book, something that was completely out of place among all those stiff, scholarly tomes. It was the novel Herman had been reading the last time we were here together: *Call It Sleep,* by Henry Roth. I remember him sitting and enthusiastically making notes in the margins, a habit I couldn't stand. When I said something about it, he had looked at me with gleaming eyes. 'Stop whining, Nathan,' he had said. 'This is work.' He had held up the book, asked me if I knew it. No. Roth, said Herman, was a forgotten writer. Sometime in the thirties he had made his debut with a novel that bore all the elements of modernism, a strikingly European novel. 'Stream of consciousness, realism, surrealism, fantasy, dialogue, the whole lot. An amazing book. Pitch-black. Terrifyingly hopeless.' And he had told me about Roth, the son of East European Jews who had gone to America and started at the bottom of the heap. He was a communist, who, because of his political convictions, came to a dead end as a writer.

He became a 'labourer,' then a chicken farmer in the wilds of Maine, and had never published another book. 'Roth's novel,' said Herman, 'can be read as a kind of sociological case history.' I had disputed this, without ever even having read it. 'Every novel is a lie, Nuncle. Fiction is, by definition, unreliable, and therefore of no use.' Herman had raised his eyebrows. 'At the very most,' I had said, 'a novel can give you an idea of a particular way of looking at things. But even then, it's all so personal and subject to demands that have nothing to do with society, politics, or reality, that any "application" of a novel is like trying to read the future in a dog's entrails.' Herman had shaken his head and immersed himself once again in his book, scribbling furiously. Now and then he seemed to remember what I had said and he pressed his lips together disapprovingly and shook his head.

This was the book I finally chose. I sat down next to Nina and, like her, was soon lost in the world behind the cover. I didn't realize how long we had been sitting there until I began to feel cold. Putting the book aside, I got up to stoke the fire, which was by now nothing more than a thick layer of smouldering chunks. It was some time before the flames shot back into the wood and the hearth began giving off heat.

'It's not a biography, N,' said Nina, when I had sat back down. 'What?' For a moment I thought that she, just as I had done at the time, was commenting on Roth's book. She held up the portion of the manuscript that she had finished reading. 'Ah. No. No, not a real biography.'

Nina unfolded. She placed her hands on either side of her in the chair and stretched her legs. For a moment she looked like a gymnast on the parallel bars. I had to resist the urge to give her a score.

'Reisele.' Nina leaned forward and bathed her face in the fireglow. 'You never saw her again?'

I shook my head. 'Schlomo Minsky had been an important man in the Bund. Many people in those circles knew him. But in America, that sort of thing didn't mean much. They already had very powerful unions over there. The Minskys just melted away into history.'

Nina looked at me uncomprehendingly.

'That's the way it goes. Life is like watching falling stars on an August night. They appear out of nowhere, draw a trail of light through the darkness, and then disappear again. The stories we tell imply that we experience an event from beginning to end, but all we really see is that briefly glowing trail. What happened before that, and what happens afterwards, we don't know.'

'So you think the world is made up of unfinished stories.'

'Yes, and what we do is extrapolate those stories. We try to give them a beginning and an end. We try, on the basis of those frag-mented stories, to understand the world.'

The upper half of her body moved gently, in an approving kind of way.

'Are you pleased?' I asked.

'With this? Yes. But it reads like fiction. This Uncle Magnus, for instance . . .'

'Cousin. Cousin Magnus and Uncle Chaim.'

'Cousin and Uncle. You have them popping in and out as if they still exist.'

I gave her a long, hard look.

'I like that,' she said, 'but it's not what you'd expect in a biography.'

'But perhaps they do still exist.'

'In your mind? Okay. But that makes it more and more fiction and less and less biography.' She drank the last few drops of wine from her glass and tipped back her head. She yawned. 'But you certainly tell a good story, N.'

'Time for bed,' I said. 'We'll make up the four-poster in the hunting room, you can sleep in there. I'll stay here in the chair.'

Nina looked at her watch. 'Twelve-thirty. God, yes, I'm tired. But N, we'll never last the next few days if one of us has to sleep in a chair. Even the bed'll be cold. The only warm spot is right in front of the fire.'

'What do you suggest?'

'We share the bed. We make a small fire in the hunting room, to take the chill off, then crawl into bed and go to sleep.'

'I've already made a fire in there. The chill is off. But the two of us in one bed? Weren't you the woman who thought, only this afternoon, that I was going to rape her?'

She raised her eyebrows.

I took the poker out of the stand next to the hearth and raked the fire. 'All right, let's go. I'm dead tired.'

Nina blew out the candles, picked up the sleeping bag, and a candelabra. I picked up a glass, got my hip flask of Jameson's and a box of Alka Seltzer out of my bag, grabbed my book and followed her into the hunting room. In the cold, cavernous hall the voice on the tape was still scraping through the darkness. We said nothing as we crossed the marble floor and opened the door on the other side.

Although the fire had been burning for some time now, the room was still freezing.

'What's that?'

I had put the hip flask on the table on my side of the bed, next to the book, the glass, the candelabra, a box of matches, and the box of Alka Seltzer. 'My nightly ritual. Irish whiskey. In case I wake up and can't fall back to sleep.'

'Don't you sleep well?'

'Old people never sleep well. It's like having a limited amount of time in which to do something and you keep putting it off until the end. Just before your time runs out you realize that you should have been better prepared, that you could have made more out of it if only you'd started sooner and now it's too late. That's how night-time feels, when you're old.'

She looked at me blankly.

'Would you like a hot-water bottle?'

'Hot-water bottle?'

'Hot-water bottle.'

'Have we got any here?'

'I'll make one.'

I took my glass and race-walked through the dark hall to the kitchen. In the kettle on the kitchen stove was enough warm water to fill one of the empty wine bottles. When I had done that, I pushed open the back door and pulled the kettle through the snow. There was a sizeable bank behind the house. If it kept on snowing all night, they would have to dig us out in the morning. I put the kettle on the back of the stove, where it started hissing fiercely, stuck a cork in the bottle, filled my glass with hot water, and went back to the hunting room. Nina lay shivering under the covers. She had spread the sleeping bag out over the bedspread. Only the top of her head was visible. I took a thick woollen sock out of Uncle Herman's cupboard, slid it over the bottle, and slipped the makeshift hot-water bottle under the covers on Nina's side of the bed.

'God, you're clever . . .' Her teeth were chattering so loudly, I could hardly understand her.

'I know.'

'And arrogant.'

'I know.'

I pulled off my shoes and jacket, put down the steaming glass, and crawled in beside her. It was like sliding under an ice floe. 'Tomorrow, let's try to remember to put a couple of these bottles in bed an hour beforehand.'

Nina didn't answer. There was only the quiet rustling of her breathing.

I stared at the brocade canopy, which was faintly lit by the glow from the hearth, and waited. It must have been nearly one in the morning. Darkness everywhere. A night as thick as treacle covered the land, no sound but the rustling of the snow, the endless stream of flakes that would keep falling, falling, falling, until things were no longer what they used to be.

An endless white plain of frozen snow, black patches of ice, stiff white grass.

'Nathan . . .'

A dot on the emptiness.

Above that: the veiled sky.

A thin black stripe that crosses the burnished ice, walks effortlessly through the frozen stalks of grass, grows biggerandbiggerandbigger.

'Nathan . . .'

The wind: a sheet of steel scraping across the countryside.

He sits at the foot of my bed.

Here.

There. At my feet, on my bed.

'Nathan . . . It's a cold, cold land.'

The darkness nestles in the corners of the room. Shadows huddle together under the four-poster bed. I peer through the slits of my eyelids at the foot of the bed and push myself up, against the wall, my head half-buried in the folds of the midnight blue canopy, in the musty smell of old velvet and mothballs and . . . I arrange the blankets and sheets, the quilted bedspread, the sleeping bag.

'Zeno.' Puffs of vapour escape my mouth. 'This isn't you. This is a dream.'

'You talk to dreams, N?'

'A trick of the light,' I said.

'And what am I? The light or the trick?'

Razor sharp. Uncle Herman was right: A *Kopf*. (But has he got a heart?)

Not light. Not light as in alightbulbgives. But still. All is clear.

He at my feet, at the foot of my bed. Me against the wall, in my cloak of deep dark blue velvet, under my baldachin of brocade, in a bed like a room, a room like a house.

He looks around.

I breathe out clouds of steam, reach sideways, unscrew the flask, and drink. As the fire starts burning inside me and my stomach tackles the whiskey, as the chill in my mouth gives way to the prickle of alcohol, he looks at me. His white face the dark eyes with the moss-green flecks the coppery hair. (Not that I can see him well enough to make out these details. It's how well I know him. Like my heart. Like my stomach. Like the depths of the depths of myself.)

Every night. Sometimes not until morning. He has the time. He can wait. Every night: 'Zeno, this isn't you.' All that time: 'It's a cold, cold land.'

My shivering brother.

'You've been exercising, Zeno. You're less transparent. You've even got a bit of colour in your cheeks.'

He looks. The Zeno-knows-something-you-don't-know look.

'Come on, Zeno,' I say. 'Rattle your chains. Let me go back to sleep.'

Motionless. Silent.

But then.

He raises his head. He tips back his head. He opens the mouth in his head. He closes his eyes.

He breathes out.

And I hear. Oh Lord of the Universe, how I hear him. From across the fields, the snow-covered roads, the sleeping cities, the oceans that glitter like mica in the blue moonlight. I hear him.

A soft, gentle exhalation like a . . . a lament from afar . . . from far across fields and villages and houses and forests and fields and . . .

Ahhhhhhhhhhhhhhhhhhhhhhhhhhhhhhhhhhhh.

BookGlassCandelabraAlkaSeltzerFlask.

Matches.

Fire shoots up, crackling and sputtering, shadows flee timidly into their corners, orange-yellow flecks dance across the bed, the velvet canopy swells, the floorboards leap. The flame licks curiously at a candlewick and jumps over.

In a small sphere of light in the darkness of the universe, a universe surrounded by endless, snow-covered plains. The clouds from my mouth, fluorescent in the trembling light. Someone out of Dante's *Inferno*, exiled to the frozen ice fields of Hell, doomed for all eternity to float through space in a clammy bed, surrounded by darkness cloaked in darkness and around that, a ring of frost. Alone all my life, even when there were people around me, but never lonelier than I feel right now . . . The last living soul.

Nina's face appeared like a smudge on the darkness.

'Nathan? Nathan. What's wrong?'

'Cold. It's cold.'

She carefully sat up. 'I thought you were talking to somebody.'

I shook my head.

Her face was right next to mine. 'Has the fire gone out?'

'In the hearth? I think so.' I rubbed my forehead and sighed. 'I'm sorry. I must have been dreaming.'

She nodded. I could hear her teeth chattering. I climbed out of bed. A tiny red eye was still glowing in the mouth of the hearth. I blew on it and laid the smallest piece of wood I could find on top. When it caught, I covered it with the rest of the chair legs and pieces of piano.

Nina was already asleep by the time I crawled back under the cold sheets on my side of the bed. Firelight rippled over the walls and ceiling. Now and then the wood snapped. There was a whispering sound, very soft, almost as gentle as Zeno's sighs. When I blew out the candle, the room went dark. Moments later the glow of the fire loomed once more.

Part Two

On Our Way (to the Middle)

AT ABOUT FIVE o'clock on our second day in Uncle Herman's house, I woke up. Nina had curled into a ball and was almost completely buried under the pile of blankets. It was so cold that I could feel the frosty air on my face. Shivering, I pulled on my clothes, went to the kitchen, made a fire in the stove, and hurried into the library to stoke up the hearth. When that was done, I got a bucket out of the cellar, grabbed the shovel, pushed open the kitchen door, which was nearly impossible by now, and filled the bucket with snow. It was pitch dark, but when I held out my arm I could feel, by the top of the wedge that the door had scraped out of the bank behind the house, how deep the snow was. We could never get out of here on our own. There was far too much snow to walk, and on our way down, down the Mountain, we would undoubtedly come upon banks as high as this one.

When the bucket of snow had melted on the stove, I diluted some powdered milk, added flour, and made dough. The kitchen warmed up, the smell of coffee began to fill the room. I put the dough in a large mixing bowl, covered it with a cloth, and stared out the black window.

In the past, I would wake up in the yellowish light of the morning sun, to the warbling (no other word for it: warbling) of birds, and feel the deep contentment that comes after a good night's sleep in a big soft bed. I slept upstairs, in the room at the front of the house, left, the one next to the bathroom. The curtains open and a splash of summer morning sun on the old wooden floor, the tousled bed. The light that caressed the walls, the wooden door frame, the sprigged wallpaper. In the bathroom, with the door wide open, I would turn on the taps, lay out my shaving things, a large towel, a small towel. Then into the bedroom again to throw back the covers, choose my clothes, and drink in the sun at the window.

And then the lazy ritual of the bath. The slow immersion in the big cast-iron tub. Early morning baptism. The mirror on the shelf above the bath, my face damp, fragrant foam whipped up with the sable brush in the porcelain shaving bowl, jaws, chin, and neck gently lathered and the first careful tracks in the creamy landscape.

When I came downstairs, Uncle Herman would be waiting in the kitchen. He'd have been awake for several hours already. Every morning at six o'clock he watched the rabbits hopping across the field behind the house, back into the forest.

He would fill a large mug with coffee, set it on the wooden kitchen table, and let me prepare my own breakfast. When I was sitting down, behind the steaming mug and the plate with two Emmenthal cheese sandwiches, always two Emmenthal cheese sandwiches, he sat down opposite me, head bowed over his book, invariably an old one, crumbling like a loaf of dry bread, turned a page, and said, 'I went in to check on you, sir. I thought you were dead. You were lying there like a kidney simmering in a pan.'

'Zakhar!' I'd cry, 'why must you torment me so?' And then he would grin, my Uncle Herman. Every morning he quoted a different line from one of the great Russian novelists and I had to come up with the appropriate response.

And there we sat. I ate my bread, he read his book. We drank our coffee and after I had put my plate on the cracked granite counter, he smoked a Partagas and I, a Belgian cigarette.

Then we got down to work. I went off to the library with a fresh mug of coffee, he disappeared somewhere into the house. As I sat at the table, reading and writing, some mornings with a window open and the scent of the sun-warmed forest drifting in now and again, I could hear Uncle Herman's footsteps on the wooden floor above me.

While the dough was rising, I gathered wood. Upstairs, where it looked as if someone had blown up a furniture shop, I stepped into the linen cupboard that had blocked my way the night before. With the hissing of the gas burner in my ears, I began breaking down the back wall. As the axe split through the wood and the large panel started coming loose, my thoughts strayed to Uncle Herman. For years we had wandered, fled, moved house, we had sought, found, and lost our fortune. But here, Uncle Herman had drawn a line in a sand. He wanted a house that would lie in the land like an anchor, a place where we wouldn't always have to be, but to which we could always return. Herman, as professor at an American university, travelled to Holland at least once a year to see us, my mother, my sisters, Zeno, and me. Usually he stayed with us for a day or two and then went up to the house. There, he would work, rest, and think. The house kept him alive, he said, and that was no exaggeration. Uncle Herman was not only a professor, and director of the Moskovitz Institute for Sociological Studies (MISS), he was also the big name in the field of urban culture, a specialized area that was apparently so much in demand that he spent as much time on a plane as other people spent in a car.

I hadn't expected there to be anything else behind the linen cupboard, but once the back wall was lying on the floor in a heap of splinters, I saw a strange gleam in the darkness. I leaned forward and peered into the depths of the cupboard. A watery eye stared back at me.

Uncle Herman once said (first to me, but when that proved to be a success he repeated it in interviews, lectures, and newspaper articles) that all our fears, however small and insignificant, could be traced back to that one fear, the fear of death. At the time I had thought it empty rhetoric, but now, peering into the half-demolished linen cupboard, which stood before me like a doorway to nothingness, staring into a glassy eye that didn't belong there, I understood what he meant. As I shrank back, my left hand flew up to my heart. At almost the very same moment – my lungs filled with air – I realized that there couldn't possibly be anyone standing behind the cupboard. There wasn't enough room.

I picked up the lantern and shone it into the cupboard. A vaguely familiar face emerged from the shadows. It was a painting, the portrait of Uncle Herman's predecessor, the last of the house of Van

Henninck, the heirless squire. It should have been hanging in one of the rooms on this floor. Zeno, said the voice inside my head, you bastard. My heart was still pounding. Zeno. I found it hard to imagine him as the special-effects expert who had transformed this place into a haunted house. I tried to picture him, heaving and hauling, plotting and grinning. I couldn't. I saw him sitting with Sophie in the corner between the wall and the mantelpiece. They were reading a book with spidery illustrations.

'And this is . . .'

'ALITH!'

'And what's the rabbit holding?'

'CWOCK!'

So small, so fragile, the perpetually tangled hair with that indescribable, coppery sheen, the clear brown eyes with their moss-green flecks . . . I shook my head and picked up the basket, filled it with pieces of wood, and went downstairs. I put some in the library hearth, the rest in the kitchen, next to the stove. Then, the dough in the oven, I drank coffee and warmed myself by the glowing Aga.

'Lithuania.'

I looked sideways. Uncle Chaim was standing at the sink, gazing out at the dark garden. Very warily, day was breaking. The treetops slowly took shape against the blue-black sky.

'What do you mean, Lithuania?'

'Where I was born. On the edge of the great Lithuanian forest. Bialowieza, you know it?'

'Was that where Magnus thought he . . .'

'No, that's further. This is the great forest, where the bison live.' He shivered.

'And what, Uncle Chaim, makes you think of the Lithuanian forest?'

He looked at me, his head to one side. 'The snow, Nathan, the snow.' He sighed, and turned away. He sat down at the wooden table and sniffed. 'Baking bread?'

I nodded.

He sniffed again. 'Smells like the challah my Friede used to bake.' He leaned his arms on the tabletop and hung his head.

A slow sadness drifted down inside me. Like falling snow.

In 1648, when Chmielnicki's Cossack hordes began plundering and murdering their way through Poland, they smothered the radiance of those hopeful years – and the light of Uncle Chaim's life. Friede was standing outside their house with a basket of washing. She had just returned from the stream and was no more than five steps away from her little house, when she heard a low, surging rumble. Uncle Chaim was sitting inside repairing a clock. He, too, heard the sound. 'Like the thunder rolling across the *puszta*,' he said, when he first told me about it, 'Pharoah's armies driving the children of Israel into the sea.' But for Friede, the waters didn't part. No Moses to lift his staff and make the churning waves rise into blue, white-crested walls, no pillar of cloud to show her the way to freedom and redemption. As the cloud of dust came rolling around the bend and changed from a tumbling brown ball into a ragged band of horsemen, you could hear them, the blackguards, above the hollow rumbling of hooves and the wind whistling through their clothes and the horses' legs, screaming and shouting. Friede didn't even have time to walk back to the house.

Less than five seconds later (but it had been a journey that seemed to last an hour) Uncle Chaim rushed out the door and saw his wife. Where once tiny black curls had graced her neck, like a finishing touch that the Lord of the Universe, in a burst of tenderness, had added to his creation, was now a pulsating dark jet of blood. The basket stood upright in the grass alongside the path. On top of the washing lay Friede's head.

It wasn't until that night, when Uncle Chaim lay drunk in a corner of Yankel the forester's house, that he realized how long her body had stood there. Once again he saw her before him, his wife, the way she always was, the straight back, the delicate curve of her shoulders. And above that, nothing. For the twentieth time that day it made him 'puke like a donkey shitting his guts out.'

1648. 'The zenith of our exile,' Magnus had once said. 'Only a few times has the tree of Jewry blossomed in another land. And this was one of those times. I'm not saying that life was good or that people were happy, but it was better than before, and much better than afterwards.'

'Nonsense,' was Uncle Chaim's response. 'Travelling amulet merchants. *Wunderrebbes*. Muddle-headed mystics. Charlatans. The year of redemption, said the Kabbalists. Redemption . . . Bah. Chmielnicki.'

And here, now, in Uncle Herman's kitchen, in the worst winter in years, Uncle Chaim was thinking of Lithuania and the air smelled of the challah that Friede had baked three and a half centuries ago. I sat down across from him at the table and lit a cigarette, a bit guiltily, because I was dipping into the rations that Nina and I were supposed to be sharing.

'*Nu*, what are you getting up to here, in Herman's attempt at nobility?'

I told him about the barricade and the stockpile of food and the tape of Zeno's voice and that we were chopping up the furniture so we wouldn't freeze to death. Uncle Chaim listened attentively. He nodded, shook his head, pursed his lips, and raised his eyebrows when I was through.

'Who did this?'

I shrugged. 'I don't know anything for certain, and to tell you the truth, I'd rather not think about it right now.'

Uncle Chaim looked up. I followed his gaze. Outside, Magnus wandered past the window. He looked around, dazed, peered nearsightedly at the trees along the edge of the forest, and then disappeared from view.

'*Gott* . . .' said Uncle Chaim.

I went to the window and tapped on the glass. It was a long time before Magnus reappeared. When he saw me, his mouth dropped open.

'If he were stupid,' sighed Uncle Chaim, 'I could accept it. But this . . .'

We heard him stumbling about in the hall. After a while he came in through the kitchen door.

'Magnus,' I said, when he was standing before me.

'Nathan.' He looked at his uncle and shrugged helplessly. 'I lost my way.'

'You thought you were in Bialystok,' said Uncle Chaim.

Magnus sat down at the table. He grinned at me. 'In Herman's house,' he said. 'What a mess up there at the top of the stairs! Who did that?'

Uncle Chaim glanced at me. I shook my head.

'Fresh bread,' Magnus said. 'Delicious.'

I smiled.

'Delicious . . .' said Uncle Chaim grumpily. 'You haven't even got a stomach, not anymore. Heart's gone, too. To say nothing of brains. There's no more delicious for you.'

I looked at Magnus. For fifty years he and Uncle Chaim had been dropping by, and their visits had become so normal that it only very rarely occurred to me that they weren't 'real.' But this was one of those moments. Suddenly I saw Magnus in all his . . . ghostliness. He wasn't tall, almost nobody was in those days, but wiry and sharp. The close-cropped brown hair, so short that his scalp glimmered through, and olive complexion gave him the look of a watchful rodent. This, and the long, curved nose and piercing brown eyes. Twenty-five, maybe twenty-six. That was about how old he looked. But why? Uncle Chaim appeared as he must have looked in the year of his death. Magnus had lived to be nearly a hundred, the longest living Hollander. This is Magnus at the moment of his departure, I suddenly thought. Twenty-five, or -six. That was when he set off. Magnus as Wandering Jew. Magnus, the first Hollander. Magnus, the flying Dutchman. All those times he had appeared to me, roaming, searching. His continual uncertainty about where he was and when. Bialystok. Where had Magnus actually gone, when he left home after Uncle Chaim's death? The wrong way, he said. South instead of west, or west instead of south. But twenty years on the road, all because of one wrong turn?

I stared at Magnus and then turned around. As I poured the coffee, I let my eyes stray to the window. The sky above the trees was bluer now. It had stopped snowing. The wind had dropped, I knew by looking at the branches. I leaned forward and peered out at the thermometer, but it was still too dark to be able to tell the mercury from the scale.

When I turned round again, my relatives were sitting in exactly the same position as before.

'What?' I said.

'How?' said Uncle Chaim.

'What are you staring at?'

He looked at Magnus, who was still waiting for an answer. 'Lower your eyes.'

Magnus started, then looked around in confusion. 'Me? But didn't we just ask who made all that . . .'

'And shut your mouth,' said Uncle Chaim.

'Zeno,' I said. 'It's Zeno's work.'

Uncle Chaim got abruptly to his feet. He went to the counter and peered out the window. 'Where are the Cossacks?' he asked.

Magnus and I looked at each other. 'Nuncle,' said Magnus.

'There are no Cossacks,' I said.

'How . . . if there are no Cossacks . . .'

Magnus's expression was a mixture of amazement and fear.

I told them how we had been snowed in, that Nina had tried to escape, that the way upstairs was barred and Zeno's voice on the tape and . . . 'Nuncle,' I said to Chaim, 'I said that Zeno did it, but that's only a guess. *Nina* thinks it was Zeno.'

He looked at me blankly. 'Nina's here?'

I nodded.

'I think you'd better take the bread out of the oven,' said Magnus.

I jumped up, grabbed the dish towel off the counter, and opened the oven. He was right. A mushroom cap of dough bulged out of the baking pan. Below it, on the oven floor, lay the flamed brown boulder that the second loaf had become. I pulled out the baking tray and turned it over on the counter. Then I loosened the other loaf with a spatula, slid it out, and placed it on the bread-board.

'The smells of happiness,' Uncle Chaim was standing next to me, sniffing like a puppy. 'Fresh-baked bread, new-mown grass, a gentle shower.'

Magnus came over and joined us. 'He's been awfully poetic lately, Nuncle Chaim.'

Chaim snorted. 'Me, poetic, you, scatterbrained. If I didn't know better, I'd say we were on our way to the end.'

'And bad-tempered,' said Magnus. 'Awfully bad-tempered.'

'Magnus, stick parsley in your ears, wash your mouth out with tar, and put your hand over your eyes. When you're able to think again, you can . . .'

'Nuncle,' I said.

My great-great-grand-uncle nodded and hunched his shoulders. He had always, as long as I had know him, looked like a cross between a scarecrow and a tailor, but today he seemed more stick-like and fragile than ever. As if his clothes were being held up by a broom instead of a body.

'I'm going to tell you something, Nathan. Sit down. No, don't talk back. Remember the commandment. There. Sit, *mayn kind.*'

Mayn kind. I was older than he had been when he left the land of the living and began wandering about the world through which he had been wandering for three centuries now, and he called me: *Mayn kind.*

He walked through the kitchen, from the sink to the door, from the door to the sink and back again.

'Two sorts of light, both of different strengths. What happens? One, visible, the other disappears in the glow of the first. That doesn't mean: the first light is the best. The strongest. The . . . most Radiant. Sometimes the weaker light is the best. What did Herman say? That you don't use your talents. That you waste them on fairy tales, when you . . . could rule the world. That's what he said.'

That was, indeed, what Uncle Herman had said. You could rule the world. I remember thinking how very American it sounded.

'I'll tell you how it was.'

'Nuncle,' said Magnus.

'*Schtil,*' said Uncle Chaim.

I sat at the table, the intoxicating smell of fresh bread around me, and listened like a child being told that there's no such thing as *Sinterklaas.*

'Zeno . . . You don't know what he was, Nathan. No one saw it.' He had arrived back at the sink, leaned his hands on the granite surface, and looked out at the grey-blue sky above the white wall of conifers. 'He was the Other.' Uncle Chaim turned round and looked at me with his faded black eyes. 'He was the Sitra Ahra.'

'Uncle . . .'

'The Other Side, Nathan. Sitra Ahra. He is the annihilator.'

'*Is?*'

'The shatterer of worlds.'

A curtain was lifted. Like clouds parting after a storm to reveal the light that was hiding behind them, a darkness brightened within me and I was in another world, not Uncle Chaim's Sitra Ahra, but the flat hard desert near S 10,000. The slender, bowed figure of Mr O., the fluttering grey suit, the sharp face against the rising light of early morning, his right hand above his eyes, peering into the distance where the swirling black mushroom was gobbling up the sky. 'I am become Death, the shatterer of worlds.'

'Nathan.' I jumped and turned my eyes to Uncle Chaim. 'You . . . the small light, tiny flame no one saw in the . . . glare of . . . of Zeno's . . .'

'We have to go now, Uncle.' Magnus had stood up and grabbed him by the sleeve. 'It's almost day.'

'Nathan . . . has . . . to know . . .'

'There's no time to lose, Nuncle.'

'What?' I asked.

Uncle Chaim closed his eyes. Magnus looked at me sharply and shook his head. He put his finger to his lips and didn't shift his gaze until I had nodded. They melted away like mist in the morning sun.

It was a long time before I could tear my eyes away from the spot where Uncle Chaim and Magnus had disappeared. I drank the last few drops of cold coffee and thought about the half sentences, the fragments of language that had come tumbling from Uncle Chaim's lips. The light, and the light that vanished within it.

My two loaves of bread were steaming on the counter. The one in the pan was split down the middle. The other one, on the baking sheet, was the sort of loaf the Dutch masters found so pleasing to the eye: round, lightly dusted with flour, pale brown around the edges, dark on top, gleaming like a piece of polished wood. I had made three slashes in the dough, which had come out as three pale stripes. I put the kettle on, sliced bread and cheese and, when the coffee was ready, set off for the hunting room with a pile of sandwiches and a steaming mug. The Small Light serves a Big Breakfast, I thought.

––––––––––

Nina woke up like someone who had just been raised from the dead. She groaned, struggled, resisted. She opened her eyes, a tiny bit, and closed them again. She lay there for a while and then said, with a crack in her voice, 'Coffee . . .'

She ate in silence. I had fetched an armload of wood and made a fire, so the hunting room wasn't quite so dark anymore.

'We've got to make it last,' said Nina, when I came and sat down on the edge of the bed. She nodded towards the hearth.

'Yes.'

She sipped her coffee and stared straight ahead. 'So?'

I shrugged. 'We'll see how it goes. If the worst comes to the worst, we can always burn the books.'

She looked at me for a long time.

'Don't worry,' I said. 'While you were sleeping I had another go at the barricade. It's bigger than I thought. There's probably enough wood there to heat this room as well. You can sleep in here tonight, I'll take the library.'

She ate her sandwiches, staring into the half-light. Suddenly she straightened up. 'I thought we didn't have any bread?'

We. Was this the first time she had used the word 'we'? Was it no longer *my* house in which she was stranded?

'This is freshly baked,' she said. 'How . . .'

'There was flour, powdered milk, we've got an oven.'

I saw a look of admiration cross her face. 'Nathan Hollander,' she said, 'what kind of a man are you that you can write fairy tales, bake bread, and make the best sauerkraut casserole I've ever tasted? What else can you do?'

'Talk to the dead,' I said.

She laughed.

'So, what's on the programme today?'

I ran my hand through my hair and smiled. 'Today, Madame, that is to say, after the house breakfast, you will be escorted to the hall, where local residents will introduce you to a quaint regional custom: Antique Bashing.'

'Antique Bashing.'

'Antique Bashing is a tradition that dates back to the time before the Iconoclastic Fury, contrary to what Professor Melchior claims in his study: "Clearing the Decks: Antique Bashing and Other Purification Rituals." Following the Antique Bashing Demonstration you will be shown to the library, where you will witness Fire Fixing. Damn.'

'What is it?'

'The fire in the library. I haven't checked it for a while. If you get dressed, I'll go and throw on some more wood.'

I stood up and walked out of the room. Just as I was about to close the door behind me, I heard Nina's voice. 'A bath,' she said. 'What did you do about a bath?'

'Nothing,' I said. 'There's no water up there. This afternoon, if we make it to the bathroom, we can fill the tub. But we'll have to carry up buckets of hot water.'

'No bath.' She wrinkled her nose. 'Yuck.'

'It'll be fine,' I said. 'As long as we both stay dirty.'

There wasn't much left of the fire in the library and the temperature in the room had hardly risen since early that morning. I began building it up again and sat there for a long time watching, now and then feeding the red, lip-smacking beast in the mouth of the hearth a piece of chair, drawer, or cupboard. Half an hour later, Nina came in. She was wearing Uncle Herman's clothes, the ones I had given her the day before, and looked strangely pale. It was a while before I realized that she wasn't wearing any make-up.

'Got a comb?' she asked, as she crouched down beside me in front of the fire.

I shook my head. 'You can always use a fork.'

'A . . . Hey, who do you think I am, Wilma Flintstone?'

'It's up to you.'

She dropped to her knees, wailing dramatically. 'Mama, Mama! What have I done to deserve this? Uncombed and unwashed, and I slept in the same bed last night with a man old enough to be my father!'

'Nina?'

'Yes?'

'Shut up.'

She clapped her hands to her mouth and opened her eyes wide. 'Uncle Nathan! Such language!'

I laid more wood on the fire and got to my feet.

'It's true,' said Nina.

'What's true?'

'That I spent last night in bed with a man old enough to be my father.'

'As long as it was respectable sex, dear girl.'

She raised a wriggling red eyebrow.

'But speaking of your mother, how is she?'

'Busybusybusy.'

'Be sure to give her my regards, will you?'

She stared at me and opened her mouth. Then she closed it again and shook her head.

'What?'

'You are un . . . You're too much,' she said. 'We've been snowed in here for more than twenty-four hours and if it doesn't rain hot water today we'll be stuck here for the rest of the week and all you can say is: Give my regards to your mother.'

'You think we're never going to get out of here?'

She stood up and sighed. 'At the moment I haven't got the slightest hope.'

I headed for the door. 'That's a shame,' I said over my shoulder, 'because apart from a supermarket full of food and a mountain of antiques, hope is about the only thing we've got.'

There wasn't much light in the hall, but enough to give the gas burner a rest. I picked up the axe, climbed the stairs, and began hacking away at what was left of the linen cupboard. When the side panels were knocked out, I found myself face to face with Squire Van Henninck. The portrait was hanging exactly at eye level. I lifted it off and passed it to Nina. She looked at me, dumbfounded. 'In the fire? Are you mad? No, just lean it up against the wall. Somewhere where it won't scare us.' I told her how it had been hung behind the cupboard, to make it look as if someone were standing there.

Nina lowered the painting. 'Trap number two,' she said.

'Three: the piano, the tape, and now this business.'

She nodded. We both realized at the same time that the tape had stopped playing. Neither of us mentioned it, but when our eyes met we each knew what the other was thinking.

A niche had formed in the barricade, a space about six feet wide, closed off on the left by the sideboard and the little red sofa, a table or two, the secretaire, and a jumble of other small pieces of furniture. On the right, our passage was blocked by a pile of chairs, a few bedside tables, one or two large armchairs, a blanket chest, and a vast assortment of odds and ends. I saw a mirror, a couple of mattresses, pillows, a hat rack and, stuck in anywhere they would fit, photographs, vases, umbrellas, boxes, a walking stick, floor lamps, clocks, a pair of scales, a 1940s radio, ashtrays. The pile nearly reached the ceiling and gave me the same feeling of despair that one has after a move, when the removal men have dumped the boxes all over the house and the furniture is standing any which way, in all the wrong rooms. Since the left-hand side of the barricade contained the most wood, and led to my bedroom, I raised my axe and brought it down on the sideboard.

When the linen cupboard and sideboard were finally out of the way, I tried the door to the attic. It was locked. When I peered through the keyhole, a tangle of chair legs loomed up in the murky light. It was as if a truckload of furniture had been dumped down the stairs from above. I didn't want to force the lock, because whatever was behind the door would come crashing down and fill the hole in the barricade. Besides, it was probably even colder under the roof than in the hallway and there would be a powerful draught through the broken door. So we went straight on.

We were making real progress now. There was a pile of dining room chairs, five or six, which we swiftly tossed down the stairs. Before long a piece of kite string came into view, tied to one of the chair-legs. I cut through it with the axe. After the chairs came the contents of my bedroom, first the mattress, pillow, sheets and night table, then the entire bed. I tried to pile up as much of the linen as I could against the wall. When I came to the bed itself, I saw the cassette recorder. It had been attached to the foot of the bed, upside-down, with long strips of tape. The string was wound around the play-button. I recognized the recorder. Uncle Herman used to use it to dictate notes. The play-button was a small metal bar you slid upwards to turn the thing on. When I had pulled a chair out of the pile the night before, it must have caught on another chair, the one to which the string was tied, and set the trap in motion.

'How much longer do you plan to go on?' asked Nina. She was leaning on the rake, looking up.

I rested the axe on the floor and looked down at her. 'I'd like to do as much as possible now. Otherwise we'll have to come back up here this afternoon.'

'Why the long face, N?' she asked. She stood the rake against the banister and came upstairs.

'I think I just don't see the humour in it anymore.'

Nina brushed aside a lock of hair and ran her eyes over the mountain of things behind me. 'How much farther before we get to the end of the hallway?'

I looked over my shoulder. The jagged outline of stacked furniture was silhouetted against the half-light. 'About twenty feet. There's a door coming up on the left, the door to my bedroom. And opposite that is another door. Then comes another bit of hallway leading to the outside wall.'

'And you're sure there's nothing up in the attic . . .'

'There wasn't when Uncle Herman was still living here, in any case. And even if there were . . . The stairs to the attic are one big rubbish chute. Did you want to empty it?'

'If there's nothing in the attic,' said Nina, 'then whatever happened to the person who piled up all this stuff?'

The question was so logical, and at the same time so simple, that at first I didn't realize what she was saying.

'Not that I'm an expert on barricades,' said Nina, 'but looking at the way everything is stacked, I'd say that whoever built this must've worked from the bottom up.'

'He started in the bedrooms . . .'

She nodded. 'He filled the right side of the hallway, little by little, until he got to the stairwell.'

'And then he went down to the other end.'

We looked at the stairwell and the intact front of the barricade to the right of it.

'And did the same thing on that side.'

'The piano,' I said.

'Where was the piano?'

'In the farthest room, on the right-hand side.'

'The first piece he had to get rid of.'

We fell silent and looked at the closed attic door. The light that streamed into the hall through the windows above the front door was just bright enough, up here, to illuminate the area around the stairwell.

'So you think,' I said slowly, 'that he crammed full both sides of the hallway, then went up the stairs to the attic and . . .'

Nina nodded.

We stood there among the chips and chunks of wood. With all that furious chopping, I had worked up a sweat. Now, in the chill of the unheated first floor, I quickly began to cool down, but when my teeth started to chatter, I didn't know whether it was the cold, or the inescapable conclusion to which Nina's analysis was leading.

'Zeno,' said Nina.

I said nothing. I leaned my axe against the wall and went ahead of her, down the stairs, to the kitchen.

We didn't speak. I sliced the bread, Nina boiled water and made tea, and when everything was ready, we sat down at the table where Zeno, my sisters and I had so often sat in the summertime, drinking the mugs of fresh milk that Mrs Sanders had poured for us, with lumps of cream floating on top. The bread she had sliced and set on the table in the wicker basket came from the village. It was heavy and brown and tasted of grain. The best bakers in the country lived here, and in the South. Everywhere else you got something that was shaped like a loaf, but which, upon coming home, turned out to be nothing more than a hard crust around greyish foam. Now we were eating large white slabs from the round loaf I had baked that morning. Nina's hair hung in spirals, her cheeks were slightly flushed. We stared past each other, in silence.

'May I tell you something?' I asked, after a while.

Nina bit into her sandwich and eyed me sceptically.

'I've never seen you looking healthier.'

She stopped chewing for a moment. 'Perhaps you should organize this every winter,' she said. 'Nathan Hollander's Beauty Farm. Hard work, wholesome food, and a healthy dose of fear.'

'I heartily recommend the SS.'

'What?'

'Freud. That's what Freud said when he was driven out of his house by the Germans. They had stolen his money, turned the place upside down, and forced him to flee. When they left the house, he had to sign a statement saying he'd been well-treated.'

'And did he?'

I nodded. 'He also wrote: I heartily recommend the SS.'

She looked hard at me. Then she smiled. 'So now you think that if the police show up in a day or two to rescue me from this madhouse, I'm going to sign a statement saying: I heartily recommend Nathan Hollander's Beauty Farm.'

'It's the very least you can do, Madame.'

She sipped her tea. Her eyes strayed to the window. 'I'm glad it's stopped snowing, anyway.'

'But it's freezing harder than ever.'

'What are we going to do this afternoon?'

I stood up and cleared away the dishes. 'Nothing,' I said. 'We've got enough wood for the whole day. I say we take the afternoon off.'

Nina went to the stove, picked up a dish towel, and laid it across the handle of the kettle. She began pouring hot water over the plates. 'As if that were any consolation,' she said out of the cloud of steam that billowed up around her. 'A whole day with nothing to do.'

'Nina,' I said. 'I've noticed this before about you. Do you know what I think your greatest fear is? Idleness. You're afraid of doing nothing.' I picked up the mugs and put them in the sink. 'There's a library here that's second to none in this country, probably even the entire continent, and you're dreading a few spare hours. But, okay, if you're so set on doing something, feel free to carry on chopping. Just make sure you stop at the wall.'

She sighed. 'That library of yours . . . Do you think I might find a couple of those light-hearted novelettes for bored young ladies?'

'Why do I suddenly have the disagreeable feeling that if *I* had said that, I would have been slapped in the face?'

She smiled sweetly. 'Let's have another chunk of that biography. If you've got any left.'

'Piles, Madame, heaps.'

And so we spent the afternoon in our chairs by the fire, reading. I had brought up the tea-lights from the cellar and floated them in a large glass bowl of water. Nina had gathered together every candelabra she could find and arranged them on the table between our chairs. In the soft glow of all that candlelight, Nina read another portion of the manuscript, while I worked my way through the pack of paper that contained three of the four fairytales that would make up my new collection.

'What have you given me?'

'Something appropriate,' I said. 'Zeno.'

Her gaze cooled. For a moment I thought she was going to hand me back the whole pile of printed sheets, but then she tucked her legs underneath her and began to read.

The Second Law of Thermodynamics

IN 1948, MANNY and Sophie went their separate ways. According to Manny, because Sophie looked down with so much European disdain on the United States that the rest of the family began to feel they were living in a monkey house.

The year before, we had returned to New York. In our old apartment in Manhattan, where Uncle Herman had spent the war years alone but was gone by the time we came back, we tried to pick up the thread of our lives. But the years on the Hill, far away in New Mexico, had changed us all. Zoe, Zelda and I had grown into half-savages and were annoyingly precocious. We began to go wrong in a most spectacular way. The only one of us who hadn't been affected by our stay in the desert was Zeno. He had been born in 1944 in the little hospital on the Hill and was too young to know the difference between wooden and brick houses, dirt streets and asphalt, a village of physicists and engineers and a city where life pumped, pounded, and sang.

Sophie's loathing for America ran deep. She hated the bigness, the muchness, the filled to burstingness, the 'you can't get any better than this.' America, to her, was: the absence of discretion. The size of the refrigerators, the cars, the cartons of milk, the glasses of beer and the steaks provoked a rage in her that none of us could understand. Zoe, Zelda and I were completely immersed in the culture of our new homeland, for Manny the transition had been a matter of course, and Herman was unavailable for comment. He didn't turn up again until the beginning of 1946.

The marriage of the light and the darkness, as Herman had described it, had only been stable for the first few years, when Sophie was still up to her armpits in nappies, bottles and talcum powder. But just before I was born, the first crisis arose. Zoe and Zelda were born one after the other and Sophie was so busy that she (and she readily admitted it) sometimes had trouble remembering her own name. Not long after the birth of Zelda, she collapsed.

One night she dreamed that she was painting. The portrait she was working on was taller than she was. She painted as she had never painted before. It was, she said later, when she told me about the dream, as if the brush, no: the paint, was a part of her. 'And then,' said Sophie, 'I realized why.'

She was painting with mother's milk.

The realization that she was using her own milk as paint came to her in the dream and although she was anxious to wake up, she couldn't. She went on working. She squeezed the milk out of her breast, onto the brush, and blended it into the thick layer on the canvas, and little by little, as she struggled to wake up, it became clear to her what she was making. From head to toe, larger than life, the figure of a woman emerged on the milk-stained canvas. It was Sophie herself, and she was naked, sagging, a skeleton hung with loose, wrinkled folds of skin. Her breasts were flattened water bags with large, dark brown nipples, her hipbones protruded and between them, like an old pillow, hung her belly.

When she finally awoke, she heard herself screaming.

The crisis lasted a year and it was a year in which she longed to paint, but with all the hustle and bustle of motherhood, was unable to. Emmanuel watched his wife and didn't know what to do. He saw her unhappiness, but knew he could do nothing to change it. He didn't earn enough to pay for a nanny. Whenever he tried to talk to her about it, her eyes grew dull and it was as if there was an empty shell sitting opposite him and that her soul was elsewhere. Herman was the only one who could get through to her.

'Not because I had a solution,' he said. 'There weren't any in those days. Crèches, part-time jobs, that sort of thing didn't exist. But, I told her, you can always draw. If you start drawing now, I said, in a few years, when circumstances are better, you'll have a clearer idea of what you want to do. I'd been wrong in thinking that she only painted as a diversion, a young lady's pastime. I tried to make up for that mistake when things weren't going so well for her, and I think I succeeded.'

Sophie began to draw, in between the feeding, washing, cooking and ironing, and after a while she had so much faith in the future that she became pregnant again. In 1935, I was born.

Once, when we had been back in Holland for some time, a friend of mine asked why it was that all the children in our family had names that began with a Z, yet I was called Nathan. 'Did they find you on a doorstep, or what?' I brought it up that night at dinner, and Sophie said, 'We just couldn't think of any more nice names starting with a Z.' I had looked at Zeno, who was sitting on the other side of the table and trying to fob off his meat on Zoe. 'It wasn't until much later,' said Sophie, who had followed my gaze, 'that we thought of Zeno. What's the matter, don't you like your name?' I had shrugged. 'It means "friend,"' she said. 'Because I thought: perhaps he'll be a good friend to me.' Zoe, who had just started on Zeno's steak, burst out laughing.

But there was another theory, Zeno's. We were quite a lot older, he fifteen and I twenty-four, when I told him The History of Names. A family legend of sorts. He waited until I had finished speaking and then shook his head.

'They called you Nathan because by that time Manny was so sure he was leaving that he had the guts to oppose another Z. Sophie, who also saw it coming, was just compliant enough to give in. But only once. After that she ran out of patience. Then I was born.'

I, he said, was Compliance; he, Indomitability.

'Manny, gone? In 1935? What makes you say that?'

'Ask him yourself,' said Zeno.

I did, later that same year, when I went to America to spend my autumn half-term with Manny and Herman.

My father heard me out and then nodded. What Zeno had said was absolutely right.

'God will call me to account!' Manny had cried, when Sophie came up with the name for the second baby. 'Another Z? That's tempting fate. Definitely not. What about Esther. Or Rebecca? Eve!'

'We've already got one of those,' his wife had said. 'Zoe means Eve. Alexandrian Jews used to call their daughters Zoe.'

'Miriam?'

Sophie had shaken her head. The baby was called Zelda.

And then I arrived. From the moment they knew that I was on the way, Manny opened fire. No more Z's. Over his dead body. The first son would be a Heijman; there *was* such a thing as family tradition. The battle lasted nearly nine months. The result was Nathan. I was, in Zeno's words, the last attempt, the sacrifice, and the straw they were clutching, all rolled into one. He himself, born when there wasn't much left of the marriage worth saving, was the symbol of Sophie's indomitability.

'Names,' said Manny, when we talked about it in New York. 'What difference does it make? If you don't like the name you've got, you can always think up your own.' We were standing in an endless queue outside Brooklyn Stadium. Whenever I was over from Holland, Manny took me to a baseball game. I looked at him, the ridiculous straw hat, the sports coat, the stubborn, grey-black curls, and shook my head. It was a mystery to me how my father, of all people, could have such unwavering faith in the malleability of his own existence.

But what Zeno had said was true: I was an N because my father had already left, at least in spirit, and my mother was willing to make one last rescue attempt, in the area of nomenclature. Zeno was the end.

Strangely enough, Sophie and Manny's marriage wasn't a bad one. They may not have been an ideal match, and they could argue long and passionately about a thing as trivial as a name, but there was no shouting, no hitting, no hating. It was as if they both understood that there was a flaw in the fabric of history and that they had been drawn to each other for reasons that, at the time, were unclear, even to them. Manny had chosen an independent, wilful woman because he thought she would leave him in peace, just as he would her. He had overlooked the possibility that children and domestic obligations might throw a spanner in the works. Sophie chose a man who could appreciate her independence and wilfulness. And although my father had always sincerely believed that women should have a life of their own, his appreciation alone was not enough.

On our way to America, on the ship, during the storm in which Sophie was the only one of us who remained on her feet, she finally realized this and began to think back to the time when she still painted, when she knew of poverty and wealth, socialism and capitalism, Mondriaan and Disney. She did drawing after drawing, covered reams of paper with her sketches. But she also foresaw that she could go on this way until she had used up an ocean of charcoal and a forest of pencils. Soon, in America, they would have to start from scratch, and she would have neither the time nor the money to paint. Once she began putting it off, she would never find her way back. This had to end.

She managed to hold out in New York, and for as long as we lived on the Hill, but when we returned to Manhattan she began churning inside, so violently that she could no longer keep still. She looked around her, saw no way out, saw nothing but superficiality, bulk, speed, and excess, and said we were leaving.

So we left.

A year later Manny returned alone to the land where he didn't need to wear a tie. He had invented something to do with mattresses. What, exactly, wasn't clear to any of us, but apparently this was what the world had been waiting for (or rather, losing sleep over), and Manny made a fortune. He bought his way out of the bosom of the family, as Zelda put it, and off he went. He never asked Sophie for a divorce ('I took a vow'), but phoned every two weeks, made over a vast sum of money every month and, for the rest, pursued his lifework in the beds of women half his age. ('If anyone profited from his invention, it was Manny,' said Zoe.)

In New York he moved into our old apartment, where Uncle Herman, who had finally resurfaced, was still living. Manny had no trouble sharing a place with his brother. Herman was hardly ever there.

Sophie accepted her newly-gained independence with amused indifference. She stayed alone for a long time, except for the occasional 'friend', and it wasn't until years later that she allowed herself the luxury of a new partner. She soon forgave her husband his desertion, but his silly invention, combined with the fact that in the years following the divorce he had begun to look more and more like a typical American sitcom character, a cross between Billy Wilder and Walter Matthau, robbed her of the last ounce of respect she still had for him. On those rare occasions when she actually saw him in person, you could have scraped the cynicism right off her face. A European lady who consumed her pleasures with taste, she saw, in Manny, everything she abhorred: garish clothing, white sports socks under dark slacks, canned beer, a passion for Jerry Lewis.

Manny's departure was as atypical as the marriage had been. We all went to see him off. At the airport, with a sudden boyish awkwardness, he kissed Zoe, and Zelda, and Zeno. Last of all, he laid his hand on my shoulder. 'Take care of your mother and the girls,' he said.

Zoe had rolled her eyes and groaned. 'My God,' she said. 'It's 1948! You don't ask a thirteen-year-old child to take care of two grown women.'

'You're not grown,' said my father.

'Wanna bet?'

He had looked at her, his eyes narrowed slightly. 'Calm down,' he said. 'This isn't the end of the world.'

'Wrong again,' said Zoe.

Manny shrugged his shoulders and kissed Sophie, who was standing to one side and watching this little scene with raised eyebrows. She offered him her cheek, tapped him on the jaw with the fingers of her kid gloves, and turned away. He grinned and picked up his hand luggage.

That was the end of the family. At my insistence we stayed to watch the plane take off, but as we stood there behind the departure hall window, it was as if we had never been otherwise: four obstinate children with an equally obstinate mother and a father who was tinkering his way through life in America.

Life went on and, contrary to what Zoe had claimed, the world kept turning.

But the world had changed. In those days people hardly ever got divorced, and if they did, it was an event that hung over their lives like an ever-present rain cloud. That this wasn't the case with our family only served to arouse the suspicions of those around us. Less than a week after Manny had left and we were living our old life again, I was walking down the street with Zeno, when I was stopped by Mrs Poppe, one of the neighbours. She bent down, stroked Zeno's hair, and said, half sobbing, 'Poor little thing.' I had no idea what she was talking about. That night at the table I told the others what had happened. Sophie looked at me steadily and then shook her head. After dinner she took me over to Mrs Poppe's house. She rang the bell and, while we were waiting, said, 'Pay attention to what I'm about to say, Nathan.'

The door opened, Mrs Poppe appeared. Before she could even say hello, Sophie asked if she had called Zeno a 'poor little thing' that afternoon. I saw the woman shrink back. She stammered out something that sounded like 'yes.'

'Would you mind explaining that to me?'

I tried to wriggle my hand out of Sophie's and slip behind her, but she wouldn't let go. Worse still: she deliberately held me in plain view. The woman began to say something about fatherless . . . 'So, just because their father happens to be away, my children are "poor little things"? Better to have a father who beats his children and drinks and commits adultery than a "poor little thing" with no father at all?' I began to wish desperately that the sky would burst open and hit me with a thunderbolt. Each time my mother repeated those words, 'poor little thing,' I saw the woman cringe and each time I saw this, I cringed too. 'My children, Mrs Poppe,' said my mother, 'are just as happy and unhappy as all the other children in the world, and they always will be. The fact that you feel you need a man around the house so your own children won't be "poor little things" says more about your inability to make something out of your life than about the circumstances in our home.'

That last sentence, I couldn't quite follow, but what I did understand was that we Hollander children were actually better off than children in other families. Sophie gave the woman a curt nod and turned around. I let her drag me back, dazed. At home, in the sun lounge, among her painting things, as she resolutely began stirring a pot of paint, she said that she was well aware that I had felt uncomfortable standing there, but that she had wanted to be very sure that I understood why it was wrong for people, for no good reason at all, to feel sorry for me and Zelda and Zoe and Zeno. Because there was nothing to feel sorry for.

'No,' I said.

Did I think I was worse off than children whose fathers were still living at home?

'No.' (But I wasn't really sure.)

Sophie smiled and began wetting her brushes.

———————

The divorce made a letter writer out of me. Manny had only just left for America (he must have been flying somewhere over England) when I asked for pen and paper and began the correspondence that turned me into the family's emotional switchboard.

'*What* are you going to do?' asked my mother, when I told her I wanted to write a letter to America. I explained it to her again. 'You can always phone him, you know,' she said. 'Not every day, but once a week . . .' I said I didn't want to phone, I wanted to write. She shook her head. 'But why? What is it you want to tell him?' 'It's confidential,' I said. Years later, when my sisters and I were long grown and I wanted to keep something to myself, they would tease me about this. 'Leave him alone,' one of them would say. 'It's confidential!'

My father was hardly the ideal correspondent. In answer to my first letter, complete with illustration (an airplane flying towards the sun and, below that, little houses and four waving stick figures with hands as big as heads), I received a postcard of Central Park.

'Hey,' said Zoe, who always collected the post. 'There's a card for you, from Papa.'

The whole family gathered around me as I made a lengthy examination of the photograph on the front and finally, at their insistence, turned over the piece of cardboard to read the text.

Regards, Papa, it said.

'Regards, Papa?' I said.

'That's what it says,' said my mother.

'That's it? Regards, Papa?'

'Good grief,' said Zoe. 'What did you expect? The Old Testament?'

'Wasn't it nice of him to send you a card?' said my mother.

'I write a letter and all I get back is *Regards, Papa?*'

'The man's got better things to do than worry about us,' said Zoe, rather smugly.

'Quiet,' said my mother. She leaned over and put her hands on my shoulders. 'He's busy, N. He has all sorts of things to arrange over there, and besides, he's never been much of a letter writer. You can't hold it against him. But I'm sure he appreciates you writing to him. You understand that, don't you?'

I didn't understand that. I had greeted someone with a bear hug and my enthusiasm had been met with a limp handshake.

'When you write letters,' said my mother, 'you mustn't have any expectations. There's no law saying that a person has to write as long or beautiful a letter back. Remember that the next time you write: you're doing it because you want to be in touch, not to get attention.' She stood up and stared briefly over our heads. 'Come to think of it,' she said, 'life is always like that.' She stroked my hair and, looking pensive, disappeared into her studio.

That night I wrote my second letter and this time I didn't worry about initiating any sort of dialogue. I had resolved, through my letters, to tell my father everything I felt he needed to know, whether he wanted to or not, in order to return to us.

When I had been writing to my father for a year, a year in which I got back a few postcards and he, each time he phoned, thanked me profusely for my letters, an airmail envelope arrived from New York. I was sitting in an old wicker chair in the sun lounge – my mother's studio – reading, when Zoe came in with the post. Zelda was walking behind her, holding Zeno by the hand. Sophie was working on a charcoal sketch for a large portrait, and looked up in annoyance.

'How many times do I have to tell you, I need quiet when I'm working,' she said. 'And no more than one at a time in the sun lounge.'

'But there's mail,' Zoe said. 'For Nathan.'

'Then give him his postcard and out you go.'

'It's a letter!' said Zoe. 'From Uncle Herman!'

Sophie lowered her charcoal and looked at me.

'I didn't do anything,' I said. 'I never wrote to him.'

Zoe handed me the letter. I took it from her carefully and looked at it. On the front, a tiny airplane cleaved the sky-blue sky of the envelope. I imagined the pilots in their cockpit staring ahead with pensive faces, over the billowing cloud banks. And the stewardess coming in to ask if it were really true, that there was a letter for Nathan Hollander in the hold.

'Aren't you going to open it?' asked my mother.

I turned the letter over and looked, a bit nervously, for a way to open it without causing too much damage. My mother leaned over, picked up a pallet knife, handed it to me, and nodded. I slipped the knife under the flap and carefully cut open the envelope. Zeno came up and leaned against my leg. He looked gravely at the pale blue paper. I felt his elbow in my thigh.

'Come on, take it out,' Zoe whined. 'It's just a letter, a plain old letter.'

'Shut up, Zoe.'

She ignored my mother and jabbed me in the arm. I slid my fingers inside the envelope and drew out three wafer-thin sheets of folded paper.

'A real letter,' Zelda said.

'What did you think it was,' said Zoe, 'a fake one?'

'Pig.'

'Cow.'

'Zoe! Zelda! Stop that bickering.'

Bold, generous handwriting.

'All right, I want everyone out of here,' my mother said. 'It's Nathan's letter, let him read it in peace.'

'Aren't you going to read it out loud?' said Zelda, her eyes wide with disbelief.

'A letter is personal,' said my mother.

Zoe and Zelda looked at her with disgust.

'My,' said Zeno.

There was an antediluvian silence.

'Dear,' said Zeno.

My mother opened her mouth. I saw my sisters do the same.

'Na-than,' said Zeno. He looked up, at me. 'Nathan,' he said again, smiling, deeply satisfied.

'He can talk,' said Zoe.

'He can read,' said Zelda.

'Zeno?' said my mother.

He turned round and looked at her questioningly.

'Did you just say something, Zeno?'

He knitted his brow and thought for a moment. Then: 'My. Dear. Nathan,' he said. My mother's right hand, in which she had been holding the charcoal, slackened. The little black stick fell to the ground and shattered to pieces. Her hand moved slowly upwards, to her mouth. Zeno leaned on my leg again and peered at the letters on the delicate paper. 'I'm writing,' he read, 'you this letter, be . . . because you . . . ap . . .'

'. . . because you, apparently, are the one who keeps the channels open . . .' I continued. I felt Zeno's weight shifting against my leg. I wrapped my free arm around him and pulled him onto my lap. Together we looked at the letter.

'. . . you, apparently, are the one who keeps the channels open in this strange family,' I read. 'Everything here is fine. Emmanuel has rented a small workshop, a block away, where he can fiddle with his inventions, while I travel from one land to the next. Because I'm so often in transit, I also have a bit more time to write than he does. That's why you're getting a letter from me this time. But there's another reason. I'll be in Holland next month and I'd like to stop by for a visit. Please be so kind as to ask your mother if that would be convenient. I won't stay long, three days at most, but at least we'll have the chance to see one other.

'Emmanuel shows me your letters – I hope you don't mind – and I must say I always enjoy reading them. It's good to get news every now and again from the old country and to hear how everyone is doing. I always say: a phone call can never compare with a letter.'

At this I looked up, at my mother, who had often asked me in the past year why I bothered to write when I could just as easily phone. She caught my glance and closed her eyes wearily.

'What I also find extremely entertaining are the subjects you write about. Most people, the moment they put pen to paper, tend to get rather solemn, which doesn't make for very pleasant reading. You, fortunately, write about the ordinary, everyday things that happen in your life, and in the lives of your family. Just the sort of things you want to hear about when you're so far away from those who are dear to you.'

Next to me, I could hear my sisters shifting in their seats. In the beginning I had always read my letters aloud before sending them, but I had stopped doing so because each time, Zoe and Zelda would roar with laughter when they heard, for instance, that I'd described how we'd decorated the living room the night before Zeno's birthday and how Zelda had fallen off the chair, streamers and all. They said I only wrote about silly things, or things they were ashamed of.

Uncle Herman went on to tell me about all the places he had been in the last few months and that he and my father had been to the play-offs together and which players they had seen. He obviously knew I still loved baseball.

'Well, it's time to stop. I'm writing this on the plane and we're about to land in New York. I hope you won't forget to tell your mother that I'd very much like to see you all next month, and needless to say, I would greatly appreciate it if you would drop me a line. Your uncle, Herman Hollander.'

Zeno, who had been sitting upright on my lap the entire time, sank back contentedly and stuck his thumb in his mouth.

'The revenge of Nathan Hollander,' said Zoe. She gave me a nudge. 'Are you sure you didn't write that letter yourself?'

My mother knelt down in front of me and looked at Zeno. 'And you, young man,' she said. 'What's going on? How is it that you can read, but don't talk? Tell me that.' But Zeno said nothing and sucked thoughtfully on his thumb.

'Leave him alone,' said Zoe on her way out, 'maybe he'll write you a letter.'

It was a big day in my life, in all our lives. I received the letter that motivated me to go on writing letters, and Zeno spoke for the very first time. My mother had already taken him to see a whole army of specialists and paediatricians, she had consulted speech therapists and neurologists, but not one of them had been able to tell her why he didn't speak. One doctor, a common-or-garden GP, as I recall, had sent her home and told her not to worry, and as it turned out, he was right. He said he had heard of this sort of thing before, a child who didn't speak, or was very late in speaking, and he had even read once that there were children who kept silent until they were certain they could speak well. That was the sort of child Zeno turned out to be. Up until the age of five he hadn't said a word, and now, now that I had received my first letter from Uncle Herman, he was speaking and reading at the same time. Why it had taken him so long (to speak – in reading he was exceptionally early) we never knew. And Zeno never told us.

That night I wrote back to Uncle Herman and told him what had happened, that Zoe and Zelda and Zeno had brought in his letter and how I had opened it and that Zeno had come over and leaned against me . . . It went on and on. In response to his own letter, Uncle Herman received a ten-page document that was more of a short story than a letter from one member of the family to another. He obviously wasn't displeased. Less than two weeks later, I received his reply.

And so Uncle Herman and I began a correspondence that lasted until his death and, according to my calculations, produced just over two thousand letters, a thousand from him and an equal number from me. I don't, unfortunately, have my letters to him, but if I were to lay them side by side with his letters to me, I'd have a complete family history.

Zeno talked. Not much, but at least he knew how. He went to school, where he hardly ever opened his mouth, he came home again, where he frowned whenever my mother asked him how it was in first year, second year, third year, and so on and so forth. He never wrote letters, as Zoe had so sarcastically remarked. He just watched and nodded.

Nevertheless, it was a great relief. Zeno had turned out to be normal after all. And that was how he grew up, as an ordinary, though extremely reticent, almost inconspicuous child. Until that day, in the autumn of 1954.

Zoe, who had come home early from school and was sitting across from him at the table doing her homework, said later that you would never have known by looking at him, he was simply drinking his milk and eating biscuits. Zeno was munching away, elbows on the table, not saying a word, when suddenly he sat bolt upright.

'It was as if he was looking straight through me,' said Zoe later. 'But he wasn't looking at anything behind me. It was more as if I were invisible. Then he smiled, and fell over.' Every time my sister told that story (and she told it often; the older we got, the more that story meant to us), every single time, she showed us how it had gone. She sat down on a chair, stared into space, laughed, a bit dazed, and then keeled over sideways, like a stone.

Zeno lay in bed for nearly a year, the first few weeks mostly sleeping, later surrounded by cars and planes and, after a month or two, immersed in books. It was the year in which he began to read, in which he, like a film in fast motion, read his way straight through my mother's books, the novels in the living room bookcase, the encyclopedia, and finally, a list of books he had compiled himself and asked us to buy for him. He turned ten, that year, and read *The Magic Mountain*, *The Wanderer*, *A Portrait of the Artist as a Young Man*, Gogol (and a handful of other Russians), *Young Törless*, Dickens, London, Kafka, Roth, Zweig, poetry by Slauerhoff. My mother watched him and frowned. There were so many books lying around him, it was as if he had risen from a hole in the ice. Whenever she came in for a chat, he answered her distractedly, irritably, as if he really didn't have time for such trifles. Doctor Harm ('Good thing you don't live in England, you wouldn't have many patients,' said

Zeno, who had taught himself so much English that year that he was soon reading in that language, too), Doctor Harm just shrugged his shoulders and ignored Zeno's mania. 'I have no idea whether it's good or bad, all those books,' he said. 'I'm just a humble family doctor. All I can do is see if he's getting better.' And he was. Zeno, who, after his fall from the chair had spent a month in the hospital, recovered before our very eyes, although in the end, it was nearly a year before he was back to normal.

No one knew quite what was wrong with him. That afternoon, after his collapse, my mother had rung the doctor, who examined him and then had him brought to the hospital in a taxi. They had to lay him diagonally across the back seat, because he was completely catatonic. 'His muscles,' my mother told us, 'were so hard, it was like carrying a statue.' The stiffness lasted until the following afternoon. Then he opened his eyes, smiled once, and fell into a deep sleep. He didn't wake up for days. By that time the first tests had been done and it was clear that Zeno didn't have meningitis, or polio, or any other immediately identifiable disorder. One of the professors who examined him – it was a teaching hospital – said that the patient appeared to have suffered a severe shock, but none of us could imagine that this was possible. He had sat at the table, drunk milk, and eaten biscuits. What could have given him such a shock?

After his year in bed and on the sofa, Zeno was a different person. He had always been fairly precocious, but now, armed with his books and encyclopedias, he verged on the unbearable. He always knew best, and if he didn't, he knew where he could find a better answer. He began devouring the newspapers and didn't seem to forget anything he ever read. He bombarded people three times his age with facts, statistics, and views that were, at the very least, painful, and nearly always unpleasant. He opposed the Russian invasion of Hungary, but jeered at my sisters when they spoke of "those Russian barbarians." He called it 'populist rubbish, not rooted in any form of knowledge whatsoever.' He said: 'Europe was divided up at Yalta. What do you suppose the Americans would do if we all turned Communist?' He nearly died laughing when existentialism gained a foothold in Europe and people in black turtlenecks started hanging around in smoky French cafes, listening to monotonous chansons and American jazz by the light of dripping candles and getting drunk on bad wine. Zoe, who was rather intrigued by the views of Sartre's followers, got into a terrible row with Zeno when he said they were a 'pack of wolves, just like the people they oppose, maybe worse, because they don't even know it.' Zeno, in the years when you could only be one thing, left-wing or right, was everything at once. Some thought he was a cynic, others, an opportunist, still others, a fatalistic realist. When Zoe told him he didn't believe in anything, Zeno replied that she believed in too many things at the same time. Zeno had become quite the little pedant.

For a while I was his teacher. Even though his knowledge had exploded in a cloud of facts and figures, he still needed someone to show him the way. We discussed politics, history and physics. I read him Uncle Herman's letters, which, at that time, were nearly all about the theory he was trying to develop.

Herman was less and less inclined to define the world in terms of class struggle (a political variation on Darwinian theory, he said). He leaned more towards modern physics. 'Naturally, it still remains a question of imagery,' he wrote. 'Ever since the Encyclopedists, we've looked at ourselves and our surroundings through the metaphorical filter of the mechanism, something which still restricts us. And then, of course, there's that whole Darwinian-Malthusian amalgam of views with which we attempt to understand one thing and another. The advantage of modern physics, however, assuming you use it in the way I wish to do, is that it offers an explanation for the component of civilization in our lives. Or rather: an answer to the question of why we're never able to achieve stability.'

The Second Law of Thermodynamics was Uncle Herman's answer to the question that preoccupied him: why was there no equilibrium?

'Entropy,' wrote Uncle Herman. 'We're collapsing under our own entropy. The more we continue to develop our society, the more advanced and sophisticated the system becomes, the greater the problems of managing it and, as a result, the greater the entropy.

We strive for the improvement of the world, of ourselves, of the way in which we organize our lives, but in doing so, we gradually lose our grip on things.'

When I first read that, I thought of my father, who saw the world as a machine that still wasn't working very well and just needed a bit of fine tuning. If Uncle Herman was right, and I believed he was, then my father was devastatingly wrong.

'What is en-tro . . .'

'Entropy,' I said to Zeno. 'It's called en-tro-py.' I explained the concept to him in light of my father's view of the world. 'So the Second Law of Thermodynamics,' I concluded my lecture, 'says that everything gets more and more complex and harder and harder to keep under control. The universe is a clock that ticks and ticks and generates more and more "time", but this means that the energy used to generate that time is lost, and eventually the alarm goes off and the maximum amount of time has been generated and the spring is stretched as far as it will go. The energy is then contained within the time that it has produced and can no longer be removed to rewind the clock. It's irreversible. That's entropy.'

Zeno nodded. I knew this meant that he had not only understood it, but had also been able to visualize it. That was his greatest talent. When he thought of numbers, he saw them, just as he could never talk about the colour red without seeing a particular shade of red. Once I was writing a letter to Uncle Herman and I devoted an entire paragraph to the storm that had raged above our house all night long and that I thought would never end. I described the thunderclaps, that it was as if someone were beating against the walls of the house with an enormous board. I told him that there was so much lightning you could no longer tell the difference between light and dark and that the room in which we all waited until the storm had passed was a frenzy of leaping blue shadows. When I read the letter to Zeno, he seemed pleased. But after a while he said, 'Of course, it's only an impression.' I explained to him that this was always the case when you were talking about reality, that one could only ever speak in terms of an *image* of that reality. He found this very disappointing.

'Flaubert,' I said, 'was Guy de Maupassant's teacher. Remember de Maupassant? We've read his stories. Anyway, Guy always let Flaubert read his texts, but Flaubert was never satisfied. One day he came along with another new piece and Flaubert said: "You describe things as if they were of no importance. If you want to write about a tree, you must go up to a tree and keep looking at that tree until you no longer see 'a tree,' but that one tree, the essence of that tree. Once you have done this, you can begin to write."'

Zeno felt that you would still only be working with an image, and even though I tried to explain that, in this case, you were no longer concerned with that particular tree, in that particular spot, but that you, as a writer, were trying to convey the feeling of 'tree,' he insisted that every text that tried to say anything other than the most trivial ('Be back soon') was doomed to failure.

'I thought you liked those de Maupassant stories!' I cried.

Yes, he had, but in retrospect he found them slightly too 'non-committal'. We stared at each other for a while, and then he came out with a pronouncement that made me realize that he was living in a totally different world than the rest of us. 'Actually,' he said, 'music and abstract painting are the only completely autonomous art forms. Since it's impossible for the musician or painter to actually talk about reality, the listener or spectator is forced to enjoy the work of art itself. What you've done, writing about a storm and trying to describe it as well as you can . . .'

'. . . the feeling of a storm,' I said.

'Same thing. What you've done is a feeble attempt to create a new reality, without ever breaking free of the reality from which you derive your images.'

'Jesus, Zeno,' I said. 'We're talking about a letter here, not linguistic philosophy.'

He looked at me with an expression in which pity and compassion went hand in hand.

Each time I think of that scene, I have to force myself to bear in mind that he was still just a little boy but — and it was several years before I was able to admit this — he wiped the floor with me.

I knew where Zeno's rigid views on art and reality came from. Years before he became ill, as his fall from the chair was thus described, the whole family went to see *Bambi*. My sisters sobbed when Bambi's mother died, I swallowed hard. We sighed with relief when the forest fire was over. Only Zeno seemed fairly unimpressed. It wasn't until months later, when we were walking through the forest one Saturday afternoon with Uncle Herman (who was over again from America), that something seemed to have stuck. Zoe and Zelda were playing tag, Uncle Herman and my mother were walking and talking, and Zeno was looking around in amazement. After a while he tugged at the sleeve of my jacket. When I stopped and looked down at him, he stood on tiptoe and whispered, 'Where's the music?'

'The what?'

'Music. Where's the music?'

'What music?'

'The music in the forest.'

I had no idea what he meant and was about to walk on, when he gave my sleeve another tug and said, 'Like in *Bambi*. The violins. And the harp.'

I should have reacted differently, taken him more seriously, but I was young: I burst out laughing. When the rest of the family came over to see what was so funny and I told them that Zeno wanted to know where the music was, they too roared with laughter, even Uncle Herman. Zeno didn't move a muscle. He looked at us as if we had just stepped out of a spaceship and had three heads apiece. 'If there's no music,' he said at last, when the laughter had died, 'why do they need it in the film?'

My mother, Uncle Herman, and I tried to explain the function of a soundtrack, but Zeno closed his mouth, pressed his lips together, and refused to listen to reason. Looking back I'd say that this was the first sign of what was to be a continuing rejection of anything that either imitated reality, or created a new reality by using elements from the existing one. Ever since *Bambi*, Zeno saw, in every attempt to create an image by non-abstract means, nothing but deception and cheap imitation. The second commandment, against the making of graven images, had found, in my younger brother, an unexpected advocate.

———————

After his illness, when he had read every book in the house, memorized the encyclopedia, and could speak fluent English, Zeno started begging for money. He even wanted Sophie to buy a car, so he could wash it. That didn't happen. Since he wasn't allowed to deliver coal for the coal merchant across the street either, Zeno thought up something else. It was a long time before we found out what that was.

One day, Sophie went upstairs to look for the Doré Bible that was usually kept in the bookcase in her study. If it wasn't there and she didn't see it anywhere else, Zeno had it. We were all readers, but Zeno was the only one who read so much and so many different books that if you couldn't find something, you could generally assume it was in his room. Zeno spent most of his free time up there and never let anyone in. The only person who did have this privilege was the housekeeper, but, as we later discovered, he had bribed her to keep her mouth shut.

We lived in a big house in the centre of town, on the corner of a quiet canal. Before we moved in, it had consisted of two separate dwellings, the remains of which were still visible on the fourth floor: a long rectangular living room with high windows and, behind that, a large, old-fashioned kitchen and modest washing facilities. The living room, after my mother had bought the house, was divided into two bedrooms. I got the one at the front, a room which, with its big bay window, looked like the bow of a ship. Zeno's room was behind mine and had a huge green marble fireplace and a row of windows along the side wall. Those windows, when Sophie walked in, were practically hidden: the sills were piled high with books. In the fireplace, Zeno had built extra shelves. The floor looked like a miniature labyrinth. At first Sophie couldn't even find Zeno's bed. Only after she had inched along the low walls of books – there were piles in the room that were taller than she was and swayed gently as she walked past – and got closer to what used to be the hearth, did she see a mattress. It was lying on a solid layer of books about two feet high.

She didn't find the bible, but after half an hour, which she spent sitting on a stack of books, staring at the unbelievable spectacle around her, she knocked on my door. When I opened it, she said nothing. She stared at me for a moment, then beckoned me with her head and walked into the hallway.

Years later, when, at Zoe and Zelda's request, I would tell that story yet again, I still couldn't describe what went through me when my mother flung open the door of Zeno's room. She had allowed me a few moments to take it all in, and then said, 'So this is new to you, too.'

We stood side by side in the doorway. I was speechless.

'How . . . Where did he get all this? Did he steal it? How did he get it in here without my noticing?' The questions of astonishment and anger and self-reproach that my mother asked herself and me.

I walked into the room, slaloming, step by step, left-right-left, because there was no other way you could walk. The ruins of an ancient city, in paper and cloth. No novels, all textbooks, scholarly books. I began searching, not for anything specific, just something to hold on to, something recognizable: theology, philosophy, anthropology, photography, bibliography, biography, psychology . . . I stooped down and picked up a folio bound in weather-beaten brown leather. I opened it. A title page I couldn't read. 'This is seventeenth century!' I cried. I walked on. Latin, Hebrew, English, German, some in Gothic print. New books, old books, very *very* old books.

There was a small fortune in that room. A complete, highly specialized library.

Zeno came home an hour later. He went up the stairs, walked into his room, whistling, and drew out three, four, five books from under his jacket. He was just about to distribute them over the piles around him, when my mother and I rose up from behind a wall of Kabbalistic mysticism. Zeno was so startled that he dropped his smuggled goods. What books meant to him was clear enough by the way he fell to his knees to examine them. He picked them up, put them in a safe place (but what is a safe place, I thought, where on earth is a safe place to put a book in this chaos?) and looked at us questioningly.

'Zeno,' said Sophie, 'is there something you'd like to tell me?'

He frowned. 'Tell you?'

'What is it you want to talk to me about?'

Zeno looked left, right, and then back at us. 'I thought there was something you wanted to talk to *me* about,' he said.

'Bloody hell!' shouted my mother. It was the first and only time I ever heard her swear.

I grabbed her by the arm, because I was afraid she was going to fly straight through the columns, over the walls of books, at Zeno. 'She wants to know where you got all these books,' I said. Sophie tried to pull her arm away. 'She thinks . . .' Just then the sleeve of her blouse ripped. She shot towards Zeno and I went flying backwards.

We landed softly, in the books. As I struggled to get to my feet I saw a pillar sailing past me. I heard Zeno shouting and looked in his direction. There was Sophie, scrambling up out of a pile of paper, while all around her, one stack after another was dominoing to the ground. It took nearly an entire minute for everything to come to a halt. Only two towers were left standing. My mother was sitting on the floor again, her legs splayed, on a layer of books. Her shoulders were gently shaking.

'You think I stole them!' cried Zeno, hurt. I was on my hands and knees on the floor and looked up. I tried to shrug. 'You think that I . . .'

My mother looked as if she was about to cry, but began quietly laughing.

'Did you?' I asked.

'Of course not!' shouted Zeno.

'But . . .'

Zeno stepped like a heron through the lake of paper. 'Most of them come from auctions, bazaars in old people's homes, markets. Some of them are from antiquarian booksellers. Not many people are interested in books like these. They're often dirt cheap.'

'And what about this one, then,' I said, burrowing around in a solid wave of book jackets. I pulled out a small volume, no bigger than my hand, bound in stiff brown cloth.

'*Der Raw*,' said Zeno, 'historio-cultural *Erzählung*, written by a certain "Judaeus," Hermon-Verlag, Frankfurt. Probably from around 1930. Got it from an antiquarian book dealer. Not the original binding, but apart from that, undamaged.'

'You got it from a . . .'

'As I said, there's hardly any interest for this type of book. Certainly not if they've got a new cover.'

That was the moment when I concluded, to my horror, that Zeno wasn't a collector: he actually read these books.

'Where do you get the money?' I asked.

'Why do you think I wash all those cars every Saturday?' He piled up several books and sat down on top of them, shaking his head. He raised his right hand and began calculating aloud. 'I do ten cars myself and I've got two assistants who also do ten each. I give them seventy-five percent of the earnings.'

He began working out how much all that yielded him and then went on to tell us that he sometimes stumbled upon a book at the market that he bought for fifty cents and sold to a dealer for fifty guilders. 'Last year,' said Zeno, 'I bought *Ulysses* for two-fifty.'

'A later edition.'

'No, Olympia Press. Got a hundred and fifty seven guilders for it. Found it in a thrift shop, in a box full of trashy novels.' I realized that my fifteen-year-old brother, in order to satisfy his craving for knowledge, had become a businessman and that he, in both the former and the latter, was doing rather well.

My mother, who had been sitting on the floor listening, brushed a lock of hair out of her face and looked up. 'I don't care about you buying and selling books, as long as you pay for them, but I don't like the idea of you hiring two boys to wash cars and then have them pay you for mediating. A person has to work for his own money.'

Zeno opened his mouth.

'And what's more,' she said, scrambling to her feet, 'I want you to go out and learn something about documentation, so you can straighten up this mess, put it in some sort of order. This isn't just a bad habit, it's terrifying! I don't want you falling through the floor with all this rubbish and I don't want you to become some dirty old man shuffling through stacks of dirty old books in a pair of mouldy slippers. You need to organize.'

'But I know exactly where everything is,' said Zeno. He looked around, at the drifting white expanse. His shoulders drooped. 'Knew,' he said.

Through one of Sophie's students, who was married to a frozen meat wholesaler, Zeno got hold of a batch of used wooden racks. Another student was a librarian and got him a job as a volunteer at the local library, where he could learn how to deal with large quantities of books. With Sophie's permission, Zeno and I tore down the unused kitchen on our floor. A plumber shut off the water supply, which we wouldn't be needing anymore. The walls were repainted and my mother had the floor laid with black linoleum. The racks weren't repainted. Bloodstains glimmered here and there, but Zeno insisted on keeping them the way they were. 'Blood and books,' he said to me. 'They go together.'

I couldn't tell whether or not he was joking.

Zeno had been working at the library for six months, every Wednesday afternoon, when one day after class, the librarian asked how Zeno was getting on with the variety show. Sophie, who was rinsing out the brushes, laughed. It wasn't until about ten seconds later that she realized what had been said.

Several weeks before, the librarian explained, Zeno had stopped coming to work. He had said he knew enough and had found another job. He wouldn't tell her what, but she and her sister's children had been to a kiddie show at the local community centre and seen him performing as the assistant to someone who called himself Mr Tony.

'That boy is driving me crazy,' said Sophie, when the four of us, Zoe, Zelda, me and Sophie, set out one Saturday morning for a school building on the other side of town. There, as we had discovered after a lengthy search through the local papers, was the forthcoming performance of Mr Tony, a man who billed himself as a 'singer-acrobat-magician-equilibrist.' What that last one was, none of us knew.

We stood in line for a quarter of an hour, along with mothers in curlers and their snivelling children, surly fathers with cigarettes dangling from their lips, and fun-loving uncles who were already trying to compete with the artist everyone had come to see. One of them even went so far as to walk down the street on his hands and, after fifteen feet, amid loud cheers and applause, capsized over a row of bicycles.

The afternoon began with a girl dressed in a handmade variety-show suit who came leaping onto the stage, made her introductions, and then cartwheeled back off. No sooner had she rolled out of sight than we heard a crash and a clatter and then silence, followed by a muffled altercation.

Mr Tony, instantly recognizable as the mousy little man I some-times saw at the baker's who only ever ordered currant buns, came on singing. It took a while for us to realize that he was doing his own version of a Las Vegas show. Half drowned-out by the orchestra tape, he sang 'There's No Business Like Show Business', interspersed with lines like 'Welcomeladiesandgentlemenboysandgirls!' and 'It's great to be here!'

'As if he ever went anywhere else,' said Zoe.

After his opening number Mr Tony did a magic act. He pulled a long silk scarf out of his pocket, waved it around in the air and, poof! a collapsible bouquet burst into flower. 'He pulled it out of his sleeve!' shouted someone in the audience. From the right-hand wing came a black-clad *Struwwelpeter*, a small, disagreeably glum-looking fellow who walked up to Mr Tony, rigid as a bar of wrought iron, accepted the artificial flowers and, aiming a deadly glare at the audience, took his place beside the artist.

'Zeno,' whispered Zelda. There was a distinct note of admiration in her voice. The audience, until then quite rowdy, had gone pin-drop silent.

No doubt Mr Tony had had something fairytale-like in mind

when he picked out a costume for Zeno, but somewhere along the line, that 'something' had gone wrong. The make-up under his assistant's eyes was smudged, giving him the appearance of a zombie freshly risen from the grave. The black suit had been washed at the wrong temperature, or bleached, and looked as if it had been sprinkled with ashes. In his hair Zeno had traces of talcum powder (for a moment Sophie thought it was cobwebs) and the white pan-cake on his face had been so unevenly applied that his cheeks looked unnaturally waxen and the hollows under his cheekbones were even deeper than usual. What stood there before us on that tiny school stage was a creature from the netherworld.

Mr Tony was just about ready to pop someone from the audience into a chest and make them disappear, 'into the ether,' as he put it, but he couldn't get a volunteer. A mother or two tried to push forward a child, but their attempts ended in whimpering and wailing. Next to me, Zoe got to her feet. Zelda tugged at her sleeve and hissed something, but Zoe, peering intently at the stage, shook her off and stepped out into the aisle. In the distance I could see Zeno's unnervingly black left eyebrow go up. Sophie said nothing.

Mr Tony welcomed Zoe with a mixture of enthusiasm and relief. He helped her onto the stage, introduced her to the audience, and showed her the huge, red-lacquered chest in which she was to disappear. Zeno stood beside it, motionless.

'Music, Maestro, please!' cried Mr Tony. Somebody offstage dropped a phonograph needle onto Beethoven's Ninth. The doors of the chest banged open. Zoe put her left foot into the contraption, looked defiantly at the audience, and let her right foot follow. No sooner was she inside than Zeno came closer, shoved her down, slammed down the lid, and began grimly locking the clamps. Restless whispers rose from the audience. Zeno glowered at the spectators, and then hoisted himself onto the lid. Mr Tony stared, flabbergasted, at the small black monster towering above him. When Zeno ignored him, he took a step back, pulled his magic wand out of his sleeve (realizing too late that he should have conjured it up), waved it back and forth and cried, 'Shaddai!' Sophie turned to me, frowning.

It began to dawn on me that Zeno had had a large hand in the staging of Mr Tony's show. Less than a week before he had told us about the seven secret names of God, and that 'Shaddai' was one of them. 'Especially popular among people who feel threatened by the devil,' he had said. I wondered to what extent the fourth-rate variety show artist in whose service my brother worked knew what he was doing.

Mr Tony's cry had barely sounded, when there was a whitish-blue flash of ignited magnesium powder and a thick ball of smoke filled the stage. Above the cries of fear from the audience was the sound of violent coughing. When the smoke cleared we saw a wildly waving Mr Tony and the impassive black figure of Zeno, still straight as a rod on top of the chest. The audience began murmuring, but Mr Tony would allow them no time to get over the shock. He motioned to Zeno to come down and unlock the clamps. Then he banged open the lid and turned the chest over. Zoe was gone.

There was a hesitant smatter of applause that quickly increased in strength as Zeno raised his right arm in a triumphant Presto! gesture. Sophie leaned towards me. 'He doesn't leave us much choice, does he?' I knew what she meant. Zeno gave the impression that anyone who didn't heed his directions would come to no good.

Mr Tony had him close the chest again, instructed Zeno to take his place on the lid, and waved his wand. The loudspeakers boomed out half a clarion call. Zeno spun around on the toes of his right foot and jumped down. Mr Tony lifted the lid and stared, amazed, into the depths. Slowly he straightened up and gave Zeno a helpless glance.

Zelda, Sophie and I looked at each other. It was no great surprise to any of us that Zoe hadn't returned from, as Mr Tony had called it, 'the ether'. What we did wonder, as Zelda said under her breath, was 'how he was planning to get out of *this* one.'

That soon became clear. Zeno raised his left hand: the restless audience fell silent. He leaned towards the magician and whispered something in his ear. Mr Tony brightened, turned to the audience, and announced that the subject had vanished into the ether and that another subject was needed to bring her back. A tremor ran through the hall. 'That young lady over there,' shouted Zeno, pointing to

Zelda. Sophie began shifting uncomfortably in her chair, a hundred and fifty faces turned in our direction. Zelda rose, beaming.

The ritual repeated itself and Zelda, too, vanished into thin air, where she remained. Mr Tony stood nervously beside his assistant. He had lost all control of his show. The audience, seeing his helplessness, grew increasingly restless. 'What have you done with those girls, you pervert!' someone shouted. Mr Tony flashed an uncertain smile into the school auditorium. When the first few men got up and started heading for the stage, Zeno took charge. He swore to everyone that the 'victims' would definitely be coming back, but that they needed just one more volunteer. 'All magic revolves around the number three,' he said. Sighing, I got to my feet.

When I climbed onto the stage, Mr Tony greeted me with a look that bordered on desperation. He pushed me hurriedly towards the chest. As I entered the red monstrosity, which stank of mothballs, Zeno came over and stood next to me. This time, he shouted, he would accompany me personally on my search for the missing subjects. Mr Tony groaned softly. 'For God's sake, come back,' he lisped. 'They'll lynch me if you don't.' Zeno grabbed one side of the lid, I grabbed the other, and together we slammed it shut. Just before it went dark, Mr Tony said: 'Hey, are you two related?' The clamps clicked, the phonograph needle slithered through the first few bars of the Ninth, magnesium exploded, and Zeno started moving. Before I knew what was happening the bottom dropped out and we were sliding down. There, in what was apparently the prompt box, I followed Zeno down a steel ladder into a dark room where Zelda and Zoe were waiting for us.

'Bitch,' said Zeno to Zoe.

She gave him a superior grin.

Zeno walked ahead of us and motioned to us to follow. And follow him we did, through a cellar-like room, where it was so dark we had to hold hands so we would know which way to go. Then we surfaced, somewhere backstage, I thought. I could hear the vague echo of excited voices.

'Quick,' said Zeno. He ran ahead of us, into a corridor. At the end was an emergency exit door that could be opened with a horizontal bar. Zeno tugged at the bar, but it wouldn't budge. I went and stood next to him and together we pulled. The door was jammed.

'Reverse,' said Zeno. He raced back, down the corridor, through a doorway, into a dressing room. He climbed onto a chair and pushed open a high little window. I gave him a shove, helped Zoe and Zelda, and then hoisted myself up. We came out onto a court-yard, which we quickly crossed, Zeno in the lead. He steered us through an alleyway, past dustbins, rotting vegetables, and two bemused-looking cats, then ran around a corner, to the front door of the school.

Our entrance, at the rear of the hall, came just as Tony was being driven slowly backwards into the wings by a group of twenty furious men and women.

'Presto!' cried Zeno.

'Bastard,' said Zoe.

The audience burst into deafening cheers.

The rest of the afternoon Mr Tony sang from his Dean Martin and Frank Sinatra repertoire and the girl who had done the introduc-tions, his niece, closed with a painfully awkward rendition of the Dying Swan. The final round of applause was, as Mr Tony himself later admitted, the most ecstatic in his career.

'And I've had some pretty wild clappers in my day, kids,' he said in the dressing room, taking a hip flask of whisky out of his suitcase and putting it to his lips. His hands were shaking. 'Jesus. For a minute I thought: they're all going to skidoo!' He laughed too loudly and took another slug.

'Angst,' said Zeno.

'Ankst, goddamit,' said Mr Tony.

'Everything revolves around angst,' said Zeno. Mr Tony lit a cigarette and inhaled, right down to the soles of his feet. 'Angst and hope.' Mr Tony nodded absently. 'One conceals the truth, while the other leads to new roads.'

'A real little philosopher,' Mr Tony said to me. 'There's more to that brother of yours than meets the eye.' He sighed. 'Ankst,' he said again.

'Zeno would make a good prophet of doom,' I said.
'A damn good prophet of doom,' said Mr Tony.
Zeno smiled like a beetle on a pile of dung.

Years passed before I saw the truth in my own remark.

One evening Sophie walked into my room. She was holding a newspaper and looked flustered. I was sitting in one of my fifth-hand armchairs reading about quantum mechanics and was slightly annoyed that she had opened the door without knocking. She failed to notice. She drifted in like a paper boat and didn't come to a halt until she had bumped into the chair opposite mine.

'Did you know Zeno was in the paper?'

I closed my eyes and let my head drop back.

Sophie sat down and put the newspaper on her lap. '"Churches warn against youth sect,"' she read. '"The chairman of the ecumenical council ... Blah blah blah. Here. These young people have found their own leader in the person of a certain Zeno, whom they regard as a twentieth-century prophet."'

'Prophet?' I said.

'"The group meets once a week in an abandoned shed in the waterfront area. Police have received complaints about noise and disorderly conduct."'

'Disorderly conduct.' I couldn't imagine Zeno doing anything excessive.

Sophie ran her finger down the column. 'And here. "These illegal gatherings are extremely popular among the youth. The group, at present, comprises nearly fifty members."'

'Jesus.'

'Yes, I thought of that too,' said Sophie.

I got up and started opening the bottle of wine that was standing on the mantelpiece. 'Twentieth-century prophet ...' I brought Sophie a glass. She began to drink, her eyes still on the newspaper. 'Oh,' she said, after two sips, 'this is wine. Since when do you keep alcohol in your room?'

I sat down in my chair and raised my glass to her. 'Since you said I might as well have my own crockery up here, since I never sit downstairs anyway.'

She looked at me blankly and then returned to her newspaper. 'There's even a picture of him. I wonder where they got it.'

I held out my hand and took the paper from her.

It was a fairly large photograph, in fact. It had been taken here, at home. Zeno was standing in the library, hands folded over his crotch, staring gloomily into the lens. He was wearing the black suit I always wore when I had to sing in public. He looked like the chairman of the Young Undertakers Association.

I shot up from my chair and roared out his name. Then I ran out into the hallway and saw him standing there. He looked as if the house were on fire.

'Sonofabitch!' I shoved the newspaper in his face. 'Who said you could borrow my suit?'

He shrank back, frightened. His face was pale. The copper-coloured hair stood out sharply against the white skin. His eyes were a dull green and darted fearfully back and forth. 'Sorry,' he said.

'That suit is my life! I earn my living in that fucking suit. Were you planning to pay the dry cleaner's if it got dirty? Next time you ask my permission!' I flung down the paper and turned round.

Back in my room I suddenly realized that I had forgotten the most important thing of all. I ran back into the hallway and found Zeno in exactly the same position in which I had left him.

'And what's all this about a twentieth-century prophet? Why do you have to go and do things behind our backs? And what the hell are you telling those people? Why all this damn secrecy? And did Sophie really have to read in the paper that you've become the Messiah? Couldn't you at least have done a little bread-and-wine stuff at home first?'

We were standing face to face, he with his back against the wall, me in front of him, nearly bending over him. There was a silence. Then I felt myself weakening. 'Sorry,' I said. 'I . . . I'm sorry. I shouldn't have got so worked up.'

'No.' He pulled himself away from the wall. 'I should've ... I should've told you.'

We looked at each other. It didn't last long, that exchange of glances, but in those two, three seconds it dawned on me, for the first time, that we had lost him, that, for a long time now, Zeno had been somewhere else. We were still his, but he was no longer ours. Zeno was in another world and it wasn't the world we knew.

A few days later the other newspapers followed suit. Then came the weekly magazines with their in-depth cover stories. Because Zeno refused to talk to anyone, the stories grew increasingly wilder. Within two months, the silent prophet, as he was soon being called, had become a figure of mythical proportions. Letters arrived, mostly from young people, telephone calls from various organizations asking him to speak on Today's Youth, Religion, Political Commitment, and Western Democracy in Our Time. One of the leading academic journals published an article in which an attempt was made to unravel 'The Zeno Hollander Phenomenon'. Our entire family history was explored. The flight to America, my father's mattress invention, my mother's paintings and Uncle Herman's success. All of us, with the exception of Zeno, read it with our mouths open. We were like a family out of a fairy tale. It didn't surprise me, as I read, that this bizarre family had brought forth a Messiah.

The uproar, because that was what it was by now, went on for almost three weeks. Then the police headed for the docks to clear out the shed. They met with a silent crowd that wouldn't give way. Several policemen began pulling people out, but stopped when they neither moved nor spoke. In the country's most popular tabloid, a senior police officer described the atmosphere in the shed as 'terrifying.' It was the silence, he explained. Scared the living daylights out of him and his men. They had faced obstinate crowds before, during football matches and carnivals, but never had the cops seen so many people gathered together in such a silent, motionless, monolith of gloom. It was because of this report that, a week later, I attended one of Zeno's meetings.

What the papers were calling a 'shed' turned out to be an abandoned warehouse with scarred, blackened walls. Two half-open doors, shreds of green paint hanging from them like autumn leaves, formed the entrance. By the time I arrived there were at least two hundred people waiting outside the building. Inside, as I was to see later, several hundred more were seated on the catwalks, loading platforms and floor. We had to wait about half an hour before we were allowed in. The crowd at the entrance was like a collection of zombies. I lit a cigarette and suddenly felt the air around me grow heavier. Four, five, and then fifteen, twenty people turned their heads in my direction. They said nothing. I blew out a puff of smoke and ran my eyes over the staring bystanders, and as I did, I noticed that a space had formed around me. No one had spoken, no signal had been given, yet they had all reacted to my transgression. We slowly moved forward, the crowd, the emptiness around me, and I. Deep down inside me, something stirred. Resistance, aversion, contempt, even a touch of fear.

When everyone was finally inside – I was standing somewhere at the back – the air was thick with silence. Now and then I heard shuffling, or a muffled cough, but apart from that, not a sound. The doors closed, a deep dusk settled above our heads. The waiting began.

For five minutes nothing happened. Ten minutes. Then, all the way at the front, where a loading platform ran diagonally upwards to a double door in the wall, two men appeared. The crowd stirred, but no one spoke. The men each grabbed one side of the door, pulled, and in the sudden glare of a floodlight, I saw Zeno's delicate frame.

I began nodding, in spite of myself. A damn good prophet of doom, I thought. A damn good prophet of doom, Mr Tony.

The doors clattered shut, the room was cloaked in darkness. I heard a woman's voice, a deep, almost sensual moan that was immediately smothered by a hand.

Much later that night – I was sitting on a waterworn, reddish-brown iron bollard, staring at the rising and falling embankment – I spoke with Zeno. Night had fallen. The sky hung violet above the city and the Maas flowed slowly, black and wide, to the sea.

'Just because it's not for you doesn't make it meaningless.'

I didn't turn around. I knew it was him. I drew on my cigarette, tipped back my head, and watched the smoke melt into the darkness. 'Who says it's not for me? I'm a follower.'

Zeno didn't react.

In the bend of the river, way off to the right, the sidelights of a barge flickered. I followed the tiny dots of light as they crept slowly over the dark water.

'It's not a good time to be the Messiah,' I said. '1965. Why don't you wait till 2000?' I threw down my cigarette and waited for the hissing of ash, but heard nothing. 'I was reminded, this evening, of your brief career as a variety show artist.'

There were footsteps behind us. I looked round, without letting my gaze rest on Zeno. Under one of the sodium lights along the kerb, Zelda appeared. The orange light fell straight down on her from above and she looked like a peculiar cross between a Cecil B. De Mille extra and my mother. She was wearing a wide black dress that couldn't conceal her ample bosom. Her dark, wavy hair was tied back in a ponytail.

When she was standing next to us, our eyes met. 'Sister Zelda,' I said after a while. Zelda didn't answer. I stood up and looked from one to the other. 'What are you doing here?' I finally asked. 'Do you wash his feet?'

'N,' said Zeno. He laid a hand on my arm.

'N?' I said. 'Shouldn't you say "brother"? Or better still, shouldn't you not say anything?'

Zeno looked unhappy. He chewed on the inside of his cheek. His eyes shot back and forth.

'Did you come here to play the cynical intellectual?' asked Zelda.

I put my hands in my pockets and sighed. 'Everyone's got their own role to play this evening. You're the prophet's handmaid, he's the seer, and I'm the churlish pleb.'

Zelda's dress fluttered gently in the breeze. She and I were nearly the same age, thirty-two and thirty, and it was clear to everyone that I blamed her for encouraging our twenty-year-old brother in his madness.

'Those people,' said Zelda, 'are searching for truth. The world isn't what it used to be. Other people smoke hash or drink and sit in jazz clubs. Or pretend to be rebels. The Churches won't accept them. Politicians don't listen. Everyone's scared of the future. Of an atomic war. Of a world divided into East and West.'

'So what do you give them? Hope? Truth?'

Zelda nodded.

'Do you know what that is, sister? Truth? Do you have any idea how complicated that is?'

She looked at me impassively.

'I don't do them any harm. I just help them think about things they've suspected all along,' said my brother.

The dark fifties were behind us. The Eastern bloc was almost completely closed off and the areas that weren't occupied by the Russians lay in the shadow of their power. Hungary had been crushed. The Suez crisis was still fresh in our minds. Holland had lost her colonies in a war they called a 'police action'. Society was choked with views and norms that stemmed from before the Second World War and the young people who had fought in that war or were born shortly afterwards, felt, after the first flush of liberation, threatened and small. Affluence had come to our part of the world, the fleshpots were filled, there was work and food for everyone, but the Establishment clung to its power. Europe was a dangerously boiling pot. Only the heavy lid of a long outdated culture of neckties, law and order, respectability and diligence and sleeping with your hands on top of the covers, could keep whatever was in that pot from boiling over.

As far as that was concerned, Zelda was right: young people were searching for new ways, new roads, new forms. But Zeno's remark, that he offered them insight, was a lie. He merely guided their uncertainty and discontent towards the path of discipledom. I had seen it that evening, the silent crowd, the open mouths when he stood on the loading platform and let the words fall from his lips like stones. I had heard him quoting the apocalyptic prophets, but in such a way that almost no one could tell.

'And the world shall be turned into the old silence, like as in the former judgements.'

Those were his first words, that night. I had recognized them. They were from the Fourth Book of Ezra, a pseudo-epigraphic text that had been written around the year one hundred and was a curious combination of early Christian and Jewish themes.

I had recognized not only the texts, but also the minute alterations that Zeno had made. His opening line was much more Messianical in the original: 'For my son Jesus shall be revealed with those that be with him, and they that remain shall rejoice within four hundred years. After these years shall my son Christ die, and all men that have life. And the world shall be turned into the old silence seven days, like as in the former judgements: so that no man shall remain. And after seven days the world, that yet awaketh not, shall be raised up, and that shall die that is corrupt. And the earth shall restore those that are asleep in her, and so shall the dust those that dwell in silence, and the secret places shall deliver those souls that were committed unto them. And the most High shall appear upon the seat of judgement, and misery shall pass away, and the long suffering shall have an end.'

'Zeno,' I said, 'all you've done is gobble up the library and spit it back out in easily digestible pieces.'

'And what have *you* done with that library?' asked Zelda. She reached behind her head and began untying the ribbon in her hair. 'Fairy tales.'

'Zel, fairy tales may be insignificant, perhaps you even think I'm exploiting all those splendid old sources to make silly children's stories, but at least my fairy tales won't poison anyone.'

Zeno had a wounded look in his eyes.

'A fairy tale,' I said. I took the cigarettes out of my pocket and lit one. 'Once upon a time there was a clever lad who went to work for a mighty sorcerer, and one day . . .'

'The Sorcerer's Apprentice,' said Zelda. She shook out her hair and looked around defiantly. 'Who's to say you're not the sorcerer's apprentice?'

'And who might the sorcerer be?'

'Think about it.' She laid her hand on Zeno's shoulder.' I saw the nearly imperceptible squeeze she gave him. 'Coming?'

Zeno looked at me almost pleadingly. What's wrong? I thought. Why are you looking at me like that? Are you asking . . . for my blessing?

They walked away from the water's edge, under the cone of sodium light, Zelda's hand still on Zeno's shoulder. My little brother, I thought. Next to our older sister he looked frail, almost childlike.

Now, all these years later, I look back at this with the same astonished, exasperated curiosity as then. And I know, too, how carefully Zeno had thought it all out. His job with Mr Tony. His collector's mania. And what he collected. His mysterious relationship with Zelda, who seemed to believe she was guiding him, the wise, older sister, while all the time he was using her as his mouth and eyes and ears. Even, I bow my head, his conversations with me. I was his gauge. He tried out his ideas on me, knowing I would probably reject them. Only then could he find out how far and how fast he could go.

In the years that followed those first gatherings in the shed, Zeno became the focus of a cult. In the late sixties, Zeno clubs were formed, several of which became fashionable when their members, in addition to their dubious philosophy, were discovered to be using free sex and LSD as a means of achieving 'depth.' Zeno could no longer go out unescorted. There were always a couple of bony teenage girls waiting for him under the chestnut trees across the street, and if it wasn't his fans, he was followed around by a photographer from one of the tabloids. Anything and everything that was left-wing and progressive embraced him. The Right, and especially the right-wing press, pounced on every indiscretion, hungry for the chance to depict 'Zenoism' as a pernicious mixture of forbidden sex, forbidden drugs and crackpot ideas. A radical change was yet to come, but in Zeno's followers the madness that, in later years, would reach completion, was already manifest, that dangerous combination of sixties optimism, a passion for mysticism and blind faith in one's own morality.

Zoe took her brother's instant fame the way she took her whole life. She saw what was happening, said 'Ha!' and then went on with things she found more interesting. Sophie spent more time than ever shut up in her studio. She had stopped exhibiting, because everyone had started calling her 'Zeno's mother'. But Zelda was all his. She took care of his correspondence, answered his private phone, and was his watchdog. And if she hadn't thought herself unworthy, she would have written every single article about him, too.

Zeno himself grew more uncommunicative than ever. He hardly came out of his room anymore, and when he did, he avoided not only the fans on the street and around the neighbourhood, but his own family as well. In those years there was only one moment of peace. At least, that's how I remember it. That was when Zeno and I went to Switzerland. Sophie had written to Emmanuel and coaxed him into giving her a few thousand dollars to send us on holiday. This was about three years after it all began. Sophie hoped that I 'could break that boy out of the prison of silence he had built around himself.' She chose her words with careful precision, but I just shrugged. Only later did I understand how acutely my mother had seen the danger Zeno was in. Her only mistake was in sending me. I was no longer capable of seeing Zeno as a brother. I regarded him with the shocked amazement of a bystander who sees someone drowning. Something inside me told me that I should jump in and save him, but somehow my body couldn't manage to put one foot in front of the other, the other foot in front of the first, and dive in.

We were walking up a mountain path, a flowering elm on one side and the deep drop of a ravine on the other, when Zeno, for the first time since our arrival, began to speak of his own accord. He asked me if I could remember his 'fall.' It was a while before I realized that he was referring to his brief illness.

'The Second Law of Thermodynamics,' he said. 'I was shocked by the Second Law of Thermodynamics. Do you know what the Second Law is?'

Above the mountaintops, in a blue sky stretched so taut that it wouldn't have surprised me, that day, if I had heard a bang and the heavens above us split in two; above the mountains hung a sun of glass. I remember thinking of *The Magic Mountain*, the book Uncle Herman had once given me, noting that it would have been quite good with half as many pages.

'The Second Law of Thermodynamics,' Zeno lectured, 'says that in a closed system, order changes to maximum disorder, from a dynamic to a static state, and that this maximum disorder is irreversible. You can only restore the state of order if you add at least as much energy as was used during the transition from order to disorder. And that isn't possible within a closed system. The universe is a closed system, one which evidently began as a system with order, otherwise it wouldn't be dynamic now, from which you can conclude that the universe isn't eternal, it has a beginning. The end is disorder, heat, death. The universe will have drowned in its own entropy.'

I looked at a cluster of caramel-coloured cows staring dopily at the grass, and as we walked on, further up the mountain, Zeno on the left, me on the right, I felt like one of those cows.

'I'd read about that in some newspaper or magazine, I don't remember which,' said Zeno. 'Anyway, I was thinking about it that afternoon. It was probably just the religious crisis that every child has, only with me, the cause was slightly more exotic.'

'Religious crisis,' I said.

'I was ten, I didn't believe in *Sinterklaas* anymore, or in happiness, but doesn't every child of ten believe, at the very least, that all this will last forever?' He made a vague gesture with his left arm.

'The world,' I said (and I thought: Happiness? He's stopped believing in happiness?).

'The world,' said Zeno. 'That's what shocked me. The world and the irreversibility of the world. When it's gone, it's gone. What's happened has happened. No hope of restoration. I was sitting at the table and I saw myself. I was sitting on a chair, in a room, and I saw the room below me, the room above, the house on the left and the house on the right. And the image started growing, expanding. I saw the neighbourhood where we lived, all the houses, all the rooms and hallways and staircases. And I saw the people in those houses. It was like a film, the camera pulling farther and farther away, only instead of the image getting fuzzier and less detailed, it grew clearer and clearer. The road in front of the house. The intersection. The shops. The whole neighbourhood. I saw the city and I saw myself in that city, at the table, on a chair, with my glass of milk, and the biscuits. Finally I saw the earth spinning through space and all the people living there and hunger and death, people walking their dogs, people sleeping, the moon suspended from the earth, the planets floating through the blackness of the universe. I thought: This is all going to end and there's nothing to be done about it. That's when I fell.'

I, accustomed as I was to Zeno's tendency to turn a thought into a story, had looked at him sideways. It didn't seem possible, a boy of ten who had attained a degree of transcendence that would take the average Hindu five reincarnations. I put it down to a very early, and very sudden, puberty.

'In the end,' he said, as we plodded along, in a world so still and empty and peaceful that for a moment I thought this bit of Switzerland had been placed under a bell-jar to test out the theory of entropy, 'in the end, I think it was an overwhelming sense of regret that made me fall off my chair. I regretted my powerlessness, the loss of everything and the complete inability to do anything about it.

'Regret,' said Zeno, 'is, as you know, the most destructive human emotion. You only feel regret when it's too late. If something can be restored, it's not a question of regret. Remorse, perhaps, or guilt. But regret, what I mean by regret, is mourning for the irreversibility of things.'

I was in my early thirties, when we walked along that mountain path playing Castorp and Settembrini, and I had just got used to a society that revolved around guilt and lust. Regret? For a world that would disappear millions of years after I was gone? Regret for things that couldn't possibly be undone?

I began talking about Epictetus and Marcus Aurelius, the Stoics, men whose ideas were perfectly in keeping with how I felt at the time. 'No use crying over spilt milk,' I said.

Zeno swung off his backpack and dropped it in the grass alongside the path. He looked at the sun, squinted, and sat down. With his face to the light, his eyes narrowed, he answered me.

'Fine,' he said. 'If we're talking about milk: fine. But what about the things that are worth more to us than milk? A human life, for example. Imagine you're guilty of someone's death, or many someones?'

I said I was a pacifist, so his example could hardly apply to me.

He turned his face away from the sun and looked at me sharply. 'Nathan,' he said, 'even the best intentions, even the most noble deed, even a good person, can be guilty of the death or suffering of another.'

'Bad luck,' I said, 'then we're talking about bad luck. What can I possibly do about that?'

'Nothing. Nothing. But the regret is there and it won't disappear. And the rest of your life is driven by that regret.'

He spoke so severely that I said nothing. I looked down into the valley and wondered how he, young and inexperienced as he was, could have such clear views on regret.

I remembered only when we had got back that I had been the one who had explained the concept of entropy to him. So why had he made such a point of explaining it to me up there on the mountain, almost as if he regarded the Second Law of Thermodynamics as the key to his soul? Was I overlooking something?

At the end of 1968, a month after our holiday in Switzerland, Zeno disappeared. A few days later the newspapers reported that in a forest in North Holland the bodies had been found of three young people who had taken their own lives. They had been missing for a month or two. A note was pinned to the chest of one of the bodies. 'We have found eternal silence,' it said.

Lacrima Christi

NINA READ AND I tended the hearth and perused the collection of books around us. I walked back and forth between the walls of books and the chair, ran my finger down the pages, leafed through the brittle old volumes, scribbled a note here and there in the margins. I didn't notice that Nina had left the room until she came back in. She was carrying a tray with a steaming teapot and a plate of biscuits.

'Hungry?'

She put the tray on the floor between us and began pouring tea. 'Found them in the cellar. A huge tin. McVitie's digestives. Sound familiar?'

'God, yes. McVitie's . . . I'm Christopher Robin!'

She handed me a cup and sat down.

'In the cellar, you said?'

She nodded.

'You went down to the cellar all by yourself?'

'Just like I did yesterday. I threw some more wood in the stove, too. You're not going to tell me it's dangerous, are you?'

'No, but it doesn't cease to amaze me.'

'You certainly don't give me much credit.'

'Don't I?'

She brought the teacup to her lips and sipped. When she had put it down again she looked at me sternly. 'Listen, Mr Hollander, I'm not the helpless type, I don't need some manly chest to bury my face in every time there's trouble. Just because I ran away yesterday doesn't mean I was scared. I just wanted to get out of here.'

'Forgive me.'

She nodded. 'Though I must admit, that cellar isn't the most cheerful place I've ever seen.' She picked up the pile of paper again.

'Are you up to Zeno yet?'

'No, not yet.' Her face was set hard. She drank her tea, put the pile on her lap, and was soon lost in the text.

We sat like that for the rest of the afternoon, she, with the manuscript, and the part that would affect her most, me, strolling back and forth between the books and the chair. We had been sitting there for nearly four hours, when Nina put the manuscript aside. 'That's that,' she said. 'And I don't want to talk about it.'

'He's your father, Nina.'

'Exactly. What are you doing?'

It was a while before the question sank in. I bit at the air once or twice, then shrugged my shoulders and began explaining.

'Are you saying that this library is so special that you'd have to travel all over the world to find these same books?'

'Yes, and then you'd probably never find everything in one place, the way it is here.'

She thought about this. 'So Uncle Herman knew what he was doing when he left you the house.'

'Uncle Herman always knew exactly what he was doing. Uncle Herman thought I had a lot to learn.'

'And did you? Have a lot to learn?'

'What do you think?'

Nina got up. She stood with her back to the fire, tilted her head to one side, and looked at me. 'What's the purpose of this library, of this house, of . . .'

'Of life?'

She ignored that.

'Whatever you think of this family, always remember: we're clockmakers.'

Nina looked away and sighed.

'God, I've become so much like my father and Uncle Herman.' Nina gave me half a glance, from under an almost imperceptibly raised eyebrow. 'Whenever you asked Uncle Herman or my father anything, they always began their answer at the beginning. Genesis, our family is obsessed by the origin of things. Everything has to be told in the form of a creation myth.'

'If that's what your father and Uncle Herman were like, you're just like your father and Uncle Herman.'

'Nina,' I said, 'the point of such a remark is that you're supposed to say it's not as bad as all that.'

She knelt down in front of the fire and threw on more wood.

'Are you cold?'

'A bit.' She got to her feet and looked at the fire. It had collapsed under the new supply of fuel, but hungry tongues were already licking at the sides of the chair legs and cracked boards. 'Why did you say we had enough to heat up the bedroom as well?'

'We've brought down a lot from upstairs, and there's more where that came from.'

She stood before me, hands behind her back, and observed me pensively. 'But not enough.'

'There's a whole glacier of chairs behind the attic door, and if the worst comes to the worst we can always burn the bed.' I grinned when I said that, but I knew she wouldn't grin back.

She went back to her chair and slowly sat down. 'One day. I think we've got enough left for one more day.'

I was silent.

'Why did you say before that we had enough?'

'Because,' I straightened up slightly so I could reach the cigarettes in my jacket pocket, 'because we've always got the library.' I took out the cigarettes, handed one to her, put one in my mouth, and gave us both a light.

Nina shook her head, very gently. I knew she had been expecting my answer. 'You said less than an hour ago that it was a unique collection.'

'Life is more unique than books.'

She said nothing. The fire in the hearth bloomed like a noisy flower. It was noticeably warmer.

'Are these books you and Uncle Herman bought together?'

'Some of them. Zeno collected most of them. He was a great authority on old books.'

'How did he know what should be part of the collection?'

I laughed a laugh that even I myself couldn't describe – a touch of pride (in my brilliant little brother, eccentric professor and false Messiah) and a touch of shame (because, in our eagerness, Uncle Herman and I had made list after list and rubbed our hands with glee each time Zeno came home with another box of old tomes).

'He had quite an impressive library of his own. He was thinking of selling it, but turned it over to Uncle Herman instead. From then on Herman and I were always looking for possible additions to the collection and we let Zeno track them down. That is, until he had more important things to do.'

'So what was the purpose of this library?'

I laid my head on the back of the chair and looked up at the ceiling, the ornamental grapevines, worm-eaten apples and laurel branches, half-visible in the dim light. 'For Zeno? A sort of exorcism, I think. An attempt to reach a state of silence, one that couldn't be affected by entropy. Besides that, he was probably just searching, like all bibliomaniacs, for the book.'

The fire crackled. The dry wood from the chairs and the piano cracked and snapped so loudly, it was as if someone were beating the flames with a whip.

'What book?'

'*The* book.'

She waited.

But what for? What could I possibly tell her about the ultimate book? What could I say to her about books that had changed, not the world, but people? Franny Glass, after reading *The Way of a Pilgrim*. Mr O. and the *Bhagavad Gita*. Danny Saunders and Freud's case histories. Uncle Herman and Tolstoy's *Family Happiness*.

'It's a kind of myth, Nina. Many, many people believe there's such a thing as The Book. The book of *Sinterklaas*. The first version of Genesis. An undiscovered text by Aristotle.'

'Without even knowing if it exists?'

'Sometimes. There are certain texts of whose existence we're quite certain. There must have been an original version of Genesis. It would tell us a great deal, if we ever got our hands on it.'

'So what book was Zeno looking for?' asked Nina.

'We don't know.'

'We?'

'I. Uncle Herman didn't either. But we could guess, based on the collection.'

I got up from my chair, joints like splintering wood, clothes of lead, and turned my back to the fire. 'Perhaps it wasn't even a very exceptional book. No one knows for certain. We do have a vague idea what it was about, though.' The heat from the flames reached my skin and began slowly penetrating into my bones. 'It's the same with books as with people: you know a person partly through his friends, through his surroundings. Haven't you ever been inspired to read a particular book because you've read about it in another book?'

'Nope.'

'Oh.'

'I don't read.'

'Everyone reads, child. Certainly you, you're my agent.'

She looked at me haughtily. 'I sell books.'

'Which means you read. What do you think you were just doing?'

She shook her head and grabbed a candelabra from one of the tables.

'We've got to make dinner,' I said.

'*I've* got to make dinner. If you insist on treating me as your under-age niece, I'm going to punish you with my cooking.'

'No! No! Anything but that!'

She gave a malicious laugh and headed for the door.

'Can I help?'

Nina glanced over her shoulder as she pushed down the door handle. 'Not with the cooking. Not with anything else, either, come to think of it. Stay right where you are.'

'I think I'll go along with you to the kitchen, if you don't mind.'

I was standing next to her, in the doorway, when she looked at me with a smile. 'Scared?' she asked.

At first I didn't know what she meant. 'Terribly. I don't want to sleep all alone in that big dark bed tonight.'

We walked through the oily darkness of the hallway. 'Shame on you,' said Nina. 'Dirty old man.'

'It's the cold,' I said. 'It's affected my manners.'

'Then come and sit down next to that nice warm stove.'

In the kitchen, she quickly began getting things ready. Then she picked up the candelabra and disappeared into the cellar. I slid more wood into the belly of the Aga and sat down on a chair. I closed my eyes, listened to the sounds Nina made when she had returned and began slicing, peeling, and stirring. The warmth of the stove glided over me like a blanket.

I haven't had a house of my own since the early sixties, but I've always returned to this Mountain, hill, in the east of Holland, and each time I see the pine trees rising and, after the long journey down winding woodland paths, arrive at the house, it's as if I have finally come home.

Here, in this spot, is where I grew up. I know exactly when I was here, whether the sun was shining, how long it rained, who came, and who stayed away, that Zeno bumped his head against the Victorian revolving bookcase in the library, how the blood ran down his face and what Sophie said. This was where I came alive. When I wasn't here, I went from hotel to hotel, from spare bed to spare bed. I had a room in Manhattan, in the apartment my father shared with Uncle Herman, a monk's cell at the house of an old girlfriend, a sofa at Zoe's. I did actually live somewhere once, but that was long ago.

Home. House.

Five years since I was last here. Circled down like a stealthy buzzard. Alone. A weary traveller with nothing but his bag, a book, a newspaper from the country he has just left, the red of the evening sky before him, the dull blue of the late winter afternoon behind him, and below him, the lead-grey sea. The narrow strip of beach, the narrow strip of dunes, the orange glow of the greenhouse roofs, the toy-town landscape of Holland.

It was cold, that day, and I was tired, the way people are tired after a long trip: too little sleep, your mind both here, in your body, and there, somewhere else, it doesn't matter where. Around me, the silent company of men in white shirts, Business Class, the *Financial Times* or *Newsweek* or an airport thriller on their lap, head against the papery headrest, mouth open slightly. Outside, under the wing lights, where the clouds grew thin, so thin that the giant Dutch scale-model glimmered through, I could see the tiny houses with their tiny gardens, the straight grey stripes of road, the floodlit well of a soccer field, wisps of white steam above chimneys. And I felt myself slipping into the comfortable coat of my native land. Half my life I had spent in other countries: I had left, as a child, with my parents and Uncle Herman, for America, returned and gone to secondary school here and then travelled the world like a man who was searching for something but didn't know what or where, yet despite all that travelling and roaming – I knew it the moment the asphalt spaghetti around Amsterdam came into view – despite all that, I was a Dutchman. Not a feeling of national pride, the Golden Age simply a curious fact in the history books, not the faintest notion of national grandeur. Cheese, order, care, coffee, sturdy dykes, hesitant forests, straight canals, square meadows, potato fields under the summer sun, slopes they called hills, hills called mountains, long rows of yellow brick houses on long red brick streets and rectangular gardens with pruned conifers.

Sunset swept over this land, while down below, toy cars went shooting along the motorways, the runway lights of Schiphol lay in the fields like a fallen Christmas tree. I thought: This is where I want to die.

It was the exhaustion. Ten minutes in a taxi, behind a humourless grouch of a driver, were enough to sober me up.

In the train, I watched the colours draining from the landscape. A dense, wintry twilight spread across the vast Dutch sky and it was as if that grey haze were settling inside me, too. Mists rose from the fields and hung low above the grass, hiding a cow here, a fence there. It grew darker and darker. I didn't wake up until the train pulled in at Rotterdam.

It was going on for seven when I met Herman in the lobby of his hotel. Each of us always knew when the other was in our home town, and the standing arrangement was that I first meet him for dinner at his hotel and then go on to mine. Herman was sitting in a big leather chair when I came in, reading. His dark brown eyes, fixed on a copy of the *New York Times*, glittered in their sockets like jet, the too-long, white hair stood out on all sides.

'Nathan,' he said, when I tapped him on the shoulder. He got to his feet and embraced me so firmly that I dropped my bags.

'Nuncle,' I said. 'How are you?'

Herman tilted his head slightly and looked at me in a way that he himself would probably have described as 'roguish,' but which looked more to me like the expression of a blackbird disturbed while pulling up a worm.

We sat down at the table and, to my surprise, he ordered an appetizer of champagne and smoked salmon. When I asked him what the reason might be for this little splurge, he said that he was getting to the age when every encounter might be his last. He had resolved to devote more time to his family.

'The last time you tried that, you had a fight with Sophie.'

'I remember.' He raised his right hand and bowed his head. I took the champagne out of the ice bucket and filled our glasses. 'But this time I'm not talking about meddling, it's too late for that anyway,' he said. 'I've spent three-quarters of my life roaming the earth, I've got to know people I didn't want to know, I've seen places and things I didn't need to see. Now I'd like to spend more time on you, for a change.'

'Herman,' I said, 'you sound like a father who feels guilty because he was always working. You're my uncle. You're under no obligation whatsoever.'

Uncle Herman choked on his champagne and coughed, loud and long. 'Damn bubbles,' he said, when he was able to speak again.

'The drink of the ruling class,' I said.

'Sometimes, Nathan, I wonder whether you ever take me seriously.'

We smiled at each other.

'But I know what you mean,' I said. 'It's the weather. The plane was landing, and I suddenly thought: This is where I want to die. It's these melancholy Dutch winters.'

Herman turned the stem of his champagne glass between his fingers and stared over my shoulder into space. 'Birds of passage, but then in reverse. We come home in the winter and suddenly feel what it is to have a house and what Holland means to us.'

'We had to get this old to find that out?'

The waiter came and cleared away our plates. He asked Herman if he might recommend a Cahors with the leg of lamb. Herman nodded absently. 'Yes, I think we did have to get this old before we could understand. We're all nomads, Nathan, from the day we're born.'

'We, the family?'

'We, the entire country. I've only just realized that all my theories about urban society are derived from my perception of Holland as a city state. A country too small for strong nationalistic feelings. A country that has to send its people abroad to seek work and earn money. Banking began in the Italian city states, then came the German merchant cities, and finally the Dutch took up the idea. Dutch investors, insurance companies, for instance, are the biggest foreign investors in America today. They simply can't get rid of their money here in the Netherlands. In a certain sense this country hasn't changed since the days of the Dutch East India Company. We send out ships to do trade, because we can't earn enough within our own borders. It's not a country. It's a city state.'

'A harbour,' I said.

'Yes.'

The plates arrived and dishes of potatoes and vegetables were set down. Herman tasted the wine, thought for a moment, then smiled at the waiter. 'Good choice, Johan. This lamb did not die in vain.'

As we ate, Herman remained pensive. 'A harbour,' he said after a while. 'You're right. It's a delta, Holland. Not much more than a delta, with a bit of surrounding land. And we've used that delta to the best possible advantage. We turned it into one big harbour, and when the age of aviation dawned, we expanded the harbour by adding a top-notch airport.'

'You ought to write about this place,' I said.

Herman straightened up and looked at me, his left eyebrow slightly raised, the barest trace of a smile on his lips. 'Perhaps I'll just leave that to you.'

I took a sip of my Cahors, a full-bodied, deep red wine that made my insides glow. I shook my head. 'I've never lived here long enough to have a clear view of the country. I'm even more of a nomad than you are.' As I put down my glass, it occurred to me that I actually meant something else. 'The only place I could ever truly write about is the house. It's what I know best. For me, the house *is* Holland.'

'Fine,' said Herman. 'Sounds fine to me. And Israel?'

I was dumbfounded. 'What do you mean, "And Israel?"'

'A country in the Middle East.'

'What, you think I'm supposed to be longing for *Eretz HaKodesh* in my old age?'

He shook his head in annoyance.

I had been there as his secretary, sometime in the mid-sixties, between two wars, when he was sent there by the UN to do research on what was already being called 'the situation.' He spoke with ministers, army commanders, left and right-wing politicians, union leaders and professors. And I sat beside him, with my memo pad, pretending to take notes and wishing I were somewhere else. One evening we were having dinner in an outdoor cafe on Ha'atzmaut Square in Netanya. We were drinking beer and dissecting an animal that, according to the waiter, was called Saint Peter's Fish. When, after a thin layer of dry white flesh, I ended up at the bone, I pushed away my plate and swore.

'Nathan,' Uncle Herman had said, 'am I right in thinking you're not having a very good time?'

I smiled wrily.

'What's wrong?'

I ordered coffee and stared at the little square across the road, where the hope of the nation was folkdancing. 'It's not my country.

They have no cheese, no decent coffee, not one slice of wholewheat bread, and they serve cucumbers and red peppers for breakfast, for heaven's sake.'

'Gastronomically speaking it may be a bit, shall we say, simple, but that's not the point.'

'That *is* the point. Everything here is geared towards grand and heroic survival in a hostile world. It's completely unrealistic. That century-long accumulation of superstition in Jerusalem, all those damn trees they keep planting, all those men walking around day and night with uzis over their shoulder. Believe me, I can do without it.'

'You don't think it's necessary to plant trees and walk around with an uzi over your shoulder?'

The coffee arrived. I stared into the gloomy black liquid and dropped in a lump of sugar. 'A necessary evil is still evil. I'm starting to get the idea that symbols are more important in this country than life itself.'

Herman had taken a cigar out of his inside pocket and was carefully lighting it.

'Be honest, Herman. Be the critical atheist you were on the boat to America. And before that. And afterwards. We're talking about a pile of stones called the Wailing Wall. We're talking about an empty cellar they call David's Tomb. And a hole in the ground called the Holy Sepulchre. Around here, it's things that are holy.'

'And you think they're not.'

'A city, Jerusalem, or a wall, even the tomb of the greatest king, isn't holy. You know that. In Judaism things have no special meaning, nor can one person be holier than another. Everyone has just as much access to God, or holiness, or whatever you choose to call it, as anyone else. But here in Israel, they defend inanimate objects, while humanity goes down the drain.'

We had disagreed before, Herman and I, but on other issues. Now he exploded like a bomb in slow-motion: I was a spectator, someone who was quick to criticize, but remained safely on the sidelines. I was totally egocentric, indifferent to the welfare and norms of others, yet fascinated by my own short-sighted, solipsistic views.

I listened to Herman's unexpected outburst, the torrent of pent-up impatience, unspoken accusations and disappointments that he now, after so many years, let fly.

'Don't you feel anything for this country, for God's sake?' he shouted. 'Aren't you the least bit proud?'

'Proud?'

'Yes, proud. Of what we've accomplished here. Look around you!'

'The Jewish deltaworks,' I said.

Herman had opened his mouth, as if to say 'yes,' but nothing came out. Then he shook his head.

'You,' I had added, 'talk about pride and necessity and "the situation" and that everything will get better soon, but now try contradicting yourself. You taught me to do that. Since we've been here all we've seen are government agencies and officials. Where's the man in the street? Where's the terrorist?'

'I take it I'm supposed to be impressed to hear you describe them as terrorists?'

'We,' I said, 'were terrorists, too. We blew up the King David.' He sniffed.

'Herman,' and at that moment, there in that cafe, I had realized that I sounded just as desperate and imploring as he had, on that night in 1939, when the rest of the family refused to understand why we had to leave Europe. 'Herman, why do we have more right to this country than they do? Why are they any different from us? And since when did you start believing in a homeland?'

He had jumped to his feet. None of the other guests seemed surprised by Herman's fury. 'Those people,' he said, pointing wildly about him, 'those people are out for our blood. This is the last refuge for the survivors of the camps, and you want to deprive them of it?'

That wasn't what I had said. I was merely trying to find reason in the midst of so much sentiment.

'And what are we talking about anyway?' shouted Herman.

'Palestinians. They're not even a people, they're a group of nomadic Arabs.'

'Well, then. Obviously, they deserve to die.'

'Your grandparents could have been here!'

But they weren't here and that explained a lot. I was tired of being reasonable. I didn't hold my tongue, even though the moment had come to do so. 'They,' I said, 'will say the same about us.'

'What? They've never had to live through a massacre like World War II. They . . .'

'Goddamit!' I'd shouted. 'You act as if they'll never be worth talking to until they've suffered enough. They live here, they lived here and, I can assure you, they're going to keep on living here. You'd better get used to it, Professor Hollander!'

After that he had stormed off and I had drunk my undrinkable coffee, paid the bill, and gone down to the dark beach to watch the sluggish foaming of the night surf.

In spite of that argument, Herman was asking me now, at this very table, what I thought of Israel. Did he expect that what had happened to him would happen to me? That the older I got, the more I would long to be among "my people"? That I wanted to go home and that my home was there?

'I feel no differently about it now than I did twenty-five years ago,' I said.

He slid his wine glass forward and looked at the tablecloth. 'You're going to be all alone. There will come a day when I won't be here anymore. Do you think you don't need anyone?' He looked up. His gaze was sharp, but there was a glimmer in his eyes that hinted at something gentle, almost compassionate. 'Do you think you're the only person in the whole world who doesn't need anyone?'

'Nina's younger. There's a good chance she'll outlive me.'

Herman picked up his glass and drank. 'She's got better things to do in this lifetime. Besides, we don't even know for sure whether she really is family.'

Although he had never treated her that way, quite the contrary, he had always been sceptical about her origins. 'Every one of that boy's half-cracked followers can claim she's the mother of his child,' he had said, when Nina's mother first tried to get in touch. Sophie thought he was wrong. Zeno didn't seem to her the type to have hordes of lady friends. 'But that's not the point,' said Herman. 'For God's sake, woman, don't you know that a missing young man like Zeno is the perfect opportunity for unwed mothers to give their child a father? They were followers! They would have loved to bear the son of the Messiah!' Sophie had replied that she thought it was too crazy for words, all this suspicion, and took both mother and child into the family circle as casually as if she were taking in a lodger.

After dinner Herman and I climbed the four flights to his floor (we were both terrified of elevators) and walked in to the chaotic mess I had expected. Herman slalomed, like a skier with back trouble, past suitcases, chairs, trays with the remains of various meals, and piles of books and newspapers. He always had his post sent on, including the *New York Times*. As soon as he arrived in Holland, an endless stream of books and newspapers began pouring in, all of which were stripped of their bubble-wrap and converted into piles.

'I'm going to the countryside for a few days,' he said, when I looked at the bag of clothes and books standing prominently on the bed.

'The house, you mean.'

'No: The Countryside. You know, forests, plants, meadows, birds? Did it ever occur to you that there are some people who see nature as more than just a fringe around the city?'

'I'm not the one who's always going on about urban society,' I said. 'The sublimation of the human pursuit for organization.'

He grinned.

I had heard him say that once during one of his lectures, in some community centre up North, where twenty elderly members of the Sociological Society sat drinking coffee and eating pound cake in anticipation of what promised, in those circles, to be a colourful evening. After he had given the audience what they came for, he set about re-educating the assembly of old men. He switched over to the social implications of his work and was able to twist it in such a way that Karl Marx would have found in him, Herman, the ideal advocate. On a wave of almost euphoric pre-war socialism, he had given a description of the city as the cultural and technological highpoint of western civilization and socialism as the only feasible ideology within that society. I have always, as far as that goes, suspected him of the same nostalgia as my father. While Emmanuel never stopped believing in the world as a machine that worked better the longer you fiddled with it, Uncle Herman had rendered his pursuit for Paradise, because that was what it was, into a scientific theory of civilization and group dynamics. Once, when we were travelling back in an oven-warm, first-class compartment, I had asked if it wasn't just a bit too much of a good thing, dangling that flashy scientific life in America in front of a bunch of ageing sociologists and then serving up marxism as the pièce de résistance.

'If, politically speaking, you don't know whether you're coming or going, you'd better just keep your mouth shut,' he had said. 'Stick to writing fairy tales.'

I was used to the disparaging view he took of my work.

Herman packed a few shirts in his half-full bag and then sat down on the edge of the bed. I drew up one of the white leather chairs. When we were sitting opposite each other, he shook his head.

'That work of yours, Nathan,' he said, 'how long do you plan on doing it? Haven't you ever stopped to think that there might be more to life than the same old melancholy phrases, year in, year out? Once upon a time . . . Long ago in a far-off land . . . And they lived . . .'

'Herman,' I said, 'what do you care how I organize my life, or don't organize it? Look at your own life. Has the revolution ever come? I sometimes wonder which of us believes most in fairy tales.'

'I've never been a revolutionary,' said Herman. He looked at me intently.

'. . . and socialism has landed half the world in camps,' I said, 'and the other half is capitalist and one half devours the bread of the other . . .'

'You could be a socialist, do you know that?' said Herman.

'Politics is nothing but . . . powerlessness. You've all got a severe case of megalomania. Who the hell can assume he knows what's best for the world?'

'Listen, Nathan,' said Herman. 'That's all very well and good, but the point is, you're throwing away your talent. I'm sure you can still do something other than write the five hundredth variation on Cinderella. You're not that far down the road.'

'Thanks,' I said. 'So what am I supposed to do, in your opinion?'

He got up. 'If I tell you that,' he said, 'nothing will ever come of it.' As he finished packing his bag, he said, 'You don't have to listen to me. I'm not saying that I live an exemplary life. But look at yourself. You go from hotel to guestroom, you've got no wife, you've got no children, you've got work that . . .' He looked at me for a moment. 'How do you want to end up? Alone in a hotel room, in a cheap hotel room?'

We stood there, face to face, in silence.

'Just who are we talking about?' I said after a while. 'You've got no wife or children either, you travel all over the place. If you don't die on a plane, there's a damn good chance it'll be in a hotel. Besides: we're old, both of us. Why are you giving career counselling to someone on the verge of retirement?'

'Maybe I just want to warn you about the loneliness. We're the last two. Soon I'll be gone and then you'll have no one.' Uncle Herman closed his suitcase and looked at me.

'Everyone's alone.'

'Yes,' said Herman. He had sighed deeply. Herman was, that day, the day he was going to die, but we didn't know that yet, even more melancholy than I was. 'Yes.' Then he leaned over his bag and picked it up. I put on my coat.

'How long are you staying?'

'Until after New Year,' I said.

'What are your plans? Are you going up to the house?'

'I don't know yet. I was thinking of taking Nina out to dinner one night. Care to join us?'

'I've arranged to see her at the house. She might even be there already.'

'She might be there already?'

'I gave her a key. She's our only remaining relative, as you just said.'

I grabbed hold of the door handle.

'Nathan? You know why I tell you these things, don't you?'

'You can't stand waste.'

'Yes,' he said. 'That, too.'

Except for the unimaginable things he had said after that (I, at least, can't imagine the conversation that must have taken place in the final hour before his death) those were Uncle Herman's last words: 'That too.'

'Maybe I just want to warn you about the loneliness. We're the last two. Soon I'll be gone and then you'll have no one,' he had said. Not until deep in the night, when I was standing at the window of my hotel room with a glass of whisky in my hand, looking out over the river and the city, did his words come back to me. Could he have sent up for a woman because . . . Was he lonely?

The day on which I, in a surge of wistfulness, had felt more at home than ever before and thought that I wanted to die here, in this land, was the day Herman died under a call girl. Zeno, I said, as I gazed out at the tiny lights, Zeno had been right when he said that our family was like a timetable. Arrival and departure. All that travelling back and forth, that constant from here to there and from the end to the beginning and back again, where had it led? Now only Nina and I were left, and when I was gone, she would be all alone in a world in which none of the Hollanders had ever truly belonged.

I thought of what had happened on the way from Herman's hotel to mine. For the second time I walked that route, only now, I was joined by Uncle Chaim. He had his head drawn down between his shoulders and held both hands under his arms. 'This is going to be a cold, cold winter,' he said.

'Uncle Chaim.'

'Nathan . . .'

'I remember a winter like this in Bialystok,' said Magnus, who had come walking up on the other side.

'Bialystok? You've never been in Bialystok. I was in Bialystok and it was so cold that your breath fell to the ground and broke in a million pieces.'

Magnus shook his head and furrowed his brow. 'But . . . I was . . . I remember . . .' he mumbled. 'Saw a man freeze to death. He felt hot. Started seeing things. When you freeze to death you see things, some people even tear off all their clothes.'

'It's terrible having so many memories,' said Uncle Chaim. 'If you've been walking around as long as we have, everything begins to look like everything else. After a while you start believing you've seen the things you've heard about. Very dangerous.'

'Herman is dead,' I said.

'I know,' said Uncle Chaim.

'We're sorry,' said Magnus, who was still brooding about Bialystok.

'A call girl,' I said in a cloud of steam that flashed red in the glow of a hamburger ad. 'At his age.'

'Yes, that Herman!' said Uncle Chaim.

'It's true,' said Magnus. 'It's true! I've never been in Bialystok.'

A road-cleaning lorry loomed up in the distance. It sniffed, waggling like a stray dog, along the gutter. The tall houses seemed to sway in its flickering orange light.

'He would have appreciated it, dying like that.'

I looked at Uncle Chaim and opened my mouth.

'I've never been in the East at all,' said Magnus. 'I mean: never farther east than . . .'

'Would you once and for all stop that whining about Bialystok, Magnus?'

Magnus mumbled something and looked over his shoulder at a drunken man in evening dress standing in front of a cash dispenser. He was weaving back and forth, back and forth. A black blazer lay across his shoulders like a cape.

'Praying at the Wailing Wall,' I said.

Magnus smiled sadly.

The street ended in a tangled maze of zebra crossings, tram tracks, and bicycle paths. We had reached the river. Across the water stood the hotel, in a pool of yellow artificial light. In front of us, half a bridge was suspended over the Maas. An enormous floating crane lay below it with a slab of roadway in its rigging. Blue welding light sputtered in the darkness and was reflected in the black water.

'Left?' asked Uncle Chaim.

We crossed the street and walked along the wide river to the other bridge, a slow, reddish arch that hung in the glow of its own lights. In the middle of the water was a patrol boat. Its searchlight pierced through the darkness and glided over black ripples. Below us, on the quay, stood fire engines and police cars. An ambulance was trying to wriggle its way through the crowd. A pair of divers were standing up to their waists in the water, guiding a steel cable on a winch. We had nearly gone past, when the headlights of a car emerged from the river. Halfway across the big red bridge I looked back and saw the ambulance scuttling along the quayside like a fat white beetle.

Uncle Chaim, Magnus and I walked across the island in the middle of the river. It grew colder and colder. We crossed the old stone bridge to the opposite bank and turned right, under a walkway, past a huge office building under construction, onto the pier. In front of the empty, rust and grease-stained warehouses lay the quay where ships once waited for the tired, the poor, the huddled masses with their canvas travelling bags and cardboard suitcases. We, too, had set sail from here, Uncle Herman, my parents, my sisters and I. In the old Holland-America Line building, a stone fortress with copper-roofed turrets, there was now a hotel. It stood at the tip of the pier. If you sat at the window in the spacious dining hall, you could look out over the water, to the sea, England and, beyond that, the ocean and America. At the time of the great emigration, there had been a hotel for refugees on this stony protuberance in the Maas, where the price of a glass of beer hung on the wall in eight different languages. Across the ocean lay a similar place, an island where people arrived and a city that was the mirror image of this one. Just as New York was the funnel of America, in which Europeans mingled and were poured into a new life, Rotterdam was the funnel of the Netherlands, through which Russians, Poles, Czechs, Germans, Austrians, Bulgarians, Hungarians and Rumanians streamed into the ships that would take them across the Atlantic. I had come to know both cities, I had arrived and departed and never settled in either one. Here, in Rotterdam, I stayed at Hotel New York, and in New York, in a room in the apartment where Uncle Herman and my father lived. Had lived.

'I have to call Nina,' I said.

Uncle Chaim nodded. 'Don't forget to make a little rip,' he said.

'A rip?'

'Sign of mourning.'

'I won't forget, Nuncle.'

He nodded at Magnus and disappeared behind him into the midnight-blue above the river.

With the mottled city darkness on the windowpanes, the Maas a slow, tar-black stream that emptied out somewhere beyond the horizon, in my room at the front of Hotel New York, the multi-coloured lights of the city to my right, the television babbling on behind me about the American stock exchange, the weather forecasts for Asia and Africa, and the latest round of European terrorist attacks, I dialled Nina's number.

'Nina? Nathan.'

'How are you, N?' She sounded almost elated.

'There's something I have to tell you. Uncle Herman . . .' In the background was the sound of . . . happiness. Voices, glasses, barely audible music. I don't know why, but it suddenly did me an awful lot of good that my niece, Zeno's daughter, had a social life, friends who laughed and drank. 'Herman is dead.'

'He's what?'

'D-e-a-d.' Died, passed on, breathed his last, I thought to myself. Gone to meet his Maker, pushing up the daisies, he's a late uncle . . .

'What happened?'

'He . . . how shall I put it . . .'

I found it rather hard to explain the circumstances. I talked about a 'young lady', saying she was 'very possibly a close friend of Uncle Herman's.' When I was finished, there was a long silence.

'So,' she said, 'he died in the act.' On the other end of the line I heard a snicker, barely suppressed. 'My God,' said Nina at last.

'What do you mean, "young lady"? Just how old was she?' Another half-muffled giggle.

'Nina, we're talking about your great-uncle.'

'Yes. It's . . . Sorry.' A brief silence. Then she said, 'Somehow it suits him, don't you think?'

'What? Herman and women? I've never actually thought of him in that light.'

'Nuncle . . .'

'I'd rather you didn't call me "Nuncle" tonight.'

'I understand. But you're wrong if you think Uncle Herman didn't associate with women. He was a charmer of the first degree.'

'A . . . No. I wouldn't know. I'm going to make the funeral arrangements tomorrow. You'll be there, won't you?'

'Yes, of course. But, Nathan . . .'

'What?'

'He wanted to be cremated.'

'How do you know that?'

'He thought burial was unhygienic and sentimental. Told me once.'

'And we're not big on sentiment.'

'What?'

'I'll call you to let you know where and when and . . .'

'Okay. Sorry it's so noisy here.'

'Are you having a party?'

'It's my birthday today.'

'God, Nina. Sorry, I . . .'

'It's okay, N. We're not big on sentiment.'

'Yes. No. I'm sorry.'

'Listen, I'll come to Rotterdam tomorrow to help you out. Maybe I can arrange the funeral and you can close accounts and notify the authorities.'

'You don't have to.'

'No, but would you like me to?'

'Yes. Er, Nina?'

'Yes?'

'Happy birthday.'

When I had hung up and was standing at the window with a new whisky in my hand, the absurdity of Uncle Herman's death finally hit me. The man who had fled the Netherlands, that ward for compulsive neurotics in 'Hospital Europe,' as he called it, and spent the greater part of his life in the USA, his 'new homeland,' had returned here to die, in the Hotel Memphis, under a hooker from an escort service dressed as a petulant teenager. I put my left leg on the windowsill and stared out at the river and the city. So much life, so deep in the night. As if death didn't exist, as if no one knew that Uncle Herman had reached the end of the end.

Five days later Nina and I heard the reading of the will. Afterwards we drank coffee at my hotel. We sat in the lounge in two easy chairs, and stared wearily in front of us.

'A biography,' I said.

Nina opened her bag and took out a lipstick and a folding mirror. As she painted her lips red, she said, 'And within five years. Thank God he didn't say how long the biography had to be. You can probably get away with thirty thousand words.'

I shook my head.

'What do you mean, "no"?'

'If it were anyone else, yes, but not Uncle Herman.'

Nina curled her lips inward and a cherry-red mouth appeared. 'N,' she said, 'your work is going so well. Pavel's film will be out soon and the Germans are already nagging the Scandinavians about the rights to the series. That'll only lead to more and more translation rights. What you really should do is write a new collection of fairy tales.'

'I want the house, Nina.'

She looked at me for a long time. 'Can you contest it?'

'The will? That particular term?' I shrugged. 'Do I really want to contest it?'

Nina ran a hand through her hair and narrowed her eyes. 'Hm. Maybe I could even sell a biography of Uncle Herman.'

'You,' I said, 'could sell the Devil a wristwatch.'

'Why that house? It's too big for you. Why don't you rent something in Amsterdam?'

Because I grew up there. I had spent my whole life travelling about. I hadn't had a bed of my own since I was twenty. I had the clothes on my back and suitcases here, there and everywhere. I'm tired, I thought. As Nina was summing up the advantages of the big city and describing a series of opulent flats in desirable neighbour-hoods, my thoughts strayed to Uncle Herman's house. I could see it before me.

I knew the house like my own body. From the moment Herman had bought it, Sophie, Zoe, Zelda, Zeno and I had gone up there nearly every year. Me, the most. The women usually stayed only a week, Zeno was still too young to be without Sophie, so I spent all my summers with Uncle Herman, which was not always to Sophie's liking. When I returned, they all, without exception, found me highly maladjusted. 'You're developing the same egocentric bachelor habits as Herman,' Sophie once said, when I told her after one of those long summers that I preferred to eat breakfast alone, with the morning paper.

I played in that rambling garden, crept along the stairways, through the rooms and under the tables and sat for hours in the broiling sun in the little tower on the roof and looked out over the treetops to the valley, far, far below me, behind the sun-baked forests and the glistening ribbon of the brook that Uncle Herman and I called the River. Behind the brook: rolling fields, covered, in spring, with a paper-thin film of tender green, in the summer, a sea of golden wheat. Around every plot of land, wooded banks. From my vantage point I could see the wheat standing tall in the fields, a farmer in a swaying tractor going laboriously about his work. I was there and yet I wasn't. A stowaway.

When I got older, I used the house to work in. Every so often Uncle Herman would arrive, fling his suitcase under the table in the great hall, throw his coat at the hatstand (and miss the hook), and sleep and eat and walk until it was time for him to leave again. And I would sit at the heavy oak table in the library and leaf through my papers, in winter, the crackling hearth fire at my back; in summer, the lawn behind the open windows, the brook, the fields.

Herman had once said, when he thought that I was old enough to have my own key, that it really should have been mine, because I was the only one who had any use for it. But I could never have afforded a place like this. Uncle Herman, on the other hand, was rich, and lived on his estate as if it were a hotel.

The library was his pride and joy. Year after year he had added to the collection along the walls, until the flow became too great and the newest additions had to be distributed between tables and small mobile bookcases. The enormous room, thirty feet wide, nearly seventy feet long, consisted of pure paper and wood. On either side of the hearth, in the middle of the long wall, there wasn't an inch of empty space: books from floor to ceiling. The short wall adjacent to the hallway was lined with bookcases that reached the ceiling and ran along the top of the doorway, which was no more than a niche in the towering cliff of leather, linen and paper spines, a dark tunnel to another world. The other short wall: books, books, books. The only blank surfaces were the heavily beamed ceiling, which disappeared twelve feet up in a nest of twilight and shadows, and the long wall that formed the front of the house and was set with four large double windows, which, at night, were hidden away behind thick green velvet curtains inside and green wooden shutters outside.

Herman had made the whole house liveable, but he himself lived just on the ground floor. He ate in the library, slept in the hunting room. My bedroom was on the first floor and I was usually the only one there. I wasn't too pleased about that. Whenever I was alone in the house, before I went to bed at night, I checked all the doors twice, felt at the espagnolettes, pulled the curtains closed and walked backwards up the big staircase, peering warily into the darkened hall.

I had a large room. There was a wooden double bed, an imposing linen cupboard, a chest of drawers and a secretaire and chair. A solid oak door led to the bathroom, with a large cast-iron bath on lion's paws and two sinks big enough to bathe a baby. The floor was laid with marble, old, yellowed, with the soft lustre that only time can give to stone. At the foot of the bath hung a prehistoric boiler that always went on with a bang. Chrome, white-glazed tiles along the walls, punctuated by a band of gleaming black. A huge mirror above the sinks, a rectangle nearly four feet high and eight feet long.

Sometimes we would spend long evenings together in the library, drinking, saying nothing, perhaps the occasional word, Uncle Herman with his head in a creaky old book, me, bent over a white sheet of paper. But nine times out of ten I was alone, so alone that I could hear the silence rustling through the rooms and, in the evening, would walk through the hallways in search of sound. Later, as I lay in my bed, in the small circle of light from the reading lamp, I felt as if I were suspended in the middle of the universe. I had an involuntary and unpleasant image of the house at night: a huge, three-dimensional labyrinth of darkness, with me in the middle, floating in a feeble pool of light. Usually I made sure I had drunk enough wine to fall straight to sleep.

'Are you listening to me, Nathan?'

I nodded. Nina had got out her address book and was listing the names of friends and acquaintants who were about to move or who might be interested in Uncle Herman's house. I smiled and made the gestures people make when they listen to someone without really listening.

Six months after Uncle Herman's cremation and Nina's attempts to put an end to my nomadic existence, I returned to the house for the first time. I had the key, I was allowed in, but something inside me resisted when I came walking out of the forest and saw it before me, on the other side of the field. Everything was the same. Everything was different. The house was a memory of a time when voices still echoed there. It was the beginning of spring and weeds were growing through the gravel. Sorrel spread its fingers over the grass, and under the aged, heavy conifer, which had always been carefully pruned and was now a frayed dark cloud, the moss had begun winning the fight that it had seemed, for so long, to be losing. No peeling paint, no saplings shooting up in the gutters, the roof still clean and secure. But that was only a matter of time. Before long the first cracks would appear. The windows would break, withered autumn leaves would tumble through the rooms, and the old floor, polished by so many generations, would grow dull, then bulge, and finally, crack and splinter. In the end, I thought as I stood there, everything goes to ruin. I turned round and walked into the forest. It was my last visit.

'Nathan?'

My neck ached. When I opened my eyes, I saw Nina standing by the stove with her hands on her hips.

'Ah. Sorry.'

'That's okay. I was just wondering if you had any particular cooking taboos.'

I didn't know what she meant.

'You know, like no milk and meat, that sort of thing.'

I scratched my head. 'Not if it's really obvious. But I refuse to fry steak in oil.'

She blew a curl out of her face. 'Hollander clarity.'

'We were a rather confused family,' I croaked, 'culinary-wise.'

Nina turned round and went on cooking.

'Zeno was a vegetarian.' She looked over her shoulder. The candlelight glided across her face and for a brief moment it was as if I saw my brother's face before me. 'And Zelda, for instance, was kosher. So: there was Zeno the vegetarian. Sophie, normal food. Zoe was always on a diet.'

'And you?'

'I went along with Zelda.'

'You, kosher?'

'Sort of. No pork, no oysters, mussels, eels, eagle, and kangaroo.'

'Why not?'

'Well, maybe kangaroo . . .'

'I don't know a single thing about the family,' said Nina. She paused. 'And when you're not around anymore, I never will.'

I shifted in my chair.

Nina looked sideways. 'What's wrong? Do you think it's so strange, my saying: When you're not around anymore?'

'No.'

'Uncle Nathan,' she said. She put the colander in the sink and poured hot water over it.

'Please . . .'

'Uncle Nathan!'

'Okay.'

'You are, as you yourself are so fond of saying, an old man.'

'Yes, I think I'll just hobble off and . . .'

She wasn't joking. Her eyes didn't betray the slightest trace of irony. 'An old man. The rest of the family is gone.'

'No.' The image of Sophie was suddenly crystal clear. I saw the curve of her cheek, the way she would offer it to me and my lips brushing the soft skin, tasting and smelling at the same time: Arpège.

'For years, I haven't wanted to be part of the family.'

'I can't blame you.'

She shrugged her shoulders. 'But now I'm . . .'

'Older,' I said.

Her gaze was stern, but softened after she had looked at me for a while. 'Older. If you don't finish Uncle Herman's biography, you won't only not have this house. I won't have a history.'

'Sometimes it's not so bad not to have a history. I could have done without one.'

She turned back to the sink, slightly bowed. 'That's like a billion-aire saying that money isn't everything.'

I stared at the orangey-red-lit figure before me and realized that I was nodding. When Nina looked sideways again, I smiled, in spite of myself.

'What?' she said.

'You probably won't want to hear this, but sometimes you look so much like your father.'

She sniffed disdainfully, but I could see the hint of a smile. She looked over her shoulder. 'Don't forget to set out the wine, will you?'

'What shall it be? Red, white? Full-bodied, light?'

'Red, on the light side.'

I got up, grabbed hold of the chair, and waited until the blackness had cleared from my eyes. In the cellar, shivering and breathing out clouds, I spent half an hour reading labels, swatting away memories of long, long ago like mosquitoes.

I chose a Barolo, about ten years old, a Barbera d'Asti and, just to be sure, a Lacrima Christi.

––––––––––––

'How do you know all that stuff you write?' asked Nina, as we sat in the library eating her pasta: penne rigate with tuna, olives, peppers, and anchovies.

'Hearsay.'

'You were around for some of it, but you were just a child. How can you know all those things?'

'That's what Uncle Herman always used to say.'

She looked at me expectantly.

'Uncle Herman was the great saviour. I'm the one who saw it all and remembered it, all of it.'

As we ate and drank the Barolo, I told her about my 'aberration.'

I am, where the history of my family is concerned, what a person with a photographic memory is to a mutual support group for Alzheimer patients. I know everything. Even things I can't possibly know. What I don't know, I find out. I'm a mnemonic wonder. Uncle Herman once asked me how the hell it was that I could remember him telling some story or other three years earlier. I told him I saved his stories on the gallery, on the side with the scaffolding. I was seven at the time. He had stared at me like a heron at a goldfish.

'I saved it in the tower,' I said.

'What tower, Nathan?'

'The Tower of Babel.'

'What did you say?'

'I was walking along the gallery.'

'The gallery . . .'

'Yes, that's what it's called.'

'I see. And now would you mind telling me what that has to do with it?'

And so I had told him about the colour plate of Bruegel's *Tower of Babel* in one of Sophie's books and that I had sat there staring at it and after a while I found that I was walking around in the painting.

I looked at Nina, filled up her glass when she nodded, and praised the pasta. 'Don't get off the subject,' she said. 'Or I'll be totally lost. What did that tower have to do with it?'

'In ancient times, when they didn't yet have the means to file things away, people developed mnemonic systems, devices to aid and expand the memory. As a child, I had accidentally devised such a system. I discovered one day that I was walking around in *The Tower of Babel* by Bruegel and as time went on I was able to call the tower to mind and store things there.'

Her eyes were wide. 'You mean that you could remember more than other people, because you had a kind of . . . a kind of warehouse . . .'

'*The Tower of Babel* by Bruegel,' I said. 'It's here in my head. I can climb up into it and put things in niches. Every gallery has its own characteristics.' I stood up and got a few more pieces of wood. As I arranged them over the layer of glowing chunks, I walked into the tower, up the first gallery, and ran my eyes over the still lifes that stood there, frozen in time, waiting to be used.

'Is there anybody in this family,' said Nina, when I had sat back down again, 'anybody at all, who isn't completely barmy? Is there one normal person?'

'Child,' I said, 'normal people . . .'

She picked up her glass and stared at me over the edge. 'You can remember stuff about . . .'

'Nearly everything,' I said.

'May I test you?'

I shrugged.

'When you and your family were on board that ship. A conversation. Between people you didn't know.'

'That's easy. Someone told a joke. Two German Jews who had spoken to us when we embarked at Rotterdam. They were standing at the railing and when we walked past one of them said to the other: "America . . . *Gott*. Moses was a blockhead." And the other one stared. "What are you saying? Moses . . . he led us out of Egypt!" "If only he hadn't done," said the first, "then I would have had a British passport!" Good enough?'

Nina took a sip of wine. 'So, I'll bet this house is packed, too, huh?'

'No, just the tower. I'm not crazy. What you're talking about is someone like the man in that book by Luria, *Mind of a Mnemonist*. Someone who remembers compulsively. I simply have a photographic memory, only not for text, but for events. This house is a feeling, more than anything else. I've always thought that my whole life was contained within the summers I spent here, as if everything that had to and ever could happen was concentrated within those days and weeks. A time of great clarity, a time of awakening. I've never felt as strongly since then that life . . . had meaning.'

She shook her head. 'Meaning,' she said. There was a long silence. Suddenly she turned to me. 'Damn. I just remembered, you once wrote a fairy tale about the Tower of Babel.' She grabbed the candelabra and went to the wall of books. 'Which one was it? Which collection, *Telltales*?'

'Don't bother.'

'I want to know.' It took her a while to find what she sought. 'Here. "The Tower." ' She walked slowly back to her chair. She put down the candles and handed me the book. 'Read.'

'Read?'

'Please?'

'If you really want me to.'

She smiled the smile of a pixie who knew she had her victim hanging by a thread.

The Tower

ONE DAY THE builders reached the clouds. It was such a long way up that the supply of building materials at the top was exhausted before a new load had even arrived. The bearers were divided into two equal crews. The first crew received mortar, wood, and bricks on the ground and carried them halfway. There they were met by the second crew, which carried the supplies higher. Gradually three distinct sectors began to evolve: those at the bottom were closest to the earth; in the middle, they carried materials to the top; and on top, where clouds drifted about the scaffolding, was where the construction was done. On top worked the bricklayers, supervisors and draughtsmen, a hundred, a hundred and twenty men who never came down. The loneliness – relieved only by the bearers – the height, the clouds and the cold, made them both modest and proud.

Strangers came from far and wide when they heard of the great work. Everyone found employment, there were never enough men. Thousands worked in the tower and tens of thousands ploughed the fields, hunted, mixed mortar, made bricks, chopped wood. Thousands died, thousands were born. Those who visited that country and saw the tower, never left the region again. They became bearers, bricklayers, hunters, farmers, and whores.

And the tower grew higher and higher. Those at the bottom could no longer see the top, those at the top forgot the earth. The galleries swarmed with groups of people who didn't know each other. The days of working together in harmony were over.

At that time a man arose and packed his knapsack with paper, stylus, bread, oil, a wooden ball, a fistful of clay. He journeyed until he saw the horizon break and the sky split in two. He would travel seven more days before he would see something so huge that it looked like the finger of the God of gods. After seven days more the tower took shape. The traveller flung his knapsack to the ground and sat down. For a whole day he gazed at the spiral of stone, soaring in the distance. Then he stood up and walked towards the tower.

The work was going more and more slowly. The people no longer knew what they were doing. Sometimes a crew had to wait days for supplies, because a message from the galleries hadn't reached the earth. Once, the bearers from the highest sector asked for fresh water, and it never came. After that men were appointed to collect dew each morning in pots they had hung on the balustrades the night before. Others became tower hunters. They built traps and hung snares from the galleries. They shot at birds with an arrow on the end of a string. The flesh of these birds was oily and bitter, but they ate it nonetheless, because they never knew when to expect new provisions.

The bricks ran out, the firewood ran out. Those who worked at the top began to throw lumber on the fires. Here, among the clouds, it was so cold that they hung up animal skins to keep out the wind. They couldn't build closed galleries, the draughtsmen feared that the tower would grow too heavy. But at this height, where the wind always blew, where it nearly always rained and the mist was so thick that they sometimes couldn't see their own hands, here, skins weren't enough. The mortar didn't dry well, which hindered construction and made the work hazardous. Two bricklayers were lost when they climbed a new gallery and the brickwork caved in like half-baked bread. After that the builders tried to dry the air and dispel the mist. In the galleries they burned pitch and wood and lengths of rope. Sometimes they pulled down the laboriously raised scaffolding and threw that, too, on the fire.

And so it was on the morning when the traveller arrived. He had unpacked his knapsack, climbed up onto a pile of bricks, and shouted out, as if the days of the prophets had already dawned. 'You there,' he said to a bearer, 'what sort of structure is this?' The bearer told him that this was the tower that would lead them to the heavens. 'Nonsense,' said the traveller. People flocked round him. 'Nonsense. Who says that this is the way to the heavens? Why not dig a hole? Or build a wall that spans the globe?' The people laughed. 'Don't you know that the earth will be thrown off balance by such a high tower?' said the traveller. He picked up the staff that was lying beside him and placed the wooden ball on top. 'This is the world.' He took a fistful of clay and kneaded it into a tower. 'This is the world. This is your tower.' He showed them his figure of clay. 'This,' he said, 'is what will happen.' He stuck his clay tower on the ball. The earth fell. 'But the earth's not round!' someone shouted. The traveller shook his head. 'Then bring me a plate,' he said. They brought him a plate. He put the plate on his staff, kneaded a new tower, and set it on the flat earth. The earth fell. Those at the top didn't hear of this until weeks later when supplies had ceased altogether. All the scaffolding had been burned, they were living on birds and insects. A man was sent down to see what was going on. Two weeks later, he returned. 'The people have rallied around a traveller,' he said. 'They've adopted strange rituals. A child has been offered to the gods.'

The bricklayers, supervisors, and draughtsmen who worked in the galleries at the top and hadn't been down below in years, laughed. 'Barbarians,' said the chief draughtsman. He shrugged his shoulders and returned to his men. In the last few weeks they had withdrawn to the second highest gallery, just below the clouds. There they sat, not saying a word. After three days the supervisors, who were waiting for plans, sent up one of their apprentices. The youth returned, white as a ghost. 'They're not speaking,' he said. 'But their thoughts are loud.' He was sent back down, home to his parents who lived far away on the plain.

Once the building had ceased, the city that had grown at the foot of the tower slowly emptied out. Labourers who had come from afar, departed for their fatherland, farmers who had left their land to build, returned to their families, and the merchants who had settled in the city closed their shops and headed for new regions.

Gradually it grew quiet around the stone colossus. The water in the bay lay calm and empty. Except for a few broken barrels and half-corroded bales of rope, the quay was a dusty wasteland of bare stone. It still smelled of tar and wood and lime, but no one came anymore.

One day the chief supervisor went up to the top. As he climbed the steep incline, he saw saplings growing here and there out of the stone. Elsewhere was a deep pool of blackish-green water. Birds had made their nests in crumbling bits of wall.

He saw the draughtsmen sitting in a circle around a fire, and wondered where they had got their firewood. The closer he came, the slower his tread. Until at last he stopped, and looked at them in silence.

They weren't speaking, but now and again one would raise his head, another would smile at him from the other side of the circle, and nod. It was as if they were having a conversation without words.

For a long time the supervisor didn't dare to speak, and when he did, the draughtsmen didn't seem to notice him. Only when he went and stood in the middle of the circle did he feel the weight of their gaze.

'There hasn't been any food for weeks,' he said. 'The last bricks were delivered months ago. There are no more plans. We have to make a decision.'

The faces of the seated men were friendly, but blank.

'Do we leave the tower, or do we go down and discuss it?'

No one spoke.

'Something must be done,' said the chief supervisor.

Two of the men turned to each other, their eyes clear and wide. One nodded, while the other looked him full in the face, in deafening silence. After a while the first man shook his head. He turned his eyes to the supervisor and looked at him.

Here, so high in the air that the clouds rent themselves on the balustrades, it was so quiet that one could hear oneself breathing. That was what the chief supervisor heard. That, and the thoughts of the draughtsman who was staring at him. He could hear his thoughts, but he didn't understand what they meant.

On his way down the chief supervisor had a vision. He saw the tower before him, from top to bottom, at a single glance, and it was as if it were a city. At the top was the palace, high, impenetrable, a place where they discussed matters of which no one knew, in a language foreign to the townsfolk. Halfway down, in the old town, were the magistrates and mercantile houses, the shopkeepers and high-ranking officials. Now and then one of them would head upwards, summoned for an explanation or eager to ask a question, and each time it was a journey to another world. At the bottom where the tall buildings lost themselves in a jumble of alleyways, huts, and finally, tents on the outskirts of the city, lived the commoners. They knew nothing of the palace and only ever went to the old town in the event of illness or foul play. This, thought the supervisor, who was approaching the gallery where they dwelled, was what had become of the tower: The people no longer understood each other, they had nothing more to do with each other. He knew, for the first time since the building had ceased, that the tower would fall, for when men have no common goal and no longer speak the same language, the foundations will crumble.

The traveller had journeyed seven days across the grass-covered land, without seeing a soul, without spotting a landmark. After a day or two he had begun to fear that he was lost, but at night, when he studied the stars, he knew that he was walking in the right direction. At the end of the seventh day he caught sight of the woods of his own country, and at that very moment he heard the thunder rolling over the plain. He looked back and saw in the distance, not thunderclouds, but a plume of dust climbing to the heavens like a mushroom. That evening, on the banks of the river, the scent of the forest already in his nostrils, it began to rain. The water that fell on him left behind traces of black and grey. It formed turbid pools that shunned the light of the setting sun. He put his finger in his mouth and tasted the taste of stone.

Quid Pro Quo

I STOOD UP and leaned over to poke the fire. Nina sat in her chair, lost in thought.

'I think I'll stay and live here.' She jumped, then looked at me questioningly. 'I don't want to travel around anymore. I don't want to keep arriving somewhere only to leave again, I want to have a place where people can come if they want to see me. And I want to sit by the window and watch the sun rise and in the evening I want to wait for the night. And every so often, once a month, maybe once every three weeks, I want to have a profound thought about life, or woodworking, or ping-pong, doesn't matter what, and then I'll walk in here, to the table I've reserved for just that purpose, and I'll sit down at that table and in the deep tranquillity of seclusion I'll write, on a large sheet of white paper: Profound thought today.'

She smiled. 'Have you ever, dear N, done anything else?'

I fished the packet of cigarettes out of my jacket and held it out to her. She got up, took one, and let me light it. We stood side by side, smoking in silence.

'For as long as I've known you, you've lived the life of a fugitive. When the going gets tough, you run away. Uncle Herman gave you this house and you haven't been back since. You were married once, but as soon as it became more than an idea, you took off.'

'An idea?'

'The marriage. To say nothing of why you ever got married in the first place.'

'I loved Eve.'

'For love you need submission, and that's something you know nothing about.' She spoke calmly, but in the even flow of her words lay something sharp. Her white hand reached out to pick up her wine glass by the stem and brought it to her lips, as if she were about to smell a tulip.

'Nina,' I said, in a cloud of grey and blue arabesques, crushing the barely smoked cigarette in the ashtray, 'just as the Pope should keep his mouth shut about people who fuck, you're better off keeping quiet about anything other than royalties. I know exactly what kind of submission you're talking about and the mere thought of it makes me sick.'

She stood there opposite me, like an ice queen, her arms at her sides, back straight, face motionless and pale. I didn't know what her stance was meant to express, inviolability or rage, but I didn't care.

I gathered up the plates and went into the kitchen. I boiled water, scooped coffee into the filter, and stared at the black square of the kitchen window.

When I returned with our mugs, Nina looked up.

'N?' I put down her mug. 'I'm sorry. I shouldn't have said that.'

'Okay.'

'But I don't understand what you meant when you said you knew what kind of submission I was talking about.'

'You don't?'

She shook her head.

I sat down. 'I thought you meant Zeno. That you were comparing my aimless rambling to Zeno's fireworks.'

'God, no. Of course not. Why would I even . . . God.'

'Then I'm the one who should be apologizing.' We drank.

'About your memory . . .' I looked at her. I knew what she was going to ask. 'How can you remember things about Uncle Chaim and Cousin Magnus? You describe them as if you've seen them.'

'That's because they're not memories. I *have* seen them. I still do.'

'Hang on a minute,' said Nina. 'You *have* seen th . . .' A wave of horror crossed her face. 'What do you mean? You see ghosts?'

'I don't know if "ghosts" is the right word. But I do talk with

Uncle Chaim and Cousin Magnus, yes.' She made a sound I couldn't quite identify. 'Do you find that strange?'

'Strange? People get put away for less!'

'If you ask me, it's a lot more harmless than, say, an army career.'

'What's that got to do with it?' She was almost shouting. 'You talk to people who've been dead for a hundred years?'

'Three hundred years. Almost three hundred years.'

'I don't care if it's three thousand!'

'I used to chat with Abraham, too.' A note of smugness crept into my voice. It did me good to pile on all the absurdities of my life, and those of the rest of the family. Liberating. In some way, it was liberating to finally tell all that nonsense to somebody else. Lord of the Universe, I thought, after fifty years, surely I'm allowed?

'Which Abraham? No! Not . . . You're not going to tell me that you . . .'

'And Jacob. Never with Moses. But he stuttered, anyway.'

Nina stood with her back to the fire, her hands held out in front of her. She was rubbing them so vigorously, she seemed to be washing them.

'Sit down, Nina.'

She shook her head.

'I was an impressionable child.'

'Impressionable.'

'I read the Torah and I lived in those books. I fled Pharoah's Egypt with the children of Israel and I travelled about with Abraham and Jacob. I heard the prophets prophesy and I saw King David leering at Bathsheba.'

'Oh God.'

'And one day, night, Uncle Chaim and Cousin Magnus appeared at my bedside.'

I had never seen the visits from my roaming relations as something that might reflect on me, probably because I couldn't talk about them, but all of a sudden I felt rather pleased with myself. Nathan Hollander, the man who hung out with the dead as if they were members of his football team.

'And you were the only one who saw them?'

'They used to drop in on Uncle Herman, too, but he didn't want any part of it.'

She shook her head. She had been shaking her head for some time now.

'Sit down, child.'

She sat down. All the strength had ebbed away from her bearing, her back was bent, arms limp at her sides.

'The past was always very much alive in our family. Travellers. All travellers. Our arrival in the Netherlands was the zenith, as my grandfather was fond of saying, the zenith of our history. A land much like us, preoccupied with time and future, a land with morals and modernity, a land that had created itself. Did you know that American democracy was based on the Dutch model? On the Batavian Republic? A guiding light. That's how the Dutch have always liked to see themselves and that's how we Hollanders regarded ourselves, too, as a family of guides. God's guides.'

Nina clapped her hand to her mouth and went on shaking her head.

'And that's why it wasn't at all strange that we went to America, the new Holland. In 1939 it hadn't even been that long ago that New York was dominated by Dutch families. If you walked through that city, you walked down Dutch streets: Broadway, Cortlandt Street, Beekman Street, Nassau Street, the Bowery, Brooklyn. The only true Protestant nation, apart from the Netherlands.'

'But the Hollanders are Jews!'

'Yes. Jews by birth, inescapable, Dutch by choice. When Cousin Magnus came here he left the name Levi behind, he left his tribe and called himself Hollander. And my father, his descendent, married a girl, my mother, who was also called Hollander, but was no relation. How Dutch can you get? Besides, you know what Spinoza said: "Holland is the only land where everyone is a Calvinist, even the Catholics and the Jews."'

'Hollanders. But when things became really bad, it didn't help a bit.'

'Ah, that. No, it didn't help. But back then nothing helped, except fleeing the country.'

A spark leapt out of the hearth. Nina slowly rose from her chair and stamped out the glowing piece of wood. She remained standing in front of the fireplace, her back to me.

'You're doomed, all of you, with those grandiose ideas you have about yourselves.'

'Child,' I said.

'Stop calling me "child".'

'Sorry. Niece . . .' She spun round. 'Your father,' I said. 'Zeno, wasn't averse to . . . er . . . the world of the intangible, either.' Her eyes flared. 'Maybe it's time you and Zeno made peace.'

She ran her hand through the long red curls, grabbed hold of them, and laid the whole bundle on her back. It was dark in the library, but in the dim light you could still make out her pale, even features. As fine and delicate as Zeno had been, so was she. For the second time since we had been together, I felt a surge of pride. A strong young woman, rebellious and sharp, a combination of Zeno's agile mind, Zoe's sense of beauty, and Zelda's seriousness. And Uncle Herman. There was something about her that reminded me of Uncle Herman, too.

'How,' she said, 'can I make peace with someone who's no longer there? With someone who would have nothing to do with me? He didn't even want me.'

I nodded. 'But he is . . . was, your father. And it's pointless to try and fight a fact. You don't have to love him, but you are a Hollander, even though you don't bear his name.'

She hissed like a cat. 'Uncle,' she said, 'Uncle Nathan.' She planted her feet slightly apart, as if to stand her ground. 'I'm not fighting the family. You, Uncle Herman, Sophie, your sisters, you've all done your best. Especially you.' I waved my hand dismissively. 'No, it's true, and I've always appreciated it. But he, he didn't do a thing.'

'He, Zeno, wasn't there.'

'He went away.'

'Sometimes I think,' I said, 'that he was never there to begin with.'

She looked down at her shoes and said nothing.

'You say you don't know a thing about the family. But you know enough about me to claim that I'm incapable of submission.' She frowned. 'What about you? You're the great unknown here. I've told you about us and about myself. I've never heard you talk about anyone.' She turned away. I went on looking at her. 'Quid pro quo,' I said, 'Something of mine for something of yours.' She didn't answer.

'Come on,' I said after a while. 'We've got chopping to do.'

The house was on the verge of collapse when Uncle Herman presented himself as a buyer. It was in nearly the same shape it had been in at the turn of the century. There had never been enough money to install central heating, the windows were made of the same bumpy glass that had been set in the frames so many years before. The only modernization was the noisy boilers that provided the bathrooms with hot water. Because he wasn't interested in the surrounding land, Uncle Herman was able to buy the house, and all that went with it, for a fairly reasonable price. Squire Van Henninck, who had stared back at me from his portrait behind the linen cupboard, had been the last remaining member of the Van Henninck family, and when he died, the foundation that administered the estate was more interested in the returns on their investment than in the house and the heirlooms within it. That was how Uncle Herman came into possession of a complete past. He slept in the squire's bed, that rampant growth of wood, velvet, and brocade. Every morning, on his way to my bedroom, he passed an ancestral painting that was as foreign to him as a picture of a Tibetan mendicant. It threw him, he said, into a pleasant state of confusion. 'You can't feel more like a stranger than this. I live here like a country gentleman, in the house of a noble family, I'm surrounded by things that all say: We're Lord and Lady So-And-So, we've been here for centuries, so long that we've become one with this region, rulers, plutocrats, leaders. It's all mine and none of it's mine.'

It meant nothing to him. That is to say: he didn't have the slightest sense of nobility. As a sociologist, he knew where the aristocracy came from, what function it served, and to what degree it conformed to the clan structure with which 'we' were much more familiar.

'Nobility?' he cried one day, when I was swooning at the thought of all that rootedness, 'Shall I tell you what real nobility is? We're nobility. We're the Levi family, Levites, priests, the Jewish nobility. And old?' He had looked around him, we were sitting in the library. 'For five, six centuries these people belonged to a clan, a group that distinguished itself from the dirt farmers by marriage, inbreeding, and meticulous property management. We've been the same for three thousand years. Nobility? Don't talk to me about nobility.'

And there he sat, in his Chesterfield by the hearth, long after the fire had gone out: Herman Hollander, from the priestly lineage of the tribe of Levi, amid paraphernalia assembled by a family that had risen to prominence halfway into the millennium, flourished briefly and, the last two hundred years, gone plunging down like a wounded pheasant. The last squire, Uncle Herman told me, had never left the property. He never married, hardly ever collected the rent, and crept about his house like a mangy dog through the gutter. In 1910 he fell under the spell of spiritualism and, some years later, become a follower of Madame Blavatsky. The last five years of his life he spent under the illusion that he was living, not in a house on a hill that was called Mountain, but in a haven, an island in the sea of madness that the world was becoming. He holed himself up in the attic, in the wooden lookout that the local carpenter had built on the roof. In that pentagonal tower, with its peaked, slate-covered roof and high windows he had stood watch. He had let his gaze travel over the wooded hill, the fields below, the long, sinuous road that led to the town, the brook, which looked almost alive, and the railway, which was still being built, that would one day link the town with the West. About a week before his death he had severed his last ties with reality. He ordered ten farmhands to hoist a sloop up onto the roof and bind it to the lookout with a length of hemp rope. The squire's final instructions were that a dovecote and a clay pot of woodland soil be placed under the canvas. The next day the forester found him, dead. A tenant, one of the few who still came round to pay his rent, had knocked at the door, but to no avail. He had walked round the back and was about to try the kitchen door, when he saw that a window had been smashed. The forester discovered the squire several hours later. He was sitting upright in the four-poster bed, his head drooping on his shoulder, his right hand on his chest like a frozen claw. The son of a local industrialist was arrested. He confessed to having broken in. On his foray through the house he had ended up in Squire Van Henninck's bedroom. They had given each other a terrible fright, but the squire had the weaker heart and succumbed instantly.

I had done extensive research into the history of the house and the family that had lived there. I spent days on end in the Public Record Office and the museum library. The journalists at the local paper greeted me with 'Nathan the Wise!' whenever I came to ask permission to look through the files. The only obligation that Uncle Herman had felt towards the house was to be a responsible owner. He had kept it in good condition, yet never ruined it with unnecessary renovations. I was young and romantic and wanted to know the story of the house. I felt that people should always know the history of things.

But here I stood, my axe raised above the umpteenth piece of furniture that had been waiting all these years to become an antique and was now nothing more than firewood, a sacrifice to life, our lives. The left side of the barricade had been pushed back nearly to the end of the hallway. We could now choose from two doors, the door to my bedroom and the one that led to a guest room. The latter was fairly accessible, but locked. The door to my room was hidden behind a linen cupboard and, in front of that, a dresser. 'Once we get through this,' I said, pointing my axe at this new obstruction, 'we can have a bath. Ready?' Nina nodded. I pulled the drawers out of the dresser – they were all empty – and, with a few strokes of the axe, smashed it to pieces. We swept the chunks of wood into a pile. 'Let's move the cupboard away from the door,' I said. 'Then we can lay it on its side. It'll make things easier.' I put down my axe, and we began pushing against the cupboard. It wouldn't budge.

'God, it's heavy.' Nina leaned against the gleaming wood and rubbed her forehead.

'It's not that heavy. I mean: it's an oak cupboard, but I should be able to move this thing all by myself.'

'What's in it then?'

'Nothing special,' I said. 'Sheets, towels, a few blankets. It's just a linen cupboard.' I tried tugging at the doors, but they wouldn't yield.

'Locked?'

'That's not possible. In all the years I've been coming here there's never been a key in this cupboard.'

We stood there and looked, silent, pensive, at the sloping lines of the cornice above the cupboard doors.

'Should we smash it?'

I shrugged. I felt uneasy. Why couldn't we move the bloody thing? What was inside that was making it so heavy?

'Nathan?'

'No. No more smashing. I'm going to try and lift the doors out of their hinges. A hammer. There's a burlap bag around here somewhere.'

I walked down the stairs and tried to remember where I had left the bag. The first day, when Nina had run away, I had brought all sorts of things from the shed, including tools. Halfway down the stairs I closed my eyes and mentally retraced my steps, out the kitchen door, through the blinding storm. Into the shed. Rake, hoe, shovel, grindstone, sharpening the hoe, hammer, screwdrivers, chisel, pliers, burlap bag. I went back, the whorling snow between the trees and the house. Then I saw myself climbing the stairs, flinging the bag aside and . . . I turned round and walked back up.

'What are you doing?'

'I'm trying to remember where I left that bag of tools,' I said.

'That one over there?'

On top of a pile of cupboards and chairs, like an obedient puppy, lay the burlap bag.

The hinges of the linen cupboard were stuck fast, but after some effort the pins slid upward. The doors stayed in place, probably because the hinges were so tight. I had to jiggle my screwdriver between the cracks to loosen them.

The cupboard was empty.

'How . . .' I grabbed hold of the side panels and tried to move it again. 'I don't understand.'

Nina stepped into the cupboard and ran her finger along the back wall. 'It's nailed to the door,' she said.

I opened my mouth, but it was a while before I could speak. 'The cupboard is nailed to the door?'

She nodded. 'Have a look.' Her hand traced a vague oblong.

'Okay. Pliers and light. We're going to take it off.'

Nina came out of the cupboard. 'Why don't we just chop it up?'

'It's probably quicker to pull out the nails. Besides, if we chop we'll have to go through the door. I'd rather keep something intact for a change.'

When the lantern had shone its white light into the depths of the cupboard, the outline of the door was clearly visible by the trail of nailheads. As I lit her way, Nina got to work with the pliers.

It took her a quarter of an hour. Then we pushed against the cupboard and moved it with no trouble at all. We examined the door. By the look of the nail-holes, whoever had thought up this obstacle was a mighty good carpenter. He had nailed the cupboard neatly to the door frame. I put my hand on the handle and pushed down. The door was locked.

'I'm getting so tired of this. All these obnoxious little pranks.'

Nina nodded resignedly. 'And there's no key, I bet?'

'The key was always on the inside.' I leaned down to look at the lock. The keyhole was dark. 'And it still is, damnit. That's impossible!'

Nina looked up in alarm.

'What's wrong?'

She took a step backwards. 'If the key is on the inside, then whoever locked this door is inside, too.'

'Perhaps,' I said.

'Perhaps? Oh no, wait. He might also have locked the door and then gone out through the wall and then bricked up the wall again and . . . Jesus!'

'Would you hand me a screwdriver?'

She turned away abruptly and groped around in the burlap bag. 'I'm going to look for a newspaper.'

As I walked down the stairs, I could feel Nina's eyes in my back.

Up until now we had been working so hard, chopping, hauling, lugging, that the cold in the unheated part of the house had been bearable. Now, with one delay after another, it felt as if my bones were encased in ice. This couldn't go on much longer. Not only were we exhausted by the cold, it also took too much time to gather firewood. At this rate we would have just enough to keep the fires burning, but we could never sit down and catch our breath, let alone cook.

When I returned, Nina was still standing there, hugging her arms. I slid the newspaper under the door and jabbed the screwdriver in the lock. I had hoped that the key wasn't turned, so I could push it out and it would drop onto the newspaper. Then we could pull the paper back out, key and all. But nothing happened.

'Should we chop it down?'

I shook my head. 'Not yet.' The hinges were on the inside, we couldn't lift out the door. Chisel out the lock with the screwdriver? 'Wire. Wire, or a bobby pin.'

'What a shame I didn't bring my vanity case.'

I ignored the edge in Nina's voice. 'Wait here.'

I was already on my way, when I heard Nina's answer. 'Don't be long. If you're not back soon, I'm off to the hairdresser's!'

Uncle Herman had smoked a pipe and I thought there might still be some pipe cleaners in the library. I couldn't find any, but my bag lay on the reading table and after rummaging around inside I found a couple of paper clips. I threw more wood on the fire and went back upstairs.

'He's going to play safecracker,' said Nina. She brought her hand to her mouth and started chewing on her nails. I had never seen her do that before.

I squatted down in front of the lock and poked around with the largest paper clip. It took me a while to figure out which way the key was turned. Then I drew the piece of wire back out and stuck it in again at an angle, just above the bit, or so I hoped. My fingers were stiff. I had to blow on my hands to keep them moving.

'In films,' said Nina, 'this is the part where the first man tries the handle just one more time, while the second man is fiddling with the lock, and the door flies open.'

'Go right ahead. Make me happy.'

I pushed up the paper clip. 'Why don't you try and bang on the door?' Nina leaned down and picked up the hammer. 'No, harder. But not too hard. Here, right around where the lock is. And now keep on banging.'

While Nina hammered at the door, I tried to jiggle the key. It took me about a minute to push it out. When I pulled the newspaper towards me, it was lying neatly in the middle. A piece of kite-string was tied around either side of the ring, just long enough to turn the key from the other side of the door.

'You amaze me, N.'

'Fortitude, my dear. And boundless intelligence.'

She picked up the key, unlocked the door, and tried to push down the handle. 'It's stuck.'

I tried too. No luck. 'Both of us. Come on, push.' We leaned heavily. There was a faint scraping sound. Slowly the door gave way. When it was open about a foot, I looked inside. It was pitch-dark in the bedroom. I squeezed through the narrow opening.

Why does the dark always sound different? I stood there in the blackness and it was as if everything was very close by. The walls leaned in, the ceiling came down to listen. My bed used to be opposite the door. I walked slowly, gropingly, forward: a heron in troubled waters. I stepped on something soft, froze, and pulled back my foot.

A bar of light moved across the wall on my right. I looked around. Nina slipped through the door. The room turned dazzling white. At the same moment she screamed, so loudly that I stepped back in terror. She dropped the lantern, and as the room went dark again, I felt her body against mine. She shoved her head so hard into the hollow of my shoulder that the pain shot through my chest. We stood there in the void, the darkness around us almost palpable. Nina shook and sobbed. Her curls brushed my chin and without thinking I buried my face in her hair, as if I were too tired to go on any longer. I laid my hand on the back of her head and held her close. 'Nina. Ninotchka. Shhhh.' She was panting heavily, I felt her body swelling, shrinking and swelling. I took a deep breath and let her go. I dropped to my knees. Soft things with sharp edges along the ground. Paper. Paper? I felt the cool, smooth curve of the gas burner. I lit it. The floor was strewn with wads of paper. Nina was standing with her hands over her face. I put my arm around her shoulder and opened my mouth to say something. Only then did I see what had frightened her so. Across from us, where my bed had once stood, was a man, nailed to the wall.

I couldn't move. I stood there in that empty room, Nina pressed against me, and I wanted to hold her and disappear into her, a frightened child in its mother's skirts. My mouth was open, but I didn't breathe, didn't speak. Breathless. Lord of the Universe. Speechless. The lantern in my hand was shaking so hard that the light was a buzzing white tremor across the bare walls, the paper-strewn floor. What kind of Hell is this, oh Lord of the Universe? Where am I, and why me, we, she and I?

I swallowed. A ball squeezed its way through my larynx, down through my gullet. Clutching the lantern, I breathed deeply, frozen air, stepped forward, and saw that the man on the wall had my face.

'It's.' I cleared my throat. 'A dummy.'

I heard Nina moving. The rustling of paper.

'It's a dummy, love. A dummy.'

She came closer. A hand clawed at my jacket. She leaned against my back and peered, half hidden behind me, at the wall.

'He's got my face.'

She was breathing heavily. I reached into my pocket, took out the cigarettes, put two in my mouth, and lit them. She took one and inhaled as if I had just given her fresh oxygen. Her eyes shot back and forth, from me to the ground and from the ground back to me.

It was a long time before either of us spoke. It was Nina who broke the silence. 'The bastard. Shit! Shit!' She stamped her foot. I could feel her tugging at my jacket. 'I'm leaving. I'd rather bloody well die in the snow than stay here and . . . God!'

But she didn't turn round. I said nothing. I drew on my cigarette. The smoke sank down inside my chest and with it, a sadness that filled me like a jug. Zeno, I thought. And: What a life, what a disaster. My eyes grew damp. I looked at the floor, and as I began shaking my head, trying to fight off the wave of misery, I felt something wet trickling down my nose. I thought: I'm crying, Lord of the Universe. Not that, anything but that.

———————

By the fire, in the glow of the impassive orange flames, we drank the Lacrima Christi. Nina couldn't sit still. She wriggled in her chair, crossed her legs, uncrossed them, sipped at her wine, wriggled, crossed her legs. I smoked and stared at the blaze in the hearth. A vague feeling of responsibility was turning round and round inside me, but I thought: I can't do this anymore, I can't protect her, not against this.

'He hated you.'

I turned my head towards her, but slowly. I had trouble focusing my eyes on her.

'He hated you,' she said, her voice toneless, hard as sheet iron, 'more than anything in the world.' I nodded. 'He hated you with everything he had.' She looked at me. Her eyes were dull. 'I hope he burns in Hell.'

'There's no such thing as Hell.'

She sniffed. 'What do you call this?'

'Nina,' I said. 'Don't hate him. Don't fall into his trap.' My God, I thought, that *is* the trap! It's all meant to ruin our lives, my life, just as his was ruined. And I thought: Zeno, wherever you are, I'll play your little game, but it won't change me. I'll do your labyrinth, the dungeons and the dragons and your clever imitation of Dante's Inferno. But I won't let it get to me. And I'll do everything I can to keep her safe.

I closed my eyes and leaned my head against the back of the chair. A house, I thought, a fire in the hearth, a wife, and peace. No more travelling. Home. I want to arrive. And at that moment I realized that this prison in the woods, Zeno's carefully constructed system of traps and special effects, already had changed me. It had made me long for a life I'd never led.

We had lost a good deal of time, up there in my bedroom, and the expedition had yielded us very little fuel. Next to the hearth was just enough wood to make it through the rest of the evening. We'd even be able to light the stove the next morning, but after that we'd find ourselves in the predicament I had feared earlier: no time to rest, forced to gather wood to keep ourselves alive.

When I said this to Nina, she stood up resolutely. 'Then let's go get some more.'

'After what we just found?'

'I want wood, fire, and a good night's sleep. Come on.' She held out her hand and motioned with her head for me to follow.

We've changed all right, I thought, on the stairs. And how.

In the bedroom, without another word, we ripped the dummy off the wall. It was made out of an old suit of Uncle Herman's that had been stuffed with wads of paper, scraps of the wallpaper that had adorned this room since time immemorial. The face was a photograph I remembered. It had been taken when I married Eve. I looked young, and slightly sceptical. I pulled it off the ball of paper wrapped with twine that served as the head and ripped it to shreds. Nina watched me, saying nothing. In the bathroom, everything was as it had always been. Even my shaving things were still beside the sink.

Since there was no wood to be found in the bedroom, I chopped up the linen cupboard that had been blocking the door. Nina gathered up scraps of wood in the dummy's jacket and bound together another pile in its trousers and then we went downstairs. We distributed the harvest among the library, the kitchen, and the hunting room. By that time it was so late we decided to go to bed. Our shoulders were hunched with cold. I made a roaring fire in the hunting room hearth, while Nina prepared two hot water bottles.

We huddled between the icy sheets, our teeth chattering. I lay on my back and watched the firelight dancing on the blanket. The dry wood from the linen cupboard crackled and snapped. 'Warm me up, Nathan,' said Nina. She slid over to my side of the bed and turned her back to me. I didn't move. 'Warm me up,' she said again. 'Please.' I rolled over on my side, so that I was lying behind her. 'Closer.' I moved up, until she lay in the hollow of my body. She took my hand and put it on her stomach. It was several minutes before we began to feel each other's warmth. I smelled the scent of her hair and felt the slow rising and falling of her belly. I tried to think about Zeno and, when that didn't work, about my bedroom in the wooden house on the Hill, long ago and far away in New Mexico. I listened to the crackling of the wood and thought of the crackling of rocks, at night in the desert, the creaking of the walls as they cooled, the soft voices of Sophie and Manny in the next room. My hand moved up and down, together with Nina's belly. I felt the soft curve of her buttocks against my thighs and blinked my eyes to dispel the image of her naked white body. I saw the long red curls hanging down along her face, as she leaned over me and looked into my eyes. My hand on her breast, the gentle swell of her breast, my fingers across her nipple, the barely audible gasp. And the sudden warmth . . .

I was sitting in bed with Molly; we were drinking Uncle Herman's champagne. She took a sip and when she kissed me I felt the wine flowing into my mouth. Our tongues glided around each other, the champagne fizzed. I drank, and kissed her nipples. The champagne ran down her breasts. I licked them until she grabbed my head and pushed it down. Across her belly, she shivered when my tongue circled her navel, and farther down. Her hands lay on my hair. She guided me gently over the landscape of her body. The inside of her thighs. She tugged at my hair, I resisted. The place where the groin begins. Her hands wanted me higher, but my tongue drew a silvery trail along her groin, to her belly, around and around and then, suddenly, I licked her. Her back arched, her legs gave way. 'Eat me.' I'd never heard her say it. I ran my tongue over her labia. 'Fuck. Mhhh.' Her clitoris. Just barely. Round and round and round.

And again. She pushed my head down and I licked her, no longer teasing and unexpected. When she came, I felt her belly tighten. 'Oh. Fuck.' She pulled me up. I lay on top of her and she guided me in. She opened her mouth and nipped at my face. Her tongue had become a separate entity, an obscene, wet thing that entered me, licked my eyes, my throat. She bit my neck as we surged and rolled on the waves of lovemaking. When I raised myself up on my hands, she opened her eyes. She looked me full in the face. I couldn't turn away. I wanted to see her, caress her. I saw her breasts, her body, the place where I had disappeared into her and then her eyes again, that penetrating gaze. She said something, without making a sound. Her lips moved and she directed her silent words towards my eyes. I looked at her mouth and suddenly lust washed over me like a tidal wave. 'I want you,' I said. 'God . . . I want you.' She went on speaking without a sound. My head began to spin. 'I'm yours,' she said, suddenly loud and clear, and as I melted into her I felt like two men: one that wanted to take her like a beast, even now, and one that recoiled at so much submission.

I woke up when Nina sat bolt upright in bed. She stared straight ahead, seemingly impervious to the cold. When I touched her arm, she looked at me in annoyance. 'What's wrong?'

She made an impatient gesture with her hand. She seemed to be listening. I leaned on my left arm and looked at the dark smudge that was all I could see of her. 'I thought I heard something. I woke up because I . . .' She hesitated.

'You'll catch a chill.'

She shook her head. 'I heard voices.'

'You heard voices.'

She lay back down and turned to me. Her face was close to mine. 'A man's voice.' She was quiet. Then she said: 'This fucking house.'

'What did he say?'

It was a long while before she answered. 'He said: I want you.'

'That was me.' My dream about Molly still echoed. I knew exactly what I had said in that dream, when she had looked into my eyes and spoken in silence.

'Who were you talking to?'

'Molly.'

Nina turned over and nestled up against me. 'I'm listening, but I'm getting cold, so I'm afraid I'll have to use you as a heater. Who was Molly?'

'My first wife.'

'Good Lord. So Anna was your second?'

'Eve.'

'Eve.'

'Eve Barlow.'

She shook her head. 'Can we keep this brief?' she asked. 'The Nathan-and-his-women part?'

'We don't have to do it at all, as far as I'm concerned.'

'No, tell me about it. I didn't even know you were married twice.'

'I hardly knew it myself.'

'Tell me.'

'There isn't much to tell. I've been married twice, the first time to a chorus girl named Molly, the second time to Eve, who ran a tourist office in Wales.'

'What have you got against Dutch women?'

'Nothing, only there weren't a great deal of them outside Holland.'

'A chorus girl.'

Molly had danced in the chorus of a terrible musical I saw in London. She was American, had red hair, and a waist so slender that I sometimes wondered how there could be a complete digestive system inside.

I had gone to stay with Uncle Herman. He was, that year, 1968, I think, a visiting professor at one of the London universities and lived in a flat on Torrington Square. We only saw each other in the evenings, and so it happened that one afternoon, alone and bored, I ended up at a musical that was more like a glorified campus riot. It took me no more than five minutes to figure out that the show was worthless, but I sat there all the same. There were two reasons for this: the fact that the exit was blocked by an usherette, and the light that, after the first few minutes, fell on Molly's hair.

She was part of the group that filled up the space, dancing and singing, behind the lead players. But once my gaze had settled on her, she was all I saw. For the next two and a half hours I stayed in my seat, even during the interval, and stared at the stage. When she danced with the rest of the company, I followed her as if I had strings coming out of my pupils that were tied to her hair.

It was a coppery, gleaming, upswept abundance of hair that, every now and then, in my imagination, seemed to take on a life of its own. The skintight costume with the tiny skirt slipped off her, melting like spun sugar, the hair floated upwards and burst into a fine cloud of pale russet smoke.

After the show I did the unthinkable. I walked out of the auditorium, went to a local pub, and phoned the theatre to make an appointment for an interview. My request, not one of the leads, but a girl from the chorus, was thought to be rather odd, but once I had explained my plan – an article about the life of a chorus girl and how much a musical like that demanded of the entire team, not just the lead players – the artistic director suggested one of her colleagues. I told her I'd rather have Molly.

'Why?'

'She's American, isn't she? In the Netherlands, where I come from, "American" stands for professionalism, flair, that sort of thing. If I write about an American girl in an English musical the article will receive more attention.'

The appointment with Molly Gelernter was set for two days later. When I left the phone booth, I was sweating like a horse.

That night Herman and I ate dinner in a local bistro. He tried to dissect his steak, while asking me what I had done that day. I told him I had been to see a musical. He stopped cutting and looked up.

'*Hair*,' I said.

'You're not feeling lonely, are you?'

'I'm bored.'

He returned to his plate and drew the knife across the greyish brown slab of meat that was floating in a puddle of blood and grease. 'So?'

'So, what?'

'So: how was it?'

'Without lapsing into four-letter words?'

'Preferably not. This is England.'

'Let's see: a plot I could write in . . . mmm . . . ten to fifteen minutes. A day or two, maybe three, and I'd have the complete text, score included. Worthless, less than worthless. Not even the suggestion of depth. But performed to perfection . . .'

'. . . all that worthlessness.'

'Yes.'

'It's not really British, you know. That whole musical business is a twentieth-century American concept. They simply imitate it here, with all their British theatrical know-how, but you can take it from me: in ten years time all those musicals will be written by Englishmen and packed with hordes of unemployed Americans.'

I was blushing. A grown man, early thirties, and I was blushing.

'Did you know,' said Uncle Herman, 'that you're turning red? Is it too hot in here?'

Molly belonged, *had* belonged, to those unemployed hordes. She had gone to dancing school in the hope of getting famous, but by her second year she had already discovered that she and fame were two different things. She was good, good enough, but not the type that would make it to the top. That was why she had gone to London. Here, she would have little trouble meeting the requirements.

She sat opposite me, in a tiny office in the cryptlike basement of the theatre, a yellow-plastered room without daylight or fresh air, and spoke in the matter-of-fact tone in which only Americans can speak about their dreams of a lifetime. Twenty-three, born in Brooklyn, the daughter of parents who had earned their living in the second-rate Jewish theatre world, her father, as a song and dance man, her mother in farcical comedy. In those days her father was working the nostalgia circuit: evenings for Jewish pensioners, in Newark and Florida, where the music was pre-war and the memories as much American as they were European.

I asked her how it was possible to combine the life of a chorus girl, all that staying in shape and rehearsing, with a private life.

'I don't have one.'

'What . . .'

'I don't have a private life. I sleep, I wake up, I go shopping, I go to work, I sleep, I wake up. That's it.' She looked me straight in the eye, and I swallowed.

'How would you like to go out after this, for a drink and a life?'

Was that question part of the interview . . .

Definitely not.

We looked at each other for a long time and although I begged, pleaded that she would look away, that I would look away, we went on staring.

'God,' I said at last.

That was what Uncle Herman said, too, when he stood in the doorway later that afternoon and found us in the big bed, Molly astride me, my hands on her breasts, groaning under the sweet weight of her hips as they glided back and forth. 'God. You could at least have closed the door.'

I grabbed the sheet and tried to pull it over us, but it wasn't easy. 'This,' I said finally, 'is Molly Gelernter. Molly, this is my Uncle Herman.' By that time she was lying next to me, the sheet up to her chin, and she waved over the edge of it with her left hand.

'How do you do,' said Uncle Herman.

They got along very well together, so well that Molly, just before we got married, six months later, was spending more time at Uncle Herman's than in her own bedsit. Nevertheless, Uncle Herman was opposed to our union.

'N,' he said one night, when I had arrived from Holland for a long stay. 'Molly's a wonderful girl. If you make her unhappy, I'll break both your legs.'

'Why . . .'

'You're *going* to make her unhappy. No doubt about it. And I'll tell you something else: you're going to make every woman you ever meet unhappy. I don't mean to sound like the bad fairy from one of your silly stories, but you're the sort of man women should avoid. They fall for you, they even grow to love you, but until you learn to love them back, you'll always make a mess of things.'

'But I do love her. I pretended to be a bloody journalist just so I could meet her.'

'And, the Lord of the Universe be praised, she forgave you. That's how much that woman already loves you. Would you get that through your head? She loves you so much, she forgives you for getting to know her under false pretences.'

'Maybe I shouldn't be saying this, Nuncle, but in an opera, a scene like that would have been the great romantic climax.'

He had looked at me, Uncle Herman, and shaken his head. 'That's the problem,' he said. 'To you, everything is a story.'

I had lost my temper. 'I sat there at that fucking musical and watched her for three whole hours! I didn't see anything but her, nothing . . .'

'Hair,' said Uncle Herman dryly.

'Yes. No!'

'Hair. That's what you saw. Red hair.'

'So?'

'Reisele's red hair.'

Reisele's red hair. 'Doctor Spielvogel,' I said, 'spare me your analysis.'

Less than a year after the wedding, in New York, in a rented hall where we were married by a rabbi who looked like Rock Hudson and Molly's father sang a version of 'Somewhere Over the Rainbow' that would have soured sugar and one of his colleagues rounded off the evening with an unintelligible 'Hava Nagila,' less than a year later, Molly was in Manhattan with Uncle Herman, crying her eyes out, and I was on the Hill. Uncle Herman, who, shortly after my arrival, had phoned me in the middle of the night, said I was the biggest bastard he had ever met. 'It's time you started asking yourself,' he roared down the phone, '*why* you fall for someone, before you make any more victims!'

'Reisele,' said Nina, 'was that the little girl on the ship?'

'Uncle Herman had a rather Freudian outlook on life. He believed that a man spends his whole life searching for one woman and if it's not his mother, it's his first great love.'

'And Reisele was . . .'

'. . . my first great love. Oh, yes.'

She looked over her shoulder. In the darkness, I couldn't make out her face. 'How far does it go, this fascination of yours with red hair?'

'I'm not at all fascinated by red hair. That's what Uncle Herman thought. Eve was as blond as can be. Besides . . .' I lowered my voice. '. . . if it were that bad, you'd have woken up bald this morning and I'd have added your hair to my collection.'

'Okay, so tell me about the blond,' she said after a while. 'It'll take my mind off things.'

'I'm not in the mood.'

'Who says A . . .'

'I'm not in the mood, Nina.'

There was a silence. Outside, the wind moved through the trees, gently and peacefully. I felt the weariness curling up inside me.

'Nathan?'

'Hm?'

'Do you still want her? Molly?'

'No. Yes, when I dreamed about her. We had great sex. Sorry.'

'Why "sorry"? Do you think I can't imagine you having a normal sex life?'

'We were never happy, Nina. I was no good for her. She deserved better. We were two strangers, *I* was a stranger. The only time we ever met was when we . . .'

'Fucked.'

I was a yo-yo. I woke up and drifted off and each time I thought I was really going to fall asleep, I woke up again. Now and then I heard Nina's voice, I felt the warmth of her body and then I was here, in the hunting room, and then it went quiet again and I slipped away.

'Uncle Herman had quite a way with the ladies,' said Nina.

I drifted through the water of sleep and sighed. 'Yes.'

'Not you.'

I didn't answer.

Her voice sounded slow and heavy. 'Nathan?'

I lisped something vague.

'Why couldn't you ever stay with anybody?'

'You want to know that now?'

'Hmm.'

'I don't know if I can really . . .'

'More or less.'

I closed my eyes and walked into the tower.

I know two different versions of Bruegel's *Tower of Babel*. In the smallest of the two, the tower is at an advanced stage of construction. An apocalyptic red hue washes over the building and the surrounding land. It's as if the light of the setting sun is brushing this cloud-high colossus just one more time, before the earth shakes and the galleries crumble and stones roll down from the heights, taking rubble, wooden sheds, and people down with them. The tower stands on the edge of a bay, or the sea, in the lower right hand corner of the painting. There are several ships lying at anchor, another ship is headed, sail billowing, to the coast. No two galleries are alike. One has high portals, another, low, there's a row of four here, two there.

In the larger painting, the tower is much lower. It only barely reaches the clouds. The construction looks sturdy and shaky at the same time. The galleries are evenly spaced, the buttresses heavy and solid. But there are entire pieces missing, as if some God has pounded his fist into the side, the right side, where the tower juts out onto a quay. The waterfront is bustling. Several ships are moored there, others lie at anchor in the bay. A large raft is floating in the greenish-blue water. The inside of the tower is visible, a spiral of increasingly smaller and narrower corridors with windows and archways. On the side of the tower directly facing us is a half-collapsed, almost boulder-like incline, maybe thirty or forty yards high. There are houses and huts on top, just as there are in parts of the gallery. Elsewhere, the gangway is blocked by enormous pulleys, winches, and cranes.

I walked into this tower, across the mountain of sand and rubble that reached to the third gallery. Because I had been stowing memories in the tower ever since I was a child, I had to go a long way up before I came to the section where I kept my stories. They lay, not only because I had stored them away at a later date, but because the spot appealed to me, in the innermost system of spiralling corridors. It was visible from the outside, like the fragile shell of a derelict building. What were they for, all those crypts and niches? Who needed those endless corridors that wound, tunnel-like, through the stone colossus?

I did.

I climbed from gallery to gallery, until I reached the place where the heart of the building pierced the sky. It was the seventh circle, on the right was a section in scaffolding, on the left, a steep stone incline that led to several portals. I went through the middle one and turned left. Darkness hung between the damp walls. A couple of workers were standing next to a pillar with a trough of mortar. I passed them and went right, deeper into the depths. An empty corridor, swathed in flickering torchlight, lay before me. Along the walls, on the dusty stone floor, pale flecks glimmered. I looked at them as I walked past. They were miniature still-lifes, about the size of the Nativity scene I had once seen at Eve's parents' house. My first fairy tale: 'Bread for God'. A man in a caftan and yarmulke, and his wife. He was carrying two challahs, braided white loaves, in his hands. Next to that: a man on top of a mesa, looking down, where another man had built a squarish woodpile and was about to set it alight. I hurried through the corridor, the dark curve with the red-lit walls. Our family portrait, the faces frozen in black and white. Zeno in Switzerland. In a room deep within the tower, the women in my life were sitting side by side. When I saw them, I felt myself filling with emptiness. 'Nina? Are you still there?'

She mumbled something.

'Do you still want to hear it?'

'Crime and punishment,' she said suddenly, very clearly. 'Nothing has changed.' Then there was silence. I heard the trees around the house, though I knew the wind was still.

This is Germany

NINA'S BREATHING WAS quiet and even. In and out. In and out. In and out. She was asleep. I closed my eyes. It was a long time before Bruegel's tower faded from my thoughts. I reached to the side, towards the little display on my night table, and found the hip flask. The whisky glowed in my head and instead of the tower I suddenly saw a church on a medieval square. All around it were coloured floodlights, so garish that the church looked as if it were made of plastic. Frankfurt. This was in Frankfurt. 'Almost makes you wonder where the air valve is,' I had said to Abram Gans. Gans was a colleague of Uncle Herman's and he was here to promote the German translation of his book, *State and Society*, already a classic upon publication. We were with a group of four others, and we'd gone on ahead to look out for a decent bar. 'That is a question which has always intrigued me,' he said, 'with regard to all of Germany.' The floodlights wrapped us in a mist of red, yellow, and blue. We walked with averted heads through the haze of light and found, back in the darkness again, the oak facade of a *Stube* called Am Kirchplatz. Gans waved to the group and ducked into the shadow of the swinging doors.

What made me suddenly think of that? I felt the gentle burning of the whisky in my stomach. Jameson's. Gans had been drinking Jameson's, there in that bar. My madeleine: the smell of Irish whisky.

We had sat at a round table in the middle of the bar, observed by a waiter in a polyester shirt and a couple of softly crooning Italian-Germans. It was late October, but already there was a plastic Christmas wreath in the middle of the table. We drank Hefe, white wine, and Jameson's. Gans and I were the outsiders in this group of novelists: he, a sociologist, me, a fairy tale writer. A deep twilight hung beneath the rafters. Someone said that this atmosphere gave him the 'Christmas Blues' and began reminiscing about a Christmas fair in a German village, stalls that sold greenery and cherubs and candles. I shivered. Gans looked at me and said, 'Did you know that Herman always said that the only real Christmas was a German one?' His gaze was heavy with irony. 'We don't always see eye to eye.' He asked me what my idea of Christmas was. 'Uncle Scrooge McDuck in 'Mickey's Christmas Carol', I said. 'Bing Crosby. Frank Sinatra singing "Have Yourself a Merry Little Christmas." Stockings over the fireplace.' Someone else made a remark about the Americanization of the world. I was about to open my mouth, when Gans said that Herman knew what he was talking about. He knew this country better than any of us, perhaps even better than the Germans themselves. I had stared at him with overly raised eyebrows. 'It's true,' said Gans. 'He knows the black and the white of it, and all the colours in between.'

Late that night I was woken up by the telephone. It took me a while to find it. I heard Gans's voice through the receiver and it sounded as if he were a continent away, even though his hotel room was directly above mine.

'Am I right in thinking, from your reaction this evening, that you don't know why Herman knew Germany so well?'

'Bram,' I said.

'Yes.'

I turned on the light and propped my pillow against the wall. 'I don't know a thing.'

'He never told you anything about it?'

'Herman only ever tells me something when he's trying to educate me.'

I picked up the phone and walked over to the mini-bar for a bottle of Coke. Outside, bluish light flickered. It was a sidestreet off the Kaiserstrasse, that shopping street awash with fur coats, Rolex watches, and Swiss chocolate. On this side were shops, hotels, and a couple of houses. The opposite side looked as if there had just been a war.

'He was sent along as a researcher with the units that liberated the camps. A misbegotten plan. They had seen such terrible things that they needed a scholar to make sense out of it. Herman was one of the first to set foot in Bergen-Belsen. It was an inferno. At the end of January there were 22,000 prisoners, at the end of February, 41,000, middle of April, 60,000. But by then, typhoid had broken out. In February, 7,000 people died, in March, more than 18,000. When Herman arrived the bodies were piled up all over the camp. There were even piles outside the barbed wire. They had run out of space. And everywhere, the smell of rotting flesh. The British soldiers checked all the barracks, but when they inspected the beds, they couldn't tell the difference between the living and the dead. Sometimes they were lying together in one bed. In some places, in the women's camp, there were no beds at all. People slept on the floor. There were so many dead, they had to use bulldozers to throw the bodies into pits. Then they transported those well enough to be moved and burned down the camp. Herman was there. He questioned the German commandant. He was there when the guards were led around and forced to see what they had done. They had no regret whatsoever, he said. Not a spark of compassion.

'Nathan, he saw this country as a well of misery, as the heart of evil. Yet he came back here after the war. He believed that we shouldn't leave the Germans alone with their guilt. He said: "The curse of Germany is romanticism. They've romanticized their own, non-existent past. They've romanticized a future. Let's not give them the chance to romanticize their guilt as well."'

Directly opposite the hotel was a large building with a badly painted sign that said Bazar Istanbul. The facade was blackened, the windows smashed. Earlier that evening, on the pavement outside the building, I had seen a roll of carpeting. The roll was moving now. A head popped out and looked at the blue light that was shooting nervously across the housefronts. Five police cars stood any old how in the middle of the street, their doors open. About fifteen feet away, a handful of policemen were holding three men in leather jackets at gunpoint. The head in the carpet roll moved slightly and then disappeared again. Sirens wailed in the distance. I drank my Coke and watched the film. I suddenly thought of the beggars I had seen in the Kaiserstrasse: three tall men dressed in rags. They had been standing outside a jewellery shop, bolt upright, completely motionless, their raised right hands like three bowls.

Gans was quiet. The silence on the line suggested a distance far greater than the one floor between us.

'I'm going back to sleep, Bram.'

It was a while before he answered. 'Yes,' he said. 'Yes.'

I finished my Coke and crawled back into bed. When I fell asleep, the memory of my night-time stroll through Frankfurt washed over me like a slow tidal wave. A taxi through the neon-lit darkness. The driver, bent over his steering wheel: Habib! Habib! 'This is the car of the Indian ambassador that you have scratched, sir!' Falling towers, streets arched their backs and reared up from the depths of the U-Bahn, the ruins of the night sky. Through gorges of concrete. Tilting flats, snarling cars emerged from the sewers. Spinning Big Mac cartons. From north to south and east to west.

In the middle of my troubled dream, the night broke in two. Day came, and then night once more.

I saw Abram Gans standing before me. He said: 'This is Germany.'

Zeno never showed up. No: 'It's a cold, cold land.' Nor my familiar denial: 'This isn't you.' The glow in the hearth dwindled, it grew colder, night bowed over the four-poster bed. I listened to Nina's breathing, waiting for the ghost of my brother, and now and then I went under and fragments of memory floated up in a half-dream: Frankfurt, America, Wales, Sophie, Rotterdam, Manhattan. It wasn't until deep in the night that I finally slipped away. I felt the sleepiness moving across my eyes like a shadow. I saw, before me, the view from the house where Eve and I had lived. The gently sloping hills, the grey ribbon of river between them and the little white shop on the far side of the valley. The image disappeared. Night fell. Behind me the sun sank into the countryside (as if it were bleeding to death on the hilltops), below me the last rays of daylight ran together in a muddled pallette of blue, yellow, orange and purple. I was floating. I was a traveller above a world without people, a world where no one had ever been.

On the screen, a pale moon hung over a dismal plain; across the aisle, fast asleep, was the only other passenger flying first class. Now and then I could feel the plane squeezing its way through the darkness. The floor quaked and an ominous tremor ran through the aluminium shell. The plane plodded on through a night as thick as treacle.

We sat next to each other, Eve by the window, me on the aisle. We stared silently at the screen. Now and then we looked at each other, and smiled, so we wouldn't have to speak.

Halfway through the movie, when it had been quiet for a long time, Eve fell asleep. She was sitting upright in her cornflower-blue seat and still seemed to be watching the adventures before her, but her eyes were closed and her face was empty as glass. I leaned over and carefully removed her headphones. Her eyebrows twitched, but she didn't wake up. She sighed once and laid her head on my shoulder.

'Can I get you a drink, Mr Hollander?'

A stewardess, who looked as if she had just been freshly unwrapped. She leaned over me. I gave her a mechanical smile.

'Whisky, no ice, a drop of water.'

Glancing at Eve, she listed the various brands in stock. I chose mine, and smiled again when she did, as if to confirm my order. A minute later she returned with my glass on a paper napkin, something I had become accustomed to in the United States. She had also brought a blanket, which she laid over Eve and tucked loosely around her.

'Would you like to see the rest of the film?'

I turned my eyes to the screen, where four silent men on bony horses were riding down the desolate main street of a shabby desert town. I shook my head.

Shortly after the stewardess had left, the picture vanished. The cabin was enveloped in the glow of tiny bulbs. I looked sideways, at the window, and saw nothing but blackness.

When we had said goodbye at JFK, Manny had clasped us, as they say, to his bosom. The departure hall buzzed around us, a cloud of voices descended from intercoms, in the background was the rattling of suitcases on wheels, the faint, faraway screech of jet engines.

'This may be our last goodbye,' he said.

At these words, I had felt my heart sink.

'What are you talking about?' I cried, too lightly, too cheerfully. 'We're flying KLM!'

There was relieved laughter. But all three of us had known what he meant. He wasn't getting any younger, we were going back to Europe, and . . .

Eve yawned and rubbed her eyes. 'God,' she said, 'I hate flying.' She had been borne to the surface of sleep on automatic pilot. Just before we left she had taken half a Mogadon, hoping she would sleep through the entire flight. Her waking up now didn't mean a thing. She always woke up after half an hour, as if she needed to have one final look around before really falling asleep. When I asked her if the blanket was too warm, she frowned, but before she could answer, her eyes fell shut again. The wrinkle between her eyebrows faded. It was as if someone had drawn a veil across her face: her features grew soft and rounded, her clenched lips relaxed. As she sank farther and farther down, her mouth falling slightly open, I felt a pang in my chest.

From the first day we met, in 1970, there had never been a moment when I felt I had to keep anything back from her. I was not the sort of man who could easily relax, I knew that, but with Eve, I came very close to finding the peace that I had been searching for all my life. We had got to know each other one summer in Ipswich, when I was wandering through a park and ended up at the tourist office where she worked. She asked where I was from. When I told her I came from the Netherlands, she was surprised. She gave me a map with the route to some local tourist attraction and a few brochures. Then, just as I was about to leave, I asked her if she might like to have a drink with me. That was the first time I had ever dared to ask such a thing of a woman I had barely met.

She looked at me for a moment, and then nodded, as if I were a supplier who had delivered a box of Xerox paper and wanted to know if he should bring another one the following week.

It was a Sunday when we set off. I sat beside her in the car and saw the asphalt lying before us like a discarded ribbon. We drove uphill and downhill, past hedges and walls and down a narrow, hollow road where Eve honked before rounding the bend. 'I come here every weekend,' she said. 'This is the best of England, I always say. Perhaps I'm wrong, I don't know, there are so many parts of England I've never seen, but still . . . Here we are.'

We'd stopped outside a small village pub. Eve parked the car on the verge and we went inside. It was a bare, empty space with an unpainted wooden floor, wobbly round tables where silent men in caps sat with women in flowery dresses, and a bar made of dark wood that gleamed like fresh dung. Eve went up to the bar and greeted the woman standing behind it. They chatted briefly. Then the woman looked over at me and nodded. I nodded back. About three minutes later Eve beckoned and we walked out through a side door, into a small garden with an unmowed lawn. We sat down at a white wooden table, while the lady with whom Eve had spoken began bringing out the tea things. As the table grew fuller and fuller, Eve and the landlady exchanged bits of news. I listened with my eyes closed, the sun on my face.

Within ten minutes we were separated by a sea of plates, forks, platters of scones and sponges, sandwiches and cream. Eve poured the tea. We drank from thick green cups.

'And what do you think of England?'

'It's the Occident,' I said. 'The land where the European sun sets. I saw a tramp in London once. A huge black fellow in a coat that was ripped at the seams, with enormous shoes, no laces of course, a ratty beard, frostbite on his face.'

'Frost . . .'

'Frostbite. Blackish patches, as if he'd been burned. You normally only see it in Eskimos and Lapps, or Austrians who've had an accident in the mountains. I realize that some people are less fortunate than others, but I'd never really thought much about it until I came here, to the land I regarded as . . . as the zenith of Western European civilization, a land that had been governed for so long by Socialists. At first I assumed it was the fault of the Conservatives, that they were the reason this country was going to the dogs, but the day after I saw that tramp, I arrived in Birmingham, and the day after that, in Manchester. It was like travelling back in time. To the turn of the century. The air smelled of carbon monoxide, the streets were filthy, cardboard boxes lying everywhere, pale, skinny children playing with a leaky football. The buildings were sooty, with smashed windows, blackened chimneys that no longer smoked, most of them half-collapsed. The walls were covered with genuine cries for help. Somewhere in one of these "Coronation Streets" I saw a blank wall with goalposts painted on it, and over that: Help us! Abandoned factories, polluted rivers, people dressed in rags. God, I mean, I've read Ford Madox Ford and Waugh and Barbara Pym and here I am in that country and nothing is what I expected. That can't all be the Conservatives' fault. The place is too far gone for that.'

'You've seen only part of the country.'

'Oh, I've been through Kent and East Anglia, too, and I've driven down seemingly endless country lanes and wandered through village after village of pastel-coloured cottages. I've seen splendid old pubs, where they still pull the beer by hand, all those things you English are so proud of. But I've never forgotten that tramp in London. I keep seeing him, a big man, slightly stooped, in a car park with three grimy walls, rubbish piled up in the corners, newspapers with pictures of naked girls blowing across the pavement. The sickly smell of rotting vegetables. England, the future of Europe.'

'Aren't you exaggerating just a bit?'

I had shaken my head.

But I didn't tell her, there on the grass, about when I had heard the church bells ringing in Ipswich. It was a Sunday afternoon, around five or six o'clock, the sun shone low in the deserted streets. Quiet, hardly any cars, the occasional pedestrian. I had drunk half a lager in a dreary pub next to the bus station. Then I had walked into town. I was standing there looking into a bookshop window, when I heard bells ringing at the end of the street. The sound came rolling down the street like a great bronze ball. The heavy peals echoed between the houses. I began walking in the direction of the sound, when I heard, in the distance, the first unsteady tones of another bell, with a slightly higher pitch. And then I heard another and another and another. After several minutes the chiming of several dozen church bells was ricocheting through the streets. I could no longer tell where the sound was coming from. It was behind me, in front of me, it rained down from the sky, it leapt up from the pavement. There wasn't a soul in sight. It was as if I were completely alone in this town, where everything was sound, spiralling streamers of sound. The street began turning beneath my feet, the houses melted, the whole town was a whirlpool of noise.

'No,' I had said, when Eve told me that the country was in a transitional phase, that things were getting better, much better, in fact. 'No, things aren't getting better. England is an example. It shows us that everything falls apart in the end. It's a law of nature, from man to mite: birth, life, death. Inevitable ruin.'

Eve had looked at me with raised eyebrows.

'Joseph de Maistre,' I said. '*Les Nuits de Saint Petersbourg.*'

I had leaned back in my chair, that afternoon, surrounded by the flowering grass and the tall privet hedge, vaguely aware that I could stay here forever, as if I had travelled through a hurricane and landed in the eye of the storm, where everything was peaceful, everything still. Birth, life, death, it was all here, but different. Here it was a natural progression, grass grew tall and went to seed, birds rose up and were caught in mid-flight by a falcon, a rabbit sat in a field staring at the horizon and was attacked by a weasel. In London and Birmingham and Manchester it had been decay, the squirming of maggots on a rotting corpse. Here, that same process was softened by the tranquillity of the countryside. The same, but easier to accept.

Halfway through tea we had to shelter from a sudden downpour. We stood side by side under a hurriedly fetched umbrella, while the rain came down around us. Eve shivered in her thin cotton dress. It was raining so hard, we couldn't see the pub. At a certain moment we had both looked sideways, straight into each other's eyes, and knew it had happened.

The rest of my holiday I spent round and about the town. We saw each other almost daily and it was as if Eve were pulling me along in her wake, straight out of the chilly rooms of my mind. I began to see through her eyes and realized that the world was worth seeing. The trees stood in clusters on the hills, like little old men hatching a plot, the sky was blue, the clouds were as creamy as Ambrosia rice. It was an English summer: twittering birds, the sparkle of sunlight on the hedges along the roads that led to the villages where Eve liked to drink tea, patches of farmland scattered on either side. The corn stood tall, the saturated yellow of old bronze. Here and there was a tractor waiting in a field, so old it was impossible to tell what colour the thing had been, and sometimes, in the distance, a long, narrow hill where oak and beech trees grew.

I felt like a blind man who opens his eyes after an operation and sees for the very first time. Everything was new, everything clean and fresh, everything equally marvellous.

The evening of my departure, in Eve's flat, we kissed goodbye and I promised to return within a month. Six months later we were living together in a valley in Wales, where she had been made director of the local tourist office. Shortly after that we got married and I became an inhabitant of the Occident, the land to which we were now headed.

Eve was asleep and not asleep. I knew she would wake up again, the way she just had, but apparently she wasn't yet ready to open her eyes. She let the tide of sleep flow through her, back and forth, back and forth, slow and pleasing. She was dreaming, I could tell, and I wondered what about. Two days earlier, while still in the U.S., she had told me one morning what she had seen in her sleep. She saw me, straight-backed, lonely, alone, on the edge of the desert. She sat in the car and looked through the windscreen at the stripe of the horizon, and at her husband, standing some thirty yards away from the car, between her and the sloping land, staring into space. The sun lay on the plain and was red as blood and the blood of the sun flowed out into the sky, over the sand and the rocks and . . . The image reminded her of something she had seen before, she said, during our first summer together. After tea we had driven to East Bergholt and got out to take a walk. As we climbed a hill covered with oak trees, we had seen the sun setting. 'Run,' I had said, 'to the top.' But as we ran, the light began to fade. We ran uphill, faster and faster, laughing, crying. By the time we reached the top, we were nearly too late. We gazed at the horizon where the orange light flowed over old England, the Isle of Gramarye, the days of King Arthur and his noble knights, a raised sword before the globe of light that . . . And there in the desert, in her dream, I had stared at the light in the very same way, said Eve, all alone, a man who would never be not-alone. Both times she had wondered why I seemed most alone when I was staring at a blood-red, setting sun. What did I see in that light? What did I see that she didn't? And why did she have the uneasy feeling that she never would?

'It was a dream, Eve, just a dream,' I had said. 'You shouldn't attach any significance to dreams.'

'Nathan, I don't know you, and you don't want to be known.' The first time that I had ever spoken about Zeno, for instance, was one evening when she was reminiscing about her youth and had told me how, as a child, she had been so impressed by the Passion that she wished she were Catholic instead of Anglican. Then she could become a nun and suffer, like Jesus, for the salvation of mankind. Apparently I had smiled at her and said there was no need, Zeno was already doing that. When she asked me what I meant, I had shrugged my shoulders and stared out the window.

'What are you trying to say?' I had looked at her, sitting there on the edge of the hotel bed, slender and blond and, despite her early-morning disarray, elegant.

'Nothing. Only, I know so little about you. I'm not "attaching any significance" to that dream, as you put it, but I do understand the symbolism. I see you standing there, but I have no idea what's going on inside you. I know every inch of your body and I know that warm weather gives you a headache and that you hate tea with breakfast and . . . All sorts of things. But I don't know what's underneath those things.'

'Do you think I know that about you? Do you think it's possible to know another person?'

'Don't turn this into a philosophical debate,' she had said, rather sharply for her. 'This isn't something you can intellectualize. I'm talking about us. I'm not talking about absolute knowledge. I'm talking about the fact that I know nothing about you, nothing about your family. I don't even understand why you've all got such peculiar names!'

That conversation, filled with memories and accumulated misunderstanding, had taken place less than two days before and still echoed in our dealings. We had been, up until then, two people who loved each other and were wise enough to leave each other alone. We didn't have the sort of modern relationship in which mutual analysis inflicted so many wounds that you stayed together for the memory of the pain alone. But the code, the unspoken agreement not to trespass on each other's mental territory, had been broken, and now we were flying back in a half-empty plane and it was as if we had only just met.

The strange thing about the sudden loss of intimacy between myself and Eve was that I didn't know what the deeper cause might be. Nothing we had said, or not said, on the plane. That was merely the completion of something that had begun earlier, an elegant sort of farewell; my balanced inner peace and her Anglo-Saxon cool, merging to form the paragon of the happy divorce.

The estrangement happened long before, I thought, as I sipped my whisky.

We had gone to spend a few days in the east of England. 'A romantic weekend,' Eve had said, adding that we 'bloody well' deserved it. She herself was tired, dead tired, but it was my silence that had been the deciding factor. The last few months, she said, I had changed, I was colder, more withdrawn, and she had reminded me how, a while back, she had come home and found me in the sagging armchair by the fireplace, staring at the chunks of wood and the wads of newspaper below them that flickered in the dusky hearth like motionless white flames. When she asked what I was doing, I jumped. Several seconds went by before I was able to tell her that I had forgotten to light the fire. 'You're just a bit overworked,' she had said, 'we ought to get away for a while.'

In Colchester we found bed and breakfast in an ancient medieval house. By the time we arrived it was dark and all the rooms were taken. We put down our bags and waited while the landlady glanced through her booking register. 'All I have left,' she said after a while, 'is the bridal cottage.' She had led the way, chatting to Eve. As we walked out the back door of the hotel and the darkness enfolded us, an image flashed into my mind, one I didn't recognize: through a window framed in weathered wood I saw a tall chair with an embroidered seat, and in that chair was Eve. She looked back over her shoulder and smiled. I suddenly thought: She doesn't belong with me.

The cottage was even older than the main building. It leaned forward wearily, sheltered by an enormous linden tree whose crown extended over the roof. The windows were small squares of bumpy glass. The landlady unlocked the door and let Eve in first. 'This way, dear.' On the first floor she showed us a room that was made almost entirely of wood. The low roof was a nest of collar beams, the floor had the patina of boards that had been trodden on by generations, the walls were panelled with gleaming dark wainscotting. There probably wasn't a splinter of wood in that room younger than Eve, the landlady, and I put together. A huge brass bed stood against one wall, and opposite that, a small wooden sideboard. Next to the window, which offered a view of the hotel, stood a little table with a chestnut gleam.

When the landlady had left us, we stood in the room and looked around in silence.

'It's almost too much,' Eve had said.

I nodded.

'I mean, it's almost a caricature of Merry Old England.'

'The Tourist Office couldn't have done better,' I said.

That was the sentence that did it. Although it had nothing to do with us, I knew for certain that this one, casual little remark had said it all. I had felt the loneliness slipping over my shoulders like an old coat. I stared at the wood and wondered where that chill had suddenly come from. Before I could think of anything the cold penetrated deeper inside me. I felt Eve drifting away. The feeling was so strong that I panicked, as if I had a great black lake inside, an internal Loch Ness whose slow current parted to reveal the soaring head of a prehistoric monster. I turned round, wanted to call her, but when I looked at her, she smiled. I stammered something and said I was going to have a shower.

In the bathroom, I had stared at my reflection in the mirror. It was as if my body had acquired a roommate who was perfectly at home in his new surroundings.

Later, when I went into the bedroom, Eve was lying naked on the big bed. She looked over her shoulder and smiled with her eyes. I saw her rosy body, soft and seductive in the light reflected by the wood, and felt the coldness whirling inside me. I thought: This used to be a sign. I heard our glass of happiness fall.

The bridal cottage in Colchester was where it had begun. This much I knew, though I didn't have the slightest notion why.

I had told myself to stay calm, to wait, let things run their course, in a few months' time I would know what I wanted and what I should do. That was how I lived my life, that was what others valued in me, what I valued in myself. The chill I felt was perfectly normal. All over the world were men and women who felt alone in the company of their partner. It was just part of being together, and probably only temporary. I knew all that. But still I spiralled inescapably downward, towards an end I didn't know and didn't want. I stood at the window of our house in Wales, next to the cold, blackened hearth, and stared out at the rain, the river, the indifferent landscape. Sometimes the grey monotony of the valley gripped me so hard by the throat that I raced upstairs and ran a bath. Once I was lying in the hot water my thoughts would drift along on the steam to the panelled ceiling and I'd remember, with painful accuracy, the wooden room in the bridal cottage.

Eve stirred in her seat.

'Are you awake?'

She opened her eyes (but slowly, the way the lights come up in the theatre) and looked at me. 'Just barely,' she said.

'Would you like a drink?'

She shook her head.

I raised my glass and sipped.

'Why don't you try and get some sleep?' she asked.

I smiled. 'I only sleep in bed. I once made a deal with myself that there had to be at least one place in the world where I could feel safe. I decided on my bed. That's where I can sleep.'

'Why shouldn't you feel safe anywhere else, N?'

I turned and looked at her. 'You really are awake, aren't you?'

She nodded.

There was a long silence. Eve, who had discovered the blanket across her legs, pushed it off. She repeated her question.

'Have you ever had a good look at my mother?' I asked. 'She takes care of everything. And when I say everything, I mean: the entire world. Not only does she keep an inexhaustible supply of canned goods, a buffer stock of toilet paper that would last an orphanage five years, and enough detergent to clean all of Europe, she keeps track of the rest of the world, too. Every night before she goes to sleep, my mother talks to God and tells him what still needs to be done. If other people think my mother is a disbeliever, it's probably because she's so critical of God. He's not doing his job. He doesn't put away his toys. God doesn't wash behind his ears. He doesn't listen to my mother.'

I paused. I noticed I was getting worked up. Then I said, 'I'll bet my mother is God's mother, too. Do you know how she sleeps?'

Eve shook her head.

'With clenched fists and gnashing teeth. Her teeth are worn down from all that gnashing.'

'So are yours.'

'That's what I'm trying to tell you. This is the world I come from, that's the way I am. Everything has to be under control, and on a plane I have nothing under control. That's why I can't sleep.'

And that's why, Eve, I thought, he always sits next to you, when you're driving, with one hand in the strap above the door, the other hand on the dashboard. That's why I hardly slept the first year of our marriage, and if I did, I woke up in the middle of the night, screaming. Terrifying nightmares, all year long. I sat bolt upright and roared to the skies. I roared so loudly I was hoarse the next morning. I had inherited that from my mother. My mother had dreamed that way all her life. Sometimes it woke us up, but after a while it didn't scare us anymore.

'You can't have everything under control, N.'

'I know.'

'We, we two, for instance. You can't have us under control.'

We looked at each other for a long time.

'I can't tell if you're happy,' she said.

I tipped back my head slightly, as if I was about to look up, but kept my eyes on her. 'Do you feel that I'm unhappier since we've been together?'

Eve shook her head. 'The point is,' she said, 'you're not *happier*.'

'Happiness doesn't exist.'

She nodded a vehement 'yes.'

'No,' I said. 'Some times are less terrible than others, sometimes it even seems as if you know why you're alive. But that's not happiness. That's the minimum requirement for going on.'

'For God's sake, N.'

I twisted round in my seat until I was sitting almost in front of her.

'Listen,' I said. 'It's 1957. Haifa. Arabian snipers are prowling about the centre of town. Shlomo Finkelstein has taken cover from the bullets in the portico of an apartment building. All of a sudden his friend Wolf Kreisky comes running into the portico. He falls against the door and stands there, panting. "My God," says Finkelstein, "what are you doing here?" His friend looks up, points to the Bay of Haifa and says, "Life has no meaning, it's hopeless, I'm going to throw myself in the water and drown!" They get into a terrible row. Finkelstein tries to convince his friend that life really does have meaning. Okay, maybe things are tough now, but after a storm comes a calm, and so on, and so on. Kreisky won't be persuaded. "After a storm comes a calm," he says, "and after the calm comes more rain. I'm sick and tired of it, I'm giving up." Finkelstein gets angry. "Fine, go ahead, drown yourself. There's the water, what's to stop you?" Kreisky looks at him, flabbergasted. He stares out at the street, where bullets are tearing up the pavement. "Are you crazy?" he says. "With those snipers?"

Eve smiled briefly. 'Why,' she asked me, 'do I get the feeling that I'm your sniper?'

Part Three/Four

Punishment

I WOKE UP alone and my face was stiff with cold. I vaguely remembered a dream, a different dream than the one about Molly, but the images had dissolved upon awakening. All I knew was that I had heard my father's voice. 'Pack your bags. We're leaving.' Those were his words. For a long time I lay on my back, thinking about the lost dream, when suddenly I was aware of the crackling of the hearth-fire. I sat up, and only then did I see the glow of the flames. A brisk, lively fire was burning in the grate, not too wild, the sort of fire that quickly heats up a room. I looked at it and thought: For two days I've been playing boy scout, I assumed I was the only one who knew the art of firemaking. I sank back and began thinking about Nina. She's a woman, not a child anymore. Thirty. I talk to her as if she's an adult, but I treat her like a child. I want to let her lean on me, when I'm the one who . . . Crime and Punishment. Those were her words. Always been alone, led my own life, looked after myself. So I wouldn't have to be dependent? So I'd never feel guilty? I frowned. 'Doctor Spielvogel,' I said, closing my eyes, 'do you think I want to sleep with my mother and murder my father?'

'Good morning.'

I shot up. Nina was standing at the foot of the bed holding a tray. She walked round to my night table, swept aside my still-life of candle, matches, hip flask, and Alka Seltzers, and put down the tray. 'You didn't tell me you were doing a correspondence course in psychology.'

She picked up the mug of coffee from the tray and handed it to me. I stared at her smiling face and moved my lips. 'Are you going to take this, or did you want me to help you drink it?'

I held out my hand.

'You'd better hurry. I've filled the bath. There's another bucket of water boiling on the stove, but if you wait too long, there won't be any left.'

'Good grief,' I said.

She was still smiling. 'But I must warn you. I took the liberty of going first and I didn't feel like lugging all those buckets upstairs again, so you'll have to make do with second-hand water.'

'God, you're . . .'

'Terrific? Good enough for now. We'll get around to fantastic.'

Zeno, I thought. Zeno, you've changed us both: me, into a bowl of mush, her, into a pillar of right-mindedness and reason.

I drank the coffee, nerves came to life, muscles filled with blood, the cobwebs of sleep melted away. Nina took the mug and handed me a plate with two thick slices of bread and cheese. I was just about to bite into one of the sandwiches, when I looked at her and said, 'I had a dream . . .'

'About Molly.'

'No, I don't mean that. I dreamed about my father. He said, "Pack your things. We're leaving."'

'And when you woke up, you thought: Why not try the Oedipal approach for a change?'

'Sorry,' I said.

'Sorry? Again?' She picked up the mug she had brought for herself and drank. 'The unimpeachable integrity of Nathan Hollander.' She put down her mug and looked at me impudently. 'If we ever get out of here, you ought to ask for the phone number of Uncle Herman's call girl.' I looked at her, unmoved. 'What you need,' she said, plucking an invisible speck of dust from the sleeping bag, 'is for someone to give you a good shaking. Honestly, Nathan, you're my uncle, and I like you for all sorts of reasons, but you're also an unbelievably bourgeois sonofabitch, with that tame life you lead and those impeccable manners.'

I lowered the plate to my lap and picked up my mug. The hearth was burning cheerfully. I had lit sound, responsible fires. Fires that didn't use too up much wood, or too little. But this: a feast of flames and warmth. Nuncle Chaim, I said to myself, Magnus, help me.

I ate my bread, finished my coffee, and climbed out of bed. Nina piled the breakfast things onto the tray and left the room. I pulled on some clothes, socks, and shoes, and went upstairs.

The bathroom smelled of sandalwood. Two large towels were hanging on the rack, next to the bath stood a wooden stool, and on top of that was my shaving gear and a washcloth. I felt the water. It was still agreeably warm.

Agreeably warm, I thought. Agreeably goddamn warm.

I started getting undressed, laid my clothes on the sink, and stepped into the bath.

For two days we hadn't been able to wash. The water felt so good, it made me want to sing. I picked up the shaving brush from the stool and wet it. Nina came in with a steaming bucket. She grabbed a towel and supported the bottom of the bucket as she lifted it above the water.

'I'll pour it in at your feet,' she said. 'Very slowly. Just say when.'

It warmed up fast, but I didn't want her to stop. By the time the bucket was empty, my forehead was beaded with sweat. I felt the warmth soaking into my bones. I laid my head on the edge of the bath, eyes closed.

'You look tired,' said Nina.

'I *am* tired.'

She rolled up her sleeves and reached for the washcloth lying on the stool. She dipped it in the water and rubbed it with a bar of soap. 'Sit up straight.'

'Why . . .' I started to sit up. 'I may be old, love, but I'm not an invalid. Leave me . . .'

'Stop whining, Nathan.'

She came and stood behind me and began lathering my shoulders. I sat up and felt the rough cloth chafing against my skin. From my head to my toes, I felt my resistance draining away. I wanted to fight this hospital treatment, but I had no strength, no will. She washed my back, my chest, dipped the washcloth into the water again and scrubbed my face. 'Lie back.' I did as she said and closed my eyes.

'Thank you,' I said after a while. My voice sounded hoarse.

'Don't you need to shave?'

I picked up the bar of soap and rubbed it between my hands. Nina sat down on the edge of the bath and watched as I lathered my jaws. Her right hand played idly in the water. I picked up the razor, placed it next to my ear, and drew the first pink tracks through the foam.

'Is it still sharp?' she asked.

I felt the water move.

'The razor. Is it still sharp?'

'Yes.' I began on the other side of my face.

The water rippled back and forth. A silky ebb and flow over my stomach and thighs. I felt something I didn't want to feel and took a deep breath. The blade scraped across the stubble, I ran my fingers over my jaws to see if I had missed a spot. Clean. I thought: dirty and clean at the same time. 'I'm coming out.' Nina stood up and grabbed one of the towels. I looked at her for a moment and then got up. If she hadn't stayed in there with me, I would probably have spent another half hour in the warm water. When I was standing on the floor, dripping wet, she wrapped the towel around me and started to rub.

'Nina.'

She was rubbing me down like a horse.

'Nina.'

'What?'

'I can do that myself. Thank you.'

'Stop whining, Nathan.'

'Your vocabulary certainly has improved in the last twenty hours.'

She turned me round and dried my legs. 'Maybe I've just realized that you're not the type that thrives on intelligent conversation.'

'Thank you.'

'My pleasure. Here, you can do the rest.'

I leaned over, splashed some bathwater on my face, and dried myself off. Then I got dressed.

I was sitting on the edge of the bed in the hunting room, putting on my shoes, when Nina came in to ask if there were any clean clothes.

'I'm using Uncle Herman's things, whatever fits, underwear and socks.'

'What about me?'

I went to the cupboard and pulled it open. 'Take whatever you need.'

She rummaged around until she found a pair of heavy tweed trousers, a couple of T-shirts, and a few pairs of socks. She laid the pile of clothes on the foot of the bed and began undressing by the fire.

Although we had been in the house for two days now and spent two nights in the same bed, I had never seen her naked. We had always gone to bed in shirts and trousers because of the cold. Now she was taking off her clothes, right here in front of me. I averted my eyes.

'N?' I looked sideways. She was wearing a T-shirt and Uncle Herman's corduroys. 'My panties and bra are lying in the kitchen. I washed them in the bath this morning and laid them out to dry by the stove. Would you get them for me?'

It was only when I was back in the hunting room and about to hand her the two wisps of lace that I realized she had nothing on under her clothes. 'I'll go get a fire started in the library,' I said, holding out her underwear.

'I've already done that.' She ignored my outstretched hand and pulled the T-shirt over her head. I turned away.

It was a while before she spoke.

'May I have my things, or are you just going to stand around playing with them?'

I held my hand out behind me, but felt nothing. When I turned around again, she was standing there naked. Before I could say a word, she took the panties, stepped into them, grabbed the bra, and put it on. I shook my head and walked out of the room.

Sure enough, the fire in the library was burning, but it had already died down a bit. I threw on more wood and stared into the hearth from my chair. In my head the trains of logic rode back and forth. They changed tracks, waited at the station, sped past each other, and disappeared from view. For a long time I sat there, a helpless victim of my own thoughts. Then I stood up and went back to the hunting room.

'Listen here, young lady,' I said, as I walked in.

Nina was sitting on the edge of her bed, wearing only her underwear.

'If you think I'm naive enough to let you practise on me, you're dead wrong. This is going to stop right now.'

She said nothing.

'Did you hear me?'

She looked at me, but I couldn't tell by the expression on her face if my words had sunk in. I felt anger rising inside me like boiling milk.

'What are you going to do about it?' she said finally.

'Do you know what you need?' I shouted. And I thought: My God, I'm shouting, I'm raising my voice. 'You should have had a stricter upbringing!' I thought it sounded rather weak myself, this continuation of my initial threat.

'And who do you think should've done it? What about you? Are you going to teach me a lesson?' She turned round and crawled onto the bed, her buttocks towards me. She pulled down her panties, and said, 'Punish me, Nathan. Go ahead, punish me.'

'Dammit, Nina.'

'Punish me.'

I took a step towards her, voices began crying inside my head. Then I raised my hand and spanked her.

She screamed.

'Jesus.' I heard myself and was shocked by the distance between the man who had spoken and the other man, within. I laid one hand on her back and brought the other down on her buttocks. Not hard, but I could hear the blows echoing in the room.

'Punish . . .'

'God.'

'Bad . . .'

I recognized something in her voice. My hand came down and whacked against the soft skin. Molly.

'Nathan,' Nina wept.

I froze, my hand in mid-air.

'Please.'

I felt the two Nathans that I was become one again.

'Punish Nina.'

I had an erection. I turned around and held my head in my hands. I crumbled like an old house. Then I felt Nina's arms around me.

'Nathan,' she said. 'Don't.'

Not my name, I thought, not my name. I shook my head. She turned me round. She was naked. 'Come.' I let her lead me to the bed, and on the way there, I became someone else. The man who forced her down on her back, took her nipples in his mouth and bit them so firmly that she whimpered, wasn't me. It was a beast that took her, as if that were simply a law of nature. He pushed her legs apart, slid into her and fucked her as if it didn't matter who she was, or what. She moved against him as if she only wanted him more, her head went from side to side. She slipped out from under him and crouched over him. Her pelvis moved. He ate her. Eat me. Eat me. Eat me up. She came, shivering, fell on top of him and lay there for a long time. Then he felt her lips around his glans. Her tongue circled around it and he felt his erection harden. She took him deep in her mouth, her head moved up and down. She got on her hands and knees. He came up behind her and slid inside. They fucked in silence, until she looked over her shoulder. He felt his heart skip a beat. He felt her hand. She was touching herself. She was panting. He felt her belly tighten under his hand. His other hand clutched at her breast. From far, far away came the tide of his orgasm. 'Nathan.' He heard himself. Breathing like a god on the last day of Creation.

A Fairy Tale

'AND NOW,' SAID Nina. It sounded like an observation, but I
heard a question. The hearth was blazing with the armload of wood
that I, in my post-coital recklessness, had thrown on the fire. And
now, meaning: what next? I closed my eyes.

'A fairy tale. A story.'

'You're going to tell me a fairy tale?'

A question like an observation. Now, an observation like a question. I closed my eyes and opened my mouth. I always tell a fairy
tale after making love, I wanted to say.

When he had reached the edge of the forest, Berg stopped running.
He looked back, but in the white mist above the snow, there was
nothing to be seen, not even the tall, angular figure of Block. The
row of pine trees curved gently towards the road in the distance,
also invisible, though Berg knew exactly where it was and which
way it went. The green of their needles was nearly black, the trunks
greyish-white from yesterday's blizzard. He took a deep breath. The
wintry air burnt his throat and came out again as smoke. He looked
back once more and then stepped between the trees.

In the old days, everything had been different. The winters, his
father had told him, were not as harsh and there was always enough
food to make it through the four white months. But his father had
disappeared, and less than a week later, Block had been appointed
as the new forester and Berg and his mother had had to exchange
the house on the common for a shack on the outskirts of town,

even farther away than the black-tarred barns, almost as far as the rubbish dump. Berg had been seven at the time. Now he was nearly a man, fourteen years old, old enough to help his mother.

He slalomed between the pine-trees like a rabbit. It had snowed for so long and frozen so hard that even here, in the depths of the forest, you couldn't see the ground. As he walked, he watched out for tracks, but it was as if even the animals had thought it too cold to leave their burrows and dens. He pulled his scarf tighter and sized up the ditch that divided the pine forest from the wooded hill, where the oaks and beech trees grew. It was quiet among the trees. Berg looked up and felt giddy. The bare trunks looked as if they were made of rope. They hung down motionlessly, held high in the air by the dark, scruffy knots of their crowns.

When he came out of the forest again and saw the snow-covered fields that ran from here to Rodel, his tempo changed. He walked more slowly now, slightly stooped, his grey felt cap with the two peaks pulled way down over his ears. With his rounded back, head bowed one minute, slightly raised the next, marching along through the snow, he looked like a rabbit. Once Block had even shot at him, but he had leapt behind an oak tree, just in time. As the shots crackled and the bullets ripped off pieces of bark, he had screamed that he was Berg, the son of Berg-Who-Was-Gone.

He walked along the edge of the forest until he came to the forked oak. Then he turned his back to the trees and crossed the rolling field.

Beneath the snow, he knew, the ground was pitch-black and barren. In the old days, when his father was still there, the farmers hadn't touched the stubble, they had left it alone until it was time to plough. During autumn and winter the brownish-yellow film over the fields slowly rotted and seeped into the ground, together with the spring rains and the meltwater. But Block, in his very first year as forester, had ordered the farmers to burn off the fields, and he had shown them himself how this was to be done. It had been a warm October evening, the light was already beginning to redden, and the full moon hung pale over the woods beyond the road to Saens. Block had started with the largest field and placed a bundle of hay in each corner. Next to each bundle stood a man, and when the forester pointed his rifle at the sky and fired, the assembled villagers saw the torches at the corners of the field go down. The four fires were small at first, barely visible, but no sooner had the shot died away when, from all four corners, a flood of red and yellow and orange swept in towards the middle and went out with a dull bang. There was a brief silence. Everyone stared at the thin mist of smoke above the field. Then someone threw his cap in the air and the first shouts rose. In the distance, the figures of Block and the other three men appeared out of the blue-grey haze. They came walking towards the barns, where the others had stood watching. It was, Berg remembered, as if they had come from another world.

That same evening they burned off all the stubble and when night fell, the sky so dark blue that the heavens looked like a gaping hole, the men gathered on the common and Block ordered them to open a cask of beer. The celebration that followed lasted until the moon sank below the horizon. Since then it had been the same every year. The fields were burned and the excitement over the firestorm that swept across the dry stubble was celebrated by emptying the biggest cask of beer they could find. For days after the new festival, which was soon known as 'Stubble Burning,' powdery ashes floated into the village and everything was stuffy and grey. Only after the first autumn rains was the village clean again.

But that festival was long past now. It was nearly midwinter, and Berg knew that they still had two bitter-cold months to go before the first green appeared on the trees and his hunger could be stilled. For weeks on end he had eaten porridge, cold porridge, because there was no more bread and the kindling he gathered wasn't enough to drive the frost from the little house. In the old days the barns on the edge of the village had been full. There was so much grain, the wooden walls bulged. But for the past few years the store had run out before the winter was over. No one knew exactly why this was because the harvests had been no worse than usual. Wood, too, was scarce, because Block had forbidden them to cut down any trees. There was enough firewood for everyone to get through the winter, he had said, and plenty of wood left over from the last coppicing. That may have been true, but that was only for the larger land-owners, who regularly cleared away the brushwood from along their fields and gathered it in bundles. Berg and his mother had, except for a tiny vegetable garden, no land at all. If Johan, the village elder, hadn't given them wood from time to time, they would only have been able to light a fire once a week.

He was in the middle of the field when he found what he was looking for. There, where the gentle swell changed to a sunken road, lay a large bundle of sticks. He looked around him, left, right, in front and behind, and when he didn't see anyone he jumped down and disappeared.

The road was hollow and sheltered, the snow lay ankle-deep. To the left Berg saw nothing but sky. To the right, the land sloped gently and he could see the brook in a shallow valley. Berg got down on his knees and began untying the rope he had tied around his waist. He made a loop in the rope and slipped it around one end of the bundle of sticks. He was just working the loop towards the middle of the bundle, when he heard a voice. Leaning forward, his legs, his arms, his whole body turned to stone, he sat and listened. From where he sat, all the way to the village, to Saens, to Rodel, he heard the silence. But no voice. He stood up and looked around. Emptiness everywhere.

When he picked up the rope and tried, for the second time, to slide it around the sticks, he heard the voice again.

'Boy.'

He was so startled that he jumped back two paces.

'Boy?'

Berg took a step forward.

'Don't be afraid. Who are you?'

He looked at the bundle of brushwood, from which the voice seemed to be coming. 'Berg.' He took another step. 'My name is Berg.'

'Hm.'

How could a pile of branches speak?

'Strange name.'

He leaned forward.

'Would you lift up those sticks, please?'

Berg straightened up and looked all around him.

'Berg? Get this wood off me.'

Something about the voice made him walk forward, without thinking, and begin picking up branches. He had removed three or four, when a wicker cage came into view. In the cage sat a hare. Berg straightened up again and frowned. The hare moved slightly. He raised his head and hopped forward an inch or two. Then Berg crouched down and began clearing away the rest of the wood.

The cage was free, and Berg and the hare observed each other for a while. Although he had distinctly heard the voice coming from the wood, the boy still couldn't believe that it had been the hare who had spoken to him. The animal stared at him with its foolish, rabbity expression, harelips folded, ears crushed against the top of the cage.

In the old days, midwinter had been celebrated with fire. Weeks before the solstice, the people of the village began building a cone of brushwood. One day, as if by some unspoken agreement, the first branch would be tossed onto the common. An hour later someone else would come along and add another stick. This went on for days. Anyone who happened to find a bit of wood, picked it up and dropped it onto the pile. When a week had gone by, Johan would bring a stake from his barn and drive it through the middle of the branches into the ground. That was the official sign to start work on the cone of wood. In the old days Berg had looked forward all autumn to the moment when the branches slowly began to pile up on the common. And when the time came, he'd build and arrange, shift and rearrange until, after two weeks, there stood a large, evenly shaped cone of branches and pieces of wood. On the west side he always left an opening, which he filled with dry moss, wisps of straw and dead leaves and twigs. When the beehive of wood was set alight through this opening, the flames swept from the inside out and after a while the pile collapsed into a glowing heap of embers that gave heat all night long.

But seven years had passed since Berg had last done this, and in the morning, as he stood in the little house where he lived with his mother, dancing with cold in front of the hearth, he had trouble remembering the last great midwinter fire.

He had woken up that morning under a thick layer of blankets and clothes and heard his mother breaking the ice in the washbasin. Then she had gone to the hearth and swept back the ashes, so she could light the wisp of straw she had laid ready.

'Not those sticks!' he cried, when his mother walked over to the bundle he had brought home the night before.

She straightened up and looked over her shoulder at the bed. He was sitting upright, hair like a clump of grass, but darker, shaking his head.

'But Berg, it's all we have left.'

There was a pounding, and he heard the door behind him creaking in its latch. Before Berg or his mother could slide back the bolt, the door flew open and the tall figure of Block stood in the blinding snowlight. Berg saw his mother take a step back.

'Come here.'

Berg remained where he stood.

'Boy! Come here.'

His mother nodded. Berg took a step forward.

'So, you think you can poach and get away with it?'

I didn't poach, he wanted to say, but held his tongue.

'Did you think I didn't see you, with your rope, out there in the field? You snivelling brat!'

Berg looked at the dark silhouette. In the dazzling light he couldn't see the forester's face, and perhaps that was why he suddenly seemed to him to be no more than a shape.

'Go away, Block,' he said. 'You have no power in this house.' He was surprised at his own calm.

'House . . .' sneered the shadow.

'House,' said Berg. He turned around and picked up the poker. He stared into the empty hearth, the forester's eyes in his back, and it was as if he could hear him speaking, though he didn't make a sound ('Watch out, Berg,' he said. 'Don't push your luck. I'm stronger than you think.') but he didn't turn round. When, at last, he leaned the poker against the wall and turned back to the forester, the door hung askew and Block was gone. The chill he had brought in with him still lingered in the little house. Berg looked at his mother, and only then did he realize what she had done. She had gone and stood in front of the bundle of sticks and hidden them behind her skirts. He couldn't help it: he laughed.

That afternoon he helped Johan with the baking. Every midwinter Johan had one of his farmhands build a fire in the big barn. Above the fire he hung a blackened iron kettle and, on a chain, an old, equally blackened milking bucket. In this bucket Johan made *olie-bollen*. For as long as he could remember, Berg had helped him. They stood together in the thin blue smoke and while Berg stirred the batter, Johan turned over the ladle and fished the brown, potato-shaped balls out of the boiling oil. They had been busy for an hour or two when the old man nodded sideways and they sat down on a bale of hay. Johan filled a stubby pipe and puffed until the bowl glowed orange. Then he wrapped his left arm around himself, rested his right elbow on that arm, and drew slowly, but evenly, on the clay pipe. 'So, you want to build a midwinter fire,' he said after a while. Berg opened his mouth. But the man was first. 'Just be sure you know what you're doing, my boy.' He closed his mouth again and looked at Johan.

Ever since his father had disappeared, Johan had looked after them. Berg knew he did this because Johan had always regarded his father, Berg-Who-Was-Gone, as his own son. Seven years earlier, Johan had been in the prime of his life, the largest landowner in the village, with the biggest barn, the most land, and twelve cows. Now he was old. Berg had seen his mother looking at Johan one day as he walked across the common, and he had wondered why she shook her head. Now that he was sitting here beside him and saw him puffing on his pipe, he understood. Johan was hunched, but it wasn't just old age. It was as if he were carrying something he couldn't put down. Berg stood up and went over to the bucket of batter. He leaned down and stirred. Though he couldn't see him, he knew that Johan was nodding. I can speak without talking, thought Berg , I can listen without hearing.

It was getting dark by the time he came out with a wicker basket full of *oliebollen*. An ash-grey dusk rose above the road from Saens to Rodel and grew fingers above the trees, fingers that reached for the village and slowly closed around it. He stood outside Johan's barn and smelled the tang of the tarred wood. The air was dry and cold. There was a pale ring around the moon. As he marched across the frozen snow, he heard the creatures of the forest. It was as if everything had awakened. A few days before, when he had gone to fetch the bundle of sticks, it had seemed as if there was no life left in this white wilderness, as if it had buried itself deep below the ground to wait until the end of the long winter. Now, the woods were humming. An owl hooted, two crows cawed in the distance. Up on the hill, he knew, the older rabbits had come out to see if there might be something tasty poking through the snow, while the youngsters hopped nervously through the white mass that covered their warrens. Deep down below the ground, the does would be sitting with their young. He shivered in his sheepskin coat and walked, without looking, past the barns to his house.

When his mother turned back the cloth on the basket, steam rose from the *oliebollen*. She set their plates on the table and Berg filled the mugs with milk.

'All the wood is gone,' said his mother, looking at the bundle of sticks. Berg shook his head.

He bit into an *oliebol* and ate. The spongy warm dough filled his mouth and whisked him back one, two, seven years. His father sat across from him. He held onto the tabletop and smiled as Berg juggled his hot *oliebol* from one hand to the other.

'I'll fetch some wood,' he said. He felt his mother's gaze, but didn't look at her. She sighed. It was a while before she, too, began to eat.

That night the frost lay across the land like glass. Even inside, you could hear how silent the world had become. It was midwinter, and Jack Frost ruled, over the heavens, the fields, the houses and the people. The sky was clear and the moon was full. The silvery light turned the snow between the houses pale blue, and the shadows of walls and barns, even Berg's own shadow, were nearly as sharp as in the harsh sunlight of a summer's afternoon.

He carried the bundle of branches on his shoulder, a smoking torch in his hand, and walked in the shelter of the barns. Just as he was walking past Johan's farm, he saw Block standing, straddle-legged, on the common. Berg stopped and looked at the forester. He was a big man. He seemed to Berg to be towering above the rooftops. The moonlight fell on his hat and his face was hidden in the shadow of the brim. There was steam coming out of his mouth, a faintly luminous cloud that enveloped him briefly and then drifted away again. Berg lowered the bundle of branches and stepped forward.

'I knew you'd come, boy.'

Berg didn't answer. He wasn't afraid. But he also wasn't so sure of himself that he found it unnecessary to speak. He simply didn't know what to say.

'It's a cold, cold night,' said the forester.

Berg nodded.

'But we don't need fire. Put down that bundle of branches, give me the torch, and get out of here.'

He spoke calmly. Berg looked up and saw the moon in the blue night sky. His breath rose like a clear white cloud. The smoke from the torch went straight up into the air. Without seeing him, though he could feel him moving, he saw the forester step forward. He hooked his fingers behind the rope around the bundle and went on gazing at the heavens. When the dark figure of the man was silhouetted against the sky, he lowered his head. For a moment he looked him full in the face, without seeing a thing, and then he was standing somewhere else. The forester turned round. His breathing was laboured. He leaned forward slightly. He took a step and Berg shot away.

They circled around one another for a while, the forester taking bigger and bigger steps, but not lunging, and the boy, panting under the weight of his load, jumping from left to right like a squirrel. Then, turning to face Johan's farm, he let out a yell.

The forester stood before him, half-crouched, ready to pounce, but when he heard Berg 's cry, he froze and glanced quickly around him. Doors swung open, there were frightened voices, feet stomped across the hard snow, a man shouted something unintelligible. Berg let the bundle of sticks slide off his shoulder and set it down in front of him. Suddenly, Johan's door opened and he came outside.

'Fire!' Berg cried again.

Block straightened up and stepped forward. 'Like hell,' he said. The anger made his voice big and hollow.

Berg thrust his torch into the snow and, still holding onto the bundle with his right arm, he pulled the rope off the branches.

'Give me that wood! You stole it.'

Berg let go of the branches and stepped back. They fell in a circle on the ground. In the middle sat the hare in his wicker cage. He sniffed at the air, his nose twitching. His neck was outstretched and his head went from left to right and right to left.

'Poacher's brat!' shouted Block. He turned. Nearly all the people of the village were there. They were standing in a circle round the white circle of snow, round the ring of branches, round the hare. Berg leaned down and opened the cage. He took out the hare and set him down on the branches. Then he picked up the torch and looked into the forester's shadowed face.

'I'm locking you up in the coalshed, boy. And tomorrow you'll get what you deserve.'

'It's midwinter,' said Berg. His voice was loud, but he wasn't shouting. 'Tonight there will be a fire.'

'There'll be nothing!' roared Block. He turned to the onlookers. 'Go home. This boy's been poaching and stealing. He's nothing but a troublemaker.'

The circle of people stirred, but no one walked away. Block took a step, then hesitated.

'Why don't you come and get me, Block?'

'I'm coming, snotnose. Just you wait.' He walked around the circle of branches, but Berg turned away from him. 'Stay right there!'

'Why don't you step over the branches?'

Block arched his back and glared at him through his lashes.

'Hazel branches. Are you afraid of them?'

Block took a step backward. Berg saw the figure of his mother appear among the crowd. Johan grabbed her by the arm and held her at his side.

They were standing face to face, the boy and the forester, the circle of hazel branches between them, but neither of them moved. Their breath glowed white in the moonlight and the flickering of the torch. After a long while, Berg bent down and took the hare in his arms.

'What have you done with my father, Block?'

The man shrank back. He kept his eyes on the boy and the hare. Then he laughed loudly. 'I never knew your father. He was long gone by the time I got here. You're mad, you little bastard.'

The circle grew smaller.

'Get the hell out of here, all of you!' barked Block. 'This isn't a fairground! Go back to your houses, till I've dealt with this nasty little bugger. Go!' He waved his arm and the circle around him grew larger again.

Berg held his torch high and cried, 'Here's the thief! He's the one who's been stealing from us. The winter storage, the sowing seed, the wood, and all the money he's got for it. For seven years he's been bleeding us dry. Block's the thief.'

The forester growled and made a movement as if he was about to rush forward, but remained where he was. 'I'll skin you alive!' he roared. He grabbed the axe that hung from his belt and raised it. 'There'll be nothing left of you when I'm through!'

'Step over the hazel ring, then!' Berg's voice nearly broke. He felt his heart pounding high in his chest.

Block shouted something and jumped forward.

Hardly had his right foot touched the wreath of branches, when he limped back, screaming. The hare's brown eyes gleamed and he twitched his nose. The boy lowered his torch and threw it into the circle. The fire shot up like a ball of flames, then sank down again and began burning brightly. Behind the cone of flames Berg saw the forester hopping up and down. The people of the village came closer and stared at the wondrous fire.

The boy took a burning branch out of the circle and walked sideways, until he saw the man.

'Come here, Block.'

'What?'

'Put down that axe and come here!'

The forester's body seemed to resist the command, it wriggled and squirmed, but finally Block dropped his axe and went to the boy, his face contorted with rage.

'Tell them. How you blinded them and stole their harvest.'

'Like hell.'

The boy raised his burning branch and pointed it at the cringing man.

'I didn't do it. *They* did.'

The circle of people closed around them. Berg could almost feel the warmth of their bodies.

'They did it themselves,' said the forester. He gave a low laugh. 'They did it. They didn't need to be blinded. They did it themselves.' He looked around the circle. He moved, without taking a step. He swayed forward and back, like someone who was about to run off. 'Every year after Stubble Burning they got blind, stinking drunk. Who cared about the price of a cask of beer? Ha! And then.' He looked around him.

'Then they came,' said Berg.

'At night. Yes, they came at night. On their black carts. And they took everything.'

'The harvest.'

Block nodded vehemently.

'And the wood supply?' asked Johan, who had come up and stood beside Berg.

Block looked about nervously. 'Tonight. Always at midwinter. Everyone's asleep. Cold. Who's out there?' It was almost as if he were getting smaller and smaller.

'A blanket,' said Berg.

Johan looked at him in amazement.

'A blanket.'

The crowd of people stirred. Moments later a grubby horse blanket was being passed over their heads. Berg took it and handed it to Block. He looked uncomprehendingly at the matted grey wool.

'Leave your coat, your axe, and your hat. Take the blanket and go.'

Suddenly the man straightened up. His chest swelled. The crowd of people quickly scattered. Only Johan and Berg were left standing opposite the dark figure. Berg jabbed his burning branch at the face beneath the green felt hat. 'Do as I say.' The forester removed his hat, unbuttoned his coat, and threw them on the ground.

'Go.'

The body opposite them wanted to move, but didn't. Berg pressed his face into the hare's neck and whispered something in his ear. The hare looked at the forester and wriggled his nose.

'Go away,' said the hare.

Johan looked at Berg, and from Berg to the hare.

'Go away and vanish into the night.'

'How . . .' said Johan.

The hare stretched out his neck and stared at the man with the horse blanket. 'Or,' said the hare, 'would you rather he draw a circle around you with that burning hazel branch and leave you here till spring?'

The forester threw the blanket over his shoulders and turned round. He took two steps and then, with one violent movement, he hurled the blanket onto the fire. Darkness fell. There were screams.

The darkness lasted only a few moments, then the blanket burned and Block was gone. The boy and the village elder stood alone on the common. Berg set the hare down in the snow. The animal lifted its paws once or twice, as if it needed to get used to the cold, then shifted its gaze to the fire.

'Come on,' said Berg. 'You can do it.'

The hare hopped forward. It pricked up its ears, sniffed at the wind, and leaped.

Above the glow of the flames, the outstretched body of the hare was an image Berg recognized, though he didn't know why. The leap seemed to go on for hours. The boy saw the jagged hind legs, the body, slender and thin at the belly and rounded and muscular at the chest, the raised head and flattened ears, the extended front legs. It was as if the hare were suspended above the fire, a memory of something that had nearly been forgotten.

*　　*　　*

There was a crackling of flames, gnawing their way through dry wood. Dishes clinking against other dishes. In the distance, the scent of warm milk and bread.

He opened one eye and peeked out from under the quilt. His mother was standing at the hearth, stirring a pot. The door opened and a gust of wind blew into the room. The fire flared.

'Cold day today. But the animals are out again. Hares and rabbits in the field. Winter's starting to turn. The boy still asleep?'

His mother looked round. Berg closed his eyes and tried to breathe evenly.

'Hey, Seven Sleeper. Out you go.'

He felt his father's hand on his shoulder. Berg opened both eyes and yawned.

'Time to eat. Bread and porridge. Come on, son, we've got work to do.'

He turned back the covers and climbed out of bed. His mother set a bowl of water on the table and he washed quickly.

As they sat at the table eating the bread, still warm from the oven, there was a knock at the door. Johan came in. He was carrying a block of wood under his arm.

'Morning,' he said. 'Berg?'

Father and son both raised their heads.

Johan smiled. 'We'll have to post a man down by the barns. Somebody's been at the wood last night.'

Berg's father nodded. 'Everyone's cold. There are probably some who haven't got any left at all.'

Johan was silent. He took out his pipe and began to fill it, the chunk of wood still clasped under his arm.

'What's that you've got there?' asked Berg's mother.

Johan stuck the pipe in his mouth and showed them the block. 'Yes, it was odd. I was shovelling away the ashes from the fire and I found this. It's badly burnt, but it looks familiar.'

He placed the charred wood on the table.

Berg, his father and his mother and Johan all looked at it. For a long time no one spoke.

'Funny,' said Berg's father. 'It's almost as if I remember something. But I don't know what.'

———————————

'I'm going to marry you,' said Nina.

I laughed.

'God, whatever happened to the men of old?'

I sat up and began hunting for my clothes. 'I have no idea, but you never knew them and let me assure you: you wouldn't have wanted to.'

'I mean it,' said Nina. 'And why are you getting out of bed?'

I turned round. She was lying diagonally across the bed, on her stomach, looking at me. She was completely serious.

'Nina.'

'Me, Nina. You, Nathan.'

'I . . .'

She rolled over on her back and spread her arms. 'Lord of the Universe,' she said. 'Not the we-can't-we-mustn't scene.'

I felt my eyes running over her body, the small breasts, the collar-bone spokes beneath her skin, her throat, the fan of hair. Can't, mustn't.

She raised herself up on one elbow. 'Nathan, come back to bed and forget all the guilt and self-punishment and obligations and God knows what other inhibitions you've got. Come lie here next to me.'

Abraham took Sarah to be his wife and lay with her and . . . Just how old was Abraham, I thought, how old was Sarah? I went back to the bed and grasped her hand. I wanted to say something, I had it all ready in my mind, my story, but it wouldn't go down to my mouth.

She pulled my hand towards her face. I felt the warmth of her cheek. My head went back. 'It's . . .' She pulled me closer to her. 'Nina . . .' My face was right next to hers. I shook my head. 'I'm an old man. The difference.' 'I'm the boss,' said Nina. 'The wicked queen has got you captive.' I was lying half on top of her and began, against my will, to kiss her throat, the velvety spot where the chin flows into the throat, I kissed her earlobe and took her ear in my mouth. She took my head in her hands and brought it to her face. She looked deep into my eyes. Then she kissed me. I sank into her like butter in a hot pan.

Long Ago and Far Away

IT WAS NEARLY noon by the time we were back at the top of the stairs, wondering where to go next. Across the hallway from my bedroom was another one just like it. I didn't expect to find much in there. Uncle Herman had always used the room for guests, but even then there hadn't been much more in it than a bed, a chest of drawers and a night table. Nina insisted on searching it anyway. 'I'd rather waste half an hour than have to keep looking at that mess.' She nodded her head to the right, to the still intact portion of the barricade, an enormous pile of junk that lay wedged between a secretaire and an old Dutch china cabinet. The other side of the hallway looked, even in the dim light, as if it were due for demolition. The wooden floor was scratched and dented and covered with splinters. The wallpaper was tattered and torn. The doorway of my room was a pockmarked wooden frame. There were nails bulging out of it, and shreds of wood. I shook my head, laid the axe over my shoulder, and walked to the room Nina wanted to check. We had already discovered, the night before, that the door was locked. Since my burglar's trick had worked so well the first time, I didn't expect much trouble now either. I was right. Ten minutes later, the key lay on the newspaper that Nina had slid under the door and we could go in.

When I tried to open the door, though, it was as if someone were holding it closed from the inside. I had to lean my whole body against it to gain even half an inch. I gave up. The door slammed shut. I was panting. Nina put her hands in her pockets and looked at me, her head to one side, eyebrows lowered. 'If you push your back against the door,' I said, 'I'll lean, and when the opening is wide enough, I'll slip inside. Then I can get rid of that spring, or whatever it is.' She raised her head. There was something alert in her gaze. We stood there for a few moments, looking at each other. Then I laid my hand on her cheek and smiled. 'I'll take the axe. I can always chop my way out.' She nodded slowly.

The door banged shut behind me. I spun round, not breathing, my heart as big as my body. 'Nina!'

'What happened?'

'Nothing. Just the door. Are you all right?'

'Yes.' Her voice was calm.

I took out my matches and struck one. The light shot up and when the tiny flame had settled down, I saw nothing but my hand. I held the bowl of my other hand behind it and tried to direct the light. A whisper of cold brushed past my perspiring forehead. The flame swayed gently. What have you got in store for me now, Zeno? I let my foot glide over the floor, boards, boards, boards, and peered into the light of the match. When the flame had nearly reached my fingers, I blew it out and lit a new one.

'Nathan?'

I shouted back.

'What are you doing?'

'I'm trying to see something.'

'Open the door.'

I reached out my arms and felt for the door handle. Pulling was harder than pushing. I hung down on the handle and Nina leaned hard against the door, but we couldn't get it open more than an inch.

'I'm going to try and work out why this damn thing won't open. Hang on a minute, Nina.'

I ran my hands along the seam between door and doorway and then over the door itself. In the middle was a sort of wooden frame, and in the middle of that, a slat of wood, about two inches thick and bending from the strain. I followed the curve downward, until I came to a similar frame, only this one was on the floor. The tough, flexible slat must have been what was keeping the door closed. I knelt down to get a better look and realized that I was nodding in admiration. I got up, placed my foot on the wooden bow, drew it back slightly and kicked it, hard. Something shot past my feet across the floor. There was a powerful rush of air.

'Nathan?'

'What's he doing in there?'

'What's he doing in there, what's he doing in there? He's building a cathedral out of matchsticks. He's lying down!'

'Why's he lying down?'

'People lie down. People stand. People sit. Some people, like you, have a head full of mush. Nathan?'

'He's not answering.'

'Oh. Is that why he's so quiet?'

'I think he's . . .'

'No.'

'No?'

'No!'

'Should we call Feynman?'

'F . . . Why should we call Feynman?'

'Because he's not answering.'

'Every time somebody doesn't jump to their feet and start telling you a story, you want to call Feynman?'

'Mr Feynman!'

'Shut up, would you.'

'MR FEYNMAN! Oh, Mr Feynman. He's not responding.'

'Oh?'

'We keep calling his name, but he won't answer.'

'Is it the right name?'

'What?'

'His name.'

'Yes! God . . . He's moving.'

'Yes.'

'He's moving, Mr Feynman.'
'I can see he's moving. It's something people do.'

There was nothing but darkness. I was lying on my back and side. On two floors. I rolled over. I couldn't roll onto my back. Not a floor. A wall.

When I sat up, I knew where I was.

I took the matches out of my pocket and lit one. My hand was an orange stain on the blackness. I held the flame just above the floor and searched. A few yards away I found a long stick and, a bit further on, part of the broken slat. I picked it up. The tip of the slat was splintered and probably wouldn't be hard to light.

There I sat, in the middle of the floor, and it took me two matches to get the thing to burn, but finally it caught fire. I held the slat upside-down and let the flame creep upward. When I was certain it wouldn't go out too quickly, I began exploring my surroundings.

What had happened, I wasn't quite sure, but after I had kicked through the slat, something had hit me and sent me flying against the door. My face and left shoulder hurt, but nothing was broken. I thrust the torch into the darkness. Against the door hung a bulging burlap sack. I wanted to get up and walk over to it, but I couldn't. Somehow I just didn't have the courage to push myself up and stand. Deep inside my chest I felt the distant flutter of rising panic. 'Careful, Nathan,' I whispered to myself. 'Look around you. Think. What's going on? What are the clues?'

The burlap sack looked as if it were filled with sand. By breaking the slat of wood I had freed the sack and it had come swinging down on its rope from one side of the room to the other and hit me full in the back. 'Smashed me against the door,' I whispered. 'Knocked the wind out of me. Must have passed out. What else?'

A bigger room and I would have been dead. Longer trajectory, greater momentum.

The bird of fear began flapping its wings. I could feel it in my lungs.

'Could be worse. There might have been rocks in the sack. Then you would have been dead.'

Something rose inside my head. As if I were slowly being filled with black water. The wall to my left began to glow. I leaned sideways and tried to support myself on my hands, but swayed like a top that was gradually winding down. 'Think. Think!' I opened my eyes as wide as I could. 'Nathan.'

Me?

'Stay awake, Nathan.'

God. The burning slat fell out of my hand and hit the floor several feet away from me. I saw the fire spreading along the planks. 'I'll stamp it out,' said Magnus. He hurried forward and brought down an unpolished boot onto the flames. 'Lie down, Nathan. You're tired. What room is this? Didn't Sophie sleep in here?'

My head drooped on my chest and I couldn't lift it up.

No, don't lie down. Stay awake.

I was still leaning on my arms, but it was such an effort that I could feel the pain creeping, inch by inch, through my hands, the muscles in my forearms, my upper arms, until it reached my shoulders. A dull ache.

'I'm going to tell you something. Close your eyes.'

I closed them.

Like a bed of the finest down, that floor. To sleep, and never have to rise again.

'Come. Long ago. Yes, long ago. That is the beginning. Long ago and far away.'

The soft hardness of the floor.

'There once was a man who didn't know what direction his life should take, so one morning, he rose up and went.

Listen. He went, like the shadow of a cloud over a cornfield. He was there and then he was gone.

For seven days he travelled. Seven nights. And when he looked up to see where he was, he saw that he was nowhere. And again: seven days, seven nights.

And after that: seven years.

Then he came to a plain that reached to the horizon and beyond.

A scudding blanket of clouds hung low above the grass and cast rippling shadows on the ground. The wind came from the west and had been blowing forever. It was a wind that had laid bare the skeleton of the plain, a hot wall of air that scorched the skin and dried the eyes. He lay down in the sand and the scalding mountain glided over him. He felt the storm, just as the earth felt him, and the warmth of the earth rose up through his skin. His belly grew soft and he heard how the blood pumped slowly through his veins, squeezed its way into his head and, buzzing and rustling, sang him to sleep.

There was no direction in the raging of the storm. There was only heat, a continually replenished supply of diabolical heat. Heat with no source, no land of origin, no goal. If not for the wind, the plain would have boiled, the sand would have melted and gone churning away in slow, fiery streams, to the land beyond the horizon and the air would have been so hot that it burned his lips and scorched his throat. The air would have burned if not for the wind, geysers would spout liquid sand, not a creature would survive, and the sun would hang directly above the plain and permit no shadow, not even that of a raised, shielding hand, or a blanket stretched over a pair of sticks.

Days with no beginning and no end. The wind blew time away and drove the sun behind a grey curtain of flying sand and dust. Those were the days when he was happy.

At night he sought out the warm springs of an oasis and washed his dusty, chapped skin. He floated on his back in water he could barely feel. He looked up at the night, the white moon and her patches of shadow. He hovered over the border between water and air and if he gazed long enough at the moon he forgot the springs, forgot he was earthbound. He seemed to float up through space and disappear forever.

But there were also days when the wind combed the steppe like a sheet of steel, bearing rainstorms that lashed him so hard in the face that his forehead was beaded with blood. It froze day and night and the rainwater hardened into the sharp ripples that the wind blew across its surface.

They were long days, bathed in the light of a bluish sun. The cold, relentless wind pierced through the blanket he had wrapped around his body and penetrated the holes in his clothes. When it rained the water ran down his throat and froze on his chest, leaving scars on his skin, as if he had burned himself. They chafed against his clothes, those scars, opening up again and again. Some nights, by the flickering fire, which always seemed on the verge of going out, he had to crack the blood out of his shirt.

But it wasn't the pain that heightened his agony. It was the ceaseless polar wind that drove him back under his blanket. It was the endless storm that forced him down on the ground and made him sit for days at a time with his head between his knees.

Whenever he went looking for firewood he wrestled, hunched, with the knife of cold that screeched across the plain, until he was forced to yield, once again, and was pushed back to the smouldering pile of ashes that was his fire. The next morning he'd wake up with his face half-sunk in a freezing puddle, chilled to the bone. All day long he had the feeling that half his head was made of wood.

Some days he had better luck and the storm blew a few branches (but from what tree?) his way. Then he would kindle the fire again, under the blanket. Over the spluttering flames he hung the small blackened kettle in which he heated water, but the heat from the boiling water never lingered long in his body and the warmth of the fire never penetrated to his bones, so he would spend the whole day shivering under his clammy blanket, until night came and sleep helped him to forget the cold.

One morning, seven years later, after half a night of trekking and a few hours of sleep, he woke up and saw a tree in the distance. He didn't know what sort of tree it was. His head whispered 'acacia', because that seemed an appropriate name for a tree in the middle of a plain, but somewhere in his breast a voice mumbled 'oak'. He didn't know.

It was a big tree, tall, with a huge crown that billowed out over the trunk and hung down at the edges like the cap of a giant fungus. The trunk was so thick, it would have taken him ten paces to walk all the way around it, if that were even possible, for the enormous roots had arched their backs above the ground and turned the earth around the tree into a choppy sea of wood, moss, and sand.

He had never seen the tree before. He didn't know the boundaries of the plain, so he wasn't sure he really knew the plain itself, but he was surprised that he had never noticed this tree. He sat down on the ground, about twenty yards away, and gazed. The wind rushed through the leaves, but the branches didn't move. The tree stood motionless in the sand.

He realized that the moment had come when he knew the plain. This was the boundary, this was the point at which the plain lost itself in another plain, where yet another tree would stand, in the middle of nowhere, and that tree would form a new boundary, beyond which a new plain would begin. There was no end. He knew all this, now that he saw the tree. He could journey through steppe after steppe, without direction, as the emptiness grew, but every tree would evoke yet another tree and every plain another plain. Was this tree a boundary? He had found it, and seen it as a boundary, but he might also have seen a clump of grass or a fleeing fox and accepted *that* as a boundary. Wherever he saw a boundary, a landmark, an imaginary demarcation of the endlessness around him, the borders would expand. What he saw would continue to reproduce itself until he had acknowledged, and accepted, the chaos, the self-generating chaos, disorder that brought forth more disorder. The tree was a metaphor. He could make it his benchmark, he could live in it, but never would this tree become the centre of the world, nor would it be the end. He would always know that the tree was one in an unverifiable, incalculable series. The plain had lost all meaning.

He sank back and closed his eyes. The blood moved in thin waves over his eyelids. He had to make a decision, a choice. Should he stay here by the tree and accept his powerlessness, or travel on and reconcile himself with his longing for an end? As he lay there on the ground, he began to understand why medieval man regarded the world as a flat surface. The comfort of finiteness. He thought of the dreams he had dreamt as a child, how he had sailed through the universe, from galaxy to galaxy, unable to find a boundary, lost in space. He rolled over and pressed his face into the ground. If he were to accept the tree as an arbitrary home in an arbitrary land, he would always wonder whether there were more trees, more lands, and he knew that, against his better judgement, he would imagine that somewhere there had to be an end to this chaos. But if he were to embark on the journey through the emptiness that stretched out beyond the tree, he would never really know if there were such an end, one that would bring him to his knees and give him peace. He rolled over on his back again and looked up at the passing clouds. He searched for a point on which to rest his gaze, but found none. The sky began tilting and for a moment it felt as if he were falling off the earth. He closed his eyes and thought of the warm water of his nightly oasis.

Then he heard the voice of God. He opened his eyes and closed them again.

"Nathan," said the voice.

He said nothing.

"Nathan!"

He hung his head between his knees and crossed his arms above his crown.

"NATHAN!"

At last he answered. "Lord?"

"Don't lean against that tree. Some dog just pissed on it."''

When I opened my eyes I could see, in full detail, the grain of the plank that my head was lying on: a sluggish river in a sunburnt landscape, a slow-flowing delta that split around the island of a gnarl, then came together again and flowed imperturbably on. The smell of dust and dry wood. Something trickled out of my mouth. I ran my finger over my cheek and tasted. Saliva.

I knew where I was and why. But how long?

Once again I followed the line of the wood grain and rested my gaze on the gnarl. It was as if all meaning were contained within that one spot, as if my why and how and where all met there, as if the currents all gathered around that knot and, babbling, gurgling, murmuring, exchanged stories of along-the-way. And I drifted with those currents, from one to the next, motionless, but in motion. Just as I began to wonder how it was that I could see in the dark, I heard the hissing of the burner and noticed the light streaked across the floor. I lifted my head, just a bit, an inch or two.

'Nathan. What the hell . . .' Nina's voice. 'I thought I'd lost you.' Her hand on my left shoulder.

I closed my eyes and let my head drop, rolled over on my stomach and sat up. Only then did I open my eyes again. Nina was sitting in front of me, kneeling. She reached out and grabbed me by the arms. 'Nathan . . .'

'How long?'

'How long have you been lying here? About five minutes. Are you in pain?'

I thought about pain. I shook my head. 'No pain. Bit fuzzy. Nothing broken.'

'Can you stand up?'

I could stand up. I got to my feet like a child showing off a new trick.

'Come on. Let's go downstairs.'

'Wait. I have to know what happened, how it works.'

She looked at me for a while, then shook her head.

Leaning on her shoulder as she turned the gas lamp to the four points of the compass, I took in my surroundings.

In the white light of the lantern the room looked like a torture chamber. The sack hung against the door from rope half an inch thick, a U-shaped frame, which had held the slat of wood, had been nailed to the floor. In the left-hand wall, about two feet above the ground, was a gaping, squarish hole, just wide enough for an adult to squeeze through. Behind it I could see chair legs and pieces of beam. Against the right-hand wall, in a neat pile, was the complete store of logs that had once lain outside, under the lean-to. The pile was nearly up to my shoulders, enough firewood to keep us warm for weeks. Leaning against the pile was a ladder. It had probably been used to screw the hooks into the hall ceiling and to attach the ring, or whatever it was holding up the sandbag, to the frame at the top of the door.

'Lord of the Universe,' I said.

I noticed how calm I was, and thought: It's finally come to this – I accept my fate.

Nina moved her head towards the jagged opening in the opposite wall.

'That's how he got out of the room. You can only block the door from the inside, with a piece of wood like that. And besides, he still had to rig up that sandbag.'

The rope from which the sack was hanging had been attached to the ceiling by a hook, exactly above the middle of the door. Then the sack had been pulled back and pushed against the wall with a stick. The stick had rested in the frame on the floor, checked by the bent slat of wood. By kicking through the wood I had set the trap in motion. Without the slat to hold it back, the stick had popped out and the sack had come sailing down. It hadn't been that great a sweep, but enough to smack me against the wall.

'I'm getting very cold. Let's take as much wood as we can and go down to the library. Is the fire still burning?'

'I haven't been in there. I was in your bedroom. I was trying to find something to get the door open.'

We made three trips back and forth. I found the burlap sack in which we kept our tools, Nina filled it with wood, and I carried it downstairs, while she followed behind me with another armload. After we had distributed a considerable supply over the library, hunting room, and kitchen, we sat down to eat.

Nina had made a plateful of sandwiches and a pot of tea and I breathed new life into the dying fire. We polished off the late lunch in silence.

'I think we've had the worst of it,' said Nina.

I shook my head. 'That's because the last bad thing always seems worse than all the other bad things that came before it. Have you forgotten that hike of yours through the snow?'

She shivered. Then she said, 'Why did that bastard have to be my father?'

'I'm going to tell you something.'

'A fairy tale.'

I laughed. 'No. Maybe. The last chapter of Uncle Herman's biography.'

'The last one?' She looked at the pile of paper lying between us on the table. 'But there's a lot more, isn't there?'

'Yes. But this chapter isn't quite finished. And chronologically, it should have come much earlier.'

'You've never really been the chronological type.'

'Far from it. Chronology is for sequence, chaos is for comprehension.'

She raised her eyebrows, then shook her head. 'Okay. Tell me your fairy tale.'

I reached for the cigarettes, lit two, and handed one to Nina. She brought it to her lips and drew on the short filter. Without exhaling, she let the smoke escape from her mouth. The blue-grey cloud rose up and glided around her face, hiding it briefly. Then she breathed out and the smoke dissolved. I love her, I thought, and I would spend my whole life with her, whatever is left of it, if it weren't so wrong.

'Tea?'

I nodded. Nina got up and filled our mugs. I looked at the fire and let the story come. It took a while, but then it rose like dough.

Nina sat down in her chair, curled her right leg under her, and turned her face to me.

'Speak, Nathan.'

Fathers and Sons

THE YOUNG HOOKER under whom Uncle Herman had died was called Rolinda. She was barely eighteen and not as stupid as I'd thought. I had walked her home that night, to a rather posh flat in the centre of town, not far from Herman's hotel. There, I poured us each a large glass of white wine – I had to search the whole place first before I found anything to drink – and she lay on the couch with a wet cloth on her forehead and told me she was at university (really?, I thought) and that a girlfriend had helped her get a job with an escort service.

'Does it pay well?' I asked, after I had handed her the glass and sat down in a Corbusier chair that I wished were mine.

'Not bad,' she said. She sat up slowly and took a large gulp of wine. She ran the wet cloth over her face, peeled off a set of false eyelashes, and wiped the lipstick off her mouth. When she was done, she blinked her eyes.

'What do you study?'

'Political science,' she said.

'Pol . . . Jesus. Then you certainly had the . . . er . . . the right man.'

'Oh?'

I told her the whole story. 'He was an extraordinary person,' I said, when I had finished – to the girl beneath whom he had died.

She swallowed hard. 'He's on my reading list,' she said after a while, and mentioned a title, something like *The Libertarian Movement After 1945*.

'Did you know who he was?'

'There was a picture on the back of the book.'

'But you and he never spoke about his work . . .'

'I wasn't with him that often. I've only seen him three or four times, at most.'

'I hope he was good to you,' I said. 'I'd like to remember him as someone who, even though he might have paid for sex, was still . . .'

'He was good to me.'

I emptied my glass and stood up.

'Don't go,' she said. 'I'd really like it if you stayed a while.' She swallowed again. 'I've never seen a dead man before.'

I sank back down in my chair and studied her. She looked much better without that painted pout and those glued-on lashes.

She got up and left the room. 'I'm just getting changed,' she called out from the other side of the wall. 'I feel a bit funny in workclothes. What do you do? Are you a political scientist?'

'Me?' I said. 'No. I write fairy tales.'

'Fa . . . You're a writer?'

'Fairy tale writer,' I said. 'I'm a fairy tale writer.'

She poked her head round the door.

'Someone's got to do it,' I said. 'Some folks are call girls, other folks write "Once upon a time, in a far-off land".'

She looked at me quizzically, then disappeared behind the door and went on talking about things I could hear but couldn't see, and I told her what I had written and where I lived and . . .

'Strange pair, you and the great old man,' she said. She was standing in the living room again, dressed in an ankle-length, flowery skirt and a pastel pink blouse. She was wearing round, wire-rimmed glasses, her hair was pulled back in a ponytail. Political science, no doubt about it.

'Good God,' I said. 'You look like a different person.'

She smiled. 'You thought I was some air-headed bimbo, didn't you, in that short black skirt and babydoll make-up?'

I waggled my head a bit.

'Men like that sort of thing,' she said. 'There are even some who'll pay extra if you show up in white kneesocks and patent leather shoes. I could tell you stories . . . things you wouldn't dream of.'

'I'm sure you could,' I said, and that was true. 'I think I'll be going now, if you don't mind.'

'I . . . Why?'

'It's getting late, it's already late, and it's been quite a night and I have to get back to my hotel.'

'How old are you, anyway?' she asked suddenly.

'That sounds as if you don't think I'm as old as I look, or that I should actually be quite a lot older.'

It took a while for my words to sink in. 'Hell, no. I mean, God . . . Do you always confuse people like this?'

'Fifty-five.'

She looked at me for a moment and then nodded.

'Does that mean, yes, you can imagine that?'

'No. Yes. You look older, but at the same time, you don't.'

'That's because I never associate with other people. Keeps you young.'

This time she gave me a long, hard look. 'And what's your name?' she asked finally.

'Nathan. Nathan Hollander.'

She looked startled.

'What's wrong?'

'I've got to phone the agency. I don't want them hearing this from the police first.'

'Sounds like a good idea.'

At the door of her flat, she stopped me. 'Mr Hollander,' she said. 'Nathan. Would you . . . Do you think we could talk again some time? I mean, there's nobody else I can talk to about it, I . . .'

'I'll be in town for a while. I still have to make the funeral arrangements.'

She nodded. We agreed to meet the following evening and I walked out onto the thick hallway carpet. In the lift, next to the polished brass panel, I suddenly remembered that Herman was dead. During my conversation with the girl I had spoken about him in abstract terms. Now I realized, only too well, that he was gone.

'Rolinda – what sort of a name is that?' I had asked her the following evening, as we drove out of town in her Beetle.

We were bumping along the country roads between the city and the village where her horse was stabled. There was sandy heathland as far as the eye could see. I clung to my seat as she talked and talked and didn't, I thought, pay enough attention to the road. She had resolutely turned down my suggestion to meet in the dining room of my hotel. That would only lead to awkward silence. It would be much better if we *did* something, and seeing as how she was going to see Olivier anyway . . .

'Some strange idea of my father's. He thought it went well with our surname.'

'And that is?'

'Kokuvacec. At school they called me Cookie.'

'Cookie. Hm.'

'My friends call me Lin.'

'Lin Kokuvacec. Good name for a stewardess.'

Her mouth fell open slightly.

'If this makes you uncomfortable, you don't have to give me an answer, but do you use your own name when you work?'

She looked left down a dark side road.

'Did he really live in New York, Herman Hollander?'

The mention of his name startled me. All day long I had been busy arranging things. Even though Nina had offered to take care of the funeral – she had arrived in Rotterdam that morning and checked into my hotel – I still had to phone banks and credit card companies, and Herman's institute.

'Yes, since 1939. He stayed on in the apartment we had all moved into after we arrived.'

'We? You lived there too?'

'Yes, me too. My whole family. Uncle Herman and my father stayed behind, the rest of us went back.'

We drove on. I welcomed the silence that had fallen. I didn't know why I preferred not to speak. Here, at my side, was an intelligent young woman, and the fact that she had been present at Uncle Herman's dying hour didn't particularly bother me. If he had died under a car, I wouldn't have envied the driver of that car either. Nina hadn't been terribly enthusiastic about my dinner with Rolinda. When I walked into her room that afternoon to tell her we couldn't have dinner together, and why, she had asked if I thought I was Jesus Christ. 'Because of the harlots and publicans?' Yes, and if I thought I owed that tart something. I hadn't answered. I told her we would see each other later that night and walked out the door. Now that I was sitting here next to the young woman who, less then twenty-four hours ago, had heard Uncle Herman's last words, I wondered if perhaps that were true, that I thought I owed her something, and what that might be. Why did she want to speak with me again? Because she had no one else to talk to about what had happened? Was that really the reason?

'I've always been mad about horses,' she said. 'I used to be one of those girls with pigtails and a hacking jacket. My idea of heaven was mucking out a stable.'

She had always dreamed of having a horse of her own, so she would no longer have to share her hero with rivals. Once she began working for the 'agency,' she saved up enough within six months for an entire horse, an ochre-yellow gelding named Olivier. She rode twice a week, lunged him every Saturday. If she couldn't come, the owner of the stable let him run around the paddock. The creature was in fine shape, that much I could tell. When Rolinda threw open the stable door, he towered over me like a nightmare of gleaming hide and shifting shadows. I instinctively took a step backwards. The stern gaze, the massive stench of manure and sweat – I suddenly remembered what it was that I had against horses. As Rolinda stepped inside and stroked the animal's neck, I felt the demanding, penetrating gaze of the big black eye. This was a horse that had very different views on domestication from mine. I moved farther away, leaned

my back against the stable wall, and dug around in my pocket for
something to smoke. From inside the stable came a faint stumbling
noise. I found my cigarettes and lit one.

'Hey,' Rolinda called out, 'could you hold him for a minute so
I can lock up here?'

I gulped.

'Come on, hurry up.'

I inched forward, until I was back at the stable door, and looked
at the gleaming patches moving about in the darkness. 'I'm not very
good with animals,' I said, as Rolinda backed out of the stable, the
reins in her left hand. She turned round and looked at me with
raised eyebrows. I threw away my cigarette and sighed.

'Here, right by the bit,' she said. 'And hold on tight, he's pretty
headstrong.'

I grinned foolishly and took the reins from her. I hadn't had the
leather in my hands for more than two seconds when I felt something
change, in the horse, in me, in the reins, in the air. The mighty
head bowed down, so low that I was almost forced to look the beast
in the eyes.

'Nice horsey,' I said. I brought my free hand up to the broad
neck and began gently patting. The head went up again, slowly,
almost carelessly. I breathed out and looked at the animal.

What happened after that, I can't say. The next thing I remember
is the stable roof tilting, the muddy cobblestoned path to the barn
and the full moon streaking across the sky. I heard Rolinda scream
as I tumbled through the darkness wondering where I was and why
I could no longer see the horse's head and then I felt a throbbing
in my right knee and Rolinda was bending over me and asking if
everything was okay. Why does she want to know that, I thought,
but when I tried to get up the pain shot through my knee and I
heard the dull clippity-clop of receding horse's hooves.

'What happened?' I shouted.

Rolinda tucked her arm under mine and tried to pull me to my
feet. Using her for support, I hoisted myself up until I was standing
on my left leg, and felt my knee.

'He tricked you,' she said. 'He's a real devil.'

My knee began to swell.

'Can you walk?'

I nodded.

'I've got to go after him,' she said. 'He's run out into the field. If I don't find him straight away, he'll get stuck in the sand drift and then it'll take me hours. Wait here, I'll go get Alice.'

'I'm coming with you,' I said.

'With that knee?'

'Do you think I'm going to let two women go wandering around the heather in the pitch-darkness trying to catch that wild beast?'

She looked at me blankly. 'Alice,' she said, 'is a horse, and there's no heather here, and Olivier is no wild beast.' She stuck her hand in her jacket pocket and pulled out her car keys. She held them up and looked me straight in the eye. 'Take the car. Drive down to the end of the path and turn left. Keep on driving until you get to the sand drift. Wait there until I've sent him your way or until I come to get you.'

'My, we're assertive. Is it those boots you're wearing?'

'Like father like son,' she said.

'What?'

She turned away. 'I said, you're just like your uncle. But you can't say like uncle like nephew, can you? Please drive carefully, with that leg of yours.'

As I limped to the car, I heard Rolinda running off. I looked back and saw her hurrying through the sodium yellow of an arc lamp.

I couldn't help it. I wondered if she ever wore those boots in bed.

I am a city person. I live in hotels, sleep at airports and stay in the flats of people who live in the centre of old cities and new, I smoke Belgian cigarettes and drink beer and wine and in the evening I listen to radio stations that turn the world into a network, a city of listeners. That's my world. In the urban jungle, which I have never really thought was much of a jungle, I can always find my way about. I know where you can buy live carp in Rotterdam, I know bars in New York that stay open all night long, where bakers and greengrocers go for a drink at five in the morning before lighting their ovens or heading for the auction. In Barcelona I know a seafood restaurant that opens late and closes late and looks like a covered market, where you can buy oysters and fresh salmon for a song and they still make a decent salade niçoise. Elderly Spanish gentlemen go there with young women in severe black suits and wealthy thirty-year-olds in designer jeans and shy young couples on a shoestring. If you need something welded, I know a smithy in Amsterdam that looks as if a stagecoach can come riding in at any moment. And in Stockholm I know a restaurant, in the Writer's Union Building, where the menus are old books. In London I know a hotel, in Kensington, that looks as if Miss Marple might pop up around every next corner of the labyrinth of corridors and staircases, and whenever I'm there I eat at an Italian restaurant in Charlotte Street and buy bagels and lox in a street off Tottenham Court Road. My greatest joy is this: early autumn, temperature still on the mild side, gentle rain, the reflection of sodium lamps on wet asphalt and a bus slowly pulling away, leaving behind a blue-grey cloud of smoke. The smell of diesel on a rainy night . . . Or men standing three hundred feet above street level, welding something on an office building, shouts from the marketplace, antiquated bicycles outside student pubs, whores loitering around Soho newsstands. I am perfectly at ease with all of this, but put me in a field with an animal that isn't sliced, pickled, or stamped with an expiry date, and I go to pieces.

Yet here I was, driving in second gear down a dark asphalt road past black, empty fields. The moon hung in the night sky like a speckled lightbulb and in the glow of that moon I saw something in the field that looked like a cracked mirror. It was a long time before I realized that it was a puddle, a puddle in a furrow that shone in the moonlight.

Fifteen minutes later the asphalt suddenly turned into a bumpy dirt road with deep tyre tracks. I steered the car with one half in the verge and the other on the hump of the path. I was perspiring heavily. Each time the car hit a bump, I felt a stabbing pain in my knee. The path ran in a gentle curve towards a grove of trees. I began to wonder where that sand drift might be. I jolted along through the grove, the road dipped, I slowed down and switched to full-beam. As I drove slowly on, I saw shadows leaping about among the trees.

After about fifty yards I caught my first rabbit. I had heard before that some animals could be immobilized by light, but this was the first time I had ever witnessed it. In the white beams, the tiny eyes glittered like shards of mica. I stepped on the brake and waited. The rabbit hopped a bit to one side and then stopped. I turned down the window and stuck out my head.

'Hey! I haven't got all day!'

The animal shivered gently and stayed right where it was. I sank back in my seat and sighed. The rabbit stared at the light. It probably thought Rolinda's Beetle was the Great Rabbit God.

'Go dig a hole!' I shouted.

By the time it occurred to me to turn off the headlights, I had been standing there in the middle of nowhere for at least five minutes. At first I couldn't see a thing in the darkness, but when my eyes adjusted, the road ahead of me was empty. I drove on with my lights dimmed, in the hope that this would make me less attractive to small game. After a while the path curved and came to an end. Before me was nothing but tangled, overgrown field. I plodded slowly on, until suddenly the car shot downwards and the sand drift unfolded before me. I drove another twenty yards, very slowly, and then turned, so that the nose of the car was pointing roughly in the direction from which I had come. I got out and smoked a cigarette next to the open door.

What made me think of that old Stones number, 'Lady Jane'? Your servant am I, and will humbly remain . . . I smoked my cigarette and stared into the darkness and asked myself what I was doing here. Why had I gone along with that hooker, why had I given in? I heard a high-pitched shriek in the distance, not quite human, but not agreeably animal-like, either. It was a disturbing scream, as if some beast or other were turning some other beast-or-other inside out. I cursed, at the trees, at Rolinda's horse, at this whole bloody countryside, that didn't smell like wet stones, as it should, but pine-scented bubble bath and shit. If Uncle Herman had seen me standing here, or, better yet: if he had seen me hobbling through the darkness, he'd have had the night of his life. But Herman was dead, and if he were laughing at all it was the relieved laughter of a man who was free of this world.

Somewhere ahead of me, where the sand drift glowed pale beneath the moon, I heard a noise. I hid my cigarette in my hand and squinted. I prayed it wasn't that damned horse. I leaned my head forward and listened to the sounds of the wild, thinking: God, if I were ever let loose out here without food and water, I'd probably die of hunger and thirst, and I wouldn't know a deer if I saw one, or what sound a horse makes. At that moment I smelled a pungent odour, a mixture of leather and Irish Moss.

It was Rolinda's horse.

Let me say first: I assumed it was her horse. Something was panting a hot, damp cloud down my neck and stank of leather and . . . and horse. When I turned round, the beast looked at me with a sardonic grin. The foam on his black lips flickered softly in the moonlight. A great, bulging eye gleamed blue.

The horse was standing in front of the driver's door, so that I would have had to walk all the way around the car to hide inside, if I didn't already know for certain that I had pushed down the lock (I'm a city person, in the city they steal cars you don't lock).

'Down, boy,' I said.

The horse bowed its neck and studied me. Then he raised his head and turned round. I got a hoof-full of sand in the face – and there was silence. She's not going to like this, I thought. Miss Kokuvacec is not going to like this one bit.

'Christ, Rolinda!' I roared, when I was back behind the wheel and pressed down on the accelerator with my sore leg.

As the car ate its way through the sand, in the direction in which the horse had disappeared, the darting headlights suddenly made me think of the lights of the patrol boat that I had seen dancing over the black water of the Maas the night before, searching for a car that had gone off the quayside.

I drove on until I came to the path where I had stopped for the rabbit. I braked, switched off the light and the engine, and waited. I couldn't imagine where the horse might have gone.

Five, six minutes I waited there in the dark, peering out at the emerging contours of the landscape. Then I started up the engine again and drove back to the stables.

As I parked Rolinda's Beetle next to the empty stable and crawled out, dragging my leg behind me, the memory of what she had said earlier flashed through my mind. Like father, like son. The thumbs. Suddenly I thought of Uncle Herman. He had what they called in my family the 'Hollander thumbs,' two wide, flattish things with odd, crescent-shaped nails. My father had been spared this identifying mark, but I had not. Nor had my sisters, though we only had one, on our right hands.

'Lord of the Universe,' I said.

'What did you say?'

I looked around and saw, in the half-light of a lamp farther down on a wall, the pale glimmer of Rolinda's hair. She was leading a slender little horse by the reins.

'Nothing,' I said. 'I waited, but you didn't come.'

'You were already gone by the time I came,' she said. 'I saw you drive off. Did you see Olivier?'

'Who?'

'The horse. Did you see him? I'm sure he must have come this way.'

I nodded.

'Yes? Did he come this way?'

I bowed my head.

'Oh God, no! I ride all over that sand drift trying to round him up and you just let him walk straight past you? You could've bloody well held onto him until I got there!'

'Dammit,' I said. 'Just because you jump on a horse doesn't make me an animal trainer. What do you know about fairy tales?'

She looked at me for a while with one raised eyebrow. It was quiet. From the stable came the fumes of manure and hay, and in the distance, a horse whinnied in his stall. The little horse behind Rolinda stuck its head over her shoulder and eyed me curiously. I smiled at the animal and shrugged.

'What are you doing?'

'I was just having a private chat with your friend here.'

'Amazing,' Rolinda said. 'You are one of the few people in this world that I don't understand a thing about. And the same went for your . . .'

'Uncle,' I said. I took out a cigarette and gave myself a light.

'Yes.' She turned away and looked at the stable.

I inhaled. The horse, which was still peering over Rolinda's shoulder, tilted its head slightly, as if it were wondering if perhaps it ought to start smoking, too. I opened my mouth, but closed it again when Rolinda looked back at me.

'Did you want to say something else to Alice, or . . .'

'Listen,' I said, 'I can understand your being angry that I let your horse get away . . .'

'Twice . . .'

'. . . okay, twice, but try and understand my situation. You hand me the reins of some monster and expect me to act like the world's best jockey. These things happen, you know.'

'Maybe we shouldn't have seen each other again,' she said distractedly.

'What?'

'I said: maybe . . .'

'I heard what you said. What does that have to do with this?'

'I don't know,' she said. 'We met under such strange circumstances. Your uncle and that hotel and . . . I don't know.'

'Then work it out,' I said.

'You don't have to be so nasty about it.'

'No,' I said. 'I don't.' I drew on my cigarette and let the smoke sink down inside me. I tipped back my head, looked at the moon, and enveloped the night sky in a dull white cloud.

'I didn't mean it as an insult.' She sounded a bit uncertain, as if, now that we were on the subject, she was no longer sure if that were really true.

'I didn't take it as one,' I said, still staring up at the sky. I thought: this is the story of my life, if I ever get famous and I'm on TV and they want to show everyone at home how I lived, it'll be over in five minutes. 'What did you want to tell me, Rolinda?'

'Nothing,' she said. 'I . . .' She sighed deeply.

I felt a great, calm rage rising within me, something made of marble, that was how it felt, cold and glittering and hard. I flicked the ash from my cigarette. 'I've got better things to do in this lifetime. If you've got something to say, then say it.'

She laid her hand on the horse's nose and rubbed it absently. I smoked and waited. Alice pressed her cheek against Rolinda's temple and looked at me with a compassionate gaze. I threw my cigarette on the ground, stamped it out, and walked off.

I could hear her calling. She asked what I was doing and, when I was a little farther away, shouted that I shouldn't be so silly and, when I was farther still, to watch out for my knee . . . And then there was darkness all around and I hobbled onto the service road, between the beech trees and the misty fields.

———

I had walked back, three miles to the outskirts of the city, where I found a tramstop, and all that time on the narrow path I had hovered between rage and self-pity. When at last I stumbled into the tram shelter and sank down on the grimy bench, the agitation was just beginning to outstrip the dejection. I sat there, as a knife plunged into my knee every now and again, and chewed, with slow, thoughtful movements, on nothing. I chewed out of anger and pain.

'I don't understand you,' said Nina, when I finally lay in my hotel room, leg stretched out on the bed, a Jameson's in my hand to kill the pain. 'That you'd even bother talking to someone like that.' She picked up the phone and called down to reception for a doctor. I protested softly. 'Yes, I know,' she said, one hand over the receiver, 'it's nothing, it'll be fine in the morning.' She spoke into the receiver and arranged, in a rather implacable tone of voice, for someone to come up, here and now and without delay. I sipped my whisky and tried to ignore the shooting pains in my knee.

'Nathan? You know why I tell you these things, don't you?' Uncle Herman's voice, less than forty-eight hours ago. I had left his hotel room and he had practically shouted it after me.

'You can't stand waste,' I had answered.

And his reaction: 'Yes.' That was what he had said. And then: 'That, too.'

How much of a margin should one allow? How great *was* my margin? Ten, maybe fifteen percent.

'Have you eaten yet?' Nina was standing next to the bed with the menu in her hand.

'No,' I said. 'We never got that far. Would you mind handing me that notepad? Over there, on the table.'

She walked across the room, picked up the pad, shot a glance at the river, and came back. 'I'll order something, I haven't eaten yet either. Think I'll try the sashimi.'

'That's not eating, that's noshing.'

She looked at me, expressionless.

'Lamb cutlets,' I said. 'And order a decent wine to go with them. This whisky tastes awful.'

She picked up the phone again and gave her order. 'The doctor's downstairs,' she said when she had finished. 'He'll be right up.'

'Thank you.'

'I've made all the funeral arrangements. I've also phoned the solicitor, he expects us on Monday.'

'Us.'

'Yes, we're the only ones left.'

The only ones left, I thought. My God, what a history.

There was a knock. Nina opened the door and a man came in, lightly tanned and clearly in a hurry. 'Grünenbaum. This is the patient? The knee. Would you remove those trousers, please?' He put his bag down next to the bed and Nina untied my shoelaces. I tried to stop her, but she ignored me. 'If you have anything to say, Doctor, say it to me, because he's one of those people who thinks he can do everything himself.' The doctor gave me a sardonic look. 'If I were you,' he said, 'I'd put myself entirely in your daughter's hands. In fact, I'll prescribe it.' He chuckled. Nina looked at me closely, but I refused to correct the error. 'Child,' I said, 'fetch me my pen, would you please? It's in my jacket.' She nodded slowly and went to the wardrobe.

The doctor felt my knee, he tapped, kneaded, and twisted it and did a variety of other things that all seemed to be geared towards hurting me as much as possible. 'Mr Hollander,' he said, 'your knee will be fine, but I'd advise you to walk with a cane for the next few weeks. And it would do you good to get some exercise. Your muscles are in very poor condition. A sedentary profession, I assume. With your height and build, the joints are easily strained.'

'A cane,' said Nina. 'How charming.' She smiled sweetly when I looked at her.

'Any history of back trouble in the family, that sort of thing?'

Herman, he was the only one I could really . . . The thumbs. The back. What that girl, Lin, Rolinda, had said. No, I thought, with everything else that has gone on in this family, that can't be true as well.

A waiter came in and began setting the table. Nina showed the doctor out. I stumbled to the table and smiled at the young man as he arranged the silverware and uncorked the wine and all the while fragments of memory drifted into my head like wisps of fog. Herman and I on a warm summer night behind the house, in wicker chairs, a cold Montrachet between us. Landing in a snowstorm at La Guardia and Herman waiting in the arrivals hall, so glad to have me home safe that he hid his relief behind grumpiness. The back, the Hollander thumbs. Suddenly I thought of my first visit from Uncle Chaim and Cousin Magnus and what Magnus had said, 'We were there when Herman was a boy, too.' Not Manny. Herman. I'm Herman's son, I thought. I'll be damned, I'm Herman's son.

'He told me,' Nina let slip, as casually as she could, when she had sat down at the table, 'that you might have to walk with a cane for the rest of your life, if you keep on like this. He didn't think there was much point in telling you that himself, but that perhaps

I, your devoted daughter, might have some influence on you. I say you should take up jogging.'

'Thank you, child. But my daughter, you're not. Far from it.'

She shook her head coolly and poured the wine. 'Hollander,' she said, 'you're hopeless.'

'This is just the beginning,' I said. 'Now all I need is a hearing aid, bi-focals and arch supports and I'll be the caricature of an old man.'

'You,' said Nina, as she sliced into a lamb cutlet, 'have got the worst self-image I have ever seen. You think those fairy tales of yours are worthless, you think you're worthless, you think everything you do is worthless.'

'Guess I've just read too much Marcus Aurelius and Epictetus.'

She raised her left eyebrow and, after a while, shook her head.

I brought the glass to my mouth. As I drank, I felt the wine filling the emptiness inside me.

The Depths of the Depths

'So you think you're Uncle Herman's son,' said Nina. She was standing in front of the fire, her back to the flames, arms folded.

I nodded.

'The evidence is a bit . . . shaky.'

'Not really,' I said. 'I had to clear out Uncle Herman's apartment in New York.'

Nina put her hands in her pockets.

'I'd hoped to find our letters, but I found something else instead.'

Nina sat down. She tucked her right leg under her and turned towards me. 'You're going to do this like a real storyteller, aren't you? With dramatic pauses and unbearable suspense and all that.'

'They wrote. He and Sophie.'

'And?'

'They loved each other.'

'I'm sure they did, but that still doesn't mean . . .'

'No, it doesn't mean a thing, but if you add it all up . . .'

Nina sighed. 'But you'll never know for certain.'

'No.'

'Just as I'll never really know if Zeno was my father.'

'No.'

'What a mess.'

'It's family life, Jim, but not as we know it.'

'How are you feeling?'

I felt good. Once the fire had warmed me, my joints were supple again and my blood, fluid. It was going on seven and I was starting to get hungry, but I couldn't think what we should eat and I had no desire to go down into the cellar. I wanted to stay right here in this warm chair and gaze at the fire. I wanted our imprisonment to come to an end, all that chopping through Zeno's barricades, the traps within his traps.

'A Parmentier,' I said.

'A what?'

'I think we should make a Parmentier.'

'I heard you, but what is it?'

I explained it to her, that one of the pilots on the record flight of the *Uiver*, the KLM DC–2, was called Parmentier and loved fried eggs and cheese and that that was why the dish had been named after him.

'*Uiver*,' said Nina.

'Stork. It's an old word for stork. Parmentier was the Dutch Neil Armstrong.'

We went into the kitchen, where I started up coffee and watched as Nina made eggs from powdered eggs and milk from powdered milk. She put a frying pan on the flame and poured the yellowy mass into the hot butter. I told her about the *Uiver*, the pride of the KLM, how Commander Koene Dirk Parmentier and his men took part in a race to Melbourne and had to make an emergency landing somewhere in Australia. That was in the town of Albury, where 2CO, the radio station, saved the plane and its crew by calling on local motorists to come to the race track and light their way with their headlights. I told her how the *Uiver* had landed in a flood of Biblical proportions, that's how hard it was raining, on a track less than three hundred yards long, and how several hundred spectators had pulled the plane out of the mud the following morning. Parmentier had to leave his passengers behind to get the plane back in the air. When the *Uiver* finally arrived in Melbourne, it finished first in the handicap section and second in the overall list of rankings. The mayor of Albury received a medal and the whole of the Netherlands contributed to a monument that was erected in the little Australian town. The Dutch consul general came to Albury to present gifts to all those who had assisted the crew.

'So, you put the cheese on top,' said Nina, who was standing by the stove.

'Yes, and then the lid on the pan, so it melts.'

'Do you think anyone will come and save us?' She picked up the jar of rosemary standing on the counter and sprinkled some in the pan.

'No.'

Nina looked over her shoulder.

'No, I don't think so. Why? Because no one knows we're here. The house has been vacant for years. If we want to get out of here, we'll have to wait until the worst of the cold is past. And even then: there's too much snow. We can't go out until we're feeling strong enough to dig.'

She lifted the pan off the stove and slid the Parmentier onto a plate. 'There's not much bread left.'

'We'll bake some more tomorrow. What day is it?'

'This is the third day. We came on Monday.'

Wednesday. The third day. The middle.

Nina got out the plates, I poured coffee.

'It hasn't been snowing for quite a while now,' said Nina, looking outside.

'Maybe we should go out tomorrow and have a look around.'

We walked through the icy-cold hall to the library. Our plates were steaming. The marble floor was strewn with splinters. I could feel them under my shoes.

While we were eating, I said, 'I think he concentrated on the entrance to my bedroom because he knew I'd want to go there first.'

'Then you're assuming that all this was meant for you.'

'Yes.'

'Why?'

The faint bitterness of the coffee and the earthy flavour of fried eggs and cheese had filled my mouth and head. I thought of all the times I had eaten this and how Nina had just sprinkled rosemary over the eggs and, in doing so, had let me taste this old, almost too familiar dish anew. Just as she let me taste life, my life, anew.

'What makes you think this is aimed against you?'

'Against? I don't know if it's aimed *against* me. If Zeno did do it, then perhaps it's a sort of . . .'

'A sort of what?'

'Have you ever heard of *The Way of a Pilgrim*?' Nina shook her head. 'It's a book. I had lent him *Franny and Zooey* . . .'

'Who did you lend what?'

'Zeno. A book by Salinger, two novellas about a sister and brother. The sister, Franny Glass, reads this little book, *The Way of a Pilgrim*, and because of this, and because she can't seem to love anybody, she becomes confused. It's a description, that book, of the attempts of a simple Russian peasant to discover the secret of the Jesus Prayer. He sets out to find a teacher and learns the prayer and . . .'

'What the hell is the Jesus Prayer?'

'The endless repetition of a line from the New Testament. I think it's something like, "Jesus Christ, have mercy on us." That one line is repeated over and over again, all day long, until it becomes automatic, as automatic as breathing, until you're saying it with your whole body.'

Nina looked dubious.

'It's an old mystical technique, a sort of self-hypnosis through repetition. In any case, Zeno read *Franny and Zooey* and I believe he identified quite strongly with those brilliantly bizarre Glass children. And being as mystically . . . er . . . inclined as he was, that Jesus Prayer was right up his street.'

'What does that have to do with the house and the traps?'

I ran my eyes over the walls of books. 'Zeno believed in submission. Only through submission, not subjection, could you experience the essence of something.' I reached for the cigarettes. Nina shook her head. I lit one and blew my smoke towards the darkened ceiling. 'Submission is the mystic's trademark. If you read the biographies of mystics, St Theresa of Avila, St John of the Cross, Luria, De León, the chassidic rebbes, you'll see that they always set off on a journey, as it were, a spiritual journey, and get lost along the way, find their way back again, meet helpful travellers and others who try to thwart their plans. Everything that happens on such a journey is part of the process that eventually leads to submission, to leaving behind what we call dignity and self-awareness.'

'In other words, if you're lying in the gutter in your own shit, you finally see God.'

'Something like that. But by that time, God is about all you have left. And that, I said to Zeno, is the danger of this type of venture. If you torment yourself long enough, mentally or physically, you leave yourself very little choice. I've always felt that the decision of a healthy, free man to embrace the Divine is far more meaningful than a cry for help from someone who's already trapped in limbo.'

'Coffee?'

I nodded.

Nina stacked up the plates, hooked her finger through the coffee mugs, and left the library.

If Zeno's submission theory was correct, I was just about halfway there. That afternoon I had reached the stage at which I had stared up from the depths, and felt a longing that, until now, I had fervently denied. A house, a place of my own where I could feel at home. It was a wish that was a contradiction of my entire life. When Nina and I made love, I had given myself to her. I had allowed her to prepare my bath, to wash me and dry me. I was sixty, but up until this morning my whole life had been dominated by independence, self-reliance, self-sufficiency. Whenever I was ill, I crawled into a corner where no one could see me and waited until I was better. No nursing. I was alone, and I was good at being alone. I didn't need anyone. I wouldn't even have wanted to need anyone. I was the helper, not the helpless. But with Nina . . . Did she love me, or did I love her, or both, and was that why I had been able to put myself in her hands? Or was it the pull of some deep-seated genetic code that compelled a young woman to care for an old man?

Why, Nathan, I asked, can't you believe that it's love? Because you have no certainty? You want certainty about something that can only ever be uncertain?

I'm no lover, I thought. I remembered Nina's words: 'Uncle Herman had a way with the ladies.' She had meant it as an antithesis. You, N, she had wanted to say, have not.

Herman had predicted that I would make Molly unhappy. 'No doubt about it,' he had said. 'And I'll tell you something else: you're going to make every woman you ever meet unhappy.'

Was I unable to love women? Women, or people in general? And if so, why?

Herman had once criticized one of my fairy tales, because he felt it lacked development. 'Kei was in love with the miller's daughter and the miller's daughter loved him, but one day Kei's love disappeared. He gazed, as always, at his young wife, but her hair was like straw, her eyes, dull grey pebbles, and her skin, unwashed linen. Kei knew this wasn't so, but that was how he saw her. He decided to go in search of his love.' That was how the story began and Herman, after reading that part aloud, had cried, 'What sort of nonsense is this? In and out of love in a single line. Where's the development?' I had my answer all ready, of course, but now, for the first time, I began to think about the question of how that worked in my own life. How did I fall in love, with whom and why and how did I lose my love? Sixty, I thought. I stood up and searched through the pile of wood for a piece suitable for the fire. Sixty years old, and for the first time in my life I'm thinking about my dealings with the rest of the world. It's too late. Everything has already happened.

I had loved Molly, but it was no great love. Herman had been right. I did make her unhappy. She came home, and went away and came home again, and each time she stood there with her hand on the door knob, I could see the uncertainty in the way she bowed her shoulders. She was thinking: When I go out, what does he do? She had no idea who I was. I thought there was nothing to know. What she saw was who I was. Or so I thought. But at night, when we sought and found each other in the darkness, at night she knew me and I didn't know her. The hair I had fallen in love with glided over my face, I pressed my eyes into that hair and closed them and thought: Who is she, to be doing this with me? When I came and her arms closed around me, when she pressed her body against mine, to feel all of me, feel me in her and on her and around her, then she was certain – she knew me – and I was uncertain, I didn't know myself. And as I emptied into her, my self-confidence drained away. She broke me down, brick by brick, and I didn't understand what was happening.

One morning, after she had left for a rehearsal with her enormous bag, I had packed my things and hailed a taxi. I drove to Heathrow, through the London maelstrom of people and cars, and all that time, forty-five minutes long, I stared out the taxi window and felt nothing. I thought nothing. I knew nothing. It wasn't until half a day later, when another taxi dropped me off at the Hill and the great stone house stared down at me, that I finally put down my suitcase. The taxi was already gone and I stood there, the woods behind me, the stone stairway and the heavy green door before me, and fell to my knees. With my head in the grass, hands over my eyes, I screamed into the earth.

Nina hated Zeno, she said, but her feelings for him could never run as deep as the hate I had felt for myself that day. I had walked to the door, opened it and gone inside, like a machine, a mechanism that can do nothing but move, and in my mind a feverish repeat of the same scene played over and over again: Molly coming home to an empty living room, empty kitchen, empty bedroom. I walked up the stairs, down the hallway, opened the door to my bedroom and put my bag on the bed. And I saw her screaming. Her eyes . . . The image was so sharp that I turned my head away, so I wouldn't have to see her eyes, far, far across the ocean.

In the bathroom, I soaked my shaving brush, lathered up, and laid the razor in a bowl of hot water. Meanwhile, in the steamy mirror, Molly went running from room to room. She pulled open drawers, didn't see my things, looked on the kitchen table, in the bookcase, next to the phone, but found no note, not even a stubbed-out cigarette in a barely soiled ashtray to say: I was here, but now I'm gone.

I ate a tin of haricot beans and drank two cold vodkas. Molly washed her face and got ready to go to the theatre. I went to the library, bottle in hand, and poured another glass. The hearth was a cold, empty hole. I drank and stood up, paced back and forth along the walls of books, and sat down again. And I drank, stood up, ran my finger along spines and went back to the bottle for more. I heard Molly's voice in the chorus. The high beam of a spotlight on her red hair.

At the end of the evening I crawled up the stairs, grinning. Halfway there I tumbled back down, and I thought it was so funny that I did it all over again. In the bathroom I stood for a long time in front of the mirror. I tried to force myself to be serious, but each time I looked myself in the eye, I burst out laughing.

In the middle of the night Herman phoned to give me hell. Molly was with him, in Manhattan. 'It's time you started asking yourself,' he roared down the phone, '*why* you fall in love with someone, before you make any more victims!' And as his voice echoed in my pounding head, I couldn't help thinking of the flaming sword at the entrance to Eden.

Less than two days later, Uncle Herman phoned again. He was curt. A letter had been forwarded to New York from a large estate agent's that was interested in the house. They wanted to send someone over to look at it. He wasn't planning to sell, he said, but he did want to know what the agent was offering. And since I was up there anyway, coming to terms with my sorrow (he sniffed when he said that), he expected me to receive this person. It would take my mind off things. He laughed a short, dry laugh and hung up.

The estate agent was a woman, and when she arrived the sun was shining so brightly that for a moment I thought Uncle Herman had appealed to the Lord of the Universe Himself to show me how little my 'sorrow' actually mattered. I stood at the foot of the stairs and watched as Miss Sanders disappeared into the woods on her bicycle, then crossed the field in front of the house and took the path that led downward. It was the height of spring. The forest was just coming to life. The sun had released scents that had been hidden all winter long and the wood, the rotting leaves and the first grasses made it smell like early May. High above me, in the treetops, the birds were telling each other about their nests and what good parents they were. Rabbits came hopping out of the woods, stopped in the middle of the path, looked about, as if wondering whether to go left or right, and disappeared again between the trees.

I had been walking for several minutes when I met a young woman. She was wearing a dark blue blazer that I could tell was much too warm. A few strands of her long honey-coloured hair lay, dark with moisture, across her forehead. I was about to pass her with a polite nod, when she stopped me.

'I'm looking for the . . .' she glanced down at the card in her hand, 'the Hollander house.' She looked up. 'Do you know it?'

'Come along with me.'

Her face clouded. 'That won't be necessary. Perhaps you could just tell me which way?'

I turned round and pointed to the path lying before her. She nodded quickly and hurried off. I watched her go, the back of her dark jacket gently fluttering.

When I got to the house, she was standing on the veranda, her back to the door. She started visibly at my sudden appearance, and my slow approach didn't make her any calmer.

'They don't seem to be home.' Her voice sounded tense.

'No,' I said. N, I thought, put the poor girl out of her misery.

'I have an appointment, but perhaps they forgot.'

'Why?'

She looked at me in terror.

I climbed the stairs. She shrank back, until she was nearly touching the door. Any minute now, I thought, she's going to threaten to call for her father. When I was standing right beside her, she let out a tiny squeak. I put my key in the lock and heard the woman sigh. She swayed slightly. I smiled and looked at her as reassuringly as I could. She held out a slim hand, 'Annelies ter Borg.'

'Miss Ter Borg. Nathan Hollander. So, you want to buy the house?'

She laughed, relieved.

'Come in.' I turned round and went ahead of her. As I swung open the door, I thought: What the hell am I doing?

In the hall, we paused for a moment. Her mouth moved. This was the point at which she was supposed to speak. If I hadn't disrupted the standard procedure and been a normal client, nervous, eager to sell, yet mute with excitement, my vanity flattered by the pretty blond estate agent, she would have made the little speech that the staff had met to discuss that morning. 'It's certainly a large house, Mr Hollander, a house with a history. But difficult to sell, I'm afraid. Huge maintenance costs. Not easily accessible.'

But she said nothing.

'Are you from these parts?'

She nodded.

I led the way to the library. The sun shone low through the windows. The walls of books glowed in the soft light. I took her jacket.

'I don't normally handle large projects,' she said.

I laid the jacket over an armchair and showed her to a chair at the reading table. She looked around in amazement. I walked out of the room, fetched a bottle of Gewürztraminer from the cellar. In the kitchen, as I rinsed the glasses, I looked out for a while at the spring grass. I'm making her wait, I thought. Why?

When I returned she was staring straight ahead and resumed the conversation she had wanted to begin earlier.

'Annelies, they said, this one's for you. At first I thought they had finally decided to give me a promotion, but then I saw your name.' I drove the corkscrew into the bottle and pulled. 'You have a . . . a certain . . .'

'Name . . .'

She nodded.

I went and got the ashtray, which was on the mantelpiece. 'Do you mind if I smoke?'

She shook her head.

'My name,' I said, as I sat down. 'What sort of a name might that be?'

'You're that poet, aren't you?'

I shook my head.

'Oh. I thought . . .'

'No.'

I smoked and looked at her. She sat across from me at the big table. Between us lay books, an empty coffee mug, a plate full of crumbs, my notepad, and a pile of paper, on top of which was a text covered with deletions. Annelies ter Borg. She looked as if she had a rough time of it, a young woman who had chosen a job in a world of men who were amazed that this girl took her career so seriously. The light shone through her hair, giving it a deep golden sheen. She smiled at me, two full lips, painted soft red, that seemed to swell as her smile faded.

'Miss ter Borg,' I said, aware of the formality in my voice, 'what exactly are your instructions?'

'Excuse me?'

'I said . . .'

'What makes you think I would tell you a thing like that?'

I reached for the bottle and filled our glasses. I slid one towards her and picked up mine. The yellowish wine smelled strongly of grass and herbs. I let the fragrance fill my nostrils and rise up into my head. Spring, nearly summer.

'It all depends on what one chooses,' I said. 'You were sent to me because apparently, I have a certain "name." A pretty girl does wonders – is that what your colleagues thought?'

She shook her head.

'No?'

'No.' She ran her hand through the shining hair. 'I'm sorry. I shouldn't have said that, about your name.'

'Just tell me your limit.'

'No.'

'Fine,' I said. 'Then tell me how far you're willing to go.'

She didn't answer.

I looked at her from beneath arched eyebrows and raised my glass. She took hers by the stem and we drank a toast.

'I'd prefer to negotiate openly,' I said. 'I'm not in the mood for wheeling and dealing. It's not my style, offering thirty-five so I can get forty. Shall we have a look around?'

We stood up and left the library.

'Five-fifty,' she said in the hall.

'Five . . .'

She shook her head. 'That's as far as we can go.'

I nodded. 'So, the associates have decided to use me as their pension plan?'

Her heels rapped sharply against the floor.

'I've told you what I know. What more do you want? For them to throw me out?'

I sat down on the stairs. Her face was on a level with mine. Lovely, carefully painted lips. I admired the angry look in her eyes. When was the last time I was angry? I wondered. God, that was ages ago. Before the Flood. Way before.

'How long have you been with the company?'

'Three years.'

'How long does it take to get a promotion?'

A wall of great coldness rose between us. I got up and went to the hunting room.

'Six-fifty,' I said. 'And why don't we call each other by our first names?'

I'm not being nice to her, I thought. I don't want to be nice to her.

One by one I threw open the doors. I showed her the kitchen and the lawn with the wooden shed where the garden things were kept. The sculleries, the attic, the guest rooms – the grand tour.

In the hunting room I pulled aside the canopy and offered her a seat on the bed. She shook her head.

'You can't stand around all day on those heels.'

She shrugged her shoulders in a weary sort of way. We stood there for a while facing each other, two animals in silent combat, and then she sat down.

'You know I can't go any higher,' she said.

'Where did you go to school?'

Her mouth dropped open, she slowly shook her head.

'I have the feeling I know you.'

'Jesus.' She sank back onto her arms, her face to the canopy. I could see that she was tired, of me, most likely, her feet were turned inward, her shoulders slightly bent. Something came to mind, the vague, fluttering image of a girl of eighteen.

'The Park School.'

'When did you graduate?'

'Would you also like to know whether I'm married and have children, and if I use a company car . . . Why are you so curious?'

I shrugged.

'Five-fifty,' she said.

I offered her a cigarette. She sat up straight. She drew one out of the packet with her fingernails.

'We went to the same school,' I said.

I walked over to the window, on the other side of the room, and sat down on the windowseat. I looked out at the woods and wondered why I had told her that we had gone to the same school. If nobody slaps me in the face, I thought, I'll just carry on until I'm somebody else.

'If you sell it,' she said, 'what will you do?'

I shrugged. 'I've never needed a house. I'm a traveller.'

'Why?'

I turned my head towards her and tried to think of an answer. Her question surprised me. Why? I was doing a scene from The Lonely Man, my version of a Swedish art film, but that one word had turned up the lights and shown me that the forest was cardboard, the rooms, painted wooden panels, and the chairs, mere imitations.

'I don't know,' I said. 'I think it's just the way I am.'

I got up from the windowseat. She got up from the bed.

'How old are you? Late thirties?'

'Something like that.'

'What are you waiting for?'

'Waiting?' I said.

'That's how it sounds.'

Waiting, I thought, she's right: waiting. But for what?

'May I ask you if you'll have dinner with me tonight?'

She nodded.

'Will you have dinner with me tonight?'

She laughed. 'I'm married,' she said.

'So?'

We walked around the house a bit more, avoiding the subjects that needed to be discussed (why did I want to eat with her? which offer was acceptable? why did she think I was 'that poet'? and why had I said that I wasn't?) and went through the rooms like two people saying goodbye.

'I have to get back,' she said finally.

We were standing in the library, next to the table. The bottle was half-empty. The prints of our fingers on the glasses looked almost guilty. The sun had disappeared behind the trees. Her face was a chalkmark in the twilight. I picked up the bottle and poured. She opened her mouth. I picked up my glass and she raised hers and drank, pensively. I put down my glass and looked at the window. The blood pounded in my head. When I reached out my hand, her hair was as soft as I had expected.

'I'm married.'

'Yes.'

From close up her face was a charcoal sketch: her eyes, dark smudges in a blurred, two-dimensional face. I saw her rounded lips. I leaned forward and kissed her.

'Oh God,' she said. She pulled away, the back of her hand against her mouth. Her eyes were wide.

The twilight turned thick and grey. Although I was standing right beside her, I could barely see her face. But I could hear her breathing, quick, agitated.

She lowered her hand and looked down. Then she raised her head. She sighed deeply. Her kiss was that of someone who, after a long desert journey, had finally reached the oasis.

Nina, where was Nina? I had been sitting here for at least half an hour, daydreaming about what had happened and why. Nina had gone for more coffee. I jumped up out of my chair, staggering slightly, grabbed the candle that was standing on the mantelpiece, and hurried out of the library.

There was no one in the kitchen. Our mugs stood on the counter, the coffeepot beside them. I put down the candle and laid my hand on the metal. Cold. I ran out of the kitchen, to the hunting room. No one. Out of the hunting room, up the stairs. Left. My room. Empty. Darkness everywhere and in the darkness the crunching of wood beneath my shoes, stumbling over bolts and hinges that had fallen from dismantled cupboards. Downstairs, into the cellar. From the cellar to the kitchen door and shivering in the frosty night. Snow, snow, snow. Untrodden snow. The front door. I sank down on my knees at the threshhold and looked out at the creamy layer of snow that rippled over the stairs. No one had come or gone. In the middle of the hall, at the foot of the stairs, my clothes frozen and my breath a fluorescent cloud, I called out her name. No, I didn't call, I shouted. The silence ripped like a piece of cloth. Her name bounced off the walls and the ceilings and the floors, it echoed through the empty rooms, bounced off icy windowpanes and disappeared into the impenetrable darkness. When the last sound had died away, silence rustled through the house once more. Nina was gone. This time she had left without a trace.

I felt guilty. The first time she had run away, I didn't know why (and she hadn't told me either, I had just assumed she had left because she was scared, wanted to get back to civilization, but that was, I realized now, a ridiculous explanation; why would she leave in secret? there was no reason at all), but this time it wasn't hard for me to work out why she had fled. She was fleeing from me.

I stood in the kitchen, in front of the glowing stove, turning the knob on the radio. A slow tapestry of notes rolled out of the speaker. After a while the voice of Billie Holiday rose up from a cloud of violins. It was a number she had recorded at the end of her career, an old standby that, in her ravaged voice, was charged with such emotion that it hit me like a blow to the neck. The words were those of a woman saying she didn't miss 'him', not at all: 'except when snowflakes fall, or when I hear someone call your name, I do.'

I had grown cold on my search through the house, on the veranda, and by the stairs behind the front door, but only now, in front of the roaring Aga, did I truly feel what cold was. The ice on my bones pierced through to the marrow. My back arched as a shiver rippled up from my toes. My hands began to shake. God, Nina, I thought. And then, clenching my teeth to hold back the tears: I love you, I love you more than you can ever imagine. I stared into the candle flame and tried to make it stop. Then I spilled over. I threw back my head and took a deep breath. There were voices inside me. One said: Sixty? You're sixty? And you're crying about love? And another whispered: It's all regret, regret for lost time. And yet another said: Letitgoletitflowjustthisonceleteverything . . . Tears welled up in my eyes. They streamed down along my nose, over my lips, past my chin, down my throat.

'This is Radio East, on the air twenty-four hours a day. Here's the weather with Ronald Jongsma.' The voice of the announcer came in loud and clear.

'Ronald, what's the story? Have we seen the end of that frost yet?'

'Don't think so, Jochem. The wind's still coming in from the east, all the way from Siberia, and everywhere between Russia and us it's freezing cold. In Poland, night temperatures have dropped to forty below and . . .'

'Now that's what I call cold!'

'Yep. Ha ha. You can say that again. But we're not doing too badly ourselves. For tonight we expect temperatures here in the East to fall to around minus twenty-five. Slightly warmer near the north coast. Tomorrow we should see a slow rise in temperature to minus fifteen, but that's about as high as it's going to go for now.'

'Great news for all you skaters out there! What do you think, Ronald, any chance of an Eleven City Marathon this year?'

'If frost were the only factor, I'd say yes, but as I understand it the organisers met earlier this evening, and they're pretty worried about all the snow. Skies are clear now and the chance of more snow is unlikely, but we've had so much in the past few days, it hasn't done the ice any good.'

'So, the snow's ended?'

'Certainly looks like it. But there's mist on the way, not too great for the skaters, either. Tonight and early tomorrow morning, it'll become dense to very dense . . .'

I turned the dial. It would be a long time before the mist had filtered through the forest, to the Hill, but if Nina ever reached the car she was in for an arduous journey.

If she ever reached the car.

I emptied the pot of cold coffee, shook out the filter, opened the door and filled my bucket with snow. As I scooped coffee into the filter, put the pot on the stove, as the snow turned to water and hissed on the hot surface, I paced up and down. I had to follow her. I couldn't follow her. But if she couldn't find ... Maybe I could ... I loved her. She ...

Then the boiling water in the percolator began to rise. The glass turned brown and there was a soft gurgling sound. The candle flame bobbed on the current of air from the windowpanes.

'Cold as a dream of ice.'

Uncle Chaim was standing beside me, staring at the bubbling pot.

'An old Dutch winter, Nuncle.'

'Bah.'

'Where's Magnus?'

'Where's Magnus? How would I know where he is? No one has ever known. He's wandering about somewhere, looking for the way back, or the way out.' He took something out of his pocket. It was a small watchmaker's loupe. I had seen him fiddling with it once. Long ago. He had been in good spirits then. The last few years I had watched him trudging down the long road to ponderous gloom.

'Nuncle?' He looked up, the loupe in his right eye. 'Where has Magnus been?' He made his eyebrows dance and caught the little copper cylinder in his hand. 'Where?'

'Before he came here?' He put his hand in his pocket and shuffled towards the table. I poured coffee. When I set down the mug in front of him, he looked up in surprise. 'We don't drink, Nathan.'

I nodded.

When I was sitting across from him, he looked at me for a long time, the old man. There was something like fear and gratitude in his eyes.

'Magnus,' I said. 'Where was he?'

Uncle Chaim shrugged his bony shoulders.

'Nuncle. You and Magnus wander around like two Beckettian

half-ghosts, all these centuries, and you've never once asked him . . .'

'Asked? Yes. Got an answer? No.' He used both hands for the dismissive gesture he made. 'Magnus,' he said. His face took on a pensive look. 'As a child,' he said. 'The light of my eyes.' He raised his head and rested his gaze on me. 'The light, I tell you. He came to us, Friede, she should rest in peace, and me. All day long. Sat beside me at the workbench. Quiet child. And a memory, oy! what a memory. Where I'd lost a screw. What was whose. Friede loved him . . .' He bowed his head and stared at the steaming mug. 'But then Chmielnicki came.'

'And Magnus left.' After Friede had felt the sword of history. After the little house, less than a year later, had been burned to the ground and Uncle Chaim was hung from a tree in the great Lithuanian forest, between a dog and a whore. After after after.

'Where is she?'

She? I looked at my great-great-grand-uncle. 'She,' I said, 'is gone.'

He stared back.

'And just as you don't know where Magnus was, I don't know where she went. She's gone.'

'A family of boy scouts.'

'A family of second-rate boy scouts, Nuncle. One is on his way for twenty-one years. Another gets lost in the snow, twice. And I don't even want to talk about Zeno.'

'Herman,' he said, 'was a good boy scout.'

I sipped my coffee and lit a cigarette. 'A terrific boy scout. Just look what he brought home with him.'

Magnus had appeared behind me. I could tell, because Uncle Chaim looked over my head, one eyebrow raised.

'You drink coffee?'

Uncle Chaim shook his head. 'Nathan poured me a cup.'

'We don't drink,' said Magnus.

'He knows,' said Uncle Chaim. 'After fifty years. You think he doesn't know?'

'I know everything,' I said, in a cloud of smoke. 'Ask away.'

Magnus grinned.

'From 1648, or even before, up until this very moment. I know.'
A look of suspicion crept into Magnus's face.

'Coffee?'

He nodded mechanically. I got up, picked up my mug and
went to the counter. As I was pouring for him and myself, I
heard the wordless conversation that took place between him and
Chaim.

'Sugar? Milk?'

'Yes, please,' said Magnus.

There was a silence. I picked up the candle from the counter and
put it on the table. 'Have a seat, Magnus. Stay a while.'

He walked round the table and sat down next to Uncle Chaim.
I brought the mug to my lips. The smell of black coffee curled
upward. I drank. The sweetness of the sugar, the smooth bitterness
of the coffee. Sweet and bitter. I looked at the men across from me.

'Fifty years. I'm sixty now. I may be younger than you, but I'm
not your child anymore. It's time to ask questions.'

Magnus wanted to say something, but Uncle Chaim was quicker.
'Ask.'

I stubbed out my cigarette. 'Was he a madman or a genius?'

This completely threw them. 'Who?' asked Uncle Chaim. 'Zeno?'

I shook my head. 'This is a question for Magnus.'

Magnus looked away. His hand moved towards the coffee, but
stopped just before it reached the mug.

'Did he know he was a fraud, or did he believe in his own stories?'

'Who?' cried Uncle Chaim. 'Who!'

'Did you believe him?'

'Nathan. Who are you talking about?'

'Magnus?'

'I believed him,' said Magnus. He was having trouble squeezing
his voice through his larynx. 'Me, and others.'

'Hordes of others,' I said.

Uncle Chaim was wriggling about in his chair like a frenzied
weathervane.

'And you went running after him,' I said.

Magnus nodded. He looked down at the steaming coffee.

'After him . . . After . . .'
'Shabbetai Zevi,' I said.

———————

Cause and effect are winding roads, history meanders. Time creeps forth like a dungbeetle, struggling to roll its ball of dung: pebbles cling, and grains of sand, and the ball grows heavier and heavier and the beetle crawls more and more slowly. Time has weight.

Through the dark catacombs of Europe Magnus Levi travelled, wooden clockmaker's chest on his back, grubby linen hose round his legs, shoes of birch bark on his feet. He didn't know where he was going. He hadn't even thought about it. When he had bent over Uncle Chaim's charred possessions and found the chest, he had hoisted it onto his back as if it were only natural that he be next to carry the weight of time. Was there a direction? Was there a road he had to follow? He had no idea. All roads, thought Magnus, were the same, and they all led to each other. With his clockmaker's mind, Magnus thought: Life is a beginning, with a middle and an end, and he now found himself in the middle and had to move on, because man's fate is to travel, he has no choice, even though he knows that he will never arrive.

And while Magnus was leaving the Lithuanian forest, choosing a path to the left here and a path to the right there, someone else was setting off as well. He, too, had found himself in the middle of his life. But whereas Magnus was thinking only of the journey itself, because he had no goal, the other traveller had a goal, and nothing else. For him, the journey was merely a way to get to where he wanted to be.

The other traveller was called Shabbetai Zevi. He was the son of Mordecai, a poor poulterer who had made his fortune when the mighty English mercantile houses left Constantinople and Salonika during the Turkish-Venetian War and settled in Smyrna. Mordecai earned his living cutting chickens' throats, but, soon after the coming of the English, was hired by them as an agent. He proved to have a talent for the twists and turns of international commerce, and before long he had become one of Smyrna's nouveau riche. Because of this, Mordecai was able to send his son to study Talmud and Torah with the great rabbis.

Shabbetai was born in 1626, on that formidable day of mourning known, in Judaism, as the Ninth of Av, the day on which, long before, the temple had been destroyed. It was a Sabbath, and the boy, as often happened in those days, was named accordingly. From an early age, the child had felt a bond with that peculiar birthday, and the stories of the old men who foretold that the Messiah, too, would be born on the Ninth of Av, also on a Sabbath, were as real to him as the wondrous accumulation of gold in his father's treasure chest.

The boy liked nothing better than to study Kabbala, and there was one book more precious to him than all the rest: the *Zohar*, the *Book of Splendour*. And while others contented themselves with studying the text, comparing interpretations and discussing difficult passages, the son of Mordecai entered the world of the words themselves and sought the Kabbala within the Kabbala. He was a traveller, in search of the heart of the heart of things, the depths of the depths. He had, like most Kabbalists, no conception of time. Just as the great mystics would traverse entire deserts, cross raging rivers, and travel from Damascus to Safed in a single night, Shabbetai wandered about the woodland of words in the *Zohar*. Time, for him, was not something that began in one place and ended in another. Time was a forest. There were clearings, paths, some overgrown, some wide and sunny. He could walk down a crooked path from 1626 to 1648. He'd come out in 1666, a meadow between oak trees, and struggle through the undergrowth to the lake of 1548.

He starved, he prayed, he strengthened and weakened himself, anything to reach where the great Kabbalists had once been: in the shadow of God's presence.

Even before he had reached manhood, Shabbetai's name was known throughout Smyrna. And not only his name. He was handsome. His voice was captivating. There were some who claimed that a heavenly scent emanated from his body.

At the age of eighteen, Shabbetai was ordained a rabbi.

Although he enchanted nearly everyone, there was no one who could enchant him. His first – arranged – marriage lasted only a few months. So did the second, which was performed shortly afterwards. Neither union was consummated.

And in the meantime Shabbetai wandered farther and farther into the tangled wood of Kabbala.

One day, on Yom Kippur, in the synagogue of Smyrna, surrounded by notable and less notable members of the Jewish community, he uttered the Ineffable Name of God.

It was 1648. It was the year of redemption, according to the *Zohar*. It was the year of the birthpangs of the Messiah, according to the Kabbalists. It was the year Shabbetai began to hear voices.

The rabbis of Smyrna sentenced him, because he had uttered the Name, to thirty-nine lashes. Shabbetai was unimpressed. He was outlawed, but remained in Smyrna. Then he heard a voice that told him that he was the saviour of Israel, the true redeemer, the only one who could bring salvation. The prophet Elijah appeared to him and anointed him Messiah. People began to demand a more suitable punishment for the young rabbi, some even wanted him put to death. But none were prepared to do the irrevocable.

The new messiah left his birthplace and went to Salonika. There, soon after his arrival, he regaled the rabbis and rich men of the city with a sumptuous banquet. As the wine flowed like a river of sweetness and the tables steamed with exotic delicacies, Shabbetai sent for a Torah scroll and, in the presence of his bewildered guests, married himself to the Torah, the daughter of God.

He was forced to leave Salonika. For ten years he wandered about, until, in 1658, he arrived in Constantinople. He walked the streets carrying a large fish dressed as a baby, in a cradle. The rabbis of the city summoned him. Shabbetai heard them out, but their words had no effect. Israel, he declared, would be redeemed under the sign of Pisces. Once again he was dealt thirty-nine lashes and, once again, outlawed.

Shabbetai began to speak in paradoxes. He praised Him who permitted that which was forbidden.

Then a scroll appeared. Abraham Yachini, an esteemed Constantinople Kabbalist, had found it in a cave. It was an age-old text, he said, and it described Shabbetai as the slayer of the great dragon, the conqueror of the serpent. He was the true anointed one, he would sit upon God's throne, his kingdom would last forever. He was the sole redeemer.

Shabbetai returned to Smyrna and from there travelled to Palestine. On the way, in Egypt, he was received by Raphael Joseph Halevi, a wealthy mystic and benefactor, who had fifty Kabbalists to dinner each night and wore a sackcloth under his fine clothes as a sign of mourning because the age of mercy still had not arrived. He was quickly won over to Shabbetai's cause and presented the Messiah with a vast sum of money. On his arrival in the Holy Land, Shabbetai distributed the money among the poor.

His name was like fire in dry straw. His followers multiplied like grasshoppers in a ripe cornfield.

In Gaza, Shabbetai met a Kabbalist and clairvoyant named Nathan Levi, who was soon his most zealous advocate. He became the voice and legs of the Messiah and travelled the world proclaiming and expounding Shabbetai's kingship.

Time crawled on. Time was a tortoise. The year 1666 was drawing near. The bride of the Messiah made herself known.

Her name was Sarah. At least: that was what she called herself. She had been found in a Jewish cemetery in Poland, wandering about in nothing but a shirt. She was sixteen years old and so beautiful that, beside her, the sun was as pale as the moon. For nine years she had been locked away in a nunnery until one day, the soul of her dead father came to her and ordered her to jump out the window. In the cemetery she had shown her rescuers her wounded body. Her father had held onto her so tightly as he lowered her out of the convent window that you could still see the marks of his nails in her flesh.

Sarah was taken to Amsterdam. There, she told all who would listen that she was destined to marry the messianic king. She travelled on to Italy, leaving behind a trail of sinful rumours and tales. She behaved like a whore. That, she said, was because she had permission to live life to the full before giving herself to the Messiah.

Magnus had been wandering about for thirteen years when, one afternoon, cold and weary, he began his descent down the Alps and, in the low light of the sinking sun, saw Italy lying before him. He was not alone. On his way to the mountains he had sought the company of other travellers headed in the same direction, and there were four of them, when they were joined by three more. They, too, were travelling from France to Rome.

Ever since leaving Lyon, Magnus and a German monk, who was on his way to his order in Lucca, had walked side by side. It had been a silent journey until the monk, miles out of Lyon, caught sight of Mont Ventoux, and a cry of recognition escaped his lips. Brother Anselm had dropped his staff and said something Magnus couldn't understand.

'Mons Ventosus,' said the monk, pointing to the misty mountain top.

Magnus gathered that this was the name of the mountain. He shrugged, the clockmaker's chest tinkled and chimed. He wanted to walk on, but the brother called him back.

Had Magnus ever heard of the great poet Petrarch?

Magnus could read – the Hebrew of the Torah, though not very well – but poetry was unfamiliar to him. The monk, who was twice his age, had motioned to him to walk on, and as they did, he told him about Petrarch and his struggle to free himself from the world, his love for Laura, his journey to Mons Ventosus, the Mountain of the Winds, which the French called Mont Ventoux. They came closer and closer to the mountain, the landscape was already bending to its flanks, and Anselm explained how the modern age had begun with Petrarch.

For thirteen years Magnus had been on the road, nearly always travelling alone, and now he was walking beside a monk who spoke of poetry and the modern age. Magnus came from the forest, where bison roamed and where the winters were so cold that people froze on their way from one village to the next, a world where God was addressed in the language of a distant land and foresters, herb gatherers and tanners longed for the supernal. Anselm was the son of a nobleman. His mother, the wife of a tenant farmer, had been seduced by her lord. When Magnus asked how the monk, or his mother, for that matter, knew who the father was, the old man had pointed to his hooked nose, a formidable beak that plunged down at the bridge and made him look rather daunting. 'The Haguenau nose,' said the brother. Magnus suddenly thought of his own thumbs, which had also been Uncle Chaim's.

At the age of seven Anselm had been set to work on the Haguenau estate, as his father's page. Every morning he had to hand the noble-man his bowl of water and wait until he had finished washing. Then he helped him dress and when that was done, he was allowed to wait on his master at the table. They were landed gentry, Anselm told him, and life in the big house, which was more of a fortified farmstead than a castle, lacked the refinement that he was later to encounter in certain monasteries. Breakfast consisted of gruel and cold meat from the day before, washed down with watery beer. But what the big house did have, and the farmers on the estate did not, was a teacher, and he taught not only the lord's legitimate children, but the bastard as well. That was how Anselm learned to read and write, Latin and astronomy. By the time he was sent to the monastery at the age of twelve, he was ready to work in the printing room.

And on they went, they traversed the forests, hills, and valleys and the monk told the clockmaker about his first few years in the monastery, how he had been put to work in the fields until one day, Brother Francesco, who was in charge of the library and the printing room, saw the novice reading a book of hours. A week later he was allowed to turn the heavy crank of the printing press, fetch blank paper and deliver it, printed. He wasn't an apprentice for long because Master Francesco let him do more and more until the young man, because that was what he was by then, became not only a monk but an accomplished printer. They used to cut their own ornaments, he told Magnus, and some were so popular that even secular printers came to buy them.

They passed the Mountain of the Winds and headed further South, towards Marseille. They were to remain there for several days, after which they would set out on the journey to Savoy. Magnus would stay behind in Turin, while Anselm travelled on to

Lucca. At the end of the first day, they were sitting in a shabby wayside inn. The weather was mild and the shutters were open. This was fortunate, because the fires in the kitchen were blazing and it was hot and smoky inside. Magnus was drinking a mug of weak beer and the monk had a jug of wine in front of him. Night fell quickly, the way it does in the South. The two men sat on the wooden bench against the wall of the inn and stared out at the blue-black sky, at the stars that were just beginning to prick through and the little bats that tumbled about in the velvet of the early night.

'You're a silent man, Magnus of the Lithuanian Forest,' said Anselm.

'No more silent than you, Anselm van Haguenau,' Magnus had replied.

A broad grin had appeared on the monk's face. 'If you mean that all my talk about Petrarch and the art of printing say about as much as your silence, you're right. Perhaps we ought to say, instead, that you are more talkative than I. What brings you to Turin?'

'I'm a clockmaker,' said Magnus.

'I know.'

'I want to see the clocks of Savoy.'

'I didn't realize that they were so special.'

Magnus drank his beer.

'You mustn't fear all men, my fellow traveller. Though you may not believe this, there are some in this world who are *not* out to get you and your kind.'

Magnus stared into the dark mug, barely visible in the dim light.

'I know what you are and I know that there are reasons to remain silent about what you are. But how much longer do you expect to walk before you reach home?'

'Maybe forever.'

The monk had shaken his head. 'So, you think you're the Wandering Jew, Magnus?'

Magnus closed his eyes and thought of clocks, he thought of a timepiece that would tell all of time, minutes, hours, days, weeks, months, years, centuries, the whole of Creation, a timepiece that, in all its completeness, would be superfluous, the clock of clocks.

'Let me tell you something. There are many among my brothers who obtain their wisdom from your books. Many of us know that you were the beginning. No doubt there are some who would say that you are the end. I myself believe that you and your people are the Petrarchs of this world. You seek a new way, a better way. But I don't think you'll ever find it if you continue wandering. One day you'll have to make up your mind to settle down. Take the advice of someone who has always lived in the home of others.'

The following day, in the tepid morning sun, they had set off for Marseille. A farmer let them ride part of the way on the back of his wagon, among a load of sloshing barrels, so that they reached the great road to Marseille sooner than they had expected.

In the city, Anselm took it upon himself to assemble a travelling party. He found two men who were on their way to Pavia with a bag of legal documents. They bought bread and wine and set out on their journey. They were a silent foursome. The two strangers came from Perpignan and spoke an unintelligible dialect. They took the coastal road, an easier route to travel. Near Toulon, a curious sight met their eyes. They were coming round the bend and walking uphill, when they saw a figure lying in the middle of the road. Two men were standing beside it. One of them had his arms folded and was looking down impassively at the figure on the ground, the other was speaking, but to no avail, because neither the first man nor the person on the ground seemed to hear him. When they came closer, Magnus could hear that they were Jews. The second man was speaking Yiddish, in a strange dialect, but Magnus had no trouble understanding him. He braced himself and began to walk more slowly. Then he saw that it was a woman, a young girl, lying there. She was staring up at the blue Mediterranean sky, completely ignoring the talking man.

'May we be of service? Gentlemen? Mistress?' It was Anselm who had spoken. He mopped his forehead and let his blue-grey eyes go from one man to the other, and then to the girl. She was a beauty: her skin was the colour of pure wax, her hair was a red shock of gleaming curls, tied back with a white ribbon, her lips were full and her eyes, black and glittering as jet, were large and shining. She didn't look at the monk.

'Good brother,' said the man who was looking down at the girl with his arms crossed, 'we are from Amsterdam and we are accompanying this young lady to Rome, but it seems that the young mistress is tired of walking. I'm afraid you can't help us.' He spoke flawless German, far better than Magnus.

'If the lady prefers not to walk, she prefers not to walk,' said Anselm. 'And then we certainly can't help you because we, too, must walk even though we'd rather not.'

The two men from Perpignan looked at the girl from under their dark eyebrows. One said something to the other and they both began to laugh.

The man who had spoken to Anselm glared at them and then turned to his companion. 'Come,' he said. 'We'll follow these gentlemen to Toulon. I'm sure the bride will follow us if she feels called upon to do so.'

'The bride? But gentlemen, surely you wouldn't leave behind a young bride?' said Anselm.

The man smiled. 'She is the bride of a man who does not yet know that he is the groom. If she, in her omniscience, has seen that she shall marry this man, she'll surely know when to start walking again.'

Anselm grinned.

The party moved off and the dust flew up from their heels and settled back down. Magnus, who was walking at the rear, heard the girl say something. He turned round and looked back.

'Dogfaces,' she said in Polish. She didn't raise her voice. It was more of an observation than a curse. Magnus grinned: 'Dogfaces? Shoe laces.' The girl laughed a tinkling laugh. She jumped up and shook the dust out of her dress. When they were standing face to face, there was something in her eyes that nearly made him recoil.

'Where are you going, *pan*?'

'Don't you "sir" me. I'm going to Turin. Where are you from?'

'From the dead.'

Although she laughed when she said it, a shiver ran down Magnus's spine.

'Come,' she said. 'The dogfaces are getting away!' She began walking briskly towards the cloud of dust in the distance. Magnus followed, hesitantly at first, then more quickly. He had the feeling, as he watched her nimble young body striding on ahead of him, that none of this was real.

———————

I had finished my coffee and watched Uncle Chaim's and Magnus's grow cold, and then, when Magnus turned his gaze to the dark kitchen window, I had got up to feed the stove. None of us spoke. I piled the logs into the black iron mouth and watched the flames die down. When I banged the door shut, the fire started raging again. I picked up the coffee mugs and put them on the counter.

'Wine, gentlemen? Or should I say: *pani*? Is that the correct plural?'

Uncle Chaim shook his head, not to say that he didn't want any wine, but in response to Magnus's account of his peregrinations through Europe.

In the cellar, I walked past the racks with a candle. Though Nina and I had polished off a good many bottles in the past few days, we had barely made a dent in Uncle Herman's wine supply. I hunted around until I found the Haut Brion I was looking for. It was a '78, an excellent year, as far as I could remember. By the time I had finished this, I would not only be glowing to the tips of my ears, I would also find the world a much more pleasant place.

At the kitchen table, I carefully twisted the corkscrew into the neck.

'You do that,' said Uncle Chaim, 'like a clockmaker.'

I smiled. 'This *is* a clock, Nuncle. The only clock that doesn't tell time, but preserves it.'

I filled my glass and took a sip. The smell of earth and grass and chocolate. The wine was on the cool side, but wouldn't be for long. I set out two more glasses and poured.

'Waste,' said Uncle Chaim.

'I know,' I said. 'But I want it this way. Think of Elijah's cup.'

Uncle Chaim grimaced.

It was my favourite part of the Seder, on the first night of Pesach, when the exodus from Egypt is commemorated with a meal that bulges with symbolism: the filling of a cup for someone who isn't there – the prophet Elijah. For thousands of years in exile, scattered all over the world, Jews have continued to fill that cup. Never actually believing that Elijah will come and take his share – but you can never know for certain. Just as, on that night, the door is left open a crack, so that anyone who happens to be passing can join us in celebrating the liberation from Pharoah's Egypt.

Years ago, when I was still a boy, when everyone was still alive and Sophie and Emmanuel were still together, Elijah's cup was, for me, the highpoint of the Seder. I was probably the only one in the family who would have thought it perfectly normal if Elijah had strolled in and drunk it down. But I was also the only one who, each night, travelled hand-in-hand with two dead men through the Kingdom of Shadows.

The thought of Nina rose up inside me like a sheet of paper tossed in the fire that went twirling up on the heat, caught, burned, and fluttered down again as brittle ash. Where could she be? Had she made it to the car and, if so, had she been able to get it out of the snowbank? Pointless thoughts. I shook my head, like a wet dog shaking its fur.

Magnus wouldn't look at his uncle and Uncle Chaim was acting as if the spot where his nephew was sitting wasn't even there.

'So,' I said, as I sat back down, 'you travelled with the bride of Shabbetai Zevi to Italy.'

Magnus nodded.

'And from there, to Cairo?'

Uncle Chaim looked up. 'How. Why don't I know anything? You do?'

'Books, Nuncle. There are so many books about Zevi. Zeno has a whole collection of them in that crazy library of his.'

He sniffed.

Sarah was a slut. No one has ever known who she really was, where she came from, or why she did what she did. What went on in her mind, was a mystery.

That evening they arrived at a coaching inn, where they rented a large room with straw on the floor and a smoking oil lamp hanging from a collar beam. Downstairs, a steaming pot hung over the fire, and from that pot they were given something to eat. It was a reddish-brown soup filled with shellfish. Although Magnus had learned to bend the dietary laws during the last few years, the sight of all those boggle-eyed crustaceans floating in the thick broth was more than he could bear. He confined himself to the heavy grey bread that had been set down on the table, along with a hunk of sheep's cheese.

Sarah ate as if she hadn't eaten in days. When she looked up and stared Magnus in the face, her mouth was a red stain, an obscene, cruel gash. She grabbed a feelered creature out of her bowl, broke its back, and sank her teeth in, her eyes never leaving Magnus's, her teeth white and bared, her lips gleaming with fat. Then she seized the jug of wine, filled her glass to the brim, and emptied it in one draught. Magnus averted his eyes and looked at the innkeeper, who was scolding a servant. A foot crept along his instep, up along his calf. He froze. Sarah was talking in a loud voice to Anselm. The foot glided over his knee. He tried to change position, but there wasn't much room on the bench. Toes ambled along the inside of his right thigh. He felt his member swelling. Sarah pulled the bread towards her and tore off a piece. She bit in and chewed. The foot rested against his groin.

Magnus sat up straight. He felt the pressure of her soft foot between his legs, the toes bending and flexing. His head seemed detached from the rest of his body. It looked around, drank beer, and took in its surroundings as if none of this must ever be forgotten. Down below, the toes glided under his groin, pressed against the spot between his anus and scrotum. He had never made love to a woman and knew that any expectations he had might be the wrong ones, but this was beyond his wildest imaginings. She was so young. How could she know that she . . . He coughed loudly. The foot crept back up until it lay against his crotch. Magnus felt the blood throbbing in his sex. It was like the handle of an axe. It ached with hardness. A thought flashed through his mind. He looked up at the ceiling. A tortoiseshell cat was sitting on a collar beam. It had its front paws together and was looking down imperiously at the rabble below.

The innkeeper had come, cleared away the plates, and set a new jug of wine on the table and more beer for Magnus. The foot slipped away, Sarah washed her face over a bowl and when she looked up, her skin beaded with water, her eyes suddenly moist and soft, she smiled at him and he knew for certain, if he had ever doubted it, that it had been her foot he had felt. He raised the tankard and buried his whole face in it.

That night he was awakened by screams. On the other side of the room, where a bed had been prepared for Sarah, stood a bowed figure. The girl's voice sliced through the darkness. Magnus was not the only one who had been startled out of his sleep. When he ran to her bedside, Anselm and the Dutchman came rushing over, too. Next to the bed stood one of the men from Perpignan. He was naked, and tried to cover his shame with his trousers. Sarah was holding on to one of the trouser legs and was tugging at it, cursing loudly.

Anselm grabbed the trousers and pulled them out of her hands. 'What's happened?'

Sarah began screaming at him in Yiddish. Anselm turned to Magnus.

The man from Perpignan had tried to lie with her, he translated, but she had woken up and pushed him away.

Anselm looked at the man. He started getting dressed, babbling in his unintelligible dialect. The monk said something in French. Sarah was still ranting and raving. 'Bastard! Do you think you're the best I can do? I'd rather have three farmhands than a piece of soft cheese like you!' Magnus grinned. Anselm and the two men from Perpignan – the other had come over and joined them – spoke at great length, in French. Then the monk turned to Magnus again. 'They can't stay here. But they refuse to leave the room. They're proud, those French. I'll call the innkeeper.' The Dutchmen protested, but Anselm was adamant. He strode into the hallway. They could hear him stomping down the stairs.

One of the Dutchmen, the one who had spoken with Anselm earlier, turned to Magnus. He spoke Yiddish. 'It's always the same with her. Everywhere we've been, we've had trouble. She doesn't seem to understand that we have very few rights and that no bailiff would ever believe her.'

Magnus nodded. He knew what the Dutchman was talking about, and why the man from Perpignan was being so obstinate. All he had to do was call the authorities, and Sarah, her escorts and probably Magnus, too, would be thrown in prison. And they'd be lucky to walk out of there alive.

Anselm returned with the innkeeper, grumpy and ill-tempered, in his wake. One of the other guests had left after receiving a message from Toulon. The vacant room was small, more of a garret. Sarah could sleep up there.

'Not alone,' said Anselm. 'One doesn't let a young bride sleep alone in such a place.' He pointed to Magnus. 'You're going with her. And one of you, too, I take it.' He looked at her escorts. The Dutchman who hadn't spoken until now was nudged by his companion. He sighed, went to his bed, and began packing his things.

Half an hour later, the three of them had been moved. The room was, indeed, a garret, but there was fresh straw on the floor and horse blankets spread out on top. A small window was open in the roof and Magnus could see the stars and the light of the moon. He put down his chest and crawled under his blanket. There he lay, his hands beneath his head, looking up at the night sky. Now and then the scent of lavender wafted in. He had trouble falling asleep, but after a while he drifted away. It was as if he rose up, grew lighter and lighter and . . .

When he opened his eyes Sarah was standing over him. She was as naked as Eve. He opened his mouth, but before he could say a word she sank to her knees. He felt her buttocks in his lap. She laid a hand over his mouth and began pulling off his blanket. He tried to push her away. He clutched at her breast. She moaned. Sounds came from his throat and she smothered them in the palm of her hand. It was as if time were changing. Time went faster than it should have done. Suddenly he felt her fingers, taking his sex, lifting and stroking it. In seconds, he was hard. Her hand closed, thumb on the shaft, fingers around his scrotum. She turned round and lowered herself onto his face. He gasped for breath. 'Your tongue,' she whispered. 'Your tongue.' She pushed down her pelvis. He tasted her. She moved her hips forward and back, he turned his head from side to side. 'Can't you do anything! Lick!' Magnus felt how quickly he was breathing. He thought of everything at the same time. Lick? But that was . . . Then he felt something soft and warm gliding over his glans. She was taking him in her mouth! No! A strange tingling ran down his spine. He opened his mouth and licked.

It was pitch-dark in the garret and before long Magnus didn't know where he was or how they were entwined. He didn't find his bearings again until he saw the open window above him, the sprinkling of stars, and a slowly rising phallus. For a brief moment he thought it was his, but as the hazy white rod came closer he realised that it was someone else. Sarah mounted him and, impaled, rode him like a horse. Her hands rested on either side of his chest. He saw her contorted face, the open mouth and closed eyes. He felt two knees drop down beside his shoulders. A hairy scrotum dangled just above his head. He panicked. Then the knees wriggled forward and he saw Sarah open her mouth wider and bite into the phallus that was presented to her. Magnus averted his head and touched the thigh of the man kneeling over him. Lord of the Universe, help me. Forgive me. Sarah rode and rode and rode and through the archway formed by the legs of the strange man Magnus saw how her mouth swallowed and released the other man's rod. His belly was on fire. He moaned. Sarah whimpered, her mouth made a slurping sound. 'No,' she said. 'Not like that.' She pulled her hips off him and pushed him away with her knee. 'From behind.' Magnus rolled over and crawled round her. She spread her legs. Her head moved up and down on the other man's sex. Magnus looked up. He saw only a black figure silhouetted against the faint light from the roof window. He kneeled behind Sarah and tried to enter her, but she moved her backside and he missed. Then he felt her hand around his rod. He glided through her slit, and then upward. She thrust back her hips. He couldn't go any deeper. She breathed in and pushed harder. He eased into her, and slowly, on his knees, began to fuck her. His hands on her hips, head back. Now and then he looked down to see her bobbing head of hair in the lap of the dark figure. The three bodies moved as one, a machine, a timepiece whose cogs were tightly interlocked and, together, formed one rhythm. Then the other man drew back. He lay down next to Magnus on the horse blanket and wriggled himself under Sarah. 'No,' she said. The man pulled her down, Magnus fell half on top of her. Only then did Magnus understand what was happening. The other man had plunged into her and was fucking her from the front. Magnus was committing the Sin of Sodom.

Realizing this, Magnus was gripped with fear, but he couldn't stop. The earth fell out from under him. He could do nothing but move. He felt her buttocks against his belly and the legs of the other man between his own. Then he exploded. He shot into her, thrust after thrust, and it was as if it would never end. When he finally dropped down and slid out of her, Sarah climbed off the man, turned around, sat on his face, and rocked her pelvis. She had him in her mouth again. Before long they were moaning, first she, then he. Magnus lay down on his back next to the pair and saw Sarah's rolled-back eyes, her mouth gripped around the wet staff, opening now and again to let out a moan. Then the man gave one loud groan and Sarah put her hand around his sex and kneaded it hard, as if she were milking him. The man thrust his hips upward and Sarah began to swallow.

The news that he had a bride reached Shabbetai in Cairo, at the house of Raphael Joseph Halevi. He gave orders to have her brought to him. His disciples were not pleased. The girl was said to be a slut who gave her body to every passing stranger. There were rumours about orgies beside which the excesses of the Romans paled into insignificance. A young, disappointed rabbi who saw in Shabbetai the light of Judaism, mustered up his courage and asked him why he would wish to associate with a harlot who had let her body be used as if it were a marketplace. Shabbetai replied that if the prophet Hosea could marry a whore, why shouldn't he do the same?

Magnus had travelled with Sarah and the Dutchmen to Rome. He had bid farewell to Anselm near Turin and the monk had thanked him for his company and cautioned him against his endless wandering. He knew nothing of the black night that Magnus had spent with Sarah and the Dutchman and so Magnus accepted his good advice with shame.

They hadn't been in Rome long when Shabbetai's orders came. The Dutchmen, who felt that they had travelled long enough and fulfilled their task, entrusted the girl to Magnus's care. He would accompany her to Egypt. They gave him a bag of gold pieces and a letter for the Messiah. This was the first that Magnus had ever heard of Shabbetai.

We sat around my kitchen table, Magnus, Great-Great-Grand-Uncle Chaim and I, all three staring down at the wood. Uncle Chaim shook his head, as he had done repeatedly in the past hour; Magnus barely moved.

'I thought I was on the path to enlightenment,' he said. 'I never touched her again after that night and I thought that this would be my victory over the sins of the flesh. If I were to stand before the Messiah, he would understand.'

'A victory,' I said. I filled my glass. 'In one night you had a taste of virtually every sexual possibility known to mankind. If you think that's the depths, you're right: things can only get better. Anyway, what's the problem? You made love to a woman who offered herself to you. There's no harm in that.'

Magnus waved aside my words. 'Nowadays,' he said. 'Nowadays, that would be true. But there was no love involved, and it was then. In your time, you'd have no problem with such things, but I . . .'

Uncle Chaim sighed.

I'd have no problem with such things, said Magnus. But that wasn't the case. I had received Nina's ... gift ... yes, gift, as if a hot potato had been thrust into my hands. My entire life, sixty years, had been shaken because of it.

'Magnus, I would have a problem, too. I *did* have a problem. Somehow or other we seem to find it easier to accept money, or goods, than love. If it *was* love.'

What Nina had offered – that was love. But why had she left?

'Lilith,' said Uncle Chaim.

Magnus and I stared at him.

'Lilith.'

Long, long ago, when the Lord of the Universe created the first human, He created a woman for him, because, He said: 'It is not good for man to be alone.' He created her from the earth, as He had created Adam himself, and called her Lilith, the Woman of the Night. But the woman would not yield to Adam's will. When he wanted to lie with her, she said: 'I will not lie beneath you.' Adam was shocked: 'I am your master. I belong on top.' Lilith was furious. 'We are equal,' she said, 'we were both created from the earth.' But Adam would not listen. This so enraged Lilith that she pronounced the Ineffable Name and flew off into the air. Adam called on his Creator. 'Lord of the Universe!' he said. 'The woman You have made for me has run away.' God sent three angels to bring her back. To Adam, He said, 'If she agrees to return, fine. If not, she must allow one hundred of her children to die every day.'

The angels overtook Lilith in the middle of the sea, in whose mighty waters the Egyptians were destined to drown. They told her what God had said, but she refused to turn back. The angels said, 'We shall drown you in the sea.' 'Leave me!' cried Lilith. And at the command of the Lord of the Universe, the angels left her.

According to Zeno's *Zohar*, the book that Shabbetai had loved so dearly, Lilith had six pendants dangling from her ears and all the jewels of the east around her neck. She wore robes of purple. Her mouth was said to be a temptation in itself, her tongue as sharp as a sword, her voice as smooth as the finest oil, her lips, rose-red and sweet with all the sweetness of the world.

And it was not only Adam who wanted her. One day the Lord of the Universe sent away His own wife and took Lilith in her place. According to Rabbi Shim'on bar Yohai, this was the real reason that God, the King, should be worshipped, so that He would remember His kingship and acknowledge His true wife, and she would return to Him.

Lilith, Uncle Chaim had said.

'Nuncle,' I said. 'Lilith is a story. Sarah is real. Perhaps she was disturbed, or perhaps she was perfectly sane, but she certainly wasn't some Biblical femme fatale who turned into a demon.'

I poured the last few drops out of the bottle. It was nearly midnight, but I had lost all sense of time. The day that lay behind me had run into the night and the way things looked now, that night was never going to happen. I'd probably be sitting here until the break of dawn, at this table, with Great-Great-Grand-Uncle Chaim and Cousin Magnus, trying to tie up the loose ends of the fabric that was our family history.

I tossed down my glass and got up. The stove was still burning, but I threw in a few more pieces of wood. Then I disappeared into the cellar for a new bottle of wine and a box of crackers.

When I came back upstairs, Magnus and Chaim were sitting in their chairs, frozen in motion. They didn't start moving again until I had put the bottle down on the table.

'Hey.'

Magnus looked sideways.

'I can't find the knife.'

'Knife?'

'The knife I always use to slice the cheese. It's supposed to be in the block.'

'Maybe it's under that cloth?'

'Magnus, it's a big knife.' I held my hands about twelve inches apart. 'It belongs in the block. Last time I saw it . . . I can't remember.' I'm old, cold, and tired, I thought. I'm forgetting things, I'm losing things, I can't even remember things that have just happened.

I got out a plate, another knife from the block, and sat down at the table.

'Hunger,' said Chaim.

'You, Nuncle?'

He shook his head.

'Me? Yes. Always at night. A few crackers or a sandwich before bed. You know that.'

He nodded. They had often caught me sitting up in bed at night with my knees raised, a book on my lap and, under the book, wedged between my stomach and thighs, a plate. I opened the bottle. The Haut Brion had been better than I'd expected. Any other French wine would have had a hard time in this weather. That was why I had chosen an old Rioja, a Marques de Caceras, Gran Reserva, 1984.

'You're not going to bed yet,' said Magnus. 'Would you like me to . . .'

'Please. I can't bear to think about that cold empty bed and I'm dying to hear more about your adventures.'

He smiled wrily.

The wedding in Cairo was beyond compare. There was gold from Africa and silver from Iraq, silk from China and damask from Syria. There were fresh figs in fresh cream. There were olives as big as goat's eyes and millstones of bread that gleamed like polished wood. There were almonds from Persia, there was dark red wine from Turkey. Magnus walked around like a child at a fair. He had never seen such riches. There were men in garments of pure silk. There were women with kohl around their eyes. He felt like a country bumpkin in a palace. He hadn't seen Sarah once since his arrival at Raphael Joseph's house. Her groom had sent his thanks and the master of the house received him at his table, but the Messiah himself had withdrawn. It wasn't until the wedding began that he caught his first glimpse of him. He had a sharp nose and heavy eyelids. A downy moustache graced his upper lip. An attractive fellow, without a doubt, this Shabbetai Zevi. Still, Magnus couldn't understand why everyone was so impressed with the vainglorious young man. They ate and drank, the certificate of marriage was read aloud and Shabbetai broke the glass under his foot. Then he addressed the guests. That was the moment when Magnus understood why men saw him as the Redeemer.

'It was a sweet voice,' he said. 'Not a cajoling voice, not the voice of a serpent. No, a sweet voice. It came to you and wrapped itself around you and rocked you in its arms. Shabbetai spoke, he spoke like a book. You could close your eyes and it was as if someone were reading to you.'

And Magnus had let himself be rocked on Shabbetai's words. He listened to his prophecy about the time that was to come and the time that had been and he was borne along, slowly, but inexorably.

Before the wedding it was as if life had come to a standstill, but less than a week later, time resumed its course and went storming ahead. Shabbetai asked his doctor's son to sleep with Sarah. He sent for three virgins, disappeared with them for three days and then returned them, untouched, to their homes. He took a second wife, one who had already been promised to someone else. Time, Magnus knew, hadn't really changed, the sun didn't rise any faster or set any more slowly. The days were as long and the nights as short. Yet it felt as if the whole world was flowing, as if life was a river that had begun as a meandering stream and now plunged down, churning, from a mountaintop, shearing away banks, uprooting trees.

In Cairo, Smyrna, Constantinople and Gaza, men, women and children were preaching about their visions. Seers and prophets had risen up in Amsterdam, Paris, Frankfurt, Warsaw and Rome. People walked the streets like rabid dogs, foaming at the mouth and screaming Shabbetai's holiness. The marketplaces were empty, the land lay fallow, and huge houses were sold off as if they were worth no more than tumbledown shacks. Some people exhumed their dead and had them brought to the Holy Land, so that their souls wouldn't have to travel underground to the Mount of Olives to witness the Day of the Lord. Some Christians converted to Judaism, others were infuriated by the sudden self-awareness of the otherwise so diffident

Jews. Ships with silk sails and Hebrew flags were sighted off the coast of Scotland. The Ten Lost Tribes, people said, were preparing to cross the mythical River Sambatyon.

Shabbetai proclaimed the Ninth of Av a festival and abolished the fast. He allowed women to read the Torah. He threatened his opponents with death and placated his disciples with positions in the rabbinate.

The year 1666 was approaching, the year of redemption, and Shabbetai set sail for Constantinople. Magnus sailed with him, his chest full of clocks and parts always at hand. He had become the Messiah's clockmaker. He looked after the time. And the time wasn't far off when there would no longer be any time, when hours, days, months, and years would have lost all meaning.

But even before they had set foot on land, Shabbetai was arrested and, three days later, brought before the Great Vizier. The man gave the travelling Messiah a few careless blows and then threw him in prison. After several months he was transferred to Abydos, where Sarah joined him, along with the rest of his entourage. The streets of Constantinople were soon teeming with followers and pilgrims. Magnus wandered through the city and lived off the goodwill of the Jews who took him into their homes and fed him. Clocks weren't popular here and he had no other means of support.

Meanwhile, in Poland, a man had appeared who proclaimed the coming of a Messiah, but never mentioned Shabbetai. The captive redeemer sent for him, Nehemiah Kohen, and they spoke and argued for three days and three nights. When Kohen came out again, he still wasn't convinced of Shabbetai's calling. This angered the Messiah from Smyrna, and suddenly Kohen's life was of little worth. He fled Abydos, converted to Islam, and informed the Turkish authorities of Shabbetai's false messiahship. The sultan sent for the prisoner and made him an offer: either he prove himself to be the Messiah, by submitting to torture, or embrace Islam. Nathan Levi begged his master to choose the first, but Shabbetai didn't have a moment's hesitation. He converted to Islam, was given a white turban and a green robe as a sign of his conversion and, under the name Mehmed Efendi, was appointed Royal Gatekeeper. Sarah converted, too, and the couple lived on the generous allowance provided by the sultan.

A period of great confusion ensued. For many, the world collapsed. They had neglected or sold everything they owned, shunned friends and disinherited relatives. But a small circle of followers still believed in Shabbetai. The false messiah visited them – to convert them, he had told the sultan – but was caught delivering a Kabbalistic discourse. The Turkish government banished him to Albania where, on Yom Kippur, nine years after his journey to Constantinople, he died alone.

Magnus didn't hear of these events until long after his redeemer had embraced that other religion. He happened to be in the synagogue one morning and as he bobbed through the service like a cork in the gutter, he heard someone cursing Shabbetai's name. He was about to address the man who had spoken, when he heard about the conversion.

Suddenly there was no more time. All the clocks stood still. The hum of voices around him, the screaming children running round the bimah, the women whispering behind the lattice, they all disappeared into the background and were replaced by a great silence. It was the silence of nothingness. He could feel it. He could see it. He opened his eyes as wide as he could and stared into the depths of that silence. Then he keeled over.

'And?'

'And then I came back,' said Magnus. 'Some people I'd met took me with them. They listened to my story, gave me food and drink, and when I was feeling stronger, they gave me money for the crossing. The rest of the way, I walked.'

I dug my cigarettes out of my jacket pocket and lit one. Now that Nina was gone, I no longer had to keep to the rations. As it was, I had already smoked my way through most of them. Any longer and I'd have to go hunting for mouldy old cigars that Herman might have left behind.

'So it was just his voice, Magnus? That's what made you follow him?'

He nodded.

That was hard for me to imagine. There must have been something in his words.

'But why did you go with Sarah to Rome and from there to Cairo?'

He shrugged. 'What difference does it make where you go?'

I forced the cork back into the wine bottle and stood up.

'Going to bed?'

I shook my head. 'I'm going to make coffee. I need something to keep me awake.'

'Nuncle,' Magnus said. I rinsed out the coffee pot and went to the back door to fill it with snow. 'Chaim?'

As I was shaking the coffee grounds out of the filter, I looked round. Magnus was lying nearly halfway across the table, his hand stretched out towards Uncle Chaim.

'What's the matter?'

'He's not answering.'

'Perhaps he's thinking about your journey, Magnus.'

Four scoops of coffee. Two strong cups.

'Nathan?'

'Hmm?'

'He's. Uncle Chaim . . .'

I spun round. Magnus was standing next to Uncle Chaim, his right hand on the old man's scrawny left shoulder. 'What?'

'He's dead.'

'He's been dead for centuries. What's wrong?'

'No, he's gone. Look.'

Uncle Chaim was hazy. He was somewhere between here and not here. A pencil drawing being rubbed out.

'Nuncle.' I heard the fear in my voice.

The old man looked up, and from out of the haze came a smile, the likes of which I hadn't seen on his face in years.

'Stay with us, Uncle Chaim. Not now.'

He shook his head. 'Late, now. Very late. Time up.' His voice came from far away. 'Too much happened. Too much . . .' He looked at Magnus. 'Too much time gone. Peace. Sleep.'

'Nuncle . . .'

He straightened up and looked at us drowsily. He was almost translucent, like glass. 'Last time, I think. Now. No more. Told everything. Doesn't matter . . .' The faint streak of his eyebrows seemed to dance up and down in amazement. '. . . at all.' He melted away like a puff of cigarette smoke in the wind.

Magnus's hand rested a few moments longer on the non-existent shoulder of his uncle. Then he lowered it and looked at me sadly. I shook my head but didn't know what to say.

We stood there for a long time staring at the empty space that had once contained Great-Great-Grand-Uncle Chaim and was now nothing more than air and absence. I motioned to Magnus to sit down. I put the coffee on, waited for the pot to start bubbling, then filled my mug. On top of the sparkling black liquid I sprinkled a bit of cinnamon. It reminded me of Nina's hair.

'What now?' said Magnus.

I had no idea. I felt as if I was here and not here. All those times jumbled together, people who couldn't be here, but were, people who should have been here, but weren't.

'Do you know the story of Rip van Winkle, Magnus?'

He thought for a moment and then shook his head.

I told it to him, that American fairy tale about the Dutchman who fell asleep and woke up twenty years later in a world he no longer knew and which no longer knew him. 'That,' I said, 'is how I feel.'

'Do you think that'll happen to me . . . I mean . . . like Uncle Chaim?'

'Perhaps. It's only human.'

He looked at me in surprise. Then his face cleared. He smiled. 'Are you going to stay up all night?'

'I'm not tired yet.'

'You really don't know where Nina is?'

'Gone home, I imagine. The question is, Magnus, why?'

He was silent. 'Why?' he asked after a while.

I took a sip of the hot coffee. The smell of the cinnamon made my head spin. 'I don't know. If I did, I'd have the key to her secret.'

'I didn't know why Sarah . . . But that was different.'

'Maybe not. The simplest answer, of course, would be Uncle Chaim's. Lilith. But I don't believe in that. To be honest, I think that we, you, Uncle Herman, Manny, Zeno, and I, the Hollander men, don't know the first thing about women.'

Magnus shook his head.

'No, I don't really believe that either. Besides: Nina just said that Herman had a way with the ladies. Could it be that you and I have both experienced a moment when it was clearer than ever how much of a stranger a person, a person you know, can be?'

Magnus's head swayed slightly.

I emptied my mug, got up, and put it on the draining board. 'I'm going upstairs.'

'Upstairs? I thought you slept in the hunting room.'

'I do. I'm going to the attic.'

Magnus's expression was as empty as a bottle after a drinking session. 'To do what?' he asked after a while. 'What are you looking for?'

'I have no idea.' I found a new candle and lit it, then slid two more in my trouser pocket. 'I think it's time.'

Magnus sighed.

'Listen,' I said. 'Three, almost four days ago, we began downstairs. We chopped our way up. Now we can get to the attic stairs, through a hole in the wall of the room we were in this afternoon.'

'A hole in the wall?'

'They're wooden walls. He had to chop a hole so he could set his trap and then leave the room. But he couldn't go back down the stairs. Which means . . .'

'He's upstairs.'

I nodded.

'He might have escaped by way of the roof.'

'Escaped?'

'Left.'

'Magnus, anything's possible in this house, but one thing's certain:

if I ever want to find out what really happened, I'll have to go upstairs.'

'Has Zeno been here?'

'The first day. Just the first day.'

Magnus nodded thoughtfully. Then he said, 'I'm going with you.'

Part Five

Stranger

THE CRICKETS, OR the grasshoppers, or the cicadas, God knows
what they're called, chirped desperately at the gathering dusk, but
the sun kept on sinking, falling, with Mediterranean relentlessness,
and now it's dark, the sky deep blue, not a breath of wind. I'm
close to my beginning. In the desert, another desert, I saw the first
light, not the light of day, the *true* light; in a desert, it shall grow
dark. The light of my life, the darkness of my life. On the sandy
plain of the desert.

An outstretched body. Prometheus on the mountain. Pale carcass
of a weary old man, laid out, but not yet dead, on a bed whose
sheets are furrowed like the sands of the . . . Night, fallen.

This afternoon I swept the sand out of the room, and as I dragged
my broom back and forth with the slow, unwieldy movements of
a man still unused to his own clumsiness, I suddenly thought, I'm
just like my house and garden. Consumed by the desert, bit by bit.
I sweep and I sweep, I dust off the books, wipe the powdery sand
from the cracks, but I'm getting older and slower and the sand keeps
blowing about at the same, indifferent pace. Every day the floor
takes longer to clean and I'm more and more tempted to leave the
broom in the corner and reconcile myself to the thought that the
sand will keep coming, whatever I do, and that I could spare myself
all that trouble by simply welcoming it in like a guest. Sand, take
me, unto you shall I return.

Like a stowaway, that was how I saw myself, then, there, like
someone who was present, but never took part. A stowaway, then
and now. This is where I dwell, a land that suits me better than all
the rest, if only because it's a refuge, and I'm not a resident. I came

when it was too late, and I remained, even though I was too old to go on living.

The heat, the heat.

And the things that grow here. Am I the sort of man who will ever get used to the idea that if you want to eat an orange, you simply walk into the garden and pick one? Am I the sort of man who can sleep at night if I hear sounds I know only from films?

That's not true. I did know them. But long ago. In a desert. The buzzing of the cicadas, or grasshoppers or crickets, or whatever they're called, the creaking of sun-dried wood as it shrinks in the chill of the night, the crackle of cooling stones. But long ago, so long ago. Ah.

Closer to the beginning than ever. When I was thirty, I knew the facts of my life: born here, raised there, childhood illnesses, holiday trips, school, friends, parents . . . But only the vaguest image of myself as . . . as something that was present within a greater whole . . . within life . . . the flow of . . . And now, a sack of blood and bones (plenty of bones, not much blood) and it's as if I'm in two places at once, here and there, then and now. A stowaway in time. I remember the House, the Ship, the Desert (the other one), my Father and my Mother, my Sisters and Zeno, especially Zeno, and I can smell and taste and feel what I once smelled and tasted and felt.

Ah.

'Shalom, Mr Hollander. Why are you lying here in the dark?'

'Reisel, the Shunammite . . .'

'Tsk. And I suppose you're King David, waiting for some young maiden to come warm you up?'

'Ha! Heat. I've got enough of that, thank you. It's coolness I need. A fresh rain shower to wash over me, this country, this whole damn world. A shower that'll turn all that blasted sand into mud, so it stays in one place for more than five minutes. Lord! Let it stick to our roofs, let it cover our roads, just as long as it stops blowing into my house and turning my books into Hungarian pastry. That's all I ask.'

She turns on the small lamp next to the sliding doors to the garden and walks through the room, in search of the basin and the bottle of distilled water. She stoops down and the lamplight sets her hair on fire. It glows . . . like a burning bush. I hear the sound of metal against glass. She has found what she sought. And now she comes and sits on the edge of my bed, the Shunammite. She bends over me and presses the switch above my head.

'Wait, Reisel. A few moments.' Squinting, I push myself up, prop my pillow against the wall and, very slowly, let in the light through the cracks of my eyelids. 'You bloom like a rose.'

'Mr Hollander, sometimes I think you really do think you're King David.'

She has the inner glow of youth, of health and strength. Her skin looks soft to the touch and her eyes shine with life. She is made of fresh milk.

'Do you know my name? Besides "Mr Hollander", as you insist on calling me?'

She rinses the syringe, takes the bottle of alcohol out of her apron and a wad of cotton wool from the bag on the table beside the bed.

'Do you?'

No, she doesn't. How could she? I'm the only one. All the rest who knew are gone.

A streak of light shoots across the raised needle, the air bubble disappears from the syringe.

'Wait, Reisel. Just a little longer.'

Finally she turns her face towards me, her eyes glide slowly through the darkness, through the light, where they begin sparkling, to my face. Twenty-five, maybe thirty, this girl, this tender plant with deep roots. She feels and drinks the water deep below us in the ground. It flows through her, upwards, to the flower of her face. (King David? No, failed psalmist. The flower of her face!)

'I'd kill for a cold glass of beer. A tall, cold glass of beer.'

She shakes her head gently.

'I know, I know.'

A moment longer.

'Nathan,' she says.

'Yes?'

'That's your name. Nathan Hollander.'

'I know that. But I had another name, a secret name.'

'You have more secrets than just your name.'

'Oh, yes. Full of secrets. Not worth a thing anymore, but secrets galore.'

She says nothing. Those who were born here, among the sands, on this dubious refuge, are hardened and steeled. I've seen the young men walking. Shoulders like . . . shoulders. Guns. What do they call those things they make here? Swaggering about, straddle-legged . . . Don't know what I would have preferred, the schlemiel in the East European ghetto or these young predators. I know, I know. There was no other way.

I am an evolutionist who believes in the Creation story. That is why I'm so worried about what has become of this country. He who develops claws to defend himself, shall live as a beast with claws. He who hides behind armour, must wear that armour forever. That is evolution. The Creation story is the victory of culture over the body. Genesis is: lowering the claws and trusting the mind. Here, they've done an about-face.

Now then.

Head back. Her cool fingers on my arm and . . . ah . . . the needle. The light touch and . . . Her hands glide through the circle of light, to the pillow, on either side of my head, and they grow longer and paler, green, the left hand on the long arm and the green hand on the right arm are nearly together. The four slanting squares on the wall fade and return. A lizard rustles on the roof, the wooden walls creak. When the green right hand and the left hand meet and Mickey Mouse is standing with his arms above his head in the centre of the clockface, I get to my feet. Trousers, shirt, socks. Shoes. Sunglasses, Swiss army knife, cap.

'Are we leaving?'

You.

'A trip down Memory Lane? Where to this time, Cain?'

Ca . . .

The darkness is like oil on water. It flows. As . . . as if time is moving.

'Towards the light? Up the stairs? Down the stairs?'

Stairs? Ah, yes.

'Mr Hollander?'

The Shunammite.

'Shall I turn off the light?'

'Hm.'

Her arm divides the room. She separates the light from the darkness.

Nothing, now. Never been.

'Is it working yet?'

'I'm everywhere at the same time.'

'I'll stay a bit longer. Until you fall asleep. May I take a book from the shelf?'

So black, the darkness. No. Place where she sits and reads, like a shaft. Squeeze through. Chairs.

'Can't you get through?'

'Through what?'

'If you crawl in. Can't you just crawl through the chair legs?'

'Magnus. Cousin. I'm sixty. Can you see me wriggling through that jumble of legs like a disoriented eel?'

Nothing but legs. A huge beast, turned to wood, curled up in winter sleep on the stairs to the attic. A backbone made of chair seats, vertebrae of curved wood, clawed mahogany paws. An upside-down puzzle. Everything upside-down. Upwards, but a journey to the depths.

The clarity of cold.

I thrust the blazing lantern into the darkness of the stairwell. Shadows dart away like rats. Downstairs, in front of the door to the attic, four chairs lie tangled in each other's legs. The top of the stairs are clear. I straighten up, raise the light, and start climbing.

'What's up there?' asks Magnus, who suddenly appears in the darkness.

'I . . . Why don't you go see for yourself? You're not hampered by doors and barricades.'

He shook his head. 'Can't. We wouldn't be in the same time anymore.'

'And that's a problem? I've seen Uncle Chaim fiddling with nineteenth-century watches, I've travelled through history, and now you're telling me you can't go first because it'll muddle up time?'

He nodded. 'An anachronism isn't so bad. But you mustn't disturb the course of things to come.'

'Magnus,' I said. 'That's all this family has ever done.'

The wintry gaslight pierces the blackness like a membrane. 'It's like being born.'

The look Magnus gives me is blank with amazement.

The inside of the attic. Rafters and beams. My head, level with the floor. I hold the lamp to one side. Freezing cold, a chill straight out of prehistoric times. In the middle of the large room, which spans the entire length and breadth of the house, lies the wreck of the tower. It has collapsed, probably under the weight of the snow, and crashed through the roof. Nothing left but a pile of snow, splintered wood, and pieces of broken glass. I step onto the floor. A few, shivering steps in the direction of the ruin.

'Lord of the Universe,' said Magnus.

My throat tightens. There's something gleaming on the pile. A hand drill and a small pulley. I don't understand. Why here? Tools that someone has used. For the piano. To hang up the sandbag. But why . . .

'Why?' Magnus spreads his arms. He gazes, with hollow eyes, at a point in the distance. I raise the lamp. Nina is sitting with her back against the far wall. White as milk. The knife I couldn't find is lying in her lap like a sacrificial sword.

'Nina . . .'

'Mr Hollander? M . . . Nathan?'

Light like a thousand times light.

'Mr Hollander? Is everything all right?'

'Reisel.'

'*Ribbono shel olam . . .*'

A feeling as if my arms and legs don't belong to me, as if they're floating off in different directions. In bed like a piece of wood washed up on the shore.

Reisel is bending over me. In her face, glints of lamplight.

'Did you say *Ribbono shel olam*?'

She shakes her head.

'I heard you.'

'I was scared.'

'Lord of the Universe. That's what we always used to say.'

'Who's we?'

'My family. The Hollanders. We said it all the time. Didn't think it would hurt. And God only knows we ... May I have some orange juice?'

She rises slowly. Her features blur, the face of a woman drowning. Arms and hands ripple. A cold glass of beer. A glass beaded with clear, cold droplets. A bitter head that fills the mouth and dissolves, instantly. And then ...

'Here you are. I'll help you sit up.'

Strange how difficult sitting up can be when you have to think about the difference between over and under.

'Drink.'

'No. You're supposed to say: *Trink, mayn kind.*'

Ah, that smile. A sucker for a smile. That's what Herman used to say. 'You're too nice. You're a sucker for a smile.' I drink from the glass she holds to my lips.

'Why, Reisel?'

'You cried out.'

'Morphine dreams.'

'But so much pain.'

'Not real pain. Not the desert in me. Pain of remembering. How long have I been asleep?'

She glances at the watch hanging from a buttonhole on her blouse. 'Two hours.'

'Has it worn off already?'

She nods her head. A cross between nodding and shaking.

'And I can't have any more?'

Now her head is shaking.

'There's beer in the refrigerator. Would you bring me some?'

She draws in a breath.

'Reisel?'

'It's bad for you.'

Lord of the Universe, if I had the strength I'd laugh my head off. 'Look at me. I don't have to worry about my health anymore. God. For the first time in my life I can smoke and drink and to hell with the consequences. The danger is past.'

She sighs, gazes for a while at the wreck on the bed, and then goes into the kitchen. When she returns, she's carrying a bottle and a lemonade glass. 'I've never seen a bottle like this before.'

'From a fan. Grolsch. The beer from the region where my Uncle Herman had a house. You have to push back the clamp.'

There's a churning in the big glass. Foam shoots up and billows over the edge. The smell of bars. Behind the window at Loos, looking out at the Parklaan. The trees. Number Five clanging around the bend. The rising and falling hum of voices.

'Sit down, Reisel. Aren't you having anything?'

'I'll make some tea.'

Why did I come here? A land where it's always warm, even in winter. A land where the hills are parched and brown. A land where I am nothing. The umpteenth old bastard come here to die. A person with no past and no history. A person who wouldn't help build this refuge, but seeks shelter here when the storm begins to rage. They look down on us, those cactus fruits. We are introverted, wary ghetto-dwellers. Or so they think. When they're the ones. Ghetto-dwellers. Not introverted and wary. God, no. They walk around with puffed-up chests and dangling balls. Abundance of adrenaline and testosterone. And yet. A Jewish sanctuary. The only place I can be. Only place in the world where a person without family can still feel at home. Land full of Sophies and Mannys and Hermans and Zoes and Zeldas.

Zenos?

Where are you, lad? Where did you go? Gone nearly half a century. A gaping hole, fifty years deep. Why?

Ninas?

No.

Little by little, my strength returns. The clay-like feeling in my limbs disappears. My head grows large and clear. It's probably night-time by now, the part of the day I was always best at. Always: at night the world unfolded and my senses were young and alert. Even now, lying here, on the ebbing swell of morphine, I can feel the world coming to life.

It might also be the beer.

'What were you reading?' I ask when she returns and sits down next to my bed. She has a paper napkin wrapped around the glass, and blows on the hot liquid. She looks around, at the chair near the bookcase, as if she needs to see the place where she was reading before she can say which book she was holding in her hands.

'*A Traveller in Time: the Life of Herman Hollander.*'

'You're reading me?'

Momentary confusion in her eyes. Then she nods.

'Good,' I say, without knowing what's good about it. 'Tell me the latest gossip.'

Her face lights up. 'They're having a fight in the kitchen.'

'What else is new?'

'No, it's serious. There's a Falasha cook and they want to get rid of him, because they're afraid he might have AIDS.'

I shake my head. 'And he doesn't?'

'No, but they say there's a lot of it among the Falashas.'

'And what if he does have AIDS? Do they think he's going to bleed all over the food?'

She sips her tea.

A fast, low, whop-whop sound draws near. It comes from the south, thunders over our heads, and disappears in the direction of the north.

'Good grief.'

'Helicopter,' says Reisel. 'On its way to the border.'

'Which border?'

She shrugs. 'This country is nothing but border.'

'What would all those soldiers ever do if there were peace?'

'You don't really like this country, do you?'

'Do you?'

She nodded. 'I love it.'

'You love a country, Reisel? A piece of land that someone

has drawn a line around and stuck a flag in? Save your love for a person.'

'Why did you come here if you hate us that much?'

Ah. She's not looking at me. Her gaze hovers in the dark void of the window at the front of the room. 'I don't hate you.'

She nods violently.

'No. I hate myths. I hate the myth of the Jew who rose up and took charge. I hate the myth of one state for all, which is really only a state for the few. I hate the myth of Aliyah. Why must we all live in one country? To make it easier for the rest of the world to find us? Why is it so important that we all be together and all marry each other? I particularly hate the myth that the followers are always right.'

'Which followers?'

'All followers. But especially the ones who follow the Law. *Verschwartze* Americans who have grown up in assimilated families, gorged themselves on cheeseburgers and Coke and without any knowledge of the past, or the workings of history, come to this country and run around wearing black suits and blocking off streets and forbidding mixed marriages and . . .'

I'm panting. As if in labour.

Reisel is silent. After a long time she says, 'Why did you come here?'

'Because there was nothing left.'

Old now. Outlived everyone and everything. Except the ghost. He who went away. Could he . . . Where? When? How?

A hole. No, emptiness. Ahhhh.

Cold as a corpse. Her stomach is moving.

'Magnus! Hold the lantern . . .'

He shakes his head sadly.

'Jesus.' I put the lantern on the ground and slip my arms under her. As if the cold makes people lighter. The knife clatters to the floor.

'Magnus, for God's sake. I can't get her downstairs without light. Help me.'

He shrugs his shoulders, palms upturned.

'Magnus, please. Magnus. I can't do it alone. I need you. Help
me.'

'No, Nathan. Trust me. Walk, *mayn kind*.'

I close my eyes. Stagger towards the stairs.

Down and up at the same time. Eyes still closed, yet I can see
the stairs, right down to the grain. I grow smaller with every step.
With every step the staircase grows. Deep as a mountain, high as
an abyss . . . so cold your breath fell in pieces on the ground. Where?
Kotzk? Bialystok?

Behind the shed where they parked a big truck that afternoon,
bright light shines from an arc lamp. I stand in the shelter of the
rubbish bins behind one of the houses and watch the men loading
crates and kit bags.

Just before Manny left, he and Sophie had spent a long time
whispering. Then he kissed us, Zoe, Zelda, me, Zeno, and walked
out. We heard his feet stumbling across the wooden floor in the
hallway. Then the door.

'Where's Papa going?' I asked.

'On a trip,' said Sophie, 'but he'll be back tomorrow.'

But he had never gone on a trip before. Since we had been living
on the Hill, none of us had ever been away. And why were all
those other men going on a trip? Some had left earlier, others were
leaving that night. That's what I had heard. There were buses leaving
that night for Trinity. What was Trinity?

The day before he had worked from dawn to dusk and when he
came home he fell asleep at the table. Sophie woke him up and
walked him into the bedroom, where it stank of tar and warm
wood, and put him to bed. She turned on the fan and tiptoed back
to the kitchen.

'I thought he was going to fall asleep in his potatoes,' Zoe
snickered.

Sophie smiled. 'Keep your voice down,' she said. 'He needs to
get some rest before he leaves.'

'Where's he going?' asked Zelda.

'Somewhere,' said Sophie.

'I thought "Somewhere" was here,' I said.

The last few bags are tossed into the truck. The soldiers check to make sure the tarpaulin is secure and then lace up the back flap. One of them takes a packet of cigarettes out of his breast pocket and offers it to the others. They gather round. Fire goes from hand to hand.

It's getting dark. The men near the truck look up. One of them says something. Three points of light float in the darkness and above that, the faint, milky glow of the moon behind a shred of cloud, a star or two. I hear a thud. Somebody curses. The men look past the truck and walk forward.

The canvas is lashed down with rope as thick as my finger, but the copper eyes it threads through are so far apart that it's easy for me to pull loose a piece of the flap. A ray of moonlight sharpens the contours of crates and kit bags. I hoist myself up on the tailgate and roll inside, over something soft. The muffled sound of talking men. There's a tug at the canvas. Somebody grumbles. 'Next time you close the flap, do it right, goddamit. Come on . . . pull!' The loud smack of rope against canvas. More indistinct sounds. A voice. And another one. The door of the truck opens. The other door. The engine starts.

'Time,' says Herman, 'can be measured in three ways. You've got what they call "rotational time", that is, how long it takes for the earth to turn all the way round, or one solar day. Then there's dynamical time, based on the movements of the moon and the planets. And atomic time, where the oscillations of the atom are the ticking of the clock. Actually, N, time, as we know and use it, doesn't really exist. We think time has a direction, that it moves forward, from the past to the present. But that's not true. Time measures the distance between two given moments. Question: Is time asymmetrical? Why do we believe that a tree falls, but not that a tree "unfalls"? Why do we consider it normal that incidents in the past affect incidents in the future, but not the reverse? Think about it. I'll give you an example. You throw a stone in the water. Ripples spread outwards from the point where the stone touches the surface. First the stone, then the ripples. If the process is reversed, contracting ripples throw the stone out of the water. Sound strange?

Think of a film, played backwards, about a stone being thrown into a pond. We'd see exactly what I've just described: the stone is thrown out of the water by powerfully contracting, concentric ripples. No one in our world has ever actually witnessed such a thing, but some scientists believe it's possible. Time has no direction. It's even possible that, elsewhere in the universe, there's a planet where entropy doesn't go from minimum to maximum, as it does here, from order to chaos, but the other way round. For the inhabitants of that planet, our future would be their past and our past, their future.'

'She's not dead.'

'No.' But she looks like a corpse.

The fires have all gone out. In the hunting room hangs the silent chill of a cellar. I lay her on the bed and stoke up the hearth.

'Nina.'

A waxwork. The soft, cold sheen on her skin, the colourless lips. I pull off my shoes, throw back the covers, and lie down on top of her. I sink into the chill that rises from her body. The breath I blow on her face comes back as frozen air.

'I wrote you that letter about entropy,' said Herman, 'at a time when I myself barely realized how far-reaching the societal ramifications of that concept actually were. The inevitability of it. The irreversibility. I didn't yet know that the process, the ineluctable road from minimum to maximum entropy, was only irreversible in practice. Scientists assume that, theoretically speaking, there *is* such a thing as the reversal of a process. If you shake two liquids together and they blend completely, so that you get maximum entropy, then you should, theoretically, be able to separate them again, return them to their original state, or minimum entropy. Atom by atom. What Zeno was trying to do with that silence . . . I sometimes think that, in choosing silence as a form, he was hoping to prevent entropy. If you don't act, you add no energy. The state of equilibrium is maintained, forever.'

'Nina. Wake up, Nina.'

'What is it?'

'Reisel. You're still here.'

'A dream?'

'Dreams are all that's left.'

I heave myself up. The black night of a place with no street lamps. The windows, holes. When I walk out the door, shuffle, no: stride, and turn left, through the squiggle of paths between the bungalows, I only have to walkshufflestride five minutes before I see the Hills of Galilee rippling all the way to Syria. Brown. Green. And dry as summer dust. When I first visited this place, the place where Sophie spent the 'twilight of her life,' I passed . . . No, let me start again. I drove up from Tel Aviv in a rented car, over the coast road to Netanya. Further north, to Hadera, and then right, into the countryside. Fruit trees, as far as the eye could see. Herman, beside me, pointed to them. 'This,' he said, 'was once barren and dry.' Past Nazareth on our right, farther north. Trees, trees, trees. 'Why are we so neurotic?' I said. 'We can't simply plant a tree. It has to be a whole bloody forest of unparalleled beauty. And all that fund-raising! Another new forest, another park. As if our lives depended on it!' 'I'm going to tell you a midrash,' said Herman.

'You?'

He nodded. 'An old man is working the patch of land next to his house. He digs a deep hole. Alexander the Great comes riding by with his retinue. When he sees the greybeard bowed over the cracked, dry ground, Alexander orders his retainers to stop. He dismounts, and says, "Old man, what are you doing?" "My Lord," says the man, "I'm planting a date tree." The emperor looks at him in amazement. "But by the time that tree bears fruit, you'll be long gone!" The old man laughs. "I may not be here," he says, "but my grandson will." The emperor rides on, the man plants his tree and devotes himself, once again, to his daily tasks. Years later, after a lengthy campaign, the emperor passes by that place again. News of his arrival has gone before him. Standing before a beautiful tree is an old man. His grandson, nearly a man himself, is holding a basket full of shiny dates. "My Lord!" cries the grandfather, "may I present you with these dates from the tree I planted when you passed by here so many years ago?" The emperor has the basket brought to him and takes a date. "You are a wise man," he says. "You thought, not only of the day, but of the years to come. You are also a fortunate man. You planted a tree and lived to see it grow, and now you can enjoy the sweetness of its fruits." Then he bade one of his men to scoop the dates into a sack and fill the basket with gold.'

Down a dusty road, stones crunching under the tyres, slowly climbing. Left, onto a path. Beth Kesher.

'Okay, Herman. People plant trees for posterity. It's a metaphor. We all have to provide for those who come after us. I didn't know you were so well up on Midrash.'

He shrugged.

'You know the rest of the story,' I said.

'What rest?'

'The old man's neighbour saw this, and he rushed home and told his wife. "Fathead!" she cried. "Here, fill this basket with dates and go after them. Now!" The man did as he was told and after a while he caught up with the emperor and his retinue. Alexander looked down at him from his white horse and nodded when the man offered him the dates. "Soldiers," he said to his guards, "bind this man to a tree and pelt him with dates until the basket is empty."'

The car came to a halt in a small clearing surrounded on all sides by lush greenery. Herman shook his head. 'You don't have a serious bone in your body,' he said.

'Herman, this *is* serious. By the way, there's more.'

'Lord of the Universe,' sighed Herman.

'The man comes home. His wife asks him what's happened, because he's staggering around and all covered with date juice. He tells her, cursing and swearing. "Oh, shut up," says his wife. "And just be glad the dates were ripe."'

Reisel moves through the light. She comes with a glass of water.

'I think I'd rather have another beer.'

She sighs.

'Child, listen. Is morphine any better? If I were living in Europe instead of here, I'd be lying in a four-poster bed with a cooler and a bottle of champagne at my side. I'd spend my last days amidst books and wine and big expensive cigars. What are you trying to do, prolong my life?'

She puts down the glass and turns round.

'Troublesome old bugger?' I call out after her. 'Is that what I heard you thinking?'

When she returns with the swing-top bottle, she's grinning.

'Bloody hell, that *is* what you thought! Shame on you.'

The beer rises in the glass, thirst rises in my gullet.

'I grew up in the region where this beer is brewed.' Ahhh. 'There, and in the city of Rotterdam. And in New York, but not very long. And on a hilltop in New Mexico. Do you think I'm delirious?'

She shakes her head, but not convincingly.

'I'm not delirious. Or perhaps I am, but it's true. That's me: the hill they call the Mountain, the New York of Holland, the Rotterdam of America and the mountain they call the Hill. What do you think of the book?'

A question, her gaze.

'My book. The one you were reading.'

She nods. 'I'm not sure. Is it a novel?'

'It reads like one. But it's the story of my Uncle Herman. His biography.'

'It's not really about him.'

'No. It was supposed to be about him, but it ended up being about the people who weren't there. That can happen with books.'

I close my eyes. I'm here in this desert, with a desert inside me, and this barren place reminds me of how like a steppe writing used to be. Whenever I began a fairy tale, it was as if I were standing on the edge of a plain. Emptiness, as far as the eye could see. Uncharted, unfamiliar territory. And then I'd gird my loins, step onto the plain, and begin my journey through the nothingness, and each step I took made the unknown more familiar and filled in the map. I looked for trees, bushes, a brook, a grassy hill. Landmarks that would show me the way across the plain. That was writing: a voyage of discovery without compass or map. I remember a story . . . Who told . . . Magnus. He once told me a story about a journey across a steppe. A man who slept on the ground and woke up with his face in a puddle.

'Hey, it's a little boy.' The glare of a flashlight.

'Jesus Christ. Who closed that goddamn tailgate? Okay, buddy, come on out. Here, I'll give you a hand.'

'What's the problem?'

'Some son-of-a . . . Mr Feynman. Jes . . . sorry. A stowaway, sir. A kid.'

'Hey, kid. Who are you?'

'Nathan Hollander, Mr Feynman.'

'Sophie Hollander's son?'

'. . .'

'Fifteen minutes, sir.'

'Come on, pal. Any of you men seen the boss?'

'General Groves? Back at the base.'

'No, the boss. Oppenheimer.'

'He's already there.'

'Never mind, it can wait. Let's go.'

The ground is wet. We wade through the puddles to a truck. Mr Feynman opens the door. He lifts me onto the front seat. When he's sitting beside me, he says, 'Listen, kid. This is a place you really shouldn't have been. So here's what we're going to do. We'll lie low. When they give the signal, we'll just stay here in the truck. What happens after that, we'll see.'

'Was it raining?'

'Hm? Yes. Thunderstorm. Do you know what's going on here?'

I shake my head.

He stares out the window, grinning into the nothingness. 'It's a bomb. You know there's a war on, don't you?'

'Yes.'

'It's a bomb for the war. If it works, the war will be over in two days. But it's a very big bomb. So do what I say. Listen, there's the siren.'

His hand on my shoulder. Not heavy. The hand of a small man.

The whitest white. Mr Feynman and I are lying on the floor of the truck. Purple spots. 'You okay? Come here.' The white changes to yellow, to orange, to clouds. A rumbling like a thousand thunderstorms. No place where it isn't light. Next to me, Mr Feynman stirs. 'Just a little longer. It'll all be over soon.' A mighty hurricane screeches around us. We shake and rock. It whistles and sighs. Something bashes against the truck. Mr Feynman leans over the steering wheel. He looks sideways, grins. 'I was right. A windshield is enough. Coming?' He opens the door and waits until I've slid over to his side. When he's standing next to the truck, he raises his arms and grabs me under mine. 'Out you go.'

The light goes dark. As if a tent has been pitched over the world. Far off in the distance everything is black and in the blackness loom the contours of an enormous whirlpool of smoke and dust and spiralling purple clouds.

'Hey, Dick, whatcha got there?'

'We had a stowaway. I kept him with me. I didn't think Groves would be too pleased if he found him.'

A man leans forward and peers into my face. 'How did you get here?'

'In the back of the truck, sir.'

'With the last crew. The soldiers.'

'Thank God,' he says. 'The soldiers. At least Groves can't put the blame on us.'

He lays a hand on my shoulder and asks me who I am.

'Nathan Hollander,' I tell him.

'Hollander. The drill man.' He looks down and smiles. 'You should be proud of your father, my boy. He did a good job.' He points to the bluepurpleblack mushroom far away on the plain. 'It worked!'

'. . . Hollander? Nathan?'

'Reisel?'

'Reisel?'

'Reisele. Nathan? Can you hear me? Move if you can hear me.'

Move. How. If this is then, how do I move? If this is now, why?

'Nathan. Can you blink your eyes?'

That's a tough one. You lift your right eyelid. Where does that begin? Above the cheek. No, higher. There. Up, and then . . .

'Nathan, thank God.'

Nina?

'Mr Hollander, can you understand me?'

Eyelid up, and then try . . .

'Very good. Can you open your other eye, too?'

What's going on? Yes. A low white ceiling. A kind of . . . bottle.

'Nathan.' Hand on my forehead. Great, now I can't see a thing.

'Miss, do you mind? Mr Hollander, I'm going to do a little test. Would you please blink your eyes if you feel anything?'

Nathan Hollander and his Blinking Eyes. What the hell is this?

'What . . .'

'He can talk.'

'Mr Hollander?'

'What. Is. This.'

'You're in the hospital. You're suffering from hypothermia.'

So tired.

'Ow.'

'Very good.'

Good? Jabbing me in the foot?

'Ow.'

'And that one works too.'

'What.'

Nina's face just above me. 'It's going to be all right. It's going to be all right.'

Not if they keep jabbing me like that. God, so tired.

———————

'You've been asleep for ages.'

Nina's face was the first thing I saw when I opened my eyes. She looked at me with the cheerful expression of someone who was actually very concerned.

'How are you feeling?'

'Hm. Not sure.'

'The doctors say you'll be back on your feet in a week or two.'

'What happened?'

I had difficulty speaking. It was like forcing rocks up through my throat.

'You nearly froze to death. But they found you in time.'

They? Me?

I wanted to say something, but couldn't bear to squeeze up another one of those boulders. I closed my eyes and began drifting away. Just before I tumbled into the dark hole, I saw Zeno, the way he lay sleeping in Herman's garden half a century ago, dappled with light, his eyes closed, the long lashes against the white skin.

———————

It was nearly two weeks before I could sit up again. A nurse wheeled me into the day room and I sat there for an hour or two looking out at the leaden sky above the rooftops. Nina usually came early in the evening. It still hurt to speak, so I just listened to her stories.

On the morning of our fourth day in Uncle Herman's house, they had begun clearing the road up the Mountain. Not because anyone thought there were people in the Hollander house, but to see if there might be anyone stranded in their car in the snow. They would never even have checked the house if, that evening, just as they were about to drive the snowploughs back to town, Nina hadn't emerged from the whiteness. She was dressed in a hodge-podge of Uncle Herman's things, including the hiking boots he had once bought in Austria. The men from the rescue team were dumbfounded. When she told them she had come from the house and was going to get her car so she could drive herself and her uncle down the hill, one of them said she could forget it. They had found the car at the foot of the hill, when one of the ploughs tipped it over. The men turned round and drove back with her to the house.

Once they were inside, it was a long time before they found me. I was lying in the attic, behind the remains of the fallen tower. When Nina laid her hand on my forehead, I was nearly as cold as the snow she had brushed off me, which had blown in through the roof. They wrapped me in blankets and drove me, first in a snowplough and, once we were down at the bottom, in an ordinary car, to the nearest hospital. On the way, Nina had given me mouth-to-mouth.

I was in the hospital for almost three weeks. When they discharged me, Nina drove me to Amsterdam. It was a long trip, through a land that was no longer white. I stared out the window and couldn't quite get used to the black fields and pale green verges. Inside my head it was still snowing.

At her house I fell straight to sleep. When I woke up two days later, I was hungry and restless. It was evening. Nina had sat by my bed nearly the entire time.

While I washed and dressed, she made coffee and sandwiches. I ate in the living room, on a big flowery sofa. It was my first visit to her house. As I sat there, it occurred to me that I knew almost nothing about her. Had I expected her to have a house like this? I chewed my bread and sipped my coffee and ran my eyes over the tranquil setting. The gleaming, pale wood floor. The large wooden table with the green glass vase full of flowers. The two sofas, the flowery one on which I was sitting and the elegant red one by the window. The paintings, all colourful abstracts, and the black hole of the hearth.

When I had finished my coffee and put the mug on the empty plate, I searched my pockets for cigarettes. Nina stood up and handed me a new packet. She hadn't said a word the whole time. I tore off the cellophane. Nina gave me a light. The first smoke after all those weeks hit me like a hammer. I coughed. Nina stood up and brought fresh coffee.

'Is it time to talk?'

I nodded.

'What are your plans?'

'Let's begin somewhere else.'

She frowned.

'Let's begin at the beginning, for a change. Chronological order.'

She was pale and tired. I felt something turning inside.

'Why did you do it?'

She stared at me with hollow eyes. 'Do what?'

I closed my eyes. 'The house, Nina. The traps. Running away. Everything.'

'You think . . .'

'I know.'

She swallowed, as if she had a live fish in her throat.

'It wasn't Zeno. Zeno has been dead for almost thirty years.' The realization sank in for the first time since his disappearance.

She opened her mouth.

'And even if he were still alive . . . Why? He didn't hate me. He didn't hate me the way you hate him. The cellar was stocked a year ago. You've got the key, you've got a car. Who else could it have been, Nina?'

'I showed you the date on the packets of coffee myself,' she said. She spoke with difficulty.

'I would have done the same thing, if I were setting a trap like that for someone.'

She shook her head and didn't stop shaking.

'What I don't understand is why you stocked up on so much. What was the plan? That I stay up there for several months? That I fall into a trap and die and that *you* stay there?'

She took a deep breath. 'Why, Nathan?'

'You tell me,' I said. 'Tell me.'

'Do you think I hate you?' Her face was contorted. Tiny spasms flickered round her eyes. 'I slept with you.'

I bowed my head. 'Why did you go away?' I said to the floor.

'I wanted to get help.' She spoke in a groan.

'The first time.'

She stood up and looked hurriedly around her. Then she sat back down again. 'I wanted to get out of there,' she said. 'Get the car.'

'You knew the car would never make it up the hill, maybe not even down. We walked through those snowdrifts together. No one could possibly think you could drive a car up there after that.'

'I'm losing you.'

'What?'

She stared straight through me. 'I've already lost Zeno. Now I'm losing you.'

It was as if it were raining inside.

'Why don't you just say you don't love me? You want to get rid of me.'

'Nothing better,' I said. 'I would have liked nothing better than to stay with you.' I squeezed up the lump of words in my throat. My voice was hoarse when I spoke. 'I love you.'

'Nathan.' She was sitting with her feet together, hands in her lap. She was crying.

'Why, Nina?'

'I didn't do it.' She spoke as if her voice didn't belong to her.

'Nina, it wasn't Zeno. I've been up in the attic.' Her. It was her I'd seen. I bowed my head and tried to recall the image. She was sitting against the wall, white as paper, the knife in her lap. The hole in the roof. The pile of snow and wood and glass in the middle of the floor. And the freezing cold. She was sitting there. I had carried her down the stairs. But she had been with the rescue team. Lilith, said Uncle Chaim. His face appeared. He looked deadly tired. It was black under his eyes. His face was wrinkled and lined. She's no Lilith, said Chaim. I heard Magnus's voice. 'I was in Bialystok. Saw a man freeze to death. He felt hot. When you freeze to death you start seeing things, some people even tear off all their clothes.'

I looked up and saw Nina. She was a statue. Had I been seeing things? I had felt hot. I was lying on a bed in the bungalow on the kibbutz where Sophie had lived when she went to Israel. Thought I was dying. Could hardly breathe. No, the cheese, she had fled. Punish me. Punish Nina, she had said. Why would I have had to punish her if she hadn't felt that she . . .

'Do you think I drove Zeno away?'

She flinched.

'Do you think it was my fault?'

She turned her head left.

'Nina!'

When she stood up, she was someone else. Her shoulders were hunched, her head went from side to side. A caged, taunted, beast of prey.

I loved her, I thought.

'No one else could've done it. Mrs Sanders didn't know I was coming. Herman was dead. Zeno has been dead for half a lifetime. Zoe, Zelda . . .'

'Not dead.'

'Who?'

'Zeno lives.'

That was what they had said after his disappearance. They continued to meet for weeks on end, in the shed, the silent followers of the silent wunderkind. Zeno lives, they cried. They had sounded like people performing a ritual that they themselves no longer believed in.

But he was dead. No one is gone for such a long time and then just reappears.

A few days after his departure, I had phoned the police.

'What do you mean, perfectly normal?' I asked the detective whom I finally got on the phone and who assured me there was no reason for concern, it was perfectly normal that . . . 'How,' I asked, 'can a person just disappear?'

'How often would you say this sort of thing happens, Mr Hollander?'

'No idea, but I have a feeling you're about to tell me.'

'Three hundred times a year,' said the voice on the other end of the line. 'And I'm talking about the ones we never see again. Three hundred a year. Six a week. Nothing special. There are about fifteen hundred a year that walk out the door and get lost. And except for those three hundred, they all turn up again, one way or another.'

But not him. Anything could have happened. He could have stumbled somewhere, in a forest, hit his head against a tree. He could have committed suicide, in some secret place. He could have drowned.

'Dead,' I said. 'For thirty years, stone cold dead.' Every word hurt me. Never before had I felt so strongly, known so deeply, that he was gone, that he was never coming back.

Nina paced about the room, back and forth, back and forth.

I lit another cigarette. The remains of the last one were still smouldering in the ashtray. 'Sit down,' I said.

She stopped and looked at me suspiciously.

'Sit.'

She sat down.

'Talk.'

Her mouth opened. Then came the sound. It was a soft, almost animal whimpering. I sat there opposite her and it was as if I were looking at someone I had never seen before. This wasn't Nina. Nina was bright, sharp, cynical and light. She was as nimble as a young girl and as strong as a giantess.

'Get a grip on yourself, Nina! Talk!'

Saliva dribbled out of her mouth. She plucked at her jacket. I stood up and knelt down in front of her. 'Nina.' I took her head in my hands. 'Listen to me. Nothing terrible has happened. Things can still be all right. But you must talk.'

Suddenly I was flat on my back, with a pounding behind my forehead. She was kneeling over me, hair like a mane. Her hands were around my throat. 'Nina . . .' I looked into her face, but her eyes saw nothing. There was a strange wind blowing through her gaze. My head was pounding so hard I thought it would burst. My legs kicked at the air.

'N . . .'

The strength flowed out of my fingertips. I felt death creeping up from my hands, into my wrists, my forearms.

'Bastard Zeno.' Her voice was tight as steel. She growled something I couldn't understand.

I felt the air forcing its way through my lungs. I pressed my head against the floor and with everything I had, brought up my left knee. She shot forward and rolled across the room.

'Shit . . .'

I was on my hands and knees. Panting like a swimmer who had shot up to the surface after a deep dive. Nina lay half under the table. The vase of flowers had fallen over and water was running off the table and dripping loudly onto the floor. I crawled over to her, grabbed her by the ankle, and pulled her towards the middle of the room. She kicked and squirmed. When she turned over on her back and tried to sit up, I lashed out and hit her on the side of the head with the back of my hand. She sailed across the room like a wounded pheasant. About six feet down she crashed into a sideboard and lost consciousness. I dragged myself towards her, examined her head and ears. No blood. Her breathing was calm and even. I sat down with my back against the wall, her head in my lap, and as I stroked the waterfall of her hair and felt the glow of her cheek through the red curls, as I sat there staring at the puddle of water by the table, at the cigarette that lay smoking on the floor and had already burned a black hole in the parquet, everything inside me began slipping. I was churning so hard inside that my head hit the wall. Boom, boom, boom. I felt everything coming loose, as if I were a building that had been falling apart for years and now, with a single tremor, crumbled like dry bread.

The windows were dark by the time I laid Nina on the flowery sofa. She rolled over on her side and stuck her thumb in her mouth. I stood there for a while looking at her, cigarette between my lips, arms folded. Then I put on my coat, picked up my travelling bag, and walked out the door.

Outside the air was mild. The light from the streetlamps shone down on the asphalt, the tramrails gleamed silver. I hailed a taxi. For the first time in my life I was grateful to have a surly driver. He drove silently through the streets of South Amsterdam, turned onto the ring road, and stepped on the accelerator. Before long I could see the mountain of light above Schiphol.

It was on the plane, looking down at the tiny lights of Holland, that I thought: I don't really know if she did it, though I can't imagine it any other way. We climbed through the clouds, darkness covered the earth. Here I am, I thought. I don't really know if Herman was my father. I don't know what happened to Zeno. I've left the woman I loved, because I didn't really know . . . There, high up in the sky, on my way, as I had been all my life, on my way so I would never have to arrive, I suddenly saw myself sitting on the lap of Schlomo Minsky, me on one knee, Reisele on the other, the smell of black tea and drying clothes around us, and thought: I'm a stowaway. I came alone, I'll leave alone.

Acknowledgements

Martin Koomen, *Het koninkrijk van de nacht*, Wetenschappelijke
Uitgeverij, Amsterdam 1978
Richard Rhodes, *The Making of the Atomic Bomb*, Touchstone
(Simon & Schuster), New York 1995
John Else et al, *The Day After Trinity* (cd-rom), Voyager, New
York 1995
Critical Mass (cd-rom), Corbis, Washington 1996
Michael B. Stoff, Jonathan F. Fanton and R. Hal Williams (ed),
The Manhattan Project, Temple University Press, Philadelphia
Don E. Beyer, *The Manhattan Project*, Franklin Watts, New York
1991
J.C.H. Blom, R.G. Fuks-Mansfield and I. Schöffer (ed),
Geschiedenis van de joden in Nederland, Balans, Amsterdam 1995
Cees Zevenbergen, *Toen zij uit Rotterdam vertrokken*, Waanders,
Zwolle
Nathan Peter Levinson, *Der Messias*, Kreuz Verlag GmnH,
Stuttgart 1994
Richard P. Feynman, *'Surely you're joking, mr. Feynman!'*, Vintage,
London 1992
Rabbi Dr H. Freedman, *Midrash rabbah*, The Soncino Press,
London/New York 1983
Ludo van Eck, *Het boek der kampen*, Kritak, Leuven 1979
Huw Price, *Time's Arrow and Archimedes Point*, Oxford University
Press, New York/Oxford 1996